MW01126790

PLAY ALONG

T L SWAN

ALSO BY T L SWAN

My Temptation (Kingston Lane #1)

The Stopover (The Miles High Club #1)
The Takeover (The Miles High Club #2)
The Casanova (The Miles High Club #3)
The Do-over (The Miles High Club #4)
Miles Ever After (The Miles High Club – Extended Epilogue)

Mr. Masters (The Mr. Series #1)
Mr. Spencer (The Mr. Series #2)
Mr. Garcia (The Mr. Series #3)

Our Way (Standalone Book)

Play Along (Standalone Book)

The Italian (The Italians #1)
Ferrara (The Italians #2)

Stanton Adore (Stanton Series #1)
Stanton Unconditional (Stanton Series #2)
Stanton Completely (Stanton Series #3)

AKNOWLEDGEMENTS

It takes an army to write a book and I undoubtedly have the best army on the planet.

To my beautiful friends who support me day in, day out: thank you.

My gorgeous Mum, you are so loved.

Vicki, Am, Rachel, Lisa D, Brooke, Jane, Nicole, Lisa K, Nadia— you girls are the best and thank you for all that you do for me. I love you all to bits.

To my gorgeous, talented friend and editor Victoria, you make me so much better than I am.

To my proof readers, thank you for stepping up and helping me. You're also the best.

To every single blogger out there who supports the indie book community, without your support I wouldn't have the dream career that I have. Thank you so much for all that you do for everyone.

To Linda, you help me reach the best version of myself and your help is invaluable. You are loved!

To my beloved gang in my Facebook reader group, the Swan Squad.
You girls give me a safe place to hang and someone to laugh with at least a thousand times a day. You have no idea how much your support means to me. Love you all.

And to my beautiful hubs,
You... you are the reason I write love stories.

And to my three little angels.
I love you. xoxoxo

GRATITUDE

The quality of being thankful;
readiness to show appreciation for, and to return kindness.

DEDICATION

I would like to dedicate this book to the alphabet.
For those twenty-six letters have changed my life.
Within those twenty-six letters, I found myself
and live my dream.
Next time you say the alphabet remember its power.
I do every day.

1

Roshelle

IN A WORLD full of deceit and lies, who do you trust?

I stand alone in the corner of the nightclub, watching him take her in his arms before he kisses her.

The air evaporates from my lungs. I can't breathe.

Despair is pumping through my bloodstream, but for some sick self-destructive reason, I can't bring myself to look away. I have to see this—see what he is capable of and exactly how far this has gone.

The signs were there, I saw them. But like a fool I ignored them for as long as my gut instinct would allow.

I believed that he loved me. I believed that she loved me.

As I stand there and watch my boyfriend of two years kissing my best friend and roommate of five years, I realize I have never felt so betrayed on so many levels. I can't even begin to comprehend what I am witnessing.

The hairs on the back of my neck stand to attention. I feel

like I am having an out of body experience watching the horrific nightmare unfold.

This can't be happening.

My first inkling was two weeks ago. Melissa, my roommate, had a date with a guy she has been seeing for a few weeks and when he arrived to pick her up, Todd, my boyfriend, was really nasty to him. I watched him glare at her as she left and I saw her practically run from the apartment just to get Todd away from that man.

Why?

Why wasn't he happy that she was dating? They had become friends and hell, had spent many nights alone in my apartment as he waited for me to get home from my nightshift. A sick thought had crossed my mind that night... was he jealous?

No, he couldn't be.

So, I thought I would test the theory. Over the following week I was overly affectionate towards Todd in front of Melissa, and every single time she went to bed early, acting happy even though I knew she was fuming inside. The catalyst came on Thursday night when I decided to call in sick for work and Todd and Melissa were both openly annoyed that I wasn't going in.

I had obviously ruined their plans of having sex, and that's when the deep sickening truth slayed me. Did they have sex in her bed or mine?

How often did my roommate satisfy my lover?

Unable to help myself, I put a tracking device app on Melissa's phone. I knew her password. Of course I did. We shared everything.

Even a cock, it seemed.

On Friday she announced that she was going away for the

weekend and Todd announced that he had a night away planned to somewhere else for work.

Coincidence? I didn't think so.

I knew they were meeting up and probably going to be fucking in a hotel room somewhere.

I took my time. I waited.

———

And now it's 11 p.m. on Saturday night and I'm in a different town, in a nightclub where I know nobody, witnessing my worst nightmare.

He can go. A leopard never changes his sickening spots... but why the fuck did he have to take her from me?

I watch them through unshed tears as my heart tries to escape my chest.

My best friend—the only constant in my life since my mother passed away five years ago. My father, an abusing control freak, left when I was a kid, and then when Mom died I moved here for college and met Melissa. My life changed that day. Mel was happy, confident, and attractive.

More than I was... than I am.

I watch her grind herself against him while he looks down on her seductively as she dances. His hands are on her behind. He's smiling as he says something and then they laugh together, and I feel myself die a little inside.

They are not just fucking.

They have feelings for each other.

He kisses her again and his hands go to the back of her head to hold her exactly how he wants her. Their kiss is long, deep, and erotic.

Through blurred vision, I try to make myself look away. No.

I can't look away because I know when I leave this night-club two of the most important people in my life will no longer be a part of it. The floor sways beneath me. How is this possible?

What have I done to deserve this betrayal?

I can't move.

He kisses her again and they fall back against a wall where he pins her and then they start to really go for it.

No. Stop it!

The tears burst the dam and I start to stride toward them as the adrenaline hits its crescendo. I need to stop them, stop everything.

Stop kissing her, you fucking asshole! Please, stop it!

But then I pause mid-step.

Don't do this. Don't lower yourself. Go home and move out. Don't give them a chance to deny or defend it.

I am better than this.

I stand for a moment and stare at the square pattern on the carpet beneath my feet. I'm dizzy and disorientated. I stay there for a while longer with my eyes firmly on the dirty treasons. He kisses her and lifts her thigh up to wrap around his, a move he always pulls on me.

Does he like to do her from behind, too?

That last thought snaps something deep inside. I don't remember getting over to them, but I push him in the back as he pins her to the wall, he falls forward and then looks around, his expression drops in horror. Before I know what I'm doing, I've punched him in the face.

Melissa's hands fly to her mouth. "Oh my God!" she gasps. "T-this isn't what it looks like," she stammers.

"You slut!" I scream, unable to control myself. I grab a drink from a man walking past and throw it in her face, following it up with a hard slap across her cheek. She staggers back in shock, her hand flying up to her smarting face.

"Roshelle," Todd cries as he grabs my arm to try and control me. "Calm down." He pulls me away from Melissa, clearly scared that I am going to hit her again.

"I will not fucking calm down." I push out as the tears fall. I turn to him and a myriad of emotions fill me, but it is his betrayal that steals my voice. I have so many things I want to say, so many things that have escaped my brain. My eyes search his and he tries to grab my hand.

"Don't touch me!" I yell as I whip my hand away from him. "Never again."

I turn to Melissa. "Get your things and get out of my house." I sneer.

"Roshelle," she whispers. "I'm so sorry." She shakes her head in disbelief. Suddenly the walls start closing in, and I know I have got to get out of here.

I have got to get away from this hurt.

I see an exit sign and make a beeline for it without looking back. I push out into the cold night air, the door slamming behind me.

———

"Shut the fuck up before I blow your fucking head off!" a man's voice yells.

"You don't have the fucking guts," someone else sneers in reply.

Huh?

I try to focus, despite my tears, and I angrily swipe them from my eyes. It's dark and there are people out here. I try to focus on the shadows in front of me, then I turn back and try to open the door I just came out of. It's locked and there is no handle on this side. It's clearly a fire door.

What? Where am I?

The tears are streaming down my face.

A gunshot rings out and a man drops in front of me clutching his stomach. My eyes widen in horror as I grasp the situation I have just unknowingly stumbled upon.

What?

Suddenly, I'm surrounded by five men on all sides. I've interrupted some kind of deal.

Oh no.

"Who the fuck is she?" one man calls out.

I shake my head in a panic. "I didn't see anything, I swear." I push through the group of men and one of them grabs me by the arm. "I need me some clean ass tonight."

I try to rip my arm from his clutches, but he hits me hard across the face with his gun, the pain ringing through my head like a lightning bolt before I fall to the ground.

"Bring her with us," someone yells.

"No, we don't need that baggage. Leave her, she said she didn't see anything."

They continue arguing.

"Yeah, well, my cock needs new pussy. "Bring her." The shooter growls.

I feel my body being lifted and then thrown into the tight space of a car trunk. "No," I whisper. "No." My handbag falls to the ground and I see someone pick it up and throw it in the car.

The trunk lid slams with a thud.

I taste blood in my mouth as I lie in a semi-conscious state in the dark.

The pain from my head throbs. What has just happened?

I put my hands up in the darkness and feel the cold metal that encases me.

The reality of the situation rings true as the car starts to drive and I hear them talking to each other in the backseats behind me. Everything is foggy and my head, it hurts so much. I feel something hot run through my hair. What is it? I put my hand up and feel a deep gash in my head, the dripping blood hot and sticky. What the fuck? Oh no. They will kill me.

With renewed purpose and splayed hands I start to hit the roof in a panic.

They just killed someone. I need some new pussy.

His words run through my head. Oh my God, they are going to rape me before they kill me, all five of them.

I start to run my hands frantically over the metal that encases me. How do you get out of a car trunk? Is there a latch? "Help!" I scream. "Help me," I call out as I slam my open hands on the roof. The car slows down. Shit! My eyes widen.

Is this it? I pant as I listen to their movements and I hear the whirl of the traffic lights walk indicator. Now! I need to scream now. We are static, stuck in traffic.

I start to bang on the roof with force. "Help me!" I scream. I lift my legs and try to push the lid open, but fuck, it's so cramped in here. I bang frantically on the ceiling and I feel around underneath me, grabbing the corner of the carpet. Tools. There will be tools under here. I half roll over and tear back the carpet and grab a metal toolbox. "Help me. I'm in the trunk. I'm being kidnapped. Heeeeeeelp!" I scream.

"Shut the fuck up or I'll come back there and shut you up," a male voice growls from inside the car.

My eyes widen. Oh, he sounds scary. I really begin to freak out. I have to get out of here. Now.

I struggle to open the toolbox in front of me in the dark, but eventually it flies open in a rush and a tire iron flings back, hitting me straight in the nose.

"Ah, fuck!" I scream.

Ouch, that fucking hurt. The impact brings tears to my eyes and I clutch my face. Oh, crap, I think I broke my own nose. I grab the tire iron and hit it on the roof with all of my strength. The impact makes it ricochet back and hits me straight in the eyebrow.

"Ahh!" I scream again. I feel a hot trickle run down the side of my face. If they don't kill me I am doing a good job of it myself here.

I keep banging the tire iron on the roof. This has got to be gaining some kind of attention. "Help me," I yell. "Someone... call the police. Help."

The car speeds up and I am flung to the back of the trunk. The lights change, the car flies around the corner, and I go flying, sending the tools scattering throughout the trunk so they hit me. The driver turns a right like a maniac and I slide and hit my head against the side.

"Fucking assholes," I scream, and I hear them all laugh inside the car. Then the vehicle flies around a left corner and I go sliding again. I can hear the tires screeching as the car races down the street.

I'm going to die. Oh God, I'm going to die. I try to grip onto the metal roof to stop myself from hitting the edge, but I can't, and as the car flies around the corner I crumple into the hard metal end of the trunk. The tools are flying around and hitting me. Shit. I feel around frantically for the tire iron again. I may need it, but I can't find it, and my hand feels around the carpeted floor.

Where are you? Where are you?

I bend and feel along the other end of the trunk and finally feel the cold hard metal. My heart is racing as the car races out of control. I need a plan, but what is the damn plan?

Think.

I clutch the tire iron in my hand with white-knuckle force as I try to stop myself from flying around. Whoever opens the trunk is getting knocked out with this fucker. My thoughts cross to Oprah and her sound advice to never go to the second location. I don't remember much from Oprah, but I do know that she said never go to the second location if being kidnapped—fight like hell to escape because they are going to kill you as soon as you get there.

Oh God, this is great.

I'm already in the fucking car on the way to the second location. I begin to get mad, like, furious mad. How dare they? I've had a really fucking bad night and I'm not in the mood for this shit. After about twenty minutes and sixty attack plans, the car slows down and goes over speed bumps.

Where are we?

Adrenaline starts to pump through my blood.

Speed bumps are in parking lots... So that must mean we are in a deserted parking lot.

The car stops and the men go silent. I close my eyes, knowing this is it.

Holy shit.

My heart is hammering and I grip the tire iron in one hand and the car jack in the other. If I'm going to die tonight, someone is coming with me. I wriggle around so my feet are facing the opening, and I pull them back towards my chest. I can hardly breathe, I'm so scared. I hold my weapons in my hand and wait. The car doors open and the whole car lifts as the men get out.

Where are we?

I hear them begin to talk as if I have been totally forgotten about and another sickening thought crosses my mind. What if they just leave me in here?

What if I just die a slow death in the car from no water or food? Oh my God.

What do I do? What do I do?

I stay quiet for five minutes as I try to think until I can't stand it any longer.

Screw this. I am not dying alone in the trunk of a car in a deserted parking lot. I put my tire iron down next to me on the floor and I bang on the trunk lid. "Help me. Let me out," I call.

The men go silent.

"Just get her out and let her go," someone says.

"I will be having some fun first," another answers.

I can't understand what is said next but they all laugh out loud and I grip the tire iron in my hand.

Assholes.

I pull my legs back, and as the trunk is opened I kick out with all my might and connect my feet with a man's face, knocking him to the ground. I jump out of the trunk and one man comes at me. I swing the tire iron as violently as I can and hit him hard in the head, watching as he falls away. The other men all laugh at their two friends on the ground. Another man comes at me and I swing the car jack as hard as I can and cut his face open.

Then I run.

As fast as I can, I run across the cement. It's dark and we are in a parking lot that seems to be near the ocean. I can smell the sea and hear the seagulls. I run with two men chasing after me. I have no defense in these damn high-heeled shoes. They catch up with me easily and tackle me to the ground.

"Get off me," I scream as I fight and kick. One man hits me

across the face and they struggle to contain me as I wrestle to get out of their grip. They are too strong.

They drag me up from the ground, one on each arm, as I kick my legs out and wrestle to try and get away. They fight with me through the darkness, guiding me back to the car.

One man has his t-shirt off and is holding it up against his face to try and stop the bleeding from my car jack attack and the other two men watch.

One man is leaning on the car watching me intently. I glare at him and he smirks back.

"Let me go!" I yell as I try to break the gorilla grip the two men have on me. I bend down and they struggle. I kick out again and connect with the man on my left, hitting his balls and he cries out and doubles over. The distraction lets me rip from the other man's grip and I punch him hard in the face. The man who I hit with the tire jack comes to their aid and helps them hold me down.

"You're coming with us, bitch."

"She's going to be fun to break in." The man on my left laughs.

"Fuck you!" I scream as I kick him in the balls again.

He doubles over in pain and the man leaning against the car laughs out loud.

My eyes glance over to him. He's tall, scary looking, and the other men all seem to be looking to him for guidance. He's calm and controlled, not like them. He's clearly the alpha of the group.

Their leader.

He smirks as he watches me and lights a cigarette as if thinking and shakes his head.

"I don't have time for this shit." He sighs.

I kick out and connect with the other man's shin, he cries

out. "I'm going to fucking bash you in a minute, bitch." He growls. "What are we fucking doing with her?" he yells at the man leaning on the car. "She's out of fucking control."

The tall man takes a drag of his cigarette, his eyes dropping to my feet before rising back up. He smirks darkly. "Bring her."

I shake my head and start to fight. "Like fuck you will," I scream as I kick out.

His eyes hold mine, and he smiles darkly and takes another drag of his cigarette. He licks his lips as his eyes drop to my breasts.

Fear runs through me. I start to go animalistic and fight like hell.

"Get the cloth," he says to the two other man standing next to him. The guy disappears to the car and shuffles around as I fight and kick the two men on either side of me. He reappears with a black cloth and holds it over my face as I struggle with the two men who are holding me down.

"No." I scream as I try to move my head out of their reach. I can't get away from the black cloth that smells like chemicals.

I struggle.

I fight.

I feel faint.

I lose consciousness.

———

I wake as a wave of nausea rolls through my stomach and I go to wipe the perspiration from my forehead. I can't move my arm.

Huh? I pull my arm, but it won't move, and I glance over my head to see it is tied to a post.

I struggle and look down at my body. Horror dawns on me. Oh my God.

I'm tied to a bed by my hands.

My eyes flicker nervously around the room as I try to focus. I see the tall man leaning up against a dresser in the corner, completely shirtless. He is looking through my wallet from my handbag.

What the fuck?

I start to struggle frantically. I have got to get out of here. I jiggle my whole body to try and loosen the ties. "What do you want?" I cry.

He ignores me and pulls my licence from my wallet. He holds it up and reads it.

"Roshelle Meyers," he murmurs.

"Get out of my things," I snap.

He lies next to me on the bed and rests up on his elbow. He looks down at me as his hand slides back up my body to cup my breast. "Let's get one thing straight." He sneers.

I turn my head away so I don't have to look at him and he grabs my face and drags my eyes to meet his.

"I'm the boss here."

I glare at him.

"You do what I want, when I want."

"Like fuck I do," I whisper angrily.

He smiles an evil smile. "If what I want is my cock splitting your virginal ass in two... then that's my call. Not fucking yours."

I swallow the fear in my throat as his cold eyes hold mine.

"Go to Hell," I whisper.

"I'm the gate keeper of Hell, baby. Welcome home."

2

Roshelle

HIS EYES HOLD mine before he stands and pulls a t-shirt over his head and zips up his jeans. He walks toward the door.

"Where.... where are you going?" I stammer. "Out," he grunts.

I look around the cold room. "You can't leave me here like this. Please. Please let me go. Untie me." I shake my head in a panic. "I won't say anything to anyone. I swear, I won't."

His eyes hold mine for a moment before he turns toward the door again.

"I'm cold. Please. Let me get some clothes on," I plead.

Without a care or one smidgen of remorse, he disappears out the door. It clicks as he turns the lock from the outside.

Silence.

The sound of my breath quivers through the air. I pant as I try to control my erratic heartbeat. Petrified tears of despair roll down my cheeks.

What do I do now?

The glow of a small lamp is the only light in the large room and it's been hours since my captor left. To the right of the door is a sliding doorway that I'm assuming leads to a bathroom. I can see the reflection of a towel hanging up in a mirror. A small desk, lamp, and chair are in the corner and a small two-seater lounge is at the foot of the bed. The room is cold and unwelcoming. The walls are painted a dark, charcoal grey, and I have this weird sensation that the room is moving. I know it can't be, it must be the drugs they gave me to knock me out. It feels as though it's nearly morning, although I have completely lost track of time. I hear a commotion outside and then the key turning in the door.

Oh no. He's back. My heart rate picks up and I stop breathing as I watch the door slowly open. He comes into sight and flicks the light on, smiling darkly as his eyes scan my body.

"Honey, I'm home." He smirks.

Fucking asshole.

I turn my head away from him and stare at the wall. I can't even look at this monster. Suddenly, a group of drunk men stumble into the room behind him and I screw up my face in fear. The smell of alcohol is pungent and I know they are here to take turns.

"We came for our dessert." One of the men smiles as he unzips his jeans.

They all start to wolf whistle as one gropes my breast and another puts his hand between my legs.

"No," I whisper. "Please, no."

"Hands off." The tall man growls. "Get out."

"Fuck off, man. You've had your fun. It's our turn." He unzips his pants and holds his dick above my face.

The tall man pushes him away from me. "I said... get the fuck out. I'm not sharing. I told you already."

Another man takes my breast in his mouth and the tall guy pushes him to the floor violently and kicks him while he's down. Another one launches himself over my body and the tall guy punches him hard in the face. They all start to argue.

"We brought her here for all of us," one man yells.

"The rules have changed. Get out!" He growls angrily as he pushes one man toward the door.

Another man takes one last attempt to touch me and the tall guy goes ballistic and punches him hard three times in the face. After a lot of pushing, shoving, and arguing, the men finally leave. He locks the door behind him and then turns back toward me.

I let myself breathe and then I see arousal flash across his face and my relief is short lived.

Now he's going to have his fun.

I feel sick.

I can't do this.

He walks over to the side of the bed and stares down at me.

I look at him through blurred vision.

"Drug me," I whisper as I turn my head away from him. "Knock me out."

"You don't want to enjoy me?" he asks flatly.

I swallow the lump in my throat as I stare at the wall, the tears running down my face. I can't believe he just asked me that.

I turn back to look at him and my cold eyes hold his. "If you think being tied to a bed is every woman's fantasy, you're as dumb as you fucking look." I sneer.

His face remains emotionless. He bends and begins to untie

one of my wrists. He loosens it and I just want to kick him in the head.

Stop it. Wait until you are completely free, I remind myself. He moves to my other wrist and unties it. Ouch, I'm sore from being stretched out for so long. I sit up and instantly grab the blanket to cover my body.

"Where are my clothes?" I whisper with shame.

He shrugs, turns to face away from me, and takes his shirt off over his head. "I don't know. I don't care. Get out." He's finished with me.

Hatred drips through my every pore. Unable to help myself, I push him hard in the back. "Who the fuck do you think you are?" I snap.

He turns on me like the devil himself and I instinctively flinch away from him.

"Be very careful, Miss..." He pauses for effect. "Roshelle."

"Is this how you get your pathetic kicks? Kidnapping and raping girls?" I murmur.

His lip curls in disgust. "Don't flatter yourself."

I glare at him.

"You don't have what I want." He smirks sarcastically as his eyes drop down my naked body and I try to cover myself with my hands. "I like my women to be..." He pauses again. "Women."

My heart drops.

Of all the things he could have said.

His words cut me like a knife and my thoughts go to Todd, my boyfriend... ex-boyfriend, now. I obviously wasn't woman enough for him, either. I drop my head as sadness steals the air from my lungs. Just shut up and get out of here. He drops his pants and his large erection hangs heavily between his legs. He walks into the bathroom and turns on the shower.

I stand still as I try to regain some sort of composure. The tears are running down my face. I have never been so humiliated in all of my life.

A rapist doesn't want me.

He hops into the shower and under the water, facing away from me, I see he's huge and muscular and his whole back is covered in tattoos. If he wanted to kill me with his bare hands... he could.

I wouldn't stand a chance against him.

I walk around the room in search for my clothes. I have got to get the hell out of here. Suddenly frantic, I open a drawer and quickly pull the t-shirt over my head as he walks out of the bathroom. Shit, that was the quickest shower in history.

"Where you going?" he asks as he dries his hair with the towel.

"Home," I snap as I pull up the shorts.

He raises an eyebrow. "You a good swimmer?"

I frown. "What's that supposed to mean?"

"We are fifty miles from shore."

Huh? I frown.

"You're on a container ship."

I start to look around in a panic. "W-what do you mean?" I stammer. Oh my God.

I run to the cabin door and jiggle the handle. "Let me out. Let me out," I cry.

He opens the door. "Have fun with the crew." He pushes me out and slams the door behind me.

My eyes dart from side to side as I try to focus on my surroundings that are all metal. It's dark with only a row of small orange lights on the floor along the wall. To the left is a wide corridor that must be at least one hundred meters long and I can see a large lit up room at the end. Noise and laughter echoes down the corridor. I can hear men's loud laughter. Oh God, those are the animals that were just in my room. I look to the right and see an exit sign. I have got to get out of here. I quickly dart across the hallway to the safeness of the dark and make my way up toward the exit sign.

He was lying.

He had to be lying. I'm not on a boat. I can't be on a boat.

I tiptoe like a mouse up the three flights of stairs until I get to large double doors with small round windows in them. I peer through and my heart sinks.

It's dark and raining, and for as far as I can see shipping containers are piled up miles high on top of each other.

Oh my God, what do I do?

I stand back as I think. I know one thing for certain: if I stay on this ship I will be dead before I see land again.

Fuck this. I burst through the doors and run outside into the pouring rain as I frantically look around at the surroundings. I run to the side of the ship and look over the side... water for as far as I can see.

With my heart hammering in my chest, I run to the other side of the boat... water for as far as I can see. I look to the back and see a tower with lights on in it and I know that the captain must be in there. He will have a radio.

Yes.

He will help me.

I run toward the watchtower and trip over a large rope thingy that is raised from the metal deck and I go flying across and fall onto the hard floor.

I lie for a moment in the rain as despair fills me. I can't do this. I'm not strong enough to get through this.

My head hurts from earlier and I feel disorientated. I don't need this fucking shit.

What am I going to do? I have no idea how I am going to get myself off this ship.

How did they get an unconscious girl onto a shipping deck through customs? What the fuck is going on with our border protection? With renewed purpose, I stand and start to head toward the control centre. Somebody from there will help me. I know they will. They have phones and can call for help. I open the door and am greeted by another large metal staircase. I take the steps two at a time until I get to the top. I look around nervously and I see a man sitting behind the control centre of the boat.

"Hello." I pause. "Can you help me?" I ask.

The man turns around and my face drops. Oh God, it's the man who tried to rape me on the bed downstairs. I step back in fear and he picks up the radio.

"He's finished. She's out of his room." He hangs up and smiles darkly as his hungry eyes drop down my body.

Oh my fucking God, he just called for the other men. I turn and run.

I run for my life down the stairs two at a time and I can hear men yahooing in the distance.

No. No.

I run as fast as I can and I burst through the doors and back out onto the deck. I run over to the side and hide behind one of the shipping containers. The rain is coming down really hard.

I hear the double doors burst open and all the men yell excitedly. "She's here somewhere. Find her."

Mac

I am just drifting off to sleep when I hear a commotion outside in the hall. The boys are all cheering.

I hear her scream. They found her.

I roll over and shake my head as uneasiness passes over me. She screams again and I hear one of the men cry out in pain. I smirk to myself. She's obviously just hurt someone. Feisty little bitch, I will give her that.

I start to drift off again and I hear her cry out in pain.

I frown. For fuck's sake, I don't need this shit. I'm tired.

For another ten minutes, I doze, and then the sound of a frantic bang on the door wakes me.

"Help me. Help me!" she screams as the door handle jiggles

frantically.

Go away.

I close my eyes again.

"He won't fucking help you," I hear Ian call out. The hairs on the back of neck stand to attention. Fuck, I hate that guy.

I roll onto my back and stare at the ceiling through the darkness with my hands behind my head as I listen.

I hear her struggling and fighting the group of men in the hallway. She's a hellcat all right.

I should have let them kill her. It would have been way less dramatic.

I don't have the time or energy for this shit. "Please. No," she cries.

Fucking hell. Annoyed, I hop up and pull on my shorts. I stand behind the door with my hands on my hips as I listen for a moment. "Oh, I'm going to give it to you good." Ian growls. "You're going to pay for that bitch."

That's it. He's not fucking getting her. I open the door in a rush and the boys look up from their spot on the floor where they are struggling to hold her down.

"Get off her," I snap.

"M-mac," Ian stammers as he looks up. "You don't want her."

I glare at him.

"We do," Mike replies. "She's good to go. You've already finished with her."

I turn my attention to the annoying little fuck. "Give me a reason to kill you. Make my fucking day." I growl.

He narrows his eyes at me.

"Let her go."

They stand and let her up off the floor and she practically jumps onto me and throws her arms around my neck for protection. She's wet and cold and shaking in fear. My hand instinctively snakes around her waist.

I glare at my crew mates. "Next person who touches this girl is going to fucking die. Do you all hear me?"

"Is that a threat?" Ian sneers.

I grab him by the throat and squeeze hard as I slam his head against the metal wall behind him. "That's a fucking promise, cunt."

The men all step back and glance at each other.

"Do not fucking piss me off!" I growl.

They take another step back and I open the door to throw her into my room just as Ian makes another desperate grab for her. I close the door behind her and then I turn and punch him hard and he doubles over in pain as he clutches his face.

I then turn to Mike. "Who's next? You want to fucking go at me. Let's go?"

The wimps all back down and begin to walk back up the hallway. Just as I thought they would... soft cocks.

I walk into my room, closing the door behind me before I turn to see her lying on the bed in the foetal position, crying.

I close my eyes in annoyance. Fuck this shit.

Roshelle

I pant and shake uncontrollably. I'm lying on the bed and the tears won't stop.

I have never been so frightened in all of my life.

He walks back in and stands at the end of the bed for a moment as he watches me. Then he disappears into the bathroom and turns the shower on.

I shiver and shake, unable to control it. I'm so cold.

He reappears and watches me for a moment. "Get in the shower," he demands.

I can't get up, the shaking is so violent.

After watching me for a moment he picks me up and carries me into the bathroom and I cling to his neck for protection. The tears are running down my face.

"Stop shaking," he snaps, annoyed.

"I can't...I can't help it," I stammer. My teeth are chattering and the shudders through my body are violent.

"Christ," he mutters to himself, and with an exhale of breath, he walks in under the water with me pressed against him. Both of my arms are around his neck and he is holding me like a bride.

He doesn't speak, and for a long time we stay under the hot water as I cling to him. Eventually my shudders subside. I don't know if it's the shock or if I'm so physically exhausted from fighting, but I am struggling to stay awake. My eyes keep closing by themselves.

"Can you stand?" he asks as he puts me down.

I nod sadly as my feet touch the cold, hard tiles on the floor.

"Let's get these wet clothes off you."

My haunted eyes meet his. Is this it? Is this the part where I lose all dignity?

He bends and takes the t-shirt over my head and slides the shorts down my legs.

I stand before him totally naked.

"Are you hurt?" he asks as he inspects the cut on my head. I don't answer, I just hang my head and let the hot water run over me, hoping it will wash away this nightmare of events. "Looks like it will be okay," he replies as he inspects the wound from the pistol whip from the gun.

My arms hang by my side. I am absolutely defeated. I don't have the strength to fight him. I know that.

He knows that.

He takes his t-shirt over his head and my eyes tear up. Here we go.

He slowly slides his wet shorts down his legs and my eyes drop to his groin. He's hard.

I close my eyes in pain.

He pulls me back to his large bare chest and we stand still under the water for an extended time. I can feel his huge erection pressed against my stomach.

Next thing I know, I am wrapped in a towel and being carried to the bed. He carefully dries me and pulls back the blankets and lies me down. I can feel his hungry eyes scan my flesh as I lie naked on my back in his bed. The same bed that, only hours ago, he'd tied me to.

I try to fight it, but my eyes keep closing by themselves.

"Go to sleep," are the last words I hear.

I wake alone and sit up with a start. What? Was that a nightmare? Then I feel the pain shoot through my head and I look around to the cold metal can I am in and my heart drops.

It's true. Oh God, it's true.

"Hello?" I call. Is he here? Maybe he is in the bathroom? I stand groggily and shuffle to the bathroom. I'm so bloody sore. Every muscle in my body feels like it has been ripped from the bones. The bathroom is empty and I sit back onto the bed. What the hell am I going to do?

I frown as I try to remember how last night ended?

I don't even remember falling asleep.

I'm naked and I run my fingers through my sex to see if I am wet. Have I had sex? Did he have sex with me while I was unconscious?

I get a visual of how hard he was in the shower and my stomach drops. Of course we had sex. Men like him take what they want, when they want it.

They called him Mac.

I make my way over to a porthole and I stand on the bed to peer through it. The view is about a meter above sea level and I can see the sea lapping closely as rain pelts down.

Fucking hell, this is a nightmare.

I slump back onto the bed and look around at my surroundings. I need a weapon... but am I really going to be able to kill ten men? Even if I do, who is going to steer the ship back to shore?

I blow out a defeated breath and stand, going back to the drawers to take out a large sweater and put it on. This ship is freezing.

The door opens and I step back. It's him.

His eyes hold mine and he dips his head in acknowledgment.

I nod and drop my eyes.

He puts a plate of food onto the desk. "Eat," he murmurs.

I drop to a seated position on the bed and he turns and puts his hands on his hips as he watches me. For the first time since my capture I take a good look at him. He is tall, maybe six-foot four, muscular with honey blonde hair that is about three inches long and has a curl on the ends. His skin is olive and his large eyes are brown. In any other circumstance, he would be handsome. Now I know that's far from the truth. Looks can be deceiving. He's a murdering criminal.

"Stay in the room," he murmurs.

My eyes meet his.

"You are safe in here."

I stare at him, I don't even know how to reply to that statement.

"Keep the door locked…" He pauses for a moment. "Or they will come and get you."

I don't answer.

"Answer me," he snaps angrily.

"Yes." I nod.

He turns and with one last lingering look, he leaves and I hear the door click as he locks it behind him.

I sit in the semi-darkened room for a moment as I try to process what he has just told me. Keep the door locked or they will come and get me. I am safe in this room, but I'm not safe enough. He told me I'm not woman enough for him. For the first time, my thoughts go to Todd and Melissa who are probably in the throws of passion right now. They wouldn't even know I'm missing yet and probably think I have just taken off somewhere in anger. Sadness fills me as I realize that they probably wouldn't even care if I did.

I curl up into a ball in his cold, hard bed of a prison and allow myself to weep.

I've never felt so alone.

I think I've finally hit rock bottom.

I am woken as I feel the bed dip. I pry open my sleepy eyes

to see Mac sitting on the bed next to me. By the lighting I can tell it's dark and he has been gone all day.

"You haven't eaten."

I look away from him and stare at the wall.

He stands and goes into the bathroom and showers. Still, I face the wall.

I have no words. Nothing to say to him, anyway.

He walks back into the room with a towel around his waist. "We get to Puerto Rico in twenty-eight days. You can get off there."

I roll onto my back and turn to face him, frowning in question.

He drops the towel to dress and without thinking my eyes scan his body before I snap my gaze away.

"You are on your own when we get there, though. I want nothing to do with it," he says.

I shake my head. Typical. What kind of man kidnaps a girl and then dumps her alone at a dock in Puerto Rico?

"I'm going to dinner," he states as he pulls his pants up around his waist.

My eyes hold his as hatred drips through my every pore.

Fuck you.

He gestures to the plate of cold food on the desk. "You know where yours is."

I roll my eyes and turn my back to him and face the wall again.

I hear the door click as he leaves.

I feel more human, having eaten and showered. I'm lying with my back to the door when I hear him come in. The room is lit by the lamp on the desk and he's been gone for a few hours.

I roll onto my back and look at him.

"You ate?" he asks.

I nod.

He undresses to his briefs and then goes into the bathroom. He washes his hands and then I hear him brush his teeth. He then comes and climbs into bed next to me.

We lay in silence for a long time.

Finally, he breaks it. "Why were you crying?"

I frown over at him in the darkness.

He lies on his side facing me and fiddles with the blanket. "When you came out of the nightclub onto the back dock... why were you crying?"

I hesitate before I answer. "I didn't like the song they were playing," I whisper into the darkness.

He doesn't question my lie and I don't elaborate.

3

Roshelle

MAC IS READING on the bed while I sit at the desk. We haven't spoken. I mean, what could we possibly have to say to each other? Unfortunately for me, there has been a weird development. An elephant has moved into the room. He's big and pink and smells a lot like sexual chemistry. It's not. I know it's not. It couldn't possibly be, but when he looks at me, for some reason, my stupid heart races.

Can he feel it?

Can he feel the way my body is reacting to his? It's bloody uncomfortable, especially in this situation. I mean we are sleeping in the same bed. The worse thing of all is that I am finding myself wanting to make conversation. Even though I know it's because there is nobody else and it is just human nature to want to communicate, it's unsettling.

"I'm going to sleep," he announces before standing. He slowly takes his t-shirt over his head. Instinctively, my eyes drop down his torso before I catch myself and look away. The heat of his gaze penetrates the air and I look up to find his dark eyes fixed on mine.

The electricity zaps between us and my heart starts to thump in my chest. He clenches his fists as they hang down by his sides as if trying to control himself. Air... there is no bloody air in here. For a long time, in the silence, our eyes stay firmly locked.

He's just so.... masculine. I can't believe this.

What a nightmare. This whole situation disgusts me. I walk into the bathroom and get into the shower as I try to calm my anxiety.

I don't need this shit.

I pace back and forth in the room that has been my prison for the last four days. He locks the door behind him in the morning and doesn't come back until late at night, only returning to bring me food. My only solace is that he doesn't touch me when he returns. It's a toxic environment and I am quite sure if I stay here for another twenty-four days I will go insane. The more I think about it, and I have thought about it a lot, the more I know I need to try and call someone for help. I witnessed a murder and there is no way in hell they are going to let me walk away from all of this. I'm a witness who is still alive and that makes me a massive threat. Perhaps they are going to push me overboard after they have had their fun... nobody would ever know.

The perfect crime.

My mind goes to Melissa and Todd. I'm positive that they are aware I'm missing by now and it boils my blood to think that they know that I know what assholes they both are. I bet they think I'm lying in a hotel broken hearted somewhere on the verge of suicide.

Stupid fucks.

I'm furious, not heart broken. I couldn't care less about the two of them.

I suppose that's probably the only good thing that has come of all this. I've gained a new perspective on life.

People who fuck you over are just not worth it.

I'm done with being a doormat. I'm done with fake friendships and sleazy boyfriends whose brains are in their dicks. When I get off this ship, I am going to kick some serious ass, and Todd and Melissa are at the top of my fucking list.

First, I need to think of a way to get to the control tower.

Leaving this room unnoticed isn't going to be easy. I've debated every escape plan possible and all of them seem too risky. I'm not sure how much of a risk anything is, though, as I seem to have lost all perspective on this situation.

I hear the key turn in the lock, the door opens, and he appears. Having just finished working for the day, his hair is messed up and he has what looks like engine grease on his face.

I frown when I see him. He doesn't normally look like this when he gets home from his day's work.

"What do you do on this boat?" I ask.

His eyes flick to me in surprise that I am addressing him.

"I'm a Nautical Engineer," he replies.

My face falls in surprise. Well blow me down. I raise my eyebrows. "You?" I question.

He curls his lip. "What's that supposed to mean?"

I fold my arms in front of me and raise an eyebrow in question. "Nothing."

His eyes hold mine.

"I just didn't take you to have much of a brain, that's all," I murmur under my breath.

He shakes his head, unimpressed. "I was going to take you

to the common room for dinner tonight." He takes his shirt off over his head and my eyes drop to his large, broad chest. "But seeing that you are being a smart ass, you can stay here alone again." He disappears into the bathroom and I hear the shower turn on.

He was going to take me out. My mind starts to tick. He was going to take me out. What if I went out with him and somehow slipped away for a minute to call for help? Would that work?

I glance into the bathroom. He's naked. Nothing new, he has undressed in front of me all week. He begins to rub soap over himself and my eyes flicker up between his legs. Fuck, he's huge. I've never seen a man like this and the more I think about it, the more I seriously doubt he raped me. I would be sore if he had and I'm not.

He looks up and I snap my eyes down to pretend I wasn't looking and when I slowly glance up, he smiles broadly.

"Like what you see?" he asks.

I look at him, deadpan. "No. Actually, I would like to gouge my eyes out."

"Why are you looking then?" His soapy hand strokes his dick as he washes it.

"I wasn't," I murmur distracted by his hand jerking.

"My cock feels better than it looks." He smirks as he washes himself.

I swallow the lump of nerves in my throat and my eyes drop to the floor to stop my wayward eyes from watching. I stare at the tiles on the floor for a while as I wait for him. "Where is dinner at?" I ask. I need to be nice and get him to take me out. He is the only person who can get me out of this room unnoticed.

"We have a large dorm and entertainment area at the other end of the boat."

I frown as I think. "How many people work on this ship?" I ask.

"You're very chatty tonight," he replies dryly.

God, too much, too fast. I haven't talked to him all week and now I'm sucking up. He's right. I need to calm down and use my head. I stay silent for a while.

"Twenty–four," he finally replies.

I think for a moment. I can't actually remember how many men were involved with attacking me the other night and I feel my apprehension rise at just the memory of it. Maybe I should just stay here. I can't stand the thought of facing them. I stand and then sit back down onto the bed. A few minutes later he walks into the room and drops the towel to dress. His wet curls hang down over his face and his tanned skin has a sheen on it from his shower. He smells like clean soap. Frigging hell.

"Do you have to be naked all the time?" I snap, agitated by his good looks. "I don't want to see your junk."

"I'm getting dressed, and for the record, you were just checking out my junk in the shower."

I screw up my face in horror. "I was not."

"You were too."

I narrow my eyes. "Whatever."

He smirks knowingly and takes out a pair of black tight underpants. I watch in slow motion as he bends and pulls them up his legs and readjusts his dick.

Hmm.

He retrieves his dark jeans and a light blue t-shirt, and after dressing he sits on the bed to put his shoes on. I watch him quietly.

"Do you want to come or not?" he asks. "Will..." I hesitate.

"Will what?"

"Will they be there?"

He nods as he ties a shoe.

"Oh." I pause. "Probably not then."

"They won't hurt you." My eyes search his. "I will be there." He replies.

I stay still, I don't know if I can honestly make myself leave the room. They terrify me.

He stands. "Okay, suit yourself. Stay here."

Shit, I need to get to the control tower. I stand abruptly in a panic. "What would I wear?" I stammer in a fluster.

His eyes drop down at my attire of his baggy pyjama bottoms and t-shirt. He frowns as if thinking. "Come with me."

"Where? Where are we going?" I ask as I twist my hands in front of me nervously. "Is this a trick?" I whisper.

He frowns. "A trick for what?"

I swallow the lump in my throat as my eyes flicker to the door. "To hand me over to them?"

He shakes his head, annoyed. "No. If I wanted to hand you over, I would just hand you over."

My eyes hold his. Why isn't he handing me over? I don't understand this at all.

What are his plans for me?

"Coming or not?" he asks again.

Bloody hell, this may be my only chance to get off this ship alive. I nod quickly before I change my mind.

He opens the door and walks out into the corridor and I peer around the door jamb. My heart starts to hammer.

"You coming?" he snaps.

I tentatively follow him as he strides down the corridor towards the big room I heard the partying come from the other night. We arrive at a set of stairs and I frown at him.

"Up here." He gestures to the stairs.

Oh my God. Where is he taking me? My heart is going to go

into cardiac arrest at any moment. We get to the floor above us and he walks down the corridor and knocks on a door. My eyes widen and I take a step back. Oh no. What is he doing?

The door opens and a pretty blonde girl stands before us.

"Hey, Mac." She smiles sexily.

"Hey, Chels." He gestures to me and her face falls. I fold my arms nervously in front of me. What's a girl doing on this horror ship? "Have you got any clothes she can borrow?" he asks.

She looks me up and down and I shrivel on the spot. Who is this? She hesitates for a moment. "Yeah, I guess." She opens the door and gestures for us to come in.

He grabs my hand and leads me into her room. I nervously look around as I cling tightly to his hand. There are mirrors on the wall and a fancy lace lightshade that hangs down low. A large bed. The room is feminine. Huh? Does she live on this ship? She disappears back into the bathroom and takes out her mascara and begins to apply it. "The clothes are in the wardrobe, help yourself," she calls.

He opens the wardrobe and begins to search through drawers and pull things out as he inspects them.

Okay, what is going on here? I don't understand this at all. I glance into the bathroom and she is applying red lipstick. She's wearing a tight, low-cut, black dress that leaves nothing to the imagination. She's gorgeous. She reappears from the bathroom and puts her small, gold handbag over her shoulder.

"I'll meet you both up there."

"Yeah, okay," he calls after her, distracted at the task at hand.

She leaves the room and closes the door behind her.

I wait for a moment as he keeps looking at the clothes.

"Who is she?" I ask.

"Chelsea," he replies as he hands me some clothes. "She lives on this ship?" I ask.

"Aha."

I take the clothes he has passed to me.

"Put them on," he demands.

I frown. I'm not getting dressed here in front of him. He rolls his eyes. "In the bathroom."

"Oh. Okay," I whisper. I disappear into the bathroom and put on the clothes he has selected for me. A short, pink and purple tartan skirt with a dropped waist and box pleats, and a white flowing singlet with shoestring straps. I need a bra. I stick my head around the corner of the bathroom door and he looks up from his sitting position on the bed. "Umm."

"Umm, what?"

"I need some underwear," I whisper through embarrassment.

He raises an eyebrow and tries to hide his smirk. He stands and rustles through a drawer and passes me a pair of panties. "You won't fit her bra." He smirks.

I stare at him blankly.

"She has big tits."

"Oh." Oh God, how embarrassing. I walk back into the bathroom, closing the door behind me to put on the white lace panties. I glance at myself in the mirror and cringe. I look like shit. I have a black eye and a small cut on the bridge of my nose. What must I have looked like four days ago when this first happened? I grab some concealer from her makeup bag and try to fix my face a little. I brush my long dark hair, which is frizzing to oblivion from his shitty shampoo, and I grab a hair band and tie it back into a high ponytail.

I walk back out into the room and his eyes drop to my feet and back up to my face, a trace of a smile crosses his face.

I hold my breath as I wait for his reaction. His dark eyes slowly undress me.

He stands abruptly and steps forward, bringing him way too close. "You look edible," he whispers as his huge frame invades my space.

I step back without thinking, our eyes locked on each other. My eyes drop to his tongue as it darts out to lick his bottom lip.

The hunter and his prey.

The electricity zaps between us.

"Do you want to stay alive pretty girl?" he asks as he dusts the backs of his fingers down my face.

I nod subtly. My eyes drop to the floor as his breathing becomes magnified. His fingers burn my skin.

"We need to show the crew who you belong to," he whispers.

My eyes meet his and I frown. What is he talking about? The primal urge to kick him in the balls is overwhelming, but I know to stay alive I need him on my side.

He bends and puts his mouth to my ear and his breath causes goosebumps to scatter up my spine. I close my eyes in dismay. Damn it.

"I need to show my crew mates who you belong to." His breath dusts my neck and I get a tingle all the way to my toes.

My horrified eyes meet his.

"Let's see how good an actress you are," he whispers darkly.

"What do you mean?"

"I mean, if you want to survive, you need to play along."

"Play along?" I frown.

"Play along that you're mine," he murmurs, distracted, his eyes following his fingers as he brushes them over my lips. "Pretend that you like me touching you." His fingertips run down the length of my neck and I close my eyes. "Although you wouldn't have to act much." He leans in and gently kisses my ear. "Would you?" he whispers.

I drop my head in dismay, knowing I need to change the subject or I'm going to be on my back on that bed in one second flat.

He rubs his hand through my long ponytail and down over my breast.

My eyes rise to meet his and disgust fills me as I feel my nipples harden under his touch.

In seemingly slow motion he leans in and whispers in my ear. "You like my touch." His breath on my neck sends goosebumps scattering down my spine again.

I shake my head nervously. "No, I... I don't." I stammer.

He rolls my nipple between his large fingers and it hardens even further.

Oh God.

"Yes, you do." He growls before sinking his teeth into my ear.

"No," I breathe as my knees feel like they might collapse beneath me.

"Liar," he whispers as he licks my ear again.

Dear, God. I close my eyes. "Please," I hesitate as I try to think. "Please, leave me be."

He grabs my jaw aggressively and pulls my face so that our eyes meet.

My fight instincts start to fire up but I try desperately to control them. Control it I remind myself. "Please," I whisper.

His eyes drop to my lips and he smiles sardonically. "For now." An uneasy feeling washes over me. I'm disturbed by the way my body reacts to him, the way my heart races when he looks at me. His touch is electric.

As if reading my mind, he smiles sexily and takes my hand and pulls me with him out the door.

We walk into the large, messy hall and I see everyone's eyes lift as they see us. I feel sick. What the hell am I doing here? He towers above me and holds my hand in his. I glance around the room. To the right is a big kitchen where a male chef is cooking. In front are six tables and chairs where some people are eating. To the left is a super large plasma television. Lounges are in front of that and scattered in no particular order. At the back is a bar with a pool table and a table tennis table. The room is huge and nice... not at all what I was expecting. In fact, this whole ship isn't what I was expecting. I thought container ships were supposed to be dirty and unkempt? I stand nervously as I await his instruction and he walks us over to the kitchen.

"Just two?" the chef calls.

I stare at the chef. Is he in on this? Will he help me?

"Thanks," Mac replies.

He then leads me by the hand to the back bar and another man smiles from behind it. I step back when I see him. He is one of the men from the other night.

Mac feels my fear and puts his arm protectively around my shoulders.

I drop my eyes to the floor as I try to concentrate on the task at hand.

"What do you want to drink?" Mac asks. "Diet Coke," I reply without emotion.

I glance over to the pool table where I see six girls in sexy clothing playing. I frown. More girls... Oh, thank God. They will help me. I just need to talk to them alone. Mac tightens his grip around my shoulders. I glance around the room and see approximately fifteen men. Some I recognize, some I don't.

None of them are at all surprised to see me here. They all know I am taken and they don't care.

What fucking kind of ship is this?

He gets our drinks and takes them over to the dining table area and pulls a chair out for me. I sit down. I can feel the eyes on my back. He sits down opposite me and picks up his Coke. "You're drinking Coke?" I ask. Every night this week he has come back to the room smelling of beer or Scotch. Why is tonight different?

"I'm on call tonight," he replies.

"Oh" I frown. I forget this is actually a job.

My eyes roam to the girls playing pool and I can see them looking over and talking to each other. What are they saying? Are they going to help me?

"Who are the girls?" I ask.

He sips his drink as he seems to contemplate giving me the answer. "The crew's girls."

I frown. "What do you mean?"

He sips his drink again.

"Are they the wives of some of the men?" I ask.

He smirks as his eyes hold mine. "They are the whores of all of the men."

Horror dawns.

I lean forward. "Prostitutes?" I whisper in mortification.

He raises an eyebrow. "We are a long time at sea."

I sit back in disgust. I have no words. I glance over at them again. "So you all just fuck whoever you want?"

He smirks.

"The girls sleep with all of you?" I frown.

"They have fun and are well looked after." He shrugs.

Fear fills me. "Were they taken? Is that the plan for me?" I whisper in a panic.

He frowns. "No." He shakes his head. "They come and go as they like. We always have six, but the girls change at different ports."

I sit back in my chair. I can't get my head around this type of lifestyle.

"They all have their own shit they are trying to escape. This boat is their safe place. Most do a few trips a year. They rotate." The chef brings out two plates of a beef and vegetable stew with mashed potatoes and vegetables, leaving us to eat in silence, although my mind is in overdrive at the lives those women must live. We eat and then have dessert, and I have to admit the food is much better when hot.

A man comes and sits next to Mac and they begin to talk. My mind starts to buzz and I look around at the exits. How do I get to the control tower from here? My heartbeat rises as I imagine the scenario of getting caught. To the right is a bathroom and then the main door is where we came from. If I go back that way, it's about one hundred meters down the hall, then up the stairs and then back another hundred meters to the other end. By my calculations we are closer to the control tower from here. Where is the door? I keep looking around casually. Bloody hell, it's so confusing. I pull my chair out.

"Where are you going?" he snaps.

"I..." I hesitate. "I need to go to the bathroom."

His knowing eyes hold mine. Shit.

"I will show you where it is," he says.

"Thank you," I reply. Damn it.

He takes my hand and walks me over to the bathroom and then follows me in.

I frown. "It's okay. I can go to the bathroom on my own."

He has a quick look around before he walks back out. He was checking nobody was in here with me. I go to the bathroom and exit to find him sitting on a barstool at the bar. He holds out his hand for me to join him. Bloody hell, why is he watching me like a hawk? I slowly walk over. He positions me between his legs and he snakes his arms around my waist as he talks to another man I haven't seen before.

I keep searching for an exit over his shoulder. "What do you want to drink?" he asks.

I glance up at all the alcohol.

"She will have a Scotch and Coke, please," Mac says before waiting for my answer.

I frown. "No, I won't. I don't like Scotch," I reply. "But I do and I want to kiss you."

My brain misfires. Huh?

The man he is talking to smirks. "Catch you later, man." He gets up and leaves.

The barman leaves to make my drink.

He slips his hand underneath the band of my skirt and rubs down my stomach, his fingers skim my pubic hair before he kisses my ear from behind. "You feel good," he whispers.

Crap, crap, crap.

I have to get out of here. I turn and lean into his ear and whisper. "What are you doing?" I whisper.

"I'm showing them you're mine," he whispers back into my ear as he bites it. "This is where you show them you like it."

"By running your fingers through my pubic hair?" I whisper angrily.

He smiles into my neck. "Yes, exactly. You are getting the hang of it. You need to play along."

"Nobody even cares," I whisper angrily into his ear.

He licks my neck in an upstroke and cold chills cover my body. Why does he have to affect me like this? "Everybody in this room is watching. If you are not mine, they will assume you are theirs," he whispers.

I pull back and my scared eyes hold his.

"Kiss me," he whispers darkly. "W-what?" I stammer in fear.

He pulls my face toward him and his lips gently dust mine. Oh God.

His tongue slowly enters my mouth and, unable to help it, my eyes close. His tongue delves deeper and deeper and I lose all sense of reality. His arm tightens around my waist and he pulls me closer to him. My breasts are squashed up against his chest and his hand is crushing me to him. Oh hell, I've never been kissed like this. I feel his large erection up against my thigh and my insides start to melt.

Reality sets in and I pull away. What the hell am I doing?

"I just lost my fucking appetite. I'm going back to the room."

"I'm not ready to go back yet," he snaps, angry that I stopped his kiss.

"I didn't ask you to come." I sneer.

"If you are not with me—"

I cut him off. "I'm not with you. Get it through your fucking head." I pull out of his grip and storm back to the room alone as everyone in the room watches. I will take my chances with the others. I am not standing there and making out with that fucking asshole.

I storm back to the room with him hot on my heels.

I'm angry, fucking furious with myself, actually.

He opens the door and pushes me in as he stays in the corridor and without a word locks the door behind me.

4

***

Roshelle

REALITY HITS hard when I hear the cold click of the door as he leaves. I walk into the bathroom and turn on the shower, undress, and slowly get in as the tears begin to fall. I grab the soap and rub my skin in a panic. I wash and wash and wash until my skin is red raw. I need to get this dirty, slutty feeling off me.

He knows, too. He knows I enjoyed that kiss. He felt it. In that moment, he owned me.

I lie in the darkness with my back toward the door when he comes in five hours later. The room is silent and heavy from my tears. I have cried a river tonight.

Not because I am the victim in this shitty circumstance, but because I was a willing participant.

I kissed him without a fight. I gave in to my lust.

Something that I vowed I would never do. I'm as bad as

Melissa when she gave in to her lust. Her body led her to temptation.

He comes in and puts his keys on the desk and I can feel his eyes watching me in the darkness. After a moment he walks into the bathroom and I hear the shower turn on. My heart is beating so fast and I know he will be washing himself for what's to come. Oh God, no. I can't do this. Please don't make me do this.

The shower turns off and a few minutes later he crawls naked into bed next to me. I scrunch my eyes shut and pretend to sleep.

He lies on his back for a few moments and I stay silent.....can he tell that I'm awake?

He blows out a heavy breath and then rolls so his back is to me. I frown.

What's he doing?

I lie still, but my heart and mind is scrambled as I wait for the attack. I wait and I wait.

It doesn't come and ten minutes later his regulated breathing tells me he is asleep.

I wake and feel something warm and hard under my head. I doze for a few minutes, feeling contented. Hmm, this is nice.

Hang on a minute. I jump, what the heck is going on here? I am wrapped around Mac and he has his arm under my head. Our legs are entwined and my body is splayed half over his.

He's hard.

I jump back from him in a panic and look up to his face to see he is still sleeping.

Thank God. I get up and go to the bathroom and then grab a blanket and wrap myself in it to sit at the desk. I sit in the semi-dark as I watch him. His curled, sun-kissed hair is scattered

across his pillow and his skin is golden brown. A three-day darkened growth shadows his square jaw, hiding his large dimples...
just. He's a big man, standing over 6'4", with a broad build. His
body is rippled with muscles and he has the distinct V that runs
from his lower stomach down to his groin. My eyes drop lower
and I feel the dull ache deep within my body. My memory takes
me back to how hard he was last night and how good he felt
underneath me on that barstool... how hot he had me for his kiss.

That kiss.

If that's what it's like when we are acting, imagine when
we're alone in the room. I close my eyes in regret.

Stop it.

His back is covered in tattoos and he has a few strewn down
his arms. A large, thick, purple scar wraps around his ribs on
his left side. I wonder what it's from? It isn't that old by the
looks of it. Has he been stabbed or in a fight? I stare straight
ahead as I think. I've got bigger problems on my mind than
Mac. It's day six. There could be a full scale search for me back
home in action by now. My car could have been found. My
bank accounts or phone haven't been touched. I know Melissa
and Todd would have fessed up to police about their sleazy
affair. They wouldn't want to be implicated in any of this. The
police probably think I have committed suicide somewhere.

Nobody would ever know if they did kill me out here. I have
literally disappeared without a trace. I wonder if there was any
CCTV from the back of the alleyway at the nightclub, and who
was the guy that they killed?

Who actually pulled the trigger?

Did he die? Did they know him and why did they kill him? I
wish I could remember that night, but it was all such a blur.
Today, I'm going to get to the control tower if it's the last thing I
do. I need to find a way off this ship. Actually, I haven't checked

for land in a while. I stand and go over and peer out of the port-hole. Water as far as I can see. Damn it. As soon as I see land I'm going to run and jump over the side. I'm taking my chances with the sharks. Anything is safer than this.

My eyes roam over the naked man in bed, fast asleep and on his back. His prominent stomach muscles show through his skin and his broad chest rises and falls as he breathes. One hand is on his dick and the other hand is behind his head. Uneasiness fills me, not because I'm afraid of what he will do to me. More because I'm afraid I will like it. He is unlike any man I have ever known. Hardened, rough, sexual. He makes other men I have been with seem like little boys.

For a moment, I let myself imagine what sex would be like with him and I get a visual of him throwing me around and giving it to me hard. God, it would be so fucking hot. He's so strong and hung. I picture myself on my knees going down on him, him looking down at me with his hand tenderly on the back of my head.

I snap my eyes away in disgust. Will you listen to yourself, Roshelle, you fucking idiot? You are trying to stay alive here, not star in a Pirate of Penzance Porno. I know now why they call it cabin fever. I'm getting delusional.

He stirs and I sit still. He grabs his dick and strokes a few times as he wakes up. Eventually, his sleepy eyes open and find me across the room.

"What are you looking at?" He yawns with a stretch.

"Nothing," I reply.

He casually gets up and strolls to the bathroom, butt naked.

I stare at the floor so I can't look and I hear him go to the toilet and then wash his hands. I wrap the blanket around myself protectively. I just wish he wasn't so comfortable being naked around me.

He comes back out and puts a pair of boxer shorts on.

"Chelsea is going to come and get you and watch out for you at lunch today," he tells me casually as he flicks the kettle on. "I'm working and won't have time."

"She said she would be here about twelve."

I frown in question.

"I called around and saw her on my way back here last night." He makes the two cups of coffee.

I stare at him. He went to her room. He had sex with her last night, that's why he didn't touch me.

I stand, unsure what to think. This should be a relief, but somehow it feels... I don't even know. I go into the bathroom and close the door behind me. I get into the hot shower and let the water run down over my head for ten minutes as I think. My heart is hammering and I don't know why. I try to think rationally, but I just can't. She saved me from having to do it? This is a good thing. If he's fucking them, he's not fucking me. That's all that matters. How regularly does he fuck them... her? The door opens and he comes in, fussing around before he grabs his deodorant. His eyes drop down my body and I glare at him and raise a brow.

"Go away."

His eyes drop down my body.

"Get out," I snap.

With a smirk, he walks back out into the bedroom.

I finish my shower and walk back into the bedroom, just as I see him lifting a chair back to the desk. Huh? He had the chair in front of the wardrobe. What was he looking for in the wardrobe? I pretend I don't notice and go to get something to wear from his drawers, but he picks up a bag and throws it at me. "I got you some clothes."

I really want to say, why, so you can imagine I'm a fucking

prostitute? I hold my tongue. I don't give a fuck about him. I want to go home. I snatch the bag up, annoyed at my stupid feelings, and go back into the bathroom and pull out the clothes he has given me. I go through the bag and pull out the skimpy clothing. Screw this. He's kidding. I stick my head around the door jamb. "I hate these clothes. They scream that I would fuck anything."

A trace of a smile crosses his face. "Would you?" I frown. "Would I what?"

"Fuck anything."

I narrow my eyes. "No, I would not." I go back to dressing in the bathroom.

I pull on a short, floral, peach-coloured dress.

I eventually walk back into the room and I find him dressed for work. "I got to go."

I nod once.

"See you tonight."

"Whatever," I reply, monotone. "I don't think I'm coming to dinner tonight."

"Suit yourself." With that he leaves the room, but today he doesn't lock the door.

I Frown. What? I stand and open the door and it is open.

He turns to face me.

"Where are you going?" he asks.

I shrug. "You didn't lock the door?"

"No." He turns back to me. "I have staked my claim. You should be okay now."

"Oh." I frown in confusion. "Staked your claim?" I ask.

"I will kill anyone who touches you and they know that."

"But if they have already killed me, what is the point?"

"They won't."

I frown. "Are you sure?"

He nods once with a shrug.

I turn and go back into the room and close the door. I drop to the bed and think on that for a moment. Does that mean the word is out that I am off limits? Will I be safe to walk around now? He seems to think I will, but then maybe he just doesn't care if they get me. Hmm, interesting. My eyes look up to the wardrobe. What was he doing up there? I open the double doors and peer up. It's high... whatever he was looking at is high. I lock the front door and pull the chair over to the cupboard and stand on it to peer in. Sweaters and folded clothes are in neat rows. Wow, pretty neat for a guy. I carefully take out the sweaters and clothes. No, nothing here. He must have been looking for a sweater. I get down and frown. He didn't wear any warm clothes and his work clothes aren't kept in this cupboard. I get back up onto the chair and feel around again. What was he damn well doing up here? I bang on the back wall and it makes a weird sound. I frown. Huh? I knock and it echoes. My eyes widen.

Shit, this is a fake wall. With renewed purpose, I start to feel around in desperation. Maybe he has a weapon up here and I can use it to make them call for help. I feel around the sides and it also makes a weird noise. I am perspiring as I stretch to reach up. I push up on the ceiling and somehow it lifts up. Oh shit. I slide it to the side a little and put my hand up and feel around in the timber panelling.

I glance at the door. If he gets back now he will kill me for sure. I feel a shelf and I can't see what in the hell I'm doing, but I fumble around and find something.

Shit.

I pull down a small, black zip-lock bag and quickly hide it under my pillow. I then climb back up and feel around again and find an iPhone.

Jackpot.

I jump down and hide it under my pillow and then I put everything back in its place and move the chair back to its usual place. I close the wardrobe and then take my stash into the bathroom and close the door. I swipe the phone on and it lights up.

I smile broadly.

Yes.

I go to call and the message comes up no service. Fuck. I try again and still nothing. Bloody hell. I move to the zip-lock bag and I open it.

Passports. Two passports.

Hmm. I open the first one. Joel McIntyre. His strong face stares back at me from the photo. It's his passport. I open the second one and the same face stares back at me but with the name Stace Williams.

I frown. That's weird. Why does he have two passports in different names?

Fuck, who is this guy? I look at the dates they were made. The Stace passport is seven years old, but the Mac one is only twelve months old.

Mac is a fake name.

I think on this for a moment. Mac is an alias. You would have the real passport first. I look at the birth date, September 12th 1989.

That would make him 27, which seems about right. I would have guessed that was his age.

I pick up the phone and swipe through it. Nothing irregular. I go to his images and see a picture of an attractive girl and a little boy.

My heart drops. Oh God. He has someone at home and a

son. I feel sick for this poor girl. My mind goes to scuz bucket Chelsea and what she did to him last night.

I hate her. ...I hate him even more.

Rattled that this photo annoyed me, I keep swiping through the images. Images of a piece of paper. Why is he taking images of a piece of paper?

I click on it to enlarge and I frown. It's a report of some kind.

1267 - CC - Pick up 10th - Coffee

1208 - H - Pick up after delivery - Tea

1190 - I - Pick up 14th - Statue

1211 - H - Pick up 11th - NA

1130 - CC - non disclosed - Book

1140 - DMD - Pick up after delivery - Statue

1289 - WP - PAD - Flooring

I frown as I read through the list....what does that mean and why has he taken a photo of it?

I have absolutely no idea what I am looking at or for here.

I keep swiping and see another photo of the girl and the boy, but this time they are with another man. I smile before I catch myself. This is this man's family, but who is he?

Hmm. I swipe through to the emails... nothing unordinary. I look through his emails and images for over an hour and with a little more information on Mac—or Stace—and a million more attempts to get range, I put the things back where I found them. I will check them again tomorrow if I am still here.

At twelve o'clock sharp, a knock bangs on the door. I don't want to go to lunch with this stupid bitch, but if I can get her trust, she might help me get off the ship. A faint, annoying little voice whispers from deep within so she can have Mac again tonight.

It bothers me that him sleeping with her annoys me.

It shouldn't annoy me. I should be elated. I blow out a dejected breath and open the door.

Three girls stand before me. "Hello," I murmur.

"Hi." Chelsea fakes a smile. She is bottle blonde and busty and the other two mumble some kind of fake greeting. One has long red hair and pale skin. She's beautiful and sweet looking. The other has jet-black hair and a really hard face. She's had a tough life, I can tell.

I hold my hand out and they walk past me into the room.

"I don't need to be babysat. I'm okay." I sigh.

Chelsea rolls her eyes. "Mac told me I had to watch you." I stare at her...she pisses me off. "Well, Mac's not here."

"Hmm, pity." She smirks to the other girls as she looks around the room.

I glare at her as I feel my back prickle. "I'm glad he's not. I'm being held here against my will you know."

Chelsea smiles her first genuine smile. "Oh, you poor thing. Being held as Mac's sex slave would be such a hardship." She widens her eyes to accentuate her point. The other two giggle.

Did she sleep with him last night or not? I fucking need to know. Why is it bothering me if she did?

"Let's cut the bullshit," I snap. "Can you help me get off the boat or not?"

Chelsea sits at the desk and swings on the chair. "What has Mac said?" she asks.

"He said he will let me go at the next port," I reply.

She shrugs. "Then he will let you go."

"How do you know?" I ask.

"He does what he says." She stands. "Let's go eat lunch."

I stand on the spot, I don't want to go anywhere with these girls.

"You coming?" The red head smiles as the other two walk out the door in and down the corridor in front of us.

"What's your name?" I ask.

"Angela." She smiles shyly. "What's yours?"

"Roshelle," I reply.

She links her arm with mine as we walk down the corridor.

"Look, I know this isn't ideal, but just bide your time and then leave. If you try to run you will regret it."

My scared eyes hold hers and somehow I feel like this girl is not so bad.

"For some reason Mac is protecting you. Take it. I wish he protected me," she adds.

"How did you get here, doing this?" I whisper so that the other two girls can't hear us.

She shrugs. "A string of bad decisions."

I watch her as we walk.

She shrugs. "I live on the ship most of the year. I'm safe here, the boys look after me."

I swallow the taste of disgust in my mouth. "Do you sleep with all of them?" I ask without thinking.

"I sleep with two of them." Her eyes drop to the floor. "I care about the two of them. It's not conventional but the three of us are happy."

My eyes hold hers. I can't even get my head around this kind of lifestyle. "So the three of you have group sex?"

She shrugs. "Yes, and one on one."

I look at her as my brain misfires. "Sorry." I shake my head. "I'm just so not used to this."

"I know." She smiles and takes my hand in hers. "That's why he—" she cuts off mid sentence.

I frown as we walk into the common room. "What do you mean?" I ask her softly. "That's why he what?" I whisper.

"Mac is..." She pauses for a moment. "Different."

For some reason I like this gangbanger. She has an honest quality about her.

I glance around. "What's his story?" I ask. "Who, Mac?"

I nod.

She shrugs. "I don't know. He keeps to himself, but when he first arrived—"

"When was that?" I interrupt.

She narrows her eyes as she thinks. "I don't know. Maybe eight months ago." She pauses as if contemplating telling me the next piece of info. "There was talk that he was an AWOL marine."

My eyes widen.

"But I don't know if that's true because it came from Chelsea." She leans in to whisper so nobody hears.

I smirk. I like that she doesn't trust Chelsea, either. "Go on," I whisper.

"Apparently one of the men told her he knows too much to have had the job he claimed to have had before he was here. Something doesn't add up."

My eyes flicker to Chelsea as she walks up in front. "Does she...?" I don't want to ask how often she sleeps with him, but she seems to understand what I am thinking anyway.

"Not often," she replies as she sits at the table. "Only very rarely and when we have been out at sea a long time."

I stand, unable to sit down. "Have you...?" I ask as my eyes flash to the other girls who are now at the bar.

She shakes her head. "No. My men don't loan me out."

Oh God. Loan me out. I feel sick. This is fucked up.

"Have they?" I ask as I point to the other girls with my chin. She nods subtly. "Not for a while, though, I don't think."

I drop into the seat next to her. I can't believe I am having this conversation with her. God, I bet he fucked one of them last night. "The sooner I am off this ship the better." I sigh as my eyes stare out the large windows.

"It's a couple of weeks before we hit land."

"I know." I sigh, deep in thought.

"Do you want a drink?" she asks as she stands.

I nod. "Yes, please. Diet Coke." I watch her disappear to the bar.

The girls come back and we eat lunch in relative silence, my mind in overdrive. I don't know what has rattled me more, the comment that he will let me go and just bide my time, the fact that he may be an AWOL marine, or it could be the whole he fucks them all comment. She's right, he is different to the other men, but I can't put my finger on why. I do know one thing for sure: I don't like Chelsea. She is an outright rude bitch. The other four seem nice, but she is just... I don't even know where to start with what I don't like about her. She has this whole passive aggressive demeanour with the other girls and talks over them constantly. I walk over to the big windows that look out over the ship and I see Mac and three men standing on the deck deep in conversation about something, pointing over to the shipping containers. I watch them for a while. One man is holding flags and the other two have radio devices that they are talking through.

Mac is looking up into the air with his hand shielding his face from the sun. What's he looking for? I look into the air and

I see a helicopter hovering above the boat.

What the hell?

Help.

Help is here! My eyes dart around frantically. Help is here and I dash toward the door.

"Roshelle," Angela calls out.

I run up the hall toward the stairs and she takes chase.

"Stop!" she calls. "Roshelle, stop."

I take the stairs two at a time and get to the top just in time to see the doors open of the helicopter and two huge man with machine guns get out.

I stop dead in my tracks.

Angela grabs my arm from behind. "Are you trying to get yourself fucking killed." she whispers angrily.

"They will help me," I breathe frantically as my eyes snap between her and the chopper.

She shakes her head. "The people who come to this boat do not help you."

I watch as Mac greets a man in a suit that has gotten out of the helicopter and the two bodyguards with guns watch on. He gestures over to the containers and they all walk over and disappear out of sight.

My eyes fall to Angela. "I don't understand."

"You don't have to. Keep your head down and stay close to Mac. These people will kill you. Actually, no, you will wish you had died instead of living after they have finished with you. These are fucked up high powered criminals."

I frown, still unsure if I should run out there. The guns are putting me off.

Angela grabs my hand and tries to lead me back down the stairs. "Helicopters come to pick things up everyday." I frown. "Why?"

She shakes her head. "You can't be that stupid." I look at her blankly because obviously I am. "This isn't a normal cargo ship."

I continue to stare at her.

"This is a drug ship."

5

Roshelle

I LIE ON THE BED, deep in thought. After lunching with the girls today my mind has gone into overdrive.

He may have saved me.

Maybe he kidnapped me to save my life. They would have just shot me dead on the spot if it were up to them. There was already one dead body, what's the difference in two? For six days I have lived with him, despised him, loathed my body for being somehow aroused by him, and now I lie here feeling somehow grateful for his intervention. Things could have gone down so differently that night. I try to remember back, and although it's a blur, I know for certain he wasn't one of the men who hit me. I specifically remember him saying to leave me alone. Why?

Chelsea said she doesn't think he is who he says he is. I know that's true.

His name is Stace. I smirk. it's a much nicer name than Mac.

Where did Mac come from?

I stand and walk over to the porthole and stare out over the sea. What are you up to Stace? What's your motive?

What happened to turn you to get this lifestyle?

He should be back soon and I set about finding something in my shitty bag of clothes to wear. I take out the three dresses and the skirts and tops and lay them out on the bed. There is also a white bikini in the bag. Where the hell would I wear that? One by one, I hold them up to myself and look in the mirror. They all look like shit. The door creaks to announce his arrival and I turn to face him as his huge frame overtakes the room.

"Hey," he breathes as he walks into the bathroom and washes his hands.

"Hi," I call as I feel my nerves flutter.

He walks back into the room. "Did you go to lunch?"

"Yes, your girls took me to lunch," I reply without thinking as I sit on the bed.

"They are not my girls." My eyes hold his. "Not even close," he mutters under his breath as he lies down on the bed next to me.

I stay silent for a moment as I contemplate saying this and

I know it's probably not wise, but it's burning a hole in me. I need to just say it. "Mac?" I watch him, unsure if I am saying the right thing or not.

He raises a brow in question.

"Thank you," I murmur. His eyes hold mine. "I know you saved me."

He doesn't answer, but continues to watch me intently.

"You didn't have to save me, you didn't have to protect me from them." He rolls to his side to face me as I sit next to him.

"And..." I frown as I try to articulate my thoughts. "I'm grateful that you went to Chelsea the other night."

Surprise crosses his face. "Chelsea?" He smirks, and I hesitate unsure what to say. "You think I went to Chelsea?"

I nod quickly.

He picks my hand up and holds it in his. "Do you really think that Chelsea could put out a fire that you started?"

My brain misfires as I stare at him. "I suppose if you have an itch it needs to be scratched."

He smiles sexily as he lies onto his back, his blonde, messy curls are splayed over his pillow and he smiles broadly revealing those cheeky dimples. "If I was a nice guy I would tell you I jacked off in the shower before I came to bed to save you having to suck my cock." His eyes drop to my lips and I feel it all the way down there. I swallow the nervous lump in my throat.

"Would you be lying?" I whisper. Why are we having this conversation? It shouldn't matter to me whether he did or didn't.

His dark sexy eyes hold mine, but he doesn't reply. "Truce?" I ask, hopeful.

He nods. "I have to get you a new passport made so you can slip out of here unnoticed when we get to port. A chopper is bringing one in for you in a few days. I will get a photo of you tomorrow."

"Okay." I smile my first hopeful smile in a week. He's serious about helping me get out of here alive. Maybe he's not so bad. I feel relieved that we have had this conversation and we stay silent for a while. "Can I ask you something?" I ask. He smirks as if liking where this conversation is going. "You know how we..." I hesitate. I don't really know how to put this. "Make out to everyone that I am yours?"

He picks my hand up as he watches me. "Like when I touch you," he whispers darkly.

I nod nervously. Oh man. "I just..." I hesitate again as my heart rate picks up from his electric touch. "I'm not used to this."

"Obviously."

"I just want to be clear that you know we are not going to have sex when we get back to the room."

He stays silent and his eyes narrow as if thinking.

"I want you to be able to stop. Can you promise me that you can stop after we pretend?" I raise my eyebrows in question. I don't want to rev him up outside only to come back and find him unable to stop. If he knows the limits, maybe this will work after all.

"Can you stop?" he breathes as his eyes drop to my lips again.

I nod nervously. Of course I can.

"I want to leave this ship with my dignity," I murmur. "I'm not a sleep around kind of girl."

He smiles sarcastically. "How self preserving of you." He rises from the bed. "No need to worry yourself, Roshelle. I will get my itch scratched somewhere else." He walks into the bathroom.

"Good." That was the answer I wanted, but for some reason my heart drops. "Thank you," I call after him. I hear the shower turn on and then he drops his clothes in front of the door and I can't make myself look away. He turns to face me and his dick is hard. That thing is always bloody hard.

"Can you bring me a towel?" he asks.

What's he playing at now? I swallow nervously and nod. I get a towel from the linen cupboard and walk into the bathroom to put it on the sink.

"Are you on call tonight?" I ask.

He shakes his head as he soaps up. "No."

I smile shyly. I feel awkward with what I just said and now I'm standing here ogling this muscled sex machine. I do feel better for having said it, though. Now he knows how I feel and I won't feel like I'm prick teasing him. It's just an act, that's all.

"I thought we might have a few drinks," he says casually.

I smile.

"Watch some television."

"We shall see how the night turns out?" I murmur.

He smiles sexily as he strokes his body with his soapy hand.

"Yeah, I suppose we will."

Half an hour later, we walk into the common room hand in hand, his strong frame towering over mine. The glances of the crew members tell me they are still not convinced that he has staked his claim. "Let's get a drink." He gestures to the bar.

We make our way to the bar and he stands behind me and wraps his large hands around my waist. "Can we have two Scotch and Cokes?" he asks the bartender.

"Sure thing," the guy replies. He's a different guy from the other night and I look around to the men to see if I can recognize any of them. Mac's lips drop to my neck and his hand rises up to cup my breast. I really hate this. I do. I really do, I remind myself. His hands roam up and down my body as if he has been waiting all day to touch me, and my neck stretches out instinctively to give him room to kiss me.

"Playing along already?" I whisper.

He bites me and goosebumps scatter everywhere. "Just letting them know you're mine," he murmurs into my skin.

Oh God. My eyes close as his lips skim the length of my neck, he feels...

Hazy arousal starts to fog my brain and I panic. "I don't think that's what you mean at all," I breathe.

He pulls back to look at me and his dark eyes hold mine and he raises his eyebrow in question. "What's that supposed to mean?"

He's not telling them, he's telling me, and my damn body is agreeing. "Are you telling me that I belong to you or are you telling them I belong to you."

He grips me hard and brings me back to his body aggressively. "Let's get one thing fucking straight here."

I swallow the lump in my throat and frown as a jolt of fear runs through me.

He bends and whispers into my ear, "I don't need to tell you you're mine. I don't care if you are, but I will not be played for a fucking fool. You're getting a little self-righteous, Roshelle. It's pissing me off."

He jerks me and I frown against his mouth as it presses up against my cheek.

"When you are in this room, you are mine. You do as I say, when I say." He bites my neck hard and I shrivel. "Don't misinterpret my manners for a weakness. It will be your fucking undoing."

"But you said...?" I whisper.

"If I want to touch you out here, I will touch you out here." I stare at him as my mind malfunctions. I'm confused.

The barman comes back with our drinks and he takes them and walks straight over to the corner where two barstools wait for us, and he takes a seat.

I frown and he glares at me to follow him. I tentatively walk over and he spreads his legs and drags me in between them.

My scared eyes hold his. He's a different person out here.

"Kiss me." He growls.

"What?" I whisper.

"I want a fucking kiss." His dark eyes drop to my lips.

Oh hell. I glance nervously around at the people around us who are pretending not to watch. He grabs the back of my head violently and drags me to him. His mouth sucks on my closed lips and my eyes instinctively close. He kisses me again and again until I can't stand it. Finally, my body succumbs and both of my hands slip around his large muscular shoulders. His hands grab my behind and bring my body onto his.

"Do you know how fucking hard you make me?" he whispers into my lips as he wraps his arms around me tightly

My eyes hold his. What's he doing? Is this part of the illusion?

An idea runs through my pea-sized brain.

No, that's a stupid idea. I shouldn't incite the tiger within him. This could back fire, but he does want it to look like we are really fucking. We kiss for a moment longer. No, damn it. He wants the illusion, then I will give it to him full force.

"How hard are you going to blow tonight?" I whisper into his ear.

His eyes darken and his hands tighten on my ass. "That's more like it."

I kiss him gently as my tongue swipes through his open mouth. "I bet that big cock of yours tastes so good," I whisper into his lips.

He kisses me almost aggressively as his hand rises and grips a handful of my hair.

"I want to feel you gag around my cock," he breathes. "I could fuck your mouth so fucking good, baby."

I smile as my tongue rims his lips and my hand runs through his hair. "Please," I beg.

His eyes roll back in his head and he kisses me hard. I feel my arousal heighten and, Oh God, I am not even joking, I could take him all and I would drink it down. We make out for another ten minutes in the dark and I don't know if anyone is watching and, stupidly, I don't even care anymore. I can't remember ever being this aroused.

Finally, our dinner is called and he begrudgingly drags his lips away from mine. He runs his hands up and down my behind as he watches me intently. I would give anything to know what he is thinking. The blood is pumping hard around my body and I desperately need a cold shower. We eventually stand and he leads me to the dining area.

I'm frazzled.

I sit at the table as my arousal thumps heavily between my legs. I can't imagine what I must look like. My face is flushed and my hair is all over the place. I have never...

I stare dumbfounded at the table in front of me. I can't even pick up my knife and fork. What the hell? My body is thumping, and although he is acting to the others that he has fucked me into submission, the truth is he hasn't needed to. I'm secretly begging to suck his cock now.

I have no idea what's wrong with me. This isn't who I am. He gets our dinner and puts it in front of where we are sitting at the table and then goes back to the bar and gets two more Scotch and Cokes without a word. My eyes watch him across the room, wearing tight blue jeans and a white t-shirt that hugs his every muscle. His tattoos are peeking out from under his shirt. He towers above all the men at the bar and I feel myself flutter as I watch him. Hell, this is ridiculous. I am not sure if this dominance show is for the people around us or to let me know how badly my body wants him... and it really does. Either way, I'm totally screwed. While he's gone, Chelsea and Angela get their dinner and sit down next to me at the long table.

I'm brought back to reality with a thud. One glance of her big slutty tits in my face and my arousal instantly dissipates.

"Hello." Chelsea fakes a smile.

"Hi," I reply as I cut into my chicken.

Angela smiles warmly as she puts her hand on my leg.

"God, Mac is like an animal with you. I've been watching him."

I swallow uncomfortably. I'm a ho.

"Mac is an animal with all women. You should see him with me," Chelsea murmurs sarcastically into her wine glass.

Angela and my eyes meet and I continue to eat in silence. I know this shouldn't piss me off, but it fucking does. Mac comes back and takes his seat and my angry eyes flicker up to him. I imagine the girls on the ship all lining up to fuck him and I feel sick. What in the hell goes on around here when they are all alone at sea?

This is not who you are, Roshelle.

I've already shared one man. Why in the hell would I willingly share another?

A European looking man walks over and talks to a blonde man. Mac looks up and glares at him, his jaw clenching in anger, and my eyes follow the man across the dining table.

"Who's that?" I ask Angela.

"Stucko," she whispers as she drops her head.

"Who's he? I haven't seen him before." I frown.

"Be grateful. He's a nasty piece of work." She whispers.

I glance over at Mac who is openly glaring at him across the room. I can tell there is no love lost between these two.

"So, twenty-one days until Puerto Rico." Angela smiles as she tries to make conversation.

"Oh, I can't wait." Chelsea smiles and then she looks over to

Mac. "Mac and I have had some pretty wild nights in Puerto Rico, haven't we?"

He keeps eating with his head down. He doesn't answer and he doesn't acknowledge what she has just said.

I get a vision of them fucking in a nightclub and my blood boils, even though I know I am being utterly ridiculous. I am unable to control it.

"What have you got planned for me at this port Mac?" She smiles sexily over the table.

I chew my food in silence as I stare at my plate.

"Enough, Chels. Cut the fucking shit." He snarls.

Angela widens her eyes into her wine glass. "Awkward," she mouths at me.

We continue to eat in silence and eventually Chelsea gets up to go to the bar and Angela starts talking to a man who sits down next to her. Mac casually puts his hand on my upper thigh and I flick it off discretely under the table. He glares at me and raises his brow in a silent dare.

I lean over and whisper into his ear, "I don't appreciate your scratching post boring the fuck out of me with her sleazy tales about you. I'm going back to the room."

"The hell you are," he growls in my ear as he grabs my hand.

"Stay here and fuck her on the pool table," I whisper angrily as I rip my hand from his grip.

"Wouldn't be the first time," he fires back.

I sit back and fake a smile as my eyes hold his. I hesitate for a moment, shocked that he just said that. Shocked that anyone would even say that. "This is why I'm out of your league, but thank you for the reminder."

His face drops and he sits back in his seat. I know I've got him.

"Stick to your whores." I stand and throw my napkin onto the table and walk out of the common room and down the hallway. I feel my heart beating hard. I know he is going to lose his shit, but I can't make out with him—or should I say pretend to make out with him—knowing full well she is waiting to take her turn after I go to bed. What kind of fucked up situation is this? Why do I even care? It's seriously pissing me off that I do. I know they all share beds, but I can't even share a kissing partner. I'm just going to stay in the room for the rest of the trip.

I'm not doing this to myself again.

I can't pretend that this is okay with me. It's bloody not. I walk down to our door and then I glance up at the metal staircase leading upstairs. I need some fresh air. I head up and out onto the deck. I am greeted by a brilliant light and stare up at the full moon as it lights a blazing line in the water underneath it. The ocean breeze dusts across my face and an instant calm sweeps over me. I inhale deeply and a smile crosses my face. It's nice up here. The sound of the ocean lapping on the side of the boat is a reminder of just how remote a place on Earth this is. How do these people survive in these conditions for so long?

I walk over to the side of the ship and stare out over the dark, cold sea. The sound of the ship's engine is a drone and I can hear the sea lapping at the sides of the boat.

Pirates. Modern day pirates. Governed by their own set of rules with nobody to answer to but each other. For a long time, I stare out over the sea as I contemplate how and why the people on this ship live like this. Don't they miss land? Don't they miss having their own home, their own man or woman to love?

My thoughts go to Todd and my confusion returns - different emotions all rolled into one. I miss him. I hate him. I'm glad I found out. I wish I never found out. Part of me knows that they were going to tell me and strive to be together. I stare out over the water. Are they together now?

How long was it going on?

I turn around and lean on the side rail and look back over at the shipping containers all lined up in rows. I wonder what exciting places they have been to? The things they have seen. If only they could talk, I'm sure they would have an interesting tale to tell. I stare at the large orange container in front of me. The door has a padlock and there is a number on the top left hand side on the end.

1230

A thought crosses my mind and I frown as I look at it.

That's just like...

I bite my thumbnail as I try to remember. That image of the piece of paper on Mac's phone had numbers on it. Numbers just like this. I look around to the containers surrounding me.

1130
1163
1145

I narrow my eyes as I think. I can't remember what was written next to the numbers. I'm going to have to look at his phone again tomorrow when he goes to work.

Whose piece of paper was that and why did he take a photo of it? If it was his, he wouldn't have needed to, he would have had a hard copy.

Hmm, interesting. I stand for a while longer and with each moment my mind begins to race a little more.

I walk around in the dark as I stare up at the containers. I run my hand along the hard metal end of a container. There are millions and millions of dollars of drugs on this ship.

If my suspicions are correct, Mac knows exactly what drugs they are and what shipping containers they are kept in. I look back out over the water as I think.

And now, unbeknown to him, so do I.

Holy shit.

Victim of circumstance or has opportunity knocked? The world works in weird ways and if everything that happens has a reason, what is the deeper message behind this?

Why was I at that nightclub in the middle of nowhere on that particular night?

Why did I see what I saw? Why this particular ship? Why him?

I stare at the wall in the darkness as I troll the universe for answers. Unable to look at his hidden phone because I don't know when he's returning, I'm frustrated. Four hours have passed since I left him at the dining room and he hasn't come looking for me. Maybe he doesn't care what happens to me anymore. Maybe I was deluding myself that he ever did. Why should I care either way? I lie for what seems like hours in the darkness as I think.

I hear the key shuffle in the door and I close my eyes and pretend to sleep. He walks in quietly and I feel him stand at the end of the bed for a moment as he watches me. He undresses, goes to the bathroom, and then crawls into bed behind me. I feel my body relax now that he's home and hopefully I can finally get some sleep. He wraps his large arms around my waist from behind and snuggles into my back. I shouldn't like the way he feels around me but for some sick reason...

I do.

I don't remember anything else as I drift into slumber.

Mac

I wake to the feel of my cock straining to break free from my briefs. God, this thing has a mind of its own when I'm this close to her. I glance over to see she's awake and lying on her side facing me.

"Hi," I murmur sleepily. "Hello." She smiles softly.

Her long, dark, chocolate hair falls around her shoulders and she has that whole just-woke-up-and-I-need-to-be-fucked vibe going on. She's wearing one of my t-shirts and a pair of my boxer shorts, and I have never seen something so arousing.

This is why I'm out of your league.

Her cutting words from last night weigh heavily on my shoulders. She's right. I have no right to her and she has reminded me of just how long it has been since I have been with a decent woman.

She watches me intently and I know she has something on her mind.

"What?" I ask.

She traces a circle on the sheets underneath us with her pointer finger as she contemplates her next question. "Have you...?" She pauses. "Have you always lived this life?" she asks.

I stare at her for a moment. "Have I always been... bad, you mean?"

She nods softly.

I stare at the ceiling above. "No, I haven't." I narrow my eyes as I think for a moment. "Actually I take that back. I have always been like this."

She frowns as if not believing me.

My eyes flicker up to her. "Is this the part where you want

me to tell you I'm an undercover cop and I am here to save the world?" I ask.

A trace of a smile crosses her face. "You're not a cop?"

I smile sleepily. This woman kills me. "No." I shake my head. "Not a cop."

"FBI," she asks, hopefully.

I smirk. Stop being so damn fucking sexy. "No."

"Special Forces."

I roll my eyes. "You watch too much fucking television, Rosh."

She watches me for a moment as if thinking. "Can I ask you something, Mac?"

I nod as my eyes drop to her perfect lips. God, what I wouldn't give to have them around my cock. I get a visual of her naked and kneeling as she goes down on me and I harden even more. I subtly readjust my length under the blankets. "Yes," I reply distracted by my wayward thoughts.

"You know how you are getting me a new passport?"

I frown as I listen. Where is this going? I nod.

"Can you get me a passport in another name?" she asks.

"Why?"

She shrugs as her eyes stay glued at the blankets underneath us.

I lift my hand and cup her face. "Who you running from, baby?"

Her eyes rise to meet mine. "Me. I'm running from me."

6

Mac

THE WEIGHT of her words crush my chest like a vice. I stare at her, unable to fathom the idea. "Why would you ever want to run away from you?" I ask.

She drops her eyes back to the blankets in shame.

I reach over and rub my thumb over her bottom lip. "You don't have someone at home waiting for you?" I ask. What's going on with this girl? Something just doesn't add up here. I have always thought that she was hiding something. Although scared, she's nowhere near as terrified as I imagine a woman who has been kidnapped after witnessing a murder would be. She's learnt how to detach her emotions. Why?

She shakes her head softly.

How could that be? "What about your family?" I ask.

She hesitates for a moment before answering. "My mother died a few years ago and my father is no good."

I frown. "Grandparents. Siblings?"

Standing as if annoyed with my line of questioning. "Can you help me or not?" she snaps.

I roll my lips as I contemplate her request. "I can if you tell me a few things."

Her eyes meet mine. "Like what?"

"Like, why?" She continues to stare at me but doesn't answer. "You think you can run away from your problems?"

"I don't want to run away. I want to start again."

I raise a brow in question. "Starting again on your own would be hard."

She shrugs. "What are you going to do? Explain to me what your plans would be."

I lie back and put my hands behind my head as I wait for her answer, her eyes glance up to my biceps before she drags them away and I bite my bottom lip to hide my smirk. She can pretend to not want me all she wants. I know her body has other ideas.

She swallows as she thinks. "I'm going to get off at Puerto Rico and then I thought maybe try to get a job or something." Her large brown eyes meet mine as she shrugs. "I will work it out."

I watch her for a moment. She can't lie for shit, she already has a plan, I'm sure of it.

"So, you want to go off the grid. Become invisible, bad even?"

I ask sarcastically.

She smiles sadly. "I think being bad would be easier."

"Why is that?"

"At least I would know what to expect from people."

I frown as I watch her. What's happened to make her like this? My mind immediately goes to the night where we found her at the nightclub and the tears that were streaming down her face as she stumbled out that back ally way door.

"What do you mean by that?" I ask.

"Well..." She hesitates as she articulates her thoughts. "If I expect the worst then I will never be disappointed."

I raise a brow in question. "The worst?"

"Lies." She stands and picks up a towel from the floor.

I lean up onto my elbow as I watch her. "People lie to you?" I ask.

"Everyone," she murmurs as she disappears into the bathroom to discard the towel.

"That's not true. I never have," I call.

She reappears and leans on the door jamb and smirks. "Yes, you have."

"When?"

"When you told me your name was Mac."

I raise my eyebrows. How does she know my name isn't Mac? "I never introduced myself to you, and why do you think my name isn't Mac?"

"Is it?" She smiles sexily with a raised brow.

I smirk and shake my head. "No."

"Thought not." She bends and picks up my clothes on the floor and starts to rearrange them.

"Can you just stop cleaning and come and talk to me for a moment?"

"Nothing to talk about. You either want to help me, or you don't."

"And if I don't?"

"Then I will be crippled by student loans and dealing with a jerk of an ex-boyfriend."

A smile that I am unable to hide crosses my face.

"Why are you smiling?" she asks.

"So, you do have an ex?"

"Yes." She smirks. "And this is funny because?"

I widen my eyes. "Key word ex. You're a free agent."

She looks at me deadpan. "Yes, free except for the small kidnapping being kept against my will by you part."

I smile broadly. "Minor detail. Tell me something."

Her eyes meet mine and I can tell she's fighting a smile. "If we had met under a different circumstance..."

"Which we didn't."

"But if we did."

"Yes."

"If we met say..." I hesitate while I think of a scenario. "At your work, for instance, and I asked you out on a date. Would you have gone out with me?"

A smile does find her face this time. "Would you have asked me out?" She pauses for a moment. "If you were normal and didn't like whore bags, I mean."

I laugh out loud as I pull her back over me as I grip her two hands in mine. "I am normal."

She leans over me and smiles as her hair hangs in my face. "You are not fucking normal and this whole ship from Hell thing you have got going on here is filled with whore bags. Whore bags that you share with your work colleagues." She fakes a shiver of disgust.

It would seem weird to the outside world. Truth be known, for the first time since being here, I can't wait to get back to this cabin every night after work. This beautiful, innocent, fiery woman in my bed is almost too much to bear.

I want her.

I want her to want me and I will move Hell to make damn sure that she does.

I reach up and swipe my fingers through her dark, chocolate hair as she stares down at me. "I'm not interested in the whore bags, Rosh."

"What are you interested in?" Her eyes search mine and I have to restrain myself from sitting up and taking her lips in mine. I can't touch her in the bedroom, I remind myself.

"You," I answer immediately. I can't even pretend that I don't want her. Regret fills me and I hesitate for a moment. "I wish we had met under different circumstances," I reply.

"The point is moot because we didn't." She smiles sadly as she pulls out of my grip and stands.

My face falls at her rejection.

"So, is that a yes? You will help me?" she asks.

I lie back and watch her for a moment as I tuck my two hand behinds my head. Why does the thought of being the only person on the planet who knows where she is seem so appealing to me?

"I can help you disappear," I reply.

She smiles a grateful smile. "Thank you."

I stand and wrap my arms around her from behind, and she turns and leans her head onto my chest. We stand for an extended time in each other's arms and I wish she didn't just show me that vulnerable side of her... because now, not only do I have the primal urge to fuck her, I also have the need to protect her. In the situation I am in here on this ship, I honestly don't know if I can offer her protection or which sin is the worse evil.

Roshelle

The door closes behind him as he leaves for work I wait for ten minutes and tap my foot impatiently. I'm itching to get back into his wardrobe. I tiptoe over to the door and open it to peer left down the corridor, and then right. He's nowhere to be seen. All is silent and the coast is clear.

Time for business.

I close the door behind me, lock it, and then grab the chair to lift it over to the wardrobe where I carefully climb up. I stand and peer into the darkness and feel up over my head. My clumsy hand clambers around and I just can't seem to reach the fake roofing. I stretch farther and nearly fall off the chair.

Damn it, why can't I find it today? I found it by accident last time. I jump a little and hit the roof and sure enough, it releases. I push the fake roof up and slide it to the side. I feel around and finally locate the sought after phone. My eyes glance around guiltily and I slide the roofing back into place, close the wardrobe, and put the chair back at the desk. I then take out a pen and paper, lock myself in the bathroom, and take a seat on the floor. I click on images first and go straight to the picture of the attractive girl and the young boy. Is this his family? Who is this girl? I slide across until I get to the photo of the two of them with the young man and I study it for a moment. He has his arm around her and she is leaning her head back onto him. They look like a couple... a family. I swipe through the images once more and then come back to this one again. I frown as I think. No, I am sure they are this other guy's family... not my Mac's.

I roll my eyes in disgust at myself. He's not my Mac. Oh God. Concentrate, you fucking idiot. I keep going through the images until I get to the one I am looking for. The report.

1267 - CC - Pick up 10th - Coffee
1208 - H - Pick up after delivery - Tea
1190 - I - Pick up 14th - Statue
1211 - H - Pick up 11th - NA
1130 - CC - non disclosed - Book

1140 - DMD - Pick up after delivery - Statue
1289 - WP - PAD - Flooring

Hmm, what do these mean?

Okay, so container 1267 has something in coffee. CC...what is CC? I bite my thumbnail for a moment as I contemplate this. I take out my pen and paper and start to copy down the note.

What the hell is CC?

Where is Google when I desperately need it?

Container 1208 has something in tea and the pick up is after delivery. After delivery? Does that mean after we get to Puerto Rico? And what is H?

H... H... H is for...?

My eyes widen. Holy fuck. H is heroin. I think for a moment. Shit, CC must be cocaine.

I put both of my hands over my mouth in shock. Cocaine is hidden in the coffee and heroin is hidden in the tea.

Crap. This is some serious shit. My heart rate picks up and my eyes flicker around nervously. What if I get caught copying this down?

Why does he even have it? What if he gets caught copying this down? Who did he copy this from?

Shit, I continue down the list.

1140 - DMD - Pick up after delivery - Statue
1289 - WP - PAD - Flooring

1140. DMD. What is that? What is DMD? God, I really do need to find out what all of this shit means. Whatever it is, it's in a statue. I wonder how big of a statue?

I tap my foot as I think. Okay, the first thing I need to do is find the container and try to get into it. Which container do I want? I go back through the list with my pen. It needs to be small enough for me to...

I have to ask him how I'm getting off this ship. Maybe I will be searched?

So much to think about. I put the phone back where it belongs and after carefully hiding my note, hop into the shower.

I let the hot water run over me as I try to devise a plan.

I'm going to do this, Momma. This is my chance and I'm taking it. I'm breaking free.

"Ready to go?" Angela asks from the corridor as I open the door. I smile, grateful she has been so nice to me and has come to get me to take me with her for the day.

"So where are we going again?" I ask.

"Top deck?" I frown.

"Up on top of the control room we have a place that we call top deck. Sun lounges and the gym and stuff are up there."

I raise my eyebrows in shock. "Sun lounges?"

She laughs. "Don't get too excited, it's a long way from Ibiza. You have a swimming suit, don't you?"

"Um." I frown. "Oh, I think I do in that bag of stuff. Let me check." I shuffle around in the plastic bag and find the white bikini. "Here it is." I cringe as I hold it up and inspect it.

"Put it on." She smirks

"Okay." I slip into the bathroom and put on the tiny bikini. "Hurry up," Angela calls.

"Oh God, it's fucking obscene," I shout back. "Let me see."

I tentatively open the door as I look down at myself in the white, Lycra, barely-there, string bikini.

Angela raises her eyebrows in approval. "Very nice. Mac's going to love you in that."

I frown as I try to stretch the top to cover more of my boobs.

"Do you think so?"

She smiles warmly. "I know so."

I glance over at her. I want to ask her so many things about him. Like why is he on this God forsaken boat? How long has it been since he slept with Chelsea? Does he have someone at home waiting for him? Is he really nice and insanely gorgeous, or am I becoming delusional and developing Stockholm Syndrome? I know I shouldn't care about any of the answers to my questions, and to be honest, the less I know about him the better. He is a means to an end. He will keep me safe until I get off this boat and that is all I need to know. The rest doesn't matter. I wish it really didn't matter to me... but somehow it secretly does. I grab my towel. Ten minutes later I am being led to the top deck.

"Here it is." Angela holds her arms up. "Our own special kind of paradise."

I laugh out loud. "Yes, I can see." The area is about ten meters square and there are ten white deck chairs in a semi circle, and the floor is covered in fake grass. It is the epitome of the eighties. To the left is a large glass room that houses the gym. I can see a guy in there working out. Angela spreads her towel out on a chair and lies down. "Take a seat."

I spread my towel out, sit down beside her, lie back, and close my eyes. The sun is warm and welcoming.

We lie for a long time in silence. "How long did you say you have been on this boat for?" I ask.

Angela screws up her face as she thinks. "A couple of years."

I glance over at her. "Explain this two men thing to me."

She smiles with her eyes closed as she inhales the sun. "If you had asked me ten years ago if this is the life I imagined for myself."

I watch her.

She shakes her head. "No way in Hell would I have imagined being happy here, living the way I do."

"Are you?"

"Am I what?"

"Happy?" I frown, because I can't imagine that she could be.

She smiles broadly. "I have never been so happy."

I fall back and face the sun as her words roll around in my head.

"Once I let go of my childhood aspirations and let myself live in the moment, I stopped being disappointed with everything."

I glance over at her. "What do you mean?" I ask.

She shrugs. "I thought to be happy I had to have the three kids and the white picket fence in the suburbs with the perfect husband."

"That's how I feel," I murmur. "It's all fucking bullshit. All of it."

I think for a moment. "I just don't get..." I stop myself, knowing this is none of my business and I really shouldn't comment.

"How I'm with two men?" she asks.

I bring my hand up to shield my face from the sun. "I guess."

"Neither could I for a long time. I never meant for it to turn out like this and I still remember the night I met them. It was about four in the morning and they were walking down the street after coming out of a nightclub. My boyfriend had just beat me up pretty bad and I had a bleeding lip and was running as I tried to get away from him."

I watch her as I imagine the scenario in my mind.

"Jack grabbed me and I was screaming hysterically." She pauses for a moment.

"Who, your ex?" I ask.

"Yes. He went ballistic that Jack had me in his arms and kicked me hard from behind."

"Fuck," I whisper. "Sounds hectic."

"It was. Rick went crazy and they started having a fist fight." She pauses as she thinks for a moment. "He was a nasty bit of gear my ex."

"What happened then?"

"Jack made sure I was safe and then he helped Rick fight him off."

"God." I watch her for a moment. I can't imagine being bashed by a boyfriend. How horrible?

"Anyway, to cut a long story short, I didn't want to go home because I knew he would come there looking for me. They offered to put me up for the night."

I smile.

She glances over at me. "What?"

"So you came back to the boat and fucked them both?" I laugh as I shake my head.

"No, nothing like that." She smiles broadly. "We went back to Jack's house and I slept in the spare room."

I smile as I imagine it.

"They were perfect gentlemen. Jack's marriage had just broken up and Rick was getting over a broken heart."

"Jack was married?" I ask.

She nods. "Yes, the bitch played up on him when he was out to sea."

"Oh."

"Anyway, I ended up staying in the spare room at Rick's for the week with the two of them. Just as friends."

I smile. "Yeah sure."

"No, I'm serious. We were just friends, there was no uncomfortable dating thing. They talked about their women and I talked about my guy openly. We somehow formed a bond."

I glance over at her. This story seems a little too good to be true. "Then what?"

She shrugs. "Then they had to come back to sea so they offered me to stay in the apartment while they were gone as a safe place."

"Did you?"

She nods and smiles. "Yeah and I got my shit together a bit and saved a little money to repay them when they got back."

"How long were they gone for?"

"Eight weeks."

"So you stayed in their house rent free for eight weeks?"

"Yes. They let me have a safe house."

"Wow, that's nice."

"I know. We talked on the phone while they were gone and..." She pauses as she remembers. "When they came back they were home for six weeks. I had planned to move out as soon as they got back, but they wouldn't let me."

I frown. "So how does it go from three friends to three lovers?"

"After about a month of living with the two of them I started becoming attracted to both of them. Different things in each man."

I frown. "Like what?"

She shrugs. "Jack is affectionate and sweet and caring. He dotes on me and I adore him."

"And Rick?" I ask.

"Rick is hot... like I need to fuck him all night long, hot."

I laugh. God, I know that feeling. A certain person springs to mind.

"We went out for dinner one night and we all had a few

drinks. They told me that they both had wanted to ask me out on a date, but because they knew the other one liked me, they hadn't."

I smirk. This story is kind of cool. "What did you say?"

She laughs. "I told them that I was attracted to both of them as well and that I would move out the next day as it was obvious that things were getting complicated."

I watch her as she lies with her eyes closed to shield out the sun. "Then what?" I ask.

"When I was going to bed that night Jack came into my room and kissed me goodnight. There was tongue."

I bite my bottom lip as I imagine the scenario. "Oh."

"And then Rick came in and asked me if he could kiss me, too."

"And you said yes?" I am sitting up in my chair by this time.

She shakes her head. "I still don't believe it. We sort of made out on the bed for a while... the three of us."

My eyes widen. "So the guys get it on together, too?" She shakes her head. "No. Not at first."

"God." Does that mean they do now?

"Anyway, we ended up doing the deed that night. The three of us. It wasn't sleazy and it wasn't cheap. They worshipped me and I have never felt so taken care of in my life."

I frown. "Do you take the two of them at once?"

She shakes her head. "No. Not for a long time. It started out just foreplay and I would kiss them both and they would basically take turns making love to me. I take a while to orgasm, so I can go for a long time. And then over the next year we dabbled in anal."

I sit still as I listen. This is the most interesting story I think I have ever heard.

"And then over the next year I learned how to take them both."

"What's that like?" I ask. I have only ever read raunchy books like this. I've never actually talked to anyone who does it for real.

She smiles broadly. "The best fucking thing you could ever imagine. To be able to have two men that you are in love with to be able to be inside you at the same time is insane."

"You love them both?"

"Desperately."

"And they love you?"

She nods and smiles. "And just recently they have started to love each other."

"What? Oh my God." I giggle. "Do they fuck? Like... each other?" I ask.

"No. It's been a process. They aren't gay and have never been attracted to men, but we only have sex together as three."

"It's never one on one with either of them?"

She shakes her head. "No. I won't do that."

"Why not?"

"I don't want to risk falling for one harder than the other. If it's not broken why fix it?"

I nod. "Good point."

"I've recently been thinking that it's not fair that I get to have sex with two other people and they don't. So I have asked them to experiment with each other, so to speak."

I sit up in my chair. "What did they say?"

"Well, I didn't just say it out of the blue. I'd noticed that they were more affectionate with each other. We spend a lot of time naked and in bed together. It's only natural that they had become comfortable with each other's bodies. Like, when we were in the shower they would wash me, but then they would also wash each other, and when we cuddle they would put their arms around the three of us and stuff."

I smile as I watch her.

"One night, we were in bed and I asked them if it would be alright if they kissed each other. I could tell they both wanted to but were nervous and didn't want to be labelled as gay. I told them that it would be a massive turn on and could they just try it for me. I reassured them that what goes on between the three of us stays between the three of us."

"Did they kiss?" I ask.

She nods. "It was the most beautiful, fucking hottest thing I have ever seen in my life. I think it surprised them how natural it felt."

I shake my head in disbelief. I really need to get out more. "So we are taking baby steps. We are getting close and it won't be long before the three of us do actually all fuck each other."

"What do they do... to each other I mean?"

"Don't you tell anyone any of this," she replies as her eyes flicker around.

I shake my head. "No, I would never."

"We all kiss and we all go down on each other. I can see them falling for each other a little more each day. The extended glances and the tenderness between them is clear to see. They are comfortable with fooling around, but it is a big step for a straight man to take another man anally."

I smile. God, this is not the story I imagined. I thought she was a prostitute who was paid by the two of them to stick around.

"When it does happen it will be beautiful and I am the lucky girl who gets to be there when they both lose their virginity, so to speak." She smiles.

I lie back in my chair speechless. Blow me down. That is the story of a lifetime.

"So how did you end up on the boat?" I frown.

"I couldn't be without them and I would rather be out here bored than living alone at home."

I smile and take her hand in mine. "Thank you for telling me that. You didn't have to."

"Like I said, as soon as I put my moral beliefs behind me, my happiness started. I can't imagine my life with anyone else or being with one and not the other. We are a package deal. The three misfits."

I hear a bang of a door from behind us and I turn to see Mac and three men walk into the gym. He glances up and smiles sexily as his eyes drop down my body. He gives me a subtle wave.

I feel my heart somersault in my chest and I wave back. I watch him start to stretch as he talks and laugh with his two friends. He sits down and begins to do stomach crunches and every time he leans forward and touches his elbows to his knees, I feel my insides clench. While he's wearing a white t-shirt and navy sports shorts, I can see every muscle flex in his shoulders and arms. For an extended time, I sit and watch him. I have never been with anyone like him before. He's covered in tattoos and full of mystery, and yet I think it may just be the sexiest thing I have ever seen. I snap my eyes away from him in disgust with myself. Are you fucking kidding yourself? He has kidnapped you and is keeping you here against your will. I stare out over the sea as I think. That's not true and I know it.

He kidnapped me to save my life. It's changed between us now. The feelings I have for him have changed. I don't fear him, I don't hate him, and if I am being totally honest with myself, I feel safer and happier when I'm in his company. He didn't lie to me today about his real name. Why does it make me so happy and relieved that he didn't lie?

"How are things going with you and Mac?" Angela asks, interrupting my thoughts.

"Oh." I hesitate before I answer. "Okay," I reply flatly. She raises her eyebrows. "Just okay?"

I shrug. "As okay as they can be, I suppose."

She nods, deep in thought, and we stay silent for a while longer. My eyes flicker back to him inside the gym. He's now doing chin ups on a high bar and I watch him go up and down with ease. His biceps and shoulders are huge and the veins run thickly down his inner forearms. My insides begin to melt at the sight of him. His sandy blonde hair hangs messily over his face, and his chiselled jaw has a five o'clock shadow covering it. He's just so... what would it feel like to have him inside of me? My eyes drop to his behind and I get a visual of him on top of me where I'm holding that hot ass as he pumps me hard with that huge dick. Fuck. It would be so good. I bite my bottom lip to stop myself from smiling broadly. I've never seen a criminal with such straight, white teeth. He probably had braces, which implies he grew up with a little money behind his family.

"Do you know much about Mac?" I ask.

Angela frowns with her face to the sun and her eyes still closed. "I stalked him once on Facebook when we were on the mainland. He doesn't have any social media."

"Hmm." I frown. "Does he have a girlfriend or wife?"

She shakes her head. "No, I don't think so. The boys said not."

I stay silent. The question I really want to ask is burning a hole in my tightly sealed lips.

Angela must be able to sense my apprehension in asking.

"What?" She smirks.

"How often does he..." I pause. I can't even say it out loud because it's so gross. "Does he sleep with the girls on the ship?" I murmur.

Angela shrugs. "Not often." She glances over at me. "I think it's only a desperate times calling for desperate measures, kind of thing. He is only male, remember, and we are out here for a long time."

"All of them?" I ask quietly.

She shrugs and grabs my hand in hers. "None of them for a long time."

I frown. "How long is a long time?"

"I don't know. A couple of months, I suppose. It's only ever been really late at night when he is quite drunk and seems to get the hell out of there as soon as it is finished."

"Yuck," I whisper and put my head back on my chair in despair.

"I imagine he is one hot fuck." She smirks.

I smile broadly. "Honestly?" I raise a brow in question.

She laughs and covers her face with her hands. "Oh God. Don't tell me he's a dud in bed and ruin the fantasy I have of him in my mind."

"Can you keep a secret?" I ask. God knows why but I feel closer to Angela than I probably should. She has this honest quality about her and I really, really like it.

"You know I can," she replies.

My eyes hold hers. "I wouldn't know if he's a hot fuck because we don't have sex."

Her face drops. "What?" she whispers. "I thought you two would be at it like rabbits."

I shake my head in embarrassment. "No." She screws up his face. "So... he didn't?" I shake my head quickly. "No."

"But you two are all over each other in the common room."

"I know. It's all for show so the other guys don't try to take turns of me. Mac said if he staked his claim on me that they wouldn't challenge him."

"Fuck," she whispers in shock. "It's true, they wouldn't dare." She puts her hands over her mouth and shakes her head. "How in the hell do you make out with him the way you do and not go back to the room and fuck his brains out?"

I shrug. "I don't know."

She screws up her face. "Do you want to?"

I shrug. "It's ridiculous." I pause for a moment. Why am I telling her this?

"You can trust me," she whispers.

"I'm disgusted that I am attracted to someone like him. Someone who kidnaps and kills people."

Angela nods. "Hmm. He only kidnapped you because the others would have killed you on the spot. Kidnapping girls is not his style at all."

I watch her for a moment. Can I believe what she says? "I just need to see the next couple of weeks out and get the hell out of here alive."

"You will." She replies quickly.

"Do you think they will let me go?" I ask.

"Mac has final say around here. What he says goes and if he has said you are safe then you are safe."

I nod as I lie back and inhale the vitamin D.

"Why don't you just..." she hesitates. I glance over at her.

"Just what?" "Why don't you just enjoy him?"

I frown. "What do you mean?"

"You are on this ship for a few weeks. You're obviously attracted to each other. Just go with it and have fun. This will all be a memory soon and you will be back in boring suburbia and he will be a hot guy who saved your life that you will wish you had of slept with when you had the chance."

I shake my head and smile softly. "I don't just go with it."

"And where has that got you."

I frown.

"Up until now, you have not gone with it and where has it got you? Are you happy? Is your body sated?"

"But—"

She cuts me off. "There are no buts. If you want him, take him."

For another hour we lie like lizards in the sun and I watch him like an eagle while he works out. Angela's words are ringing loud through my head on repeat. Why am I being so self-preserving? What am I expecting? A marriage proposal from Prince Harry or something? Maybe I should just go with my gut and let myself make the most of this time. What have I got to lose? I'm disappearing from life in a couple of weeks. With every exercise he does, another dirty image crosses my mind of the devious things I imagine he could do to me—What that sinful body is capable of. I don't know if it's the sun or the oil drizzled over me, or the damn hot body of his wet with a sheen of perspiration, but I am feeling very overheated by the time he comes out to get me.

"You ready to go?" he asks as he towers over my deckchair. I glance up and see his hungry eyes drop down my near naked body and then back up to meet mine as he licks his lips.

I smile and hold my hand up for him to take in his. He pulls me out of my chair and I take my dress and towel in my hand. "I'm going to head back, Ang. See you at dinner?" I ask.

"Okay." She smiles as she watches us intently.

We turn and walk to the staircase when Mac's hand drops to

my behind as I open the door. "A gentleman would open the door for me." I smirk.

He bends and gently kisses my lips. "A gentleman cannot multitask, and at this moment, this gentleman's mind is on your ass in that white bikini and the things he could do to it."

I smile into his lips and kiss him again as his hand tightens on my behind. He squeezes hard and my hormones start to pump. For a moment our eyes lock. He takes my hand back in his and we continue toward our room as my heart thumps hard in my chest. What is this?

Does he feel this attraction like I do?

I don't want to go in. I want to stay out here and play along with him touching me for a while. His hands feel so good on my skin.

We arrive at our door and I glance up the corridor toward the common room. "Do..." I hesitate. God, do I sound needy? "Do you want to go up to the common room to get a drink or something?" I ask.

A trace of a smile crosses his lips and I know that he knows exactly what I'm playing at. "Okay. Can you wrap your towel around you?"

I glance down at myself.

"I'm not putting on a show for my work mates. Your body is mine only to look at."

A rush of excitement that shouldn't be there shoots through me and I smirk, wrapping the towel around my chest as we continue down to the common room.

He walks behind the bar. "What do you want to drink?" he asks. I glance around. This is the first time I have been in this room when it has been completely empty. Not a soul is here.

"Scotch," I murmur. I know he remembers ordering me that drink so he liked the taste of my kisses the other night. I wonder will we kiss now? He pours me a Scotch and Coke and then pours himself an iced water. "You're not having a drink?" I ask, surprised. He's not working tonight.

He shakes his head as his dark, sexy eyes hold mine. "I'm not drinking tonight." His eyes fall down to my lips and back up to my eyes.

"Why not?" I ask.

He raises an eyebrow. "I have other plans." "Like what?"

"Let's just say..." He pauses for a moment. "I want my reflexes to be razor sharp."

I swallow the nervous lump in my throat. "Oh," I murmur. He picks up our two drinks and walks over to the large double lounge and pulls a coffee table over next to it, placing the two drinks down. He then lies down with his back to the

high side of the lounge and pats the lounge in front of him.

"Lie down with me?" he asks in his husky voice.

I swallow nervously. This is weird. I know we are only playing along, but this feels different. I lie down nervously on my back and he places his hand tenderly on my stomach through the towel before he leans up on his elbow above us.

"Did you enjoy your workout?" I ask nervously. He smells so damn hot.

He bends and kisses my shoulder softly. "Yes," he whispers into my skin.

I feel the air leave my lungs and I troll my brain for something intelligent to say. His hand circles on my stomach and I stop breathing all together. He bends and kisses me softly on my neck and my eyes close. God, he feels so good.

He kisses me again.

"Do you have any idea how fucking edible you look in that bikini?' he whispers into my ear.

I smile into the side of his head. "No, why don't you tell me about my bikini?" I murmur as my eyes close.

I feel him smile into my neck and I bite my lips to hide my groan. "It's not the bikini that's making me crazy." "What is it?" I breathe.

"You."

I smile. "I'm making you crazy?"

"Insane," he whispers as he takes my lips to his. His tongue gently swipes through my open mouth and he kisses me deeply. Holy fuck. I can feel his erection grow up against my leg and I have to concentrate to keep my legs together.

This is insane. "There is nobody here. We don't have to play along," I whisper into his mouth as my tongue dances with his. "I don't want to play along anymore, Rosh." He kisses me again before his mouth drops back to my neck.

"What do you want?" I breathe. He's so damn good at this. "I want you to want me for real."

I can't hold myself back and I grab the back of his head and pull him down to me. The kiss is deep and passionate and hell, if it isn't the best kiss I have ever had. His hand slips underneath the towel and roams across my naked stomach and up to my breast and then down across my hipbones.

Lower, lower. Oh, fuck. Touch me lower.

Our kissing turns desperate. He is half on top of me and I can feel his huge erection digging into the side of my leg.

"Tell me you want me as much as I want you," he whispers against my lips as his hand rubs back and forth on my skin. "Tell me."

Unable to answer through my arousal and his lips all over me, I nod. I do want him. Hell, I want him right here on this lounge right now.

"Say it," he breathes heavily.

I pick up his hand and place it over my sex. "Touch me," I whisper. "Touch me for real."

7

Roshelle

HIS EYES ROLL BACK and he slides his hand down the front of my bikini bottoms and my legs instinctively open. His large, strong fingers slide through my wet flesh.

"Fuck, yeah," he whispers to himself as his eyes close.

Oh God. My head rolls back into the lounge chair. His lips take mine with renewed purpose. "You're so wet, baby."

I try to control my erratic breathing.

He slides one of his large fingers into my body and we both inhale in pleasure.

"How's this?" he breathes onto my lips as he pumps his finger in and out. My knees lift slightly and I am suddenly aware that we are in a public place.

"The towel. Put the towel over us," I whimper. "Let's go back to the room," he murmurs.

I shake my head. "No. We will stay public for a little longer, thanks."

He smiles darkly into the side of my face. "You scared of what I'm going to do to you when I get you alone?" He bites my shoulder blade sending goosebumps up my spine.

His big lips take mine and my back arches off the lounge in arousal.

Holy fuck. "A bit," I murmur.

"You should be. I have never wanted a woman so much." He pushes three of his huge fingers deep inside of me. I moan and tense up.

"Relax. I got you, Rosh. I won't hurt you."

He kisses me gently again, and sensing my fear he keeps his fingers still as he allows my body to acclimate to his intrusion.

I nod softly as I try to calm myself down.

"You're not used to big men, baby?" he asks as if concerned.

I shake my head nervously. "No."

He smiles into my lips as he kisses me. "It's going to be fun teaching you how to take me."

My eyes close. Fucking hell, what am I getting myself into here? His frigging fingers are huge and hurting and they are nowhere near the size of his cock. Maybe this is a bad idea.

What the heck am I doing?

I pry my legs open as far as they can go and lift my behind a little to allow him greater access.

"That's it, Rosh," he whispers reassuringly. "Lie back and enjoy it. Let me relax you a bit."

He carefully slides his fingers out and then pushes them back in, making me moan in approval. He sits back and slowly pumps his fingers as he watches my face in awe.

"Does that feel good, baby?" he whispers.

"Yes." I nod as I kiss him gently, a rush of excitement running through me. I love it when he calls me baby. "Too good."

He kisses me as his perfect fingers go to work and the sound of my body's wet arousal hangs heavily as we lie in the silent room. His erection is digging through the muscle in my leg and he grinds it against me slowly.

My breath quivers and I have lost all coherent thought. His fingers work harder, more aggressive, and each pump is deeper than the last. I kiss him aggressively.

"You are so fucking tight and ready for my cock." He growls.

He picks up the pace and my mouth hangs open as the lounge rocks almost violently. Oh my God, oh my God. I start to quiver and place my hand over the back of his as it pummels through my flesh. I can feel the muscles flex in the back of his hand.

Sensing how close I am, he smiles against the side of my face. "That's it, Rosh." He kisses me. "Give it up for me, baby." His thumb swipes over my clitoris as his fingers dive deep and I lurch forward as a stronger than hell orgasm steals my ability to speak. I jerk, my body shuddering around his fingers as he tenderly kisses me and brings me back to Earth.

My heart is hammering through my chest when he kisses me softly. No aggression, no arousal, just soft, sweet kissing. That was perfect. He's perfect.

"Can we go back to the room?" he whispers into my cheek.

Oh shit. My face falls.

A frown crosses his forehead. "Why did your face just fall?"

I sit up nervously as my arousal high instantly disappears and is replaced by fear. I shake my head. "It didn't," I pant.

"I..." I hesitate. God, this sounds so lame. "I just want to take it a little slow. I'm not..." I stop myself I don't want to sound like an idiot.

"You're not what?"

"I'm not used to this sleeping around thing. I know you are, but..."

He kisses me. "I would really like to go back to the room and get rid of this hot mess in my pants. You can watch." He raises a cheeky brow to sweeten the deal.

My eyes widen. "You would let me watch you get yourself off?"

"Yes. Why not?" He seems surprised that I would find this odd. I have only had a few partners and I know I am not super experienced, but I have never been in the space where a man has jacked off in front of me. A thrill of excitement runs through me as I realize he has the confidence to have no physical hang ups. Our eyes stay locked. Holy crap. He just may be the hottest man on the planet.

"What will you do?" I whisper.

He smirks sexily. "I'm sure I will think of something."

I smile as I stand, and we kiss for a moment as he rewraps the towel around my chest and holds me in his strong arms. His pager goes off.

"Fuck's sake," he whispers under his breath. After reading the message, he rolls his eyes. "I got to go to work for a bit. I will walk you back to the room first."

We walk hand in hand until we get to the door and we turn and face each other.

"I shouldn't be long."

I feel like I am being walked home by my cute first date and I have that butterfly feeling in my stomach. I lean in and gently kiss him. I run my fingers through his two-day growth and my hand lingers on his jaw. "See you soon," I whisper.

He kisses me again and then again and he smiles as he scrunches his face up. "Screw work. Let's go inside." I laugh. "Go."

With a sigh and a roll of his eyes, he pecks me quickly and is striding up the hall and out of sight.

I stand on the chair in the bathroom as I try to catch a glimpse of myself in the smaller than small vanity mirror. I turn and look at my behind in the tight black dress. After Mac left this afternoon, I paid Ang a visit and borrowed one of her dresses. I don't know if I'm delusional, if I have cabin fever, or whether I am just going plain batshit crazy, but I feel like tonight is a little different to my other nights on the ship.

I'm nervous. I'm excited. I'm petrified.

I have never lived like this, thrown caution to the wind and not thought about tomorrow. But this afternoon was so, so nice in his arms, and I think Ang is right—I have spent my entire life saving myself for nice guys and honorable men and they have all treated me like dirt. They lied to me, cheated on me, not to mention robbed me of my self-respect. I'm done with it.

I'm done with being the victim. I'm taking back control of my life right now.

Mac's bad—a criminal, even—but he has saved my life and offered me protection when I desperately needed it. In two weeks I will be gone and nobody will be able to find me, not even him. So I'm going to take the solace of his warm arms and the feeling of safety he gives me for the short time while I can.

God knows I am going to be on my own for a long time after this in fucking Puerto Rico.

I glance at the clock on the wall. Where is he? He has been gone for a few hours and he said he wouldn't be long. I put the chair back and straighten the bed linen and fold and put away our clothes that have come back from the laundry this afternoon. I go back into the bathroom and check how I look again. Bloody hell, maybe he won't even be coming to dinner? I take a seat on the bed and stare around at my surroundings. Dead silence. No television, no radio. How does he stay sane in this environment for so long on his own? No wonder he's always horny.

A knock sounds at the door. Why is he knocking? I open the door to see Ang standing in front of me. "I came to get you for dinner."

My face drops. "Where's Mac?"

"Apparently something is going on. I don't know. The boys aren't back yet, either. Chelsea said she saw them and they said to go without them."

"Oh, okay."

"Hopefully everything is alright," she mutters as we walk down the hall.

"What do you mean?"

"Stuff happens on this ship."

"Like what?" I frown.

"Well...you know what kind of ship this is and some seedy characters fly in and out. I know a helicopter came in this afternoon. I hope the exchange went well."

"Oh," I mutter, distracted. God. "Has anything ever happened before?"

"A guy got killed once. He tried to rip off the dealer and they shot him dead."

My eyes widen in horror. "Fuck," I whisper. "Who was that?"

She shrugs. "Some idiot who worked on here. I didn't really know him. Apparently he was shifty."

"Who shot him, I mean?"

She shrugs. "I don't know. One of them."

"Mac? Was it Mac?" Is he really capable of this kind of stuff?

"Who knows? They don't tell me much. I hear most things through Chelsea."

"What did they do?"

"They threw his body overboard."

"Holy shit. I can't believe this."

"It's true."

Ang's eyes glance down at me and she smiles broadly. "You scrub up well."

I look down at myself and smile. "Thanks for loaning it to me. I would love to say I will pay you back, but I have nothing to loan you."

She grabs my hand in hers. "Your friendship is a gift and you have loaned me that."

Oh, what a nice thing to say. I get choked up. She has no idea how much that means to me. I have never felt as alone as I have in the last two weeks. It has been so nice having someone to talk to today. She squeezes my hand as if knowing that she just hit a nerve. We take a seat at our normal table with three of the girls. I haven't really paid much attention to the other girls before and I glance around at them. One has black hair and is kind of rough looking, while the other is a bottle blonde and looks like she would be in her early thirties. They are attractive, but it is blatantly obvious that they have had hard lives. The third girl is Chelsea; the boys clear favorite. She is attractive and has a banging body, but it is her confidence and outgoing personality that sets her apart from the others.

"What's going on? Where are the boys?" Angela asks.

The two other girls shrug and Chelsea leans into the table. "Apparently someone fucked up and Jack had to reprimand them this afternoon, and then Rick and he ended up fighting."

Angela's face falls. "Who... J-Jack and Rick are fighting each other?" she stammers.

Chelsea shakes her head. "No. Rick ended up getting into a fight with Stucco and then they had to call Mac to sort it."

I sit still, unsure what to say.

Chelsea points her chin toward the girl with the black hair to symbolize for her to be quiet. Oh... the dark haired girl must be close with the guy they are talking about. We wait until she gets distracted as someone comes in to talk to her.

"What happened?" Angela whispers.

"I don't know, apparently Mac ended up going fucking crazy and had to be pulled off him before he killed him."

My eyes widen. Fuck. Stucco is that sleazy guy who hit me.

I heard Mac say he wanted a reason to kill him that night.

"How did it start?" Angela whispers.

"Apparently Stucco got caught going through Simmo's cabin."

"What was he doing?" Angela whispers.

"Searching for something."

"Like what?" I whisper.

"I don't know, but it was suspicious, and to top it off, when the chopper arrived in the middle of all this chaos they couldn't find the key to the container they were here to empty."

"Fucking hell," Angela whispers.

"What happened?" I ask.

"Mac had to open the container with huge ass bolt cutters. He looked like an idiot in front of the clients. He was fuming mad."

My eyes widen. "Where was the key supposed to be?"

"All of the keys are kept in the main office, but this afternoon when they went to get the key it was missing."

"Shit," Angela whispers.

"Mac is going fucking berserk because it means we have a thief on board as one of the crew."

"Does he think it's Stucco?" I ask.

Chelsea shrugs. "Who knows, but I would hate to be whoever it is when he finds out."

I sit back and sip my drink. Hmm. Very interesting. There are keys in the office. Everybody goes in the office so everybody is a suspect. I sip my drink to hide my smirk. This could be easier than I ever imagined. But what if they lock the cupboard now?

Shit. This could really mess up my plans. "Where did he get the bolt cutters?" I whisper.

Chelsea's eyes flicker to me for asking a stupid question. "Down on level three is the maintenance level, all the tools are kept down there."

"Oh," I answer. Level three. I need to check out this level three.

The girl with the dark hair waves and stands to meet someone behind us and we all turn. It's Stucco. She kisses him on the lips and they walk over to the bar.

"So is she on with him?" I ask.

Chelsea shrugs. "They get it on, but she is with other guys, too. She sleeps most nights in his cabin now. It won't be long before he stakes his claim and refuses to share her."

I frown. God, this is a weird set up. My eyes flicker over to them as they get their drinks from the bar and take a seat on the armchair in front of it. He sits down and she sits on his lap allowing his hands to roam up and down her upper thigh.

A guy walks in. He's tall and dark and pretty damn hot to be honest. Who is this? "Hey Chels." He smiles.

She stands immediately and walks around to kiss him on the cheek, and they disappear over to the pool table.

I turn to Angela. "Tell me the high ranking of this ship. Why was Mac called to sort stuff out?"

"Okay, so there used to be a captain of the ship—"

"Who owns this ship?" I interrupt.

"Vikinos."

I frown.

Angela shakes her head. "He's a really bad dude. Mafia. He doesn't come on here. In fact, I have never met him, only heard of him." She looks around to see if anyone can hear us.

"He is known for torturing his victims to death."

My face drops and I suddenly feel sick.

"Apparently he makes billions in drugs every week. He is big... I mean huge."

"Fuck," I whisper. "Carry on. There used to be a captain."

"Oh, yes. But there was constant bickering and he couldn't control the crew, so about a year or so ago the captain got fired... or killed. We're not quite sure."

My eyes widen.

"He never came back and Mac came in his place."

"What does Mac do here?"

"His role is called the enforcer, but he is also a marine engineer so he takes care of the operations."

"Huh?"

"He enforces the rules and makes sure things run smoothly."

"How did he get the role of enforcer? What did he do to get this job?"

Angela shrugs. "That's what we would all like to know. He came from Vikinos's camp itself."

"Oh," I whisper. "So he really is bad? Like bad bad."

Her eyes widen. "Baby, everyone on this ship is fucking bad. How do you think they got this job? But I think Mac is hardcore... I don't know." She shrugs. "I do know all of the men are shit scared of him."

Bloody hell, at this point he is the only person I'm not scared of. Hell, what a mess. I am now orgasming over a hit man or something. I couldn't make this shit up if I tried.

I have enough emotional baggage. Maybe I should knock this on the head before it even begins. Before what begins? What exactly am I about to do?

No. Stop it.

Live in the moment, remember?

Have fun while you can. This is just a bit of fun. It means nothing. Stop over analysing everything.

Over the next ten minutes, I watch as man after man comes in after work freshly showered and ready for their nightly dinner. They go to the bar and get a drink and then take a seat next to their friends. I watch the door in anticipation as Angela talks to another girl who has taken a seat next to us.

Where is he? What's taking so long? My mind goes to Chelsea's words that he had to be pulled off that Stucco dude because he wanted to kill him. Does that mean they were in a fist fight? Maybe he's hurt. I begin to feel my anxiety rise and I glance back over to Stucco in the corner sitting with his back to the bar. Fuck, I hate that weasel, too. I need a drink.

"I'm going to the bar, do you guys want anything?" I ask the girls.

"Can you just get me a white wine?" Angela asks.

"Me too." The girl sitting next to her smiles. What is her name again? Damn, I have to remember this stuff. I must seem like such a bitch not remembering anyone's name.

I head to the bar and there is a bit of a line up, so I take my place at the back of the line.

"Don't worry about him," I hear the girl with the dark hair whisper.

I can hear their conversation. I glance back and see Stucco

and his girl sitting with their backs to me, unaware that I am here. I turn back towards the front and pretend not to listen.

"He is going to meet his maker very soon," Stucco whispers angrily. "The mutiny is growing."

I frown. Who are they talking about?

"Just bide your time," she replies. "You will get your chance."

"I don't know if I can."

"Stop it," she whispers.

"Next time I get him alone, I'm going to kill him. He's dead."

"How will you kill Mac without a weapon. It isn't physically possible. He is a weapon in himself."

My eyes narrow. And he will kill you first, fucker.

"How?" she asks again.

"I need a way to get back into the ammunition vault. He has the only key."

Bloody hell, he's serious. And there is an ammunition vault? I run my hands through my hair as I pretend to be unaffected by what I am hearing going on behind me.

"Where does he keep the key?" she asks.

"I don't know, but I'm going to find out, and when I do it's going to be so fun watching the cunt die."

Adrenaline starts to pump through my blood stream. It's one thing to hit me and try and rape me amongst a group of gutless men—he had payback coming for that anyway—but to plot to kill the only person I trust on this God forsaken horror ship is a whole other level.

My blood runs cold.

You can't kill Mac if you are already dead, motherfucker.

Maybe I need to speed up my plan?

I get the drinks and head back to the bar and take a seat at our table. I sit in silence for ten minutes as I try to process what I just heard.

Should I tell him, or is that idiot just blowing off steam?

Angela's words come back to me. The men are all shit scared of him. They call him the enforcer. I'm pretty sure he can handle himself, but I just don't know. I need to think on this for a while. I know he has to be careful with the keys to that ammunition vault though, so maybe I will just tell him that? Everyone seems to be here now and Angela is at the kitchen counter with her boys. I watch the three of them together. They are all looking up at the menu board and she is holding one's hand while the other is standing behind her with his hand on her ass. They look so natural together and nobody even seems to notice them. No wonder she likes it here where she can live without judgement. What is it like to have two gorgeous men in your bed who love you? I would never in a million years have guessed that her men were crushing on each other. They are both so alpha. I glance at the doorway to see Mac walk through it wearing a black t-shirt and jeans that hug in all the right places and I feel my heart skip a beat. His freshly washed hair is hanging in curls just above his collar. He towers above everyone around him and I can see every muscle through his t- shirt. He is one mighty fine specimen. His eyes find me through the room and a smile crosses his face as he gives me a wink before he walks straight over.

"Hey, sorry I'm late." He brushes the backs of his fingertips tenderly down my cheek. God, he smells so good. "Have you eaten?" he asks as he brushes his thumb across my bottom lip.

"No. I was waiting for you." I smile up at him.

"Okay." He places his hand on my shoulder as he looks up at the menu board. "What do you want?"

I screw up my face. "The chicken, maybe?"

"Yeah, okay." He disappears to the kitchen counter to order. I stay in my seat and my eyes are stuck to him like glue. He orders our meals and then holds his hand up in a drink gesture and I shake my head and point to my full glass on the table. He nods and goes to the bar to get himself a beer. He stands for a while and talks to a group of men. I watch him as something very apparent appears that I haven't noticed before. He's different to the other men here. He's quiet, reserved, and broody. It's really hard to read what he is thinking or what emotion he is holding inside. Is that a defense mechanism he uses like I do, or is it a natural behaviour?

"You can't keep your eyes off him can you?" Angela whispers, pulling me from my thoughts.

Embarrassed, I smile at the floor. She bumps me with her shoulder.

"I took your advice this afternoon," I lean in and whisper.

She frowns.

"We made out for real today."

She smiles broadly and hits me on the leg underneath the table. "Yes."

I sip my drink and try to wipe the stupid smile from my face.

"How was it?"

I shrug. "Good." I laugh and widen my eyes. "Like, really good."

"So?" She leans in and whispers, "Did you... you know?" I shake my head. "No."

"Maybe tonight?"

I shrug as I feel the butterflies rise in my stomach. "Who knows?"

She glances over at him as he talks to the other men and my eyes follow hers.

"Seriously, look at him," She mutters with a shake of her head. "You know you have a huge advantage on any girl here."

I frown. "How so?"

"I reckon you could bag him if you wanted to."

"What? No?" I shake my head. "I'm not bagging anyone."

"Think about it. He's gorgeous. You're gorgeous. He is out here all the time and I am pretty sure he doesn't have anyone at home. Who knows what could happen?"

"It's just two weeks." I roll my eyes.

He falls into the seat opposite me and I sit back guiltily, hoping that he can't tell we were just talking about him. Our eyes meet across the table and I smile, my heart rate immediately picking up. Can he tell how nervous he makes me?

He tips his head back to drink his beer and his sexy eyes don't leave mine. I can tell he's thinking about our time together on the lounge today. He was hard and above me and I was wet and open. I have thought of nothing else since.

He felt so damn good.

"How was work?" I ask as everyone disappears around us.

"It was okay," he replies, amusement crossing his face at my attempt to small talk with him.

I sip my drink and he rubs the side of his shoe against mine in a silent acknowledgement. "How was your afternoon?" he asks.

"I had other plans, but it turned out okay." I breathe.

He smirks as he lifts his beer to his lips. "That makes two of us."

Our meals arrive and we eat in relative silence. Everyone around us is talking and laughing loudly, but he is quiet and pensive. I wonder if he is thinking about his trouble at work this afternoon. I glance over at Stucco who is now talking to three other seedy looking men in the corner. Obvious bruising is appearing on his face and his remark about the mutiny growing has got me thinking. If a group of men went crazy out here, some really bad shit could go down. One of the girls has turned some music and the disco lights on, and a few people are starting to dance. Angela and the boys have gone to play pool and the table seems to have separated.

"Do you want to dance?" I ask nervously.

"I don't dance."

"Oh." I pause for a moment. "How do... I mean, what do you do to relax?"

His dark eyes hold mine and after a moment her replies. "I ejaculate."

I get a visual of this visceral beast ejaculating. Fucking hell.

"Oh," I whisper as an intelligent reply leaves my brain. "We can do that if you want?" He raises a sexy brow.

"Do what?" I breathe as my eyes drop to watch his tongue as it slips out and runs over his large bottom lip.

"Watch me ejaculate."

The air leaves my lungs. "You want me to watch?" I whisper.

"Very much," he breathes.

"Now?"

"Right now."

I swallow the lump in my throat. Holy fuck.

Before I know it I am being dragged back to his room by the hand, where he opens the door. "Take your shoes off and lie on the bed," he instructs.

Huh? I frown in question as he disappears into the bath-room and reappears with a large, white towel, which he spreads out over the sheets.

Isn't he going to touch me?

"Take your underwear off and lie down."

"Umm."

He cuts me off. "Now." He turns and switches the lamp on next to the bed and turns the main light off. The mood instantly changes to sexual.

Oh. I slide my panties down my legs and take them off and lie down on the bed in my little black dress. He stands at the end of the bed and grabs the nape of his t-shirt slowly pulling it over his head, revealing his golden, tattooed torso. My hungry eyes drop to the rippled abdomen and the V of muscle that disappears into his jeans. He doesn't have hair on his chest, but has a trail of sandy hair from his navel down to his pubic hair.

My mouth goes dry.

He kicks off his shoes and I watch as he slowly slides his jeans down his legs. He stands before me in tight black short briefs. I can see everything through the briefs, although I don't need to. His hard cock is sitting well above the waistband of his pants.

Oh dear God. I start to feel arousal pump through my flesh as a burst of cream breaks the dam.

With his eyes fixed on mine, he grabs his cock and pumps it hard through his shorts.

I've died and gone to bad boy Heaven. "What do you want to see?" he asks.

"I want to see how you make yourself come when you're alone," I whisper.

Without any expression, he slides his briefs down his legs revealing his huge, hard cock. It's thick and long and I can see every vein in its engorged head. His pubic hair is short and well kept and I have to physically hold my legs together.

I've never seen a man like this—seen a man act like this.

He turns and takes a bottle of oil from his top drawer and then sits next to me on the bed on top of the towel in the semi-darkness.

"You want to see how I make myself come?"

My eyes drop to his cock and I nod, unable to speak through my arousal.

I feel like I am having an out of body experience. This stuff doesn't happen to me. Men like this don't happen to me. Am I dreaming?

He lies back and slowly opens the bottle of oil and begins to pour it over his cock and stomach.

My chest constricts and I feel like I can't breathe. I lean up onto my elbow as I lie next to him, my eyes drinking in the visual sensation. He spreads his legs, and taking his cock firmly in his hand, slowly strokes it.

My mouth drops open.

He strokes again and the muscles in his stomach clench on the upstroke.

"What do you think about when you do this?" I whisper. His hand slides up and down as he watches me. "Pussy. Wet, swollen pussy."

My body quivers at his answer. Fuck. If this isn't the best porn I have ever watched...

His strokes get harder and harder, and the bed begins to rock and I can feel myself thumping with arousal as I watch the pre-ejaculate bead on the end of his head. The sound of the oil slicking in his hand fills the room and he leans back and closes his eyes in pleasure as his hand jerks harder. Every muscle in his torso is pumping.

The sight of him there is too much. Oh God. He pumps harder and his hips begin to lift to meet his hand to the sound of his skin slapping.

"You need to fuck me," I breathe. "I need you to fuck me now."

8

Roshelle

HE SMILES DARKLY and bites his bottom lip as his eyes close again. The bed continues to rock. "I'm not joking," I snap. He rises from his lying position and kneels next to me. "Touch me," he whispers, his eyes fixed firmly on mine. "Touch me for real this time."

Oh God.

I lean up and take him in my hand. I stroke him hard and he hisses in approval. Unable to help it, I dip my head and lick his tip and I taste the salty flavour of his discharge. My insides begin to quiver. He tastes so good. I take him deep in my mouth, and it's not easy because he is so freaking big.

"That's it," he whispers approvingly as he places his hand tenderly on the back of my head. I suck hard and he groans deeply. "Good girl," he breathes, making my eyes close in pleasure.

I take him again and again and he loses control, grabbing

my head between his two hands as he really starts to ride my mouth. He's panting, moaning in pleasure, and it only amps me up more. Each time he lurches forward, I can see every muscle in his torso flex in the semi-lit room. This is out of this world.

"I need to touch you," he whispers as he jerks himself out of my mouth and stands me up in one quick movement. He turns me away from him and slowly unzips my dress.

"Do you have a hair tie?" he asks as his lips gently dust the back of my neck.

I nod as goosebumps scatter up my spine. "In the bathroom."

He disappears and returns with my hair tie and stands in front of me as he softly pulls my hair up on top of my head and ties it up in a messy bun. Then he leans in, and with one hand on my jaw he kisses me long and slowly, his tongue dancing with mine as if asking for approval.

"That's better, baby, now I can see you," he whispers.

I frown. For some reason this seems crazy intimate. It's not, I know it's not. He's not the intimate kind of man. But, Hell, it just does.

"Kiss me," he whispers.

We kiss in the dimly lit room as we stand at the end of the bed. He is fully naked and I am fully dressed, and to be honest, if he just kissed me like this I would orgasm and be happy forever.

Anything after this kiss is a bonus.

For ten minutes we stay in this position as if time has stopped. There is no urgency to move on from this, and it's as if he is enjoying it as much as I am.

"Do you know how beautiful you are?" he whispers in between kisses.

I smile, unable to answer.

"Do you know how many nights I have laid next to you in this bed imagining just this?"

My eyes close and I grip his muscular shoulders just that bit tighter as our kiss intensifies.

"I shouldn't be doing this," he whispers again as if internally battling the decision.

"Yes, you should." I breathe. "I want this. I want you like this."

We kiss and I pry my eyes open to see his are firmly shut as he kisses me. He's right here with me. "Take my dress off."

His eyes darken as he turns me away from him and slowly slides my dress down. He steps back and smiles as he looks me up and down.

His smile is contagious. "What are you smiling at?" I ask.

"You."

"What about me?"

"You have absolutely no idea how fucking gorgeous you are." He runs the back of his fingers down over my breasts as his eyes follow his fingers. "It's like you were made from my favorite things catalogue... Just for me," he whispers in wonder.

I smile and raise an eyebrow in question.

"I like dark hair. You have dark hair." He touches my hair on top of my head. "I love brown eyes." He bends and kisses me gently on the eyelids. "I like natural, full tits, and these are the best I've ever seen." He bends and kisses each of my breasts in reverence.

My heart swells.

"I like curves." He runs his hand down to my hips. "These hips are fucking kicking."

I smile and kiss him gently. For a cold-hearted criminal this man knows exactly what to say.

He slides his hand in between my legs and rubs his fingertips through my flesh. "I didn't know how much I wanted my woman tight."

My eyes hold his. His woman.

"Until I met you, I didn't even know I liked these things."

"And now?" I whisper.

"I want to inhale them. I want to drown in your body and forget every bad thing that has ever happened."

My breath catches. "How can I make you forget all the bad?" I whisper as I take his lips in mine.

"You have this gift." Our tongues slide against each other.

"A gift?" I ask.

"Of making me forget where I am...Who I am."

Oh, that is the most perfect thing anyone has ever said to me. Our kiss turns desperate and I grab the back of his head. "You need to make love to me. Please," I beg.

He smirks sadly into my lips and his hands fall to my behind. "You will be sadly disappointed."

I frown.

"I don't make love."

"Why not?"

"I don't know how."

"Why is that?"

"I've never felt it. I have no idea what I would need to do to make someone feel loved."

My heart melts, I feel an affection roll over me like a freight train and I cup his face in my hand. "Can I tell you a secret?" I whisper.

"Yes." His eyes stare straight through me as if he can see to my very soul.

"You have just made me feel more loved than any man ever has."

A frown crosses his face as if not understanding.

"I don't know if I have ever been loved, either, Mac."

He leans in and kisses me and brings our foreheads together as if thinking.

"But I know I want to be here, doing this with you," I breathe as I kiss him softly.

He lies back on the bed and pulls me over him and we start to kiss. Not the hard, aggressive kissing I was expecting. It's tender, soft.

Beautiful and different to anything I have felt before.

"Ride me," he whispers up at me. "Take me."

Oh God. I straddle over him and run my body back and forth over his as his hands guide my hips. We kiss for a long time, and I'm swollen, wet, and ready. He rolls a condom on and grabs his base and holds it up. I have to rise on my knees to allow his entry. He guides himself into me and I stop still.

Ouch... fuck, he's big.

Sensing my fear, he whispers. "It's okay, baby, you can take me."

I nod nervously and move from side to side to try and loosen myself up as his hands gently guide my hips. We struggle for a few moments as he tries to calm me down.

It really is too big. "I don't think I can take it, Mac," I whisper in desperation as I fall onto his chest.

"Stace," he whispers into my lips. Huh? I pull back as my eyes search his. "My name is Stace."

My heart stops. "Stace?" I whisper.

He nods and his eyes search mine.

I smile softly as tears fill my eyes. He didn't lie to me. "It's nice to meet you, Stace," I breathe against his lips.

He kisses me and grabs the back of my head as our arousal hits fever pitch. Unable to control himself any longer, his hand starts to drag me back and forth against his cock and I feel like he might just break me. Oh God, he feels good.

"Open your legs." He half growls. "I want inside, now."

I open my legs as far as they go and he grabs both of my hipbones and impales me in one hard pump.

"Ahh," I cry out as my body lurches forward in shock.

"Shh," he sooths as he kisses my cheek. "It's okay. It's okay."

He stays still to let me get my bearings. I slowly lift myself and he slides out and then he slides back home. We do that slowly again and I am blessed with a rush of cream that loosens me right up.

"Fuck, yeah," he whispers as he feels it.

He lifts me and brings me back down with force. "Good girl. You feel so good."

I whimper as my whole body hums from his possession.

He quickens up the pace, and within a moment we are hard at it. His legs are spread wide underneath me and I am straddled above him. The bed is rocking hard against the wall and his jaw hangs slack as he watches me bounce above him.

"You look so fucking hot riding my cock," he pants.

If I could answer him, I would, but I'm preoccupied dealing with the best sexual experience of my life right now.

"Oh God," I cry out as my head rolls back. "I have to come already."

"Not yet." He reaches up, and in one swift movement I am underneath him and he is holding one of my legs up around our chests. His large cock is working at piston pace as it ploughs through my flesh.

"Fucking hell, Rosh," he pants as he drives into me. "I've never had sex this good."

"Oh God," I pant. "Me neither," I cry. This is absolute bull-shit sex.

The burn.

The possession.

The coming apart at the seams.

"Fucking hell," he screams as he lurches forward in a violent shudder.

"Stace," I cry out as an orgasm rips me to shreds.

He slowly eases in and out as he completely empties his body into mine.

With my heart pumping hard through my chest, I fall back and he falls on top of me. We lie silent, panting, unable to speak. I am in shock at what just happened here in this room. He is silent because... I don't know why.

What's he thinking?

With one long kiss, he slowly rolls off me and lies on his back. We both stare at the ceiling and my heart is still beating at double speed.

After an extended time of silence, I break the ice. "I thought you said you couldn't make love?"

His eyes flick over to me. "Yeah, well..." He pauses as he contemplates his answer. "You caught me in a moment of weakness."

I smile and he slowly gets up and walks into the bathroom. I lie for a moment as I listen to the shower turn on. The beautiful intimacy we shared ten minutes ago is gone.

"You getting in the shower with me or are you sleeping in oil tonight?" he calls.

I slowly get up. "Coming." I walk into the bathroom and he steps to the side in the shower and I get in beside him. He takes the soap and starts to wash me and without any words, he smiles down and kisses me on the lips.

I smile up at him and place my arms around his neck,

grateful that even though the small window of intimacy is gone, we are still okay.

Stace

I sit at the table as I drink my coffee. I've come up to the common room for breakfast to clear my head. Rosh was still sleeping when I left.

I feel like I've been hit by a truck.

In the guts, in the balls, in the head.

Why did I tell her my real name? Why did I feel something last night that I shouldn't have, and why am I aching to go back and do it again because it was just so fucking perfect?

It's never been like that before. She is just so...

I run my hands through my hair in frustration. This was not in the plan. Focus.

I blow out a steadying breath, then I pick up Rosh's breakfast and coffee from the kitchen to go, and I continue on my way back to the room. As I turn the corner back into our hallway, I notice Stucco walking ahead in front of me. What's that fucker doing down here? His room is up at the other end of the ship. I hang back and duck behind the corner so I can watch what he's up to. As he approaches my door, I peer around the corner I am hiding behind. Is he going to break into my room? I'm not in the mood for this fucking shit today. I can't wait to put a bullet through this prick. Fuck, Rosh is in there. I stay still as I wait. The door to our cabin opens and Rosh comes out in one of my t-shirts and a pair of my boxers. My breath catches as I feel my protective instincts kick in. If he touches her, I swear to God.

He's dead.

I peer around the corner as I watch.

She sees him and her eyes narrow. "What are you doing here?" she asks.

"Shut up, slut." He sneers.

"Go to Hell," he snaps and as she turns to go back into the room he grabs her arm. I step forward and then she pushes him hard and he flies back.

I wait to see what happens. She follows him out into the hall and pushes him again.

Huh? What the fuck is she doing?

She grabs him by the throat and rams him hard up against the wall.

What the...? I blink my eyes to see if I am imagining this. He grabs her around the throat and she quickly does some practiced move and flips him onto his back.

She slams his head hard up against the floor as she begins to choke him with her forearm across his throat.

He struggles as he tries to get up and yet she has him pinned down hard.

"What are you doing here?" she sneers.

"Go to Hell." He growls.

"You have no fucking idea who you are dealing with." She punches him hard in the face.

"I heard your little plan last night, asshole," she yells as she bends and grabs him by the hair and slams it back on the floor. "This is your first and only warning. You go near Mac... You even think about Mac..." She pushes him again. "You even look his fucking way and I will kill you."

"You're crazy like him." He growls as he tries to scramble to his feet to escape her attack.

She kicks him and he falls back onto the floor.

My eyes are wide. What in the fuck is going on here?

"I haven't forgotten that cheap hit you laid on my jaw the first night I was here."

"I will do it again," he retorts.

She laughs out loud as she knees him hard. "Bring it." She pauses. "Pussy boy isn't so tough when he's on his own."

I feel my cock harden.

She pushes him forward and he falls back over. "I'm watching you."

He scrambles on his hands and knees to escape her.

"Go near Mac and I promise, I will kill you."

He stands and runs down the hall and up the stairs, and after running her fingers through her hair, Rosh turns and walks back casually into our room, closing the door behind her.

I stand still, my mind in overdrive. Who the hell is she?

Roshelle

I bend and wash my legs. I'm pissed off. When I woke this morning Mac wasn't here, and I know for a fact he had the day off. Where is that gutless wonder?

He has run, scared stiff, all because we had a moment last night? It wasn't even the sex. Mind you, the sex was fucking awesome. There was a ten-minute window beforehand.

I stare into space as I remember it

"I've never felt it. I have no idea what I would need to do to make someone feel loved," he said. He's never loved anyone.

Why?

"You have this gift." Our tongues slid against each other.

"A gift?" I asked.

"Of making me forget where I am—Who I am"

Why does he want to forget who he is?

I roll my eyes in disgust at myself for feeling all attached this morning. It was just sex. Really, really great sex. It means nothing. I need to concentrate on the plan and not the monster cock I'm sleeping with.

The bathroom door opens and he comes into sight.

"Morning," he says as his eyes drop down my body.

"Morning," I reply as I continue washing myself. "Where did you go?"

"I got you some breakfast."

I smile. "Thanks."

He leans with his behind on the bathroom cabinet and he folds his arms in front of him as if thinking about something. I continue to shower and my eyes flicker back to him. He has this air about him. It's cynical and smart ass all rolled into one.

"Is something wrong?" I ask.

A cold emotion I am unfamiliar with crosses his face. "Why would anything be wrong?" he asks sarcastically.

I shrug. God, he's acting weird. "You tell me."

He continues to watch me and his smug attitude is starting to piss me off. "Are you getting in?" I ask.

He doesn't answer.

"Look. You either get in with me or you can get out, don't start your mind game bullshit."

He stands in an outrage. "Mind game bullshit?" he snaps. "What the fuck is that supposed to mean?"

"It means, if you have something to say, either say it or get out."

"I'm not in here for a conversation." He sneers.

"What are you here for then?"

"I'm looking at the ass I'm about to fuck." He growls.

Oh the hide. "Well get your dick out and put it to use."

He rips his shirt over his head angrily. "You piss me off."

I smirk. "Ditto."

He rips his pants off and throws them to the side and then he is on me. Before I can reply, he has me lifted and impaled on his cock. I cry out as he pins me against the wall and wraps my legs around his waist. His dark eyes watch my lips and his mouth hangs slack. Oh God. My eyes close at the overwhelming feeling of his claiming. He slams into me and lifts me back and forth onto him.

"Ahh, careful," I cry.

He rips through my flesh and I think I feel myself tear.

"You're hurting me," I murmur, but he's not. Not even close. It's a good pain—an addictive pain.

"Let's get one thing fucking straight." He pumps hard. "You don't act like someone you're not." He slams me again and I am dizzy from the strength of this beast. What is he talking about?

"I wasn't acting," I murmur as he hits me hard again and I feel him all the way to my neck.

"When weren't you acting?" He growls, the veins in his chest and shoulders all pump with adrenaline.

"When I told you I wanted you."

He pumps me hard again and we both cry out. This is too good. He was made to fill me.

"Do you?" he cries.

"God, yes."

He slams into me as we both hold onto each other tightly.

"More than anything I want you."

He takes my lips in his and kisses me. Unable to hold it, I shudder as an orgasm rips through me. It triggers his and he groans as I feel his hot seed burn me from inside.

Our tongues dance for an extended time and suddenly the beast is tamed. Our touch becomes gentle, tender. I kiss his cheek and then his face and, overwhelmed with emotion, I start to shower his face in baby kisses. He holds me tightly in his arms as if processing something, and I feel the desperate urge to protect him.

"Why are you being crazy?" I whisper.

He pulls his body out of mine and my legs drop to the floor.

He slowly puts me down onto the tiles.

"You're making me fucking crazy," he whispers as if confused.

"Stace." I kiss him and wrap my arms around his broad muscular frame.

"What?" he replies against my forehead as he holds me. I get the feeling that he can't even look at me.

"I got your back, baby, you can trust me."

I tiptoe down the darkened staircase as my eyes glance around guiltily. It's just on 7pm and Stace has gone to the gym for an hour, while I am supposed to be getting ready for dinner. The ship is quiet as everyone prepares for their night. The engine is the only constant sound. I'm exhausted and had the best day I think I have ever had in my life. Stace had a rostered day off and we spent the whole of it in bed.

The man is a bonafide sex god.

He makes the other men I have been with seem like really bad foreplay. I can't believe what I've been missing out on all this time. His dry sense of humour makes me laugh and it's weird between us. We talk endless small talk, neither of us asking questions about the other one's life. I'm not sure I want to know what his life has been like and how he lives or why he goes by a fake name, and I don't think he is interested in mine. Although, I'm not sure about that. He gives off mixed signals and I swing from feeling like the only woman in the world for him, back to what I really am... a roommate he is just fucking to pass the time. I'm under no illusion that this is anything more than what it is, but Hell, it's fun. I know nothing more of him than I did this morning, only that he wasn't kidding and he really does like to ejaculate to relax. Oh, and the small fact that I am probably going straight to Hell because when he jumped me in the shower this morning with no warning, we both totally forgot about a condom. He assures me he has always worn them and that I am the first, but doesn't every guy say that to stupid girls who get lost in the moment? I have had the injection so at least pregnancy isn't on my mind. I smile broadly. Baby Stace... wouldn't that be something?

I have seventeen days left on the ship. Seventeen days and I am on my way to freedom. I get to the bottom of the stairs to find big, red double doors. If I go through the doors, what happens if somebody is on the other side? Fuck, I can't see where they open. Getting into this maintenance room isn't an option. I wonder if it's manned all the time? I stand for a moment as I think. If I get caught in here, what do I say? Why would I be looking down here?

Shit, my mind is blank. Umm... I have nothing. For five minutes, I troll my brain, until finally it hits me. I'm looking for him. Stace. Shit, I mean Mac. I'm looking for Mac. Yeah, if someone asks me I am simply looking for Mac. He told me he was going to fix something and I came here looking for him. It's simple, and most importantly, believable. I tentatively open the door and peer in. The room is dark and the sound of the engines is loud and churning. It's huge with machines everywhere and doorways that lead into rooms. Okay, what am I looking for? I walk along the huge corridor as I search for what I need. I get to a room and I open the door and find desks with computers on each one. My eyes widen. Shit, do these have Internet? I close the door sit down and look at the computer in front of me. It's got red lines in swirls on it. What the hell does that mean? I go to the next computer and it has a graph of some sort on it. The third has something else with all colors and swirls. Hmm, if I hit one of the keys, will an alarm go off?

I think for a moment. This could be freedom, but do I really want to ruin the plans I have to be saved?

I'm saving myself, remember?

I decide to stick to my original plan and go back out into the main area. I see a sign 'Tools' above a doorway.

Yes.

I walk into the large room and close the door behind me. I walk along the aisles as I search for what I need. I pull out the top draw... nothing.

The second drawer slides out and I smile broadly. Bingo.

I pick up the long, pointed screwdriver, and then look at the other ones next to it. I grab another two and put them down my pants. I keep opening the drawers until I find a long blade. I hold it up and smile.

Here you are, baby. Come to Momma.

9

Stace

SHE LIES on her side and smiles softly at me as she holds my hand in hers. Her long, dark hair is splayed across my pillow and she has a sheen of perspiration dusting her skin from our carnal activities just moments ago. I have never fucked the same woman so many times in succession in all of my life. I can't get enough of her. She is blowing my mind and it is seriously pissing me off. My chest rises and falls as I try to regain my breath.

Fucking beautiful, deceiving bitch. I have so many questions. Who is she? What is she doing here and why does she feel the need to protect me? Where did she learn to fight?

I think for a moment as we lie in the stillness, hand in hand. A cop. Is she a cop?

Fuck.

She's trying to get to Vikinos.

I fell straight into the bloody trap. Fucking idiot.

She has to be a cop, who else could she be? My mind goes back to when we found her as she came out of that back door. It wasn't a coincidence at all that she witnessed that hit, but then she was crying? Why was she crying? I think for a moment. Do we have a mole on the ship that has tipped them off?

Fuck, I'm so confused.

I think about it for a moment. What if she acted vulnerable knowing that I would protect her?

She got me. She got me good. I thought butter wouldn't have melted in her mouth.

"You okay?" she whispers, breaking my thoughts.

I fake a smile and take her in my arms and kiss her forehead.

"Yeah, baby. I got a lot on my mind."

"Like what?"

My fury simmers dangerously close to the surface. Wouldn't she like to know? "Work stuff, nothing you need to worry about."

She slides her top leg over mine and I feel my cock reharden. For fuck's sake, enough with the fucking erections. My mind continues to wander. I'm going to have to kill her. Her leg slides up against mine and I feel myself harden further.

How? I need to get into the gun safe. I can't kill her with my hands. I already know that.

She softly nestles into my chest and sighs happily. Fuck.

This brings sleeping with the enemy to a whole new level.

She leans up onto her elbow and smiles down at me and then leans in and gently kisses my lips. My eyes close. I can't keep them open when she kisses me.

"I wanted to talk to you about something," she murmurs.

"Yeah?"

"Last night when I was at dinner, I overheard Stucco and that skanky girl with the black hair talking."

My eyes hold hers and I fold my arms behind my head. "And?"

"He said he was going to kill you."

"He's a fuckwit and threatens to kill me weekly." I run my fingers through her long, dark hair without thinking. Her big, beautiful eyes stare down at me and I feel my chest constrict.

"He said he needed to get into the gun safe."

I frown. She must have heard him. How else would she know about the gun safe?

"And you are telling me this because...?"

She screws up her face as if I am stupid. "Because I don't want anything to happen to you. I think you need to carry a gun to protect yourself against this pre-planned mutiny."

I smirk. She's a good actor and probably should get an Oscar. "You don't need to worry about me. I can take care of myself."

She sits up and the blankets fall revealing her breasts. My eyes instinctively drop to them and I reach out and cup one in my hand as I think.

"Stace," she whispers.

My eyes meet hers. Why did I tell her my real name? She's the first person it has ever slipped out too. Idiot.

"Baby, listen to me." She reaches out and dusts my bottom lip with her thumb. "You are in danger and I can't protect you."

"I don't need protecting."

"But, I will. Please know that."

Our eyes are locked and I want to ask who she is and why

she's here, but I can't. I know I can't trust her. I wish that I could because a woman hasn't made me feel like this... ever.

"You need to worry about your own safety," I murmur as a warning.

"Can you get me a gun?" she asks innocently.

I bite my bottom lip to hide my smile. She has got to be fucking kidding? "Do you know how to shoot?"

She shrugs. "A bit."

I run my hand up her thigh and slide my finger into her dripping sex. She is molten lava hot. I add another two fingers and she groans and spreads her legs for me. "Where did you learn?" I ask.

She closes her eyes and arches her back as I pump her with my hand. "My father used to take me to the shooting range." I give her a hard push with my hand and she cries out. I want to yell liar.

I want to kill her right now for lying to me and making me desperate to be inside her while she does it.

"Suck my cock," I demand as I grab her head and push her down. She gives me a carnal smile as she disappears down my body. She moans in pleasure and the sound releases a gush of pre- ejaculate. My mouth hangs slack in pleasure. Hmm, so fucking good.

I lie back and close my eyes as I think of a way to kill the beautiful deceiver while she sucks me dry.

I sit in my office and go through the last of the maintenance reports. It's just gone dark and I have been here all day. Shit, I have a lot to do this week. It's overwhelming, to be honest. The rotators need replacing and the bearings are all on their way out. I have six choppers coming in and I have to go through the keys and make sure they are all here. I can't stand another fuck up like the last pick up. I looked so incompetent. My mind goes to Stucco and the hiding I gave him the other night. I didn't want to stop, and if I didn't want to blow it, I wouldn't have. It's no wonder he wants to kill me. One thing is playing on my mind though... the gun vault thing. She mentioned the gun vault, which would mean she really did hear him say he wanted to get into it. He may be serious this time. Who knows? A broad smile crosses my face as I recall Rosh kicking the weak prick's ass in the corridor. Even she can beat him. An unfamiliar emotion runs through me when I think of Rosh. I get a vision of her on me laughing out loud and carefree... of us kissing. I've been let down by a lot of people in my life and I couldn't have cared less.

This one is different.

———

I'm waiting for the last of the office staff to leave their stations in the control tower so I can ring Chris, my contact on dry land.

"You want me to do anything else before I go?" Jack asks.

I smile. "No, mate, you go. I got another hours work to get through here."

"Okay, catch you later." He packs up his desk and I wait for him to walk down the stairs. I flick through my diary until I get to the phone number disguised as a product order key and I dial the number.

Ring, ring. I wait. Come on pick up, pick up. Ring, ring.

"Hello," the happy voice calls.

An instant smile crosses my face. "Yo, Chris."

"Hey," he calls excitedly. "Stace, man. Where you been, bro?"

I laugh out loud. "Missing you, you ugly prick." I swing

my chair from side to side. It's good to hear his voice. Chris was my best friend all through school, and even now as I live in an ulterior universe to him, he is still my best friend. He works for the United States Government and has contacts everywhere. A diplomat, no less.

"Hey. I got big news."

I smile. "Yeah, what's that?"

"I'm getting married."

"What? No way?" I laugh. "Tell Elsa deepest condolences."

"She's the luckiest bitch on Earth to get to bang me for life." I can hear the happiness in his voice.

"Congratulations, man." I smile. Elsa is his high school sweetheart; he has loved that girl since he was twelve years old.

"You going to be my best man?"

My face falls as I am overcome with emotion. "Really?"

"Really."

"I'd be honored." I pause. I can't believe he asked me. "Thank you, it means a lot."

Chris knows I have fallen on the wrong side of the track, and yet his loyalty has never wavered once. He doesn't ask questions and I would literally lay my life down to protect him.

Justin, my brother, and he and I were inseparable all though school. The things we got up to.

God, we wreaked havoc.

"The wedding is next year in April. Make sure you are home."

I smile. "Okay."

"You still on that ship?"

"Yeah."

"You okay?"

"Yeah, I'm doing good. Have you seen Mom?" I ask.

"Mom has said she is doing okay. Missing you, of course."

Guilt fills me. I should be around for her. "Listen, man, I need a favour."

"What?"

"I met this chick—"

"No, I can't fuck her. I'm taken," he interrupts.

I laugh. "She wouldn't have you anyway, you fat prick."

"Anyway." He laughs. "Go on."

"Something is not adding up. Can you run a background check on her for me?" I hold her licence up and read the details.

"Yeah, no worries. What's the name?"

"Roshelle Myers."

"How do you spell it?"

"R.O.S.H.E.L.L.E," I spell out. "M.Y.E.R.S."

"Date of Birth?"

"14th of October 1993." Her birthday is in four weeks. I do the maths. She's 24 turning 25.

"Address?"

I read her address out.

"So what's the deal with this chick?" he asks.

"I hooked up with her a couple of months ago and we have been chatting online, but I get the feeling she is not who she says she is. I just want to check everything before we go on vacation together to save myself some hassle later."

"You think she's married?"

I screw up my face. "Yeah, maybe." I try to think what else I need. "I want all the details. Job, current and past relationships, convictions. Memberships, stuff like that."

"I'm on it. I will put it through now but it takes about 24 hours to come back."

"So if I ring you tomorrow night you should have it?"

"Yep." He pauses. "It's good to hear from you, man."

I smile sadly, I wish things could go back to the way they were.

"You, too. Take care of that beautiful girl of yours."

"Any luck she will be pregnant and horny this time next year."

I laugh and rub my eyes with my hand. "Oh God. I can't even imagine your poor kid dealing with you as a dad. Poor fucker."

He laughs. "Speak tomorrow."

"Bye." I hang up.

And silence falls in the office again. Soon, Roshelle Myers, I will know who you really are.

I put my hands behind my head and inhale deeply as I lean back on my chair.

It's going to be a long twenty-four hours.

Roshelle

I walk along the deck of the ship in between the containers as the light fades. Dusk is the quietest time of the day here as everyone goes back to their cabins to prepare for dinner. Stace is still working and something is going on with him. He's different to the first night we slept together. Something changed yesterday morning when he went to get me breakfast. Did he see me hit Stucco?

Fuck. Why did I do that? I nearly blew my cover.

I'm going to have to take Stucco out before he kills Stace or the plan is out the window.

I don't need this shit.

I smile softly to myself as I get an image of Stace—beautiful, sexy Stace. The only regret I have is that we didn't meet under different circumstances like he said. If he wasn't a murderer connected with this ship.

We are so good together. We could have had something.

Damn it.

Right now, though, I need to focus on my task. I continue to walk slowly through the deserted deck. The sun is just dipping below the water line and light is fading fast. I look up at the numbers on the top of the containers as I walk between them all. Where is it?

I keep walking and walking. I thought I saw it over here the other day. I stop on the spot and look back from where I came, and then forward. It's like a puzzle memory game. Everything looks the same. I thought it was over here near this red one and I go back over toward that direction. There it is.

1140

My eyes glance around to see if anyone has spotted me, but I don't think they have. I quickly dart across the alleyway in the shadows and pick up the padlock and inspect it. It's just a normal key.

Right.

I narrow my eyes as I think. I need to get into the control centre to find that key cupboard. But how will I do that?

Stace is in there now.

I can pretend to go visit him? Yes, why not?

Within five minutes I am at the bottom of the stairs of the control centre and knocking on the door. No answer. I knock again as I look up at the windows above. Hmm, maybe he has gone for the night? I wait for a few more minutes. Bloody hell, this was the perfect opportunity to get in there while nobody else was around.

I knock one last time.

"What are you doing?" a stern voice from behind me commands my attention.

I jump in fright and turn to see Jack, Angela's man, standing behind me.

"Oh, hi." I smile. "I was looking for Mac. Do you know if he's in here?"

He opens the door with his key. "Yeah, I think so. Come in"

Great. "Okay, thank you." I follow him up the stairs and we get to the top level to a large computer room with machines, computers, and workstations everywhere. My eyes find him across the room as he sits at his desk, and when he looks at me I feel myself melt a little. It's been a long day without him.

Stop it.

Wearing a high visibility work shirt and navy blue cargo pants, his sandy blonde hair hangs over his forehead. Those chocolate eyes and square jaw melt me. How is any woman on Earth supposed to block this out? Even in work clothes and steel capped boots, he looks orgasmic.

Christ almighty. Focus.

"Hello." I smile, secretly hoping he will rush to take me in his arms.

"Hi," he murmurs before turning back to his computer. My heart drops and I stand nervously waiting for his instruction. God, this isn't going to work at all.

"Mac, did you see that email?" Jack asks. "I came back to make sure you did."

"Which one," he replies, distracted. "Vikinos is flying in on the 29th."

Macs eyes fly up to Jack and then to me... Shit. "Rosh can you give us a minute?" he asks.

"Um, sure. Do you have a bathroom up here I could use?" He frowns distracted. "Yeah, up the corridor to the left."

"Thanks."

I turn and walk up the corridor. Shit, I wanted to hear that conversation. The 29th. How many days away is that? I don't even know what fucking day it is. I scan the office for a key board or something. Nothing. I walk up the corridor and see two offices. I bite my lip and turn back toward the men. Can they hear me if I open this door?

Shit.

I slowly open the door and it's empty except for staff lockers. I move onto the next room and open the door. My mouth drops open.

Bingo.

The whole back wall is a board with keys that have numbers above them.

Shit, shit, shit, I'm going to get caught. I quickly scan for the one I want.

Where is it? Where is it? My eyes dart around frantically, and finally, on the bottom right corner, I find the first one and then the other.

1140 and 1289

I take the keys and I walk back to the door and look back. Damn it.

It is blatantly obvious that the top key is missing. What do I do? My eyes widen. I know. I take out my room key and quickly slide it from its key ring and put it onto the hook below the number 1140. The second key is not so noticeable as it is on the top row. I then slide the container key onto my room key ring... nobody will ever know.

I slip out of the room and then duck into the bathroom. I sit on the toilet with an over the top smile on my face.

James Bond, eat your heart out.

He lies next to me in bed as he reads his book. The room is darkened, lit only by the lamp by the bed. It's 10pm and he's in boxer shorts and a t-shirt. I am showered and smelling like soap, naked, yet he hasn't even looked in my direction.

He's different.

Something has changed.

Two days ago I couldn't fight him off me if I tried. Now... nothing.

"That Divinci Code must be an interesting book, hey?" I ask.

"Very," he murmurs as he turns the page without looking up.

"I wouldn't know." I pause as I try to get him to look at me. "I've never read it."

He rolls his tongue in his mouth as if thinking, but doesn't answer.

I turn on my side and put my hand behind my head to lean up on it as I purposely let the blankets drop to reveal my breasts.

He catches the side of his bottom lip in his teeth as if trying not to react, but still doesn't flinch. What are you doing, asshole? "I'm not tired," I announce.

"Read a book." He gestures to a box filled with books under his desk.

I roll my eyes and get up out of bed. I'm naked and I purposely bend over and slide the box out with my behind towards him. I can see him in the bathroom mirror behind me and his eyes rise to watch me, although he pretends not to.

I smirk. I sit on the floor and start to go through the books.

I read the titles out loud.

"The Devil in Silver, by Victor LaValle. The October Country, by Ray Bradbury. Broken Monsters, by Lauren Beukes. Last Days, by Brian Evenson."

I curl up my lip in disgust. "This is your reading style?" I frown.

He glances up. "I like horror."

I widen my eyes. "Boring."

His jaw ticks in annoyance. "What do you like to read?"

I purposely bend over, revealing my naked ass. "I like raunch."

"Figures," he replies as he flicks the page angrily.

I put my hand on my hip. "Why would that figure?"

"Because you're a sex maniac."

I smirk. "Can you tape that please and show it to my ex-boyfriends."

"Why would I do that?" he replies flatly.

"Because they all complained that I hated sex."

His eyes rise from his book as if suddenly interested. "Did you?"

"With them?" I ask.

He nods.

"Pretty much."

His eyes hold mine. "Do you hate it with me?"

"You're the first man I have enjoyed it with."

"Why is that?"

"I don't know." I pause for a moment. "Maybe because I know we can never amount to anything and I have to say goodbye to you soon."

We stay still as we stare at each other, the air crackles between us.

"You go alright for someone who supposedly hates sex," he murmurs.

"It's easy once you find a man who knows what to do." He raises a brow. "You know how to make me ache for it."

He readjusts his length beneath the blankets. "Ache for it?" he questions.

"God, I ache for it," I breathe.

"It?"

"You, Stace. I ache for you."

He grabs his cock through the blankets and his haunted eyes hold mine.

"Why are you looking at me like that?" I ask.

"Like what?"

"Like I'm the enemy."

"Are you?"

I frown. Why is he talking in riddles?

"I suppose so. I am someone you took against their will who is now..." I trail off. I don't understand this myself.

"Who is what?"

"Who only feels safe when she is in your arms and I know that's wrong." He frowns. "I'm going fucking crazy." I throw the book back into the box in disgust. "I feel sick when I hear myself say it out loud."

"I make you sick?" he asks.

I smile sadly. "You should."

"That wasn't what I asked."

I shake my head, our eyes are locked, and after a moment I reply, "No."

"What do you think?" he asks.

"That's the thing. I can't think when I'm with you."

He frowns as if understanding.

"When you touch me, nothing else matters," I breathe.

143

He stays silent.

"I missed you when you were at work today." He drops his head. "Don't."

"I know I shouldn't have." I fake a smile as I try to justify my feelings. "I should hate you."

"You should," he snaps.

I walk over and sit on the bed next to him. His eyes meet mine. "Kiss me," I breathe.

The room is filled with unbridled desire, so thick you could cut it with a knife.

He puts his hand up, cups my face, and gently kisses me.

My eyes instinctively close. "Stace," I breathe. I feel like I'm about to break, this is too much. The intimacy I feel from him is too much. I need to hate him. How am I going to do this?

As if sensing my fear, he whispers, "Shh."

I screw up my face as we kiss. "This has to stop," he breathes.

"I know."

"Last time," he murmurs into my lips.

I kiss him and feel myself lift off the floor. "Okay."

———

I look left, I look right. It's just past noon and the coast is clear.

Stace has called a meeting about Vikinos' visit next week. They need to get everything in ship shape. This is probably my only chance where everyone is preoccupied. The girls are up on top deck sunbathing, and all of the staff are on the maintenance level going through operations. I told everyone I was going to be sleeping.

I walk along the rows until I get to the container I need and

I take out the two keys. I don't know which one is which. I turn the first key and it doesn't work. Fuck.

I take the second key and jiggle it a bit and it opens. I smile as my guilty eyes dart around. I open the padlock and remove the key and then put it back on the lock and swing it until it looks closed. I then open the door and peer in. Pitch black, I take out the small flashlight I took from the maintenance floor the other day and peer around. It said under the floor. I walk in and slowly pull the door to so it looks like it is closed from outside.

I put the flashlight in my mouth and bend down and tap the floor. Yep... It's under the flooring. I walk around the perimeter of the container concentrating on the floor. I need to find a bit I can jimmy off. How do I do this without making noise?

Fuck it.

I think for a minute.

Behind me are some timber crates. Perhaps under those I will find a place to lift. I move one to the side, and then the one under it, and then the bottom box is really long and has a crack in the top. Yes... I put the flashlight in the crack and pull it up as I use it as a tool. After ten minutes of hard work the timber lid lifts.

I pull the shredded cardboard back and I smile.

A crate of Barret's M98B—Sniper rifles. Yessss.

Thank God they were where they were supposed to be. I rummage through the crate but there aren't any bullets.

Fuck.

I pull the crate above it apart and still nothing. Holy shit, screw this.

I pull apart the top box and finally find a metal case containing the ammunition.

I stand still for a moment and let the euphoria sink in. I take the rifle apart and load the gun. I load another and take all of the bullets. I then stand and put the crates back where they were.

My heart is pumping hard. I walk to the front of the container and stand with my back to the door. I frown.

I can hear footsteps.

I hold my breath and close my eyes. Shit, shit, shit.

"Who goes there?" the male voice shouts.

10

Roshelle

OH MY GOD.

I close my eyes and grip the gun hard enough to break my fingers.

"It's me," a man's voice replies.

"Did you fucking hear him?" one growls.

"Yeah, I did."

"How?" the other man asks.

I frown. Who is this and what are they talking about? Why are they meeting next to this particular container? Oh, God, I'm screwed. They are breaking in here to get the guns.

I stay dead still as I try to contain my frantic heart.

"It has to look like an accident."

Who is out there? Who are they talking about?

"When?"

"I'm not sure. This week. He has to be gone before Vikinos arrives so we can blame it on him."

"That fucking girl we supposedly picked up by accident is a cop."

"What?" the other man snaps.

My eyes widen. Holy fuck... why would they think I'm a cop?

"Yeah, she fucking attacked me the other day, warning me against going near him."

Oh shit. They're talking about Stace.

I hold my breath. Please don't find me.

"He's brought her on here as a little fuck buddy bodyguard. That was no accident she came out of that door at just that moment."

I frown.

"I will make an engine malfunction call this week sometime in the middle of the night, and when he comes out we will take care of it."

"It has to look like an accident."

"Yeah, it will. He will be going in the drink."

"Okay."

"Stucco?" Stace's voice comes through the radio one of them is wearing.

"Yeah?" Stucco replies over the sound of the static.

"Why aren't you down here in the meeting?" Stace snaps angrily.

"I'm coming now."

"Fucking hurry up." He growls before hanging up.

"Fuck. I can't wait to kill this cock. He's fucking asking for it." Stucco growls.

"Yeah, well, make sure it happens."

"I'm on it," Stucco replies. "He's dead."

My heart beats frantically and I know I need this gun now

more than ever. They are going to kill him. I knew I wasn't imagining it.

"We better get back."

"Okay, see you down there." The man's voice replies. Who is the other man? Stucco is working with someone. What are they up to and what do they plan on blaming on Stace?

I wait for ten minutes in the silence. Are they gone?

I'm starting to sweat, it's so fucking hot in here. My mind goes to the refugees who have been forced to travel in these things for months. I can't imagine such horror. I slowly push the door open a few inches and peer out. The wind is picking up, but the coast seems clear. I dart out and put my two guns down and quickly re-lock the container. I bend and pick up the guns and look around nervously. Please don't let me get caught. I wrap the guns in a towel I have brought and quickly walk back to our room. I push the door open. I was unable to lock it because I don't have my damn key, and that's risky in itself. That stupid Stucco could be sneaking around in here. I throw the guns under the bed and then I put another towel over them. I haven't got time to hide them now. I need to get to the other container while they are all busy. I wonder how long this meeting is going for?

The guns were the main thing I needed to get... now for the cherry on top.

I walk back up onto the deck and glance around, seeing it is still deserted. I take out the other key and walk along the back row of the containers. This one is easier to go undetected, being right up in the back row. I open the lock and go through the same procedure and pull the door closed behind me.

I blow out a breath as I turn my flashlight on. Fuck, it's hot.

I'm sweating like a pig.

Okay, what am I looking for? Statues.

It said statue.

There are boxes in this container, probably about twenty in total. I open the top one and find the box has been partitioned into twelve squares with cardboard. In each little square is a small pottery cat statue standing about fifteen centimeters tall. I go through the box and take them out one by one and shake them. Nothing. They all seem empty.

If I was going to hide something in a statue, where would I put it?

I think for a moment. The bottom box. I quickly begin to move the boxes to the side one by one until I get to the very bottom box. I rip it open and take out the cat statues one by one and shake them.

Nothing.

Fuck.

I open the next box and the next box. Maybe there isn't anything here? I scratch my head in frustration as the perspiration drips from my forehead.

Oh shit, maybe I misread the picture. Did I get the container right? I open another box and the first statue I pick up and shake clangs as something hits the inside edges.

My eyes widen and I shake it again. Clink, clink, clink.

Yes, this is it. I quickly check the others in the box. Nothing.

This must be it.

I quickly put the boxes back as they were and go to the door again. I slowly open the door and peer out. The coast is clear. I wrap my small figurine in my towel and exit and quickly re-lock the container.

My heart is beating so fast and I can't believe I am actually fucking doing this.

Who am I?

I hot foot it back to the room and get in and shut the door behind me and lean up against it in relief as I pant.

I stink. I'm wet with perspiration. I grab my cat statue and walk into the bathroom and close the door, locking it behind me. I turn on the shower and look around. I need to break the statue open. I will do it later.

When?

When am I going to get the chance when I know Stace is occupied?

Just do it now. I open the bathroom door and peer out to make sure he hasn't come home and I close it again, lift the statue above my head and throw it on the floor. It bounces.

Shit.

I lift it again and throw it and it bounces again. Fuck it.

I lift it again and really throw it down hard and it smashes across the floor.

I stare at the broken pottery for a moment in shock.

My eyes widen. Holy shit... I was right.

Diamonds.

Diamonds that are bigger than my thumbnail. Light golden and misty pink. Some are brilliant white. Oh my God, these must be worth a bomb.

I can hardly breathe.

I walk into the bedroom and grab a sock from Staces' underwear drawer and then back into the bathroom and re-lock the door. I sit on the floor and sift through the broken pottery and pick up the diamonds, putting them into the sock one at a time.

Forty-two diamonds in total. Whose are these?

I carefully tie the sock off at the end and pick up the broken pottery and put it into a plastic bag. I'm going to have to throw this overboard as soon as I get a chance.

I get into the shower and let the cool water run over me as it sinks in.

Holy shit. I did it.

Sometimes life surprises me, but not nearly as much as I surprise myself.

How stupid can a girl get?

Why on Earth did I honestly think that there was something between this criminal and me?

———

I eat the last of my potatoes and veg as I watch him with her. We are at dinner, it's 8pm, and Stace arrived late after working all day. I would have assumed that he would have gotten his dinner and then taken a seat next to me as he has done every other time.

Guess not.

Tonight he got his dinner and then went and sat next to Chelsea, while I sit alone. He hasn't even acknowledged me and I am sick of his mind games.

Fuck him.

This is the final nail in his sleaze bag coffin. Who in the fuck does he think he is?

I'm livid. Livid that he thinks he can treat me like this. Livid that I didn't see it coming. Livid that my feelings are hurt by yet another asshole.

I'm so done with men.

Angela comes over and sits down beside me. "What's going on with you two?"

I shrug. "Nothing."

She watches him as he talks and laughs with Chelsea and another blonde girl. "Are you fighting?" She frowns.

"Not that I know of."

She screws up her face. "Weird," she mutters.

I drink the last of my drink. "I might head back to the room. I can't get off this fucking ship soon enough," I mutter.

"Yeah, I bet." She sighs.

I stand.

"Are you going to say something to him?" she asks.

"No. Why bother?"

"You should ask him what his problem is."

"I don't care," I reply dryly. "He can fuck her all night."

Her eyes hold mine. "You don't mean that."

I fake a smile. "Yeah, actually, I do."

I stand and make my way over to the kitchen, order a dessert to go, and wait for them to cut the cheesecake for me. If I'm going to be depressed tonight, I may as well do it in style. I get my cheesecake and as I am on my way out, he catches my eye.

"I'm going," I announce.

He nods, unaffected. "See you." He goes back to his conversation.

Is he fucking kidding? What is his problem? "Can I speak to you for a moment please?" I ask.

"What about?"

I glare at him and he rolls his eyes and stands begrudgingly. I walk out of the common room and he follows.

I turn to face him. "What are you doing?" I whisper.

He frowns. "What do you mean?"

"Why aren't you talking to me?"

"I didn't know I had to."

I fold my arms angrily in front of me. "Is that so?"

He shrugs. "I'm going to hang with Chelsea tonight." My

eyes hold his. "I'm kind of bored in the same old cabin." He pauses for a moment. "If you know what I mean?"

If he had hit me in the stomach, it would have been less painful.

"Hook up with someone if you want," he replies nonchalantly. "I'm sure someone else can get the job done."

I swallow the lump in my throat. That hurt.

Of all the things he could say to me... the fact that he thinks I'm a slut is the worst.

I drop my head in shock. How do you even respond to that? I turn and walk away before he sees the tears that are welling behind my eyes.

I'm done.

Stace

Standing still on the spot, I watch her walk down the hall away from me.

I should feel something other than what I do. I should be elated to get rid of the conniving bitch, not remorseful.

What I should be doing is hooking up with Chelsea for real, not standing here wishing I was going home with Rosh.

Fuck you for being a cop.

Fuck you for being the first chick I have dug in forever.

Regret swirls deep in my stomach that I'm not a better man, that she was right. Fuck her for showing me time and again why I am out of her league.

She deserved that, I remind myself. She deserved to feel betrayed by me because that's what I feel from her. The act she showed to me in those first few days is what captured my attention. She had this strong willed vulnerability, and I found it so damn arousing.

What an actress.

Anyway, I don't have time to worry about her now. I head to the control tower to ring Chris. I am anxious to see who Little Miss Innocent really is.

Two hours later I sit at my desk as I watch the clock. I have rung Chris every half hour and the results are still are not in. I blow out a frustrated breath. Come on, come on. I tap my pen as I think. If she is a cop, I have to kill her. I don't have a choice. She has seen too much. I know she hasn't had a radio to contact back so they know nothing yet. If she leaves, though, they will for sure. I rub my forehead in frustration. I don't want to kill her. Fuck, what the hell does she think she's doing out here, anyway? I hold my bottom lip between my fingers as I sit deep in thought, wondering if she is working with someone. Do we have a mole on this ship that has called the authorities? I narrow my eyes as I remember her coming out of that back door that night.

She was crying. She did put up a good fight. I should have known then that she was no normal chick.

The phone rings and I pick it up first ring. "Hello."

"Hey, Stace." It's Chris.

"Are they in?" I ask.

"Yep."

He hesitates and I frown. "What?"

"How long since you have heard from this girl?"

I bite my lip as I think of my answer before I reply.

"A while."

"I know why," he replies.

"Why?"

"She's reported missing. It's all over the news."

I screw up my face. Of course he was going to find that out.

"What happened?"

"She apparently caught her boyfriend making out with her best friend in a nightclub."

I frown as I listen.

"Took off and they think she has committed suicide somewhere."

Her best friend and her boyfriend. What the fuck? That's why she was crying.

"Anyway, she's a nurse," he continues.

I frown again. "Nurse?"

"Yeah, ICU."

"I thought she was a cop?"

"Nope, did she tell you that?"

I shake my head distracted by the best friend and boyfriend thing. "No, I just sort of thought..."

"Thought what?"

"I sparred with her in the gym once and she could fight. I assumed she was a cop."

"No, not a cop. She does have a membership to a kickboxing gym. Works out regularly."

"Does she have any family?" I ask.

"That's the weird thing. There is no trace of her before her eighteenth birthday."

I frown. "What do you mean?"

"I mean she didn't exist until she turned eighteen."

"I don't understand." I frown.

"In most cases, that means she has changed her name as soon as she was old enough."

"Why would she do that?"

"Who knows?"

"Who was she before?" I ask.

"I can find out, but that info takes about a week or so.

They have to go through records and stuff. Does it really matter anyway?"

I hold the phone to my ear as I think.

"I mean she's probably dead," he replies.

I shake my head. God, nobody is even looking for her. No wonder she wants a new start.

"Who does she live with?" I ask.

"She lived with her best friend."

"The chick who was fucking her boyfriend." I frown. This is unbelievable.

"That would be her."

My heart drops. "How do they know she killed herself?"

"They don't. Apparently the friend and boyfriend had gone out of town together and she had followed them and went berserk right before she went missing. The police found her car in the nightclub parking lot when she was reported missing two days later."

"Apart from the appearing at eighteen thing, is there anything else unusual?" I ask.

"No. She's a nurse and works hard. Goes to the gym. Keeps to herself and never been in trouble with the law. A few boyfriends. Five to be exact."

"How long was she with this last guy?" I don't know why I want to know that, but I do.

"A couple of years."

Regret fills me. She probably loved him. I picture her face when she walked though that back door, and I just told her I was bored and going to spend the night with Chelsea tonight. What a weak prick. She really is out of my fucking league.

"Listen, I've got to go into a meeting. I will ring you as soon as I get her birth information."

"Okay, mate. Thank you. About a week, hey?"

"Yeah, speak soon."

He hangs up, and I sit for a moment in the semi-lit office as I process her story. I shake my head in disbelief. Her boyfriend must be fucking batshit crazy to play up on her. Stupid prick. I think for a moment. I need to get her off this ship before Vikinos arrives. I don't want her here after the shit goes down. I sit back in my chair and blow out a deep breath.

What do I do?

I bite my thumbnail and think for a moment. I do need a new part for the engine. Although it's not urgent, I could pretend it is. I turn on my computer and type an email.

To: Colombia Docking Security
  Subject: Request

Permission requested to port for 48 hours for unscheduled urgent engine maintenance.

I look forward to your reply.

Mac.

I walk into the cabin to find Rosh laid facing the wall with her back to me, the desk lamp on and the room dimly lit.

"Hi," I wait for her reply, but it doesn't come. She stays silent.

I can tell she is awake. Unsure what to say, I take a shower without saying anything else.

After getting into my boxers I lie down beside her. She

gets up violently and grabs a blanket and pillow and lies down on the floor.

"Are you mad?" I ask.

"Go back to Chelsea, you scuz bucket." She growls.

I smile into the darkness. There she is—the fiery little witch I like so much.

"You sleep on the bed and I will sleep on the floor," I reply.

"Fuck you. Don't do me any favours."

I lie down on the floor along the bottom of the bed. "I'm out of the bed, you have it." It's bloody hard on this floor, I shuffle around to try and get comfortable.

"I would rather die than sleep in your bed," she snaps.

I chuckle and she kicks me hard with her foot.

"Ouch."

We both lie on the cold, hard floor staring at the ceiling above.

"I thought you were a cop," I mutter into the darkness.

She stays silent.

"I saw you kick Stucco's ass... which I loved by the way." I add.

Still, she says nothing.

"I had a search done on you. I was waiting for the results tonight."

She sits up in an outrage. "You didn't think to just fucking ask me?"

"I will repeat, I thought you were a cop. I didn't think I could trust you."

She flops back down onto the floor in a dramatic fashion. "You can't."

"Good. You can't trust me, either," I reply.

"I never did. I'm tired, so go back to Chelsea. Your jabbering is annoying." She sighs.

I smile broadly into the darkness and silence falls over us once more.

"They think you committed suicide."

She hesitates for a moment. "I knew they would," she whispers almost to herself.

"Do you want me to kill him?"

Again, a long pause.

"I will. I can knock her off, too, if you want," I add with a smirk.

"Don't tempt me." She sighs.

"So, you are a nurse?" I ask as I look over at her in the darkness.

"Yes."

"That's a cool job." I shrug to myself. "Must be rewarding saving lives."

"I save the lives that scum drug dealers like you take."

A swift kick to the stomach hits me.

"I don't deal drugs."

"You ship them. Same thing."

I think for a moment. "Who were you before you turned eighteen?"

"I don't know what you're talking about," she fires back immediately.

"Yes, you do. It came up that you had an identity change at the age of eighteen. What are you hiding?"

She stays silent.

"I am about to help you disappear from the planet. I deserve to know the truth."

"You deserve Chelsea, that's all you deserve. Go back to her truth."

"I want yours."

"I don't want yours, so leave me alone."

For ten minutes we lie in the darkness lost in our own thoughts.

Mine are regrets, hers are... I don't know what.

Eventually, after a long silence, she speaks. "My father was bad."

I frown.

"He was always a petty criminal but my mom thought she could change him. She fell pregnant with me by accident..." Her voice trails off as if she is far away.

I lie patiently waiting for her to finish. "So she married him?" I ask.

"Yes."

I frown. I can tell this is hard for her to revisit.

"When I was a little baby, he started getting into organised crime and Mom threatened to leave him." She pauses. "He beat her so bad, she spent a week in hospital.

The more she tells me, the colder the room becomes.

"When I was two, he got locked up and Mom saw it as a way to escape. We ran to a country town and changed our name."

Silence falls again.

"When I was five he found us."

I frown and she stops talking. After a long pause I ask, "What happened?"

"He shot my mother and kidnapped me." "She died?" I whisper.

She shakes her head. "No. The police were somehow tipped off where he had me hidden and they got him. He went back to prison."

"Was your mom okay?"

"She survived but was never good after that. We lived on the edge of fear, changing cities and names every few years. We never had any long-term friends and we were always broke. Not even our family knew where we were."

I can't imagine growing up like that. For all of my flaws, my childhood was a dream.

"Then three days before my eighteenth birthday he found us again."

I sit up and look over at her in the darkness. Her eyes are glazed over and her voice is faint. This is a painful memory for her. She has a distracted air about her as if many tears have been shed.

"He tied me up so I had to watch." She pauses and I know she is right back there as if it is happening again. "He cut her throat and let her bleed out."

Fuck.

"I watched as the life drained out of her."

This time it is me who has no words.

"She was so beautiful," she whispers. "The one person who I could always trust."

I don't know what to say, so I stay silent, and after about ten minutes I reply, "What did he do to you?"

"Nothing, he just took me to get back at her for leaving him. I was taken to a hotel by two of his men."

I frown. "He has men?"

"He does now. In the beginning it was just him, but now he has help. They took me to a hotel and he was going to pick me up in a few days, but fortunately for me someone got murdered in the room next door so the police came and did random searches of all the rooms. They found me and put me into the witness protection program."

I frown as I look over at her. God, this is not what I was expecting. "And you became Roshelle Myers?"

"Yes."

"You have always been alone?"

"Yes," she replies, monotone. "I used to have this perfect little scenario in my head. It used to get me through the hard days."

"Like what?"

She smiles. "I was out to dinner with my mom and my dad at an expensive restaurant, my Dad was a well respected doctor. He loved my mom and we lived in a fancy house. We had no worries and life was perfect."

I smile as I imagine the scenario she is setting.

"This gorgeous guy would come up to us at dinner and ask Dad if he could dance with me and my dad would say no because he was too protective."

My heart sinks.

Her sad smile fades. "He loved me too much to let me dance with someone."

"Is that how you wish it was?"

"It was just a stupid fantasy. My lifeline." She sighs

"Is that why you know how to fight, to protect yourself in case he came?"

"Yes." She wipes her eyes angrily. "I'm going to kill him one day. I have to."

"Yes. You do," I mutter into the darkness. "Revenge is a powerful motivator," I whisper.

"He's going to suffer."

"I will make sure of it," I breathe.

11

Roshelle

I clutch the party invitation tightly in my hand. It's taken me eight years to get an invitation to a party—my first one.

I'm so excited and I run all the way home with my friends to tell Mom. I come around the street corner and my face falls as I see mom dragging a large suitcase down the front steps.

Oh no, not again.

"Mom?" I ask as I walk toward her.

She fakes a brave smile. "We have to go, sweetie."

I shake my head. "But..." I don't want to go. I finally have friends. I have a party. I glance to my three friends who live on my street. They have no idea what she is talking about. I wish I didn't.

"Say goodbye to your friends, baby." She gestures to them as she grabs my hand and brushes my hair back from my face. Tears fill my eyes. "I have a party on Saturday. Ellen invited me to her party. Can we just stay until Saturday?" I whisper.

Mom's face falls and her eyes flicker up to my friends as they all wait. "Next time," she murmurs.

There will be no next time.

"Say goodbye, Rosh," she urges as she squeezes my hand in hers.

"Here, you are going to need these." He passes me a large yellow envelope. "Inside you have your new passport and three utility bills in your name so you can open a bank account."

"Thanks." I look down at the envelope in my hand, my ticket to freedom, and I clutch it tightly. The boat is docking in Colombia as we speak and Stace—I mean Mac—is letting me off the ship. The plans have changed and now I'm not going to Puerto Rico, apparently, but that suits me fine. It gets me away from him quicker... him and Chelsea. I'm pissed at myself that his words last night about being bored in our cabin cut me like a knife, and I just want to get the hell away from him as soon as possible.

He is not good for my sanity, but then again I'm not sure Colombia is a much safer option. I will, however, be glad to rid myself of this cabin fever bullshit.

"You will have to apply for a driver's licence yourself and you may have to go through your learner program again, we can't get past that one."

I nod. "Okay."

"It's probably best to open a few bank accounts as soon as you get to mainland because the utilities are still in date now."

"Yes, okay." My eyes hold his. "Thank you."

A frown crosses his brow as he looks down at me.

"I sincerely mean that. You didn't have to save me, yet you did." I smile softly.

He puts both of his hands into his pockets as he stares down at me as if scared to touch me. He has a good reason. I'm feeling unstable after he went to Chelsea last night. If he touches me, he's going down.

"Can I have a goodbye kiss?" he asks hopefully.

The electricity zaps between us.

"No." I cut him off before he has time to retaliate. Why would I want to kiss him? So another fucking asshole can bring me undone? No, thank you. Alone and safe is a much better option.

He frowns in question.

"I don't want to kiss you. I'm done with us. It was fun while it lasted, let's just leave it at that?"

He shakes his head in frustration as if knowing that I am lying through my teeth.

The horn on the boat sounds loudly.

I look toward our cabin door and screw up my face as I feel the adrenaline shoot through my blood stream. "This is it?"

He nods.

"How will I get off the ship. Are they going to search me or anything?"

He shakes his head. "No, they will think you are one of the girls who travels with us. We come here regularly. They know us."

I nod as I think.

"So, you will show your passport to them."

"Oh. What's my name?" I quickly open the envelope and then the passport. My face drops in horror. My deadpan, horrid face stares back at me, and I look like something from America's most wanted. "C-could you not have picked a worse photo?" I stammer. "Oh, that's woeful." I scan down at the name, Rebecca Williams.

He gave me his surname, although he doesn't know that I know what it is.

"Rebecca?" I ask.

He shrugs as if embarrassed. "I can't really imagine you with a name not starting with R."

"Where did Williams come from?"

"I just like it, that's all," he replies casually.

I smile broadly. "It's a nice name." I narrow my eyes at the photo again and I wince. "God, that's hideous."

He takes it from me and studies it with a sarcastic smile covering his face. "That's not so bad?"

My eyes widen. "Not so bad? It's fucking evil."

He laughs out loud and it's a sound that permeates through my bones. "It is a bit evil looking, if I'm honest."

My mouth drops open in shock that he just said that. "You are no gentleman. You could at least pretend it's a good shot."

He drops his hand to my behind. "I never said I was a gentleman."

I look up at him and it's there again—the electricity zapping between us. We both stay still as we feel it, our eyes searching each other's.

If only...

No, stop it!

I break from his clutches and he drops his head.

"I need to go to the bathroom," I murmur.

"Okay." He hesitates for a moment as he watches me. "I will meet you on deck?"

I nod and walk into the bathroom and hear the click as he leaves. I wait for a few minutes and run to my hiding spot and grab my diamonds in my sock. Where the hell am I going to put these babies? The bulge in the bottom of the sock is big, too big to put you know where, as I had planned. Maybe I should leave some behind? No!

Fucking hell, am I really going to sneak stolen diamonds into Colombia?

My heart is hammering. What if I get caught?

What if I don't?

I let myself imagine getting away with it. My life will take a completely different turn. I will have money, lots and lots of money. No identity, I can travel the world alone and be pain free.

I untie the sock and slide out the diamonds and put them onto the sink one by one. I then take off my bra and feel around on the inside of each cup. This should do it.

Using Stace's razor, I nick a little hole in the top of each cup and slide the diamonds into the lining of each bra cup. I put it on and then push them down so they sit underneath my two breasts. I jiggle my boobs around to see if they are going to come out and I smile broadly.

I should be a fucking inventor or something.

I grab my handbag and take one long last look around the cabin that has been both my Heaven and my Hell for the past fourteen days. I started this journey being tied to his bed and ended it wishing I was tied to him.

Even in my wildest dreams I couldn't make this shit up. Couldn't make him up.

I get a vision of the beautiful man above me, his body in mine.

The way he looked at me, the way he made me feel.

With one last, deep, regretful inhale, I leave my prison and make my way up on deck.

It's hot, so bloody hot.

In fact, I would say molten lava doesn't get this fucking hot. I am waiting in line outside the custom office on the Colombia side of the dock to get off the ship, and I am sweating like a pig.

Oh dear God, just let me get out of here alive. If they find the diamonds on me, I'm dead. They probably just shoot people on the docks here.

No questions will be asked and even he won't protect me, I know that for sure.

I count the people in front of us. One, two, three... Ten, there are ten that are in front and another eight have gone through already. Everyone is super keen to get on dry land, so it seems.

I watch the cement ground underneath us, petrified to make eye contact with anyone in case they can tell I'm lying... or stealing, or whatever the hell this is.

There is a woman and two men checking passports and they seem to know everyone as they chat and laugh happily with the crew as they walk through.

Stace squeezes my hand that is nestled tightly within his and he bends and kisses my cheek. "Will you relax?"

I fake a smile and nod.

He slings his arm around my shoulders casually. "What do you want to do today, baby?" he asks in a loud voice so others can hear.

I force a fake smile. "I don't know. I have never been here before I am so excited. When do we have to be back on the ship?" I reply.

"We leave port at 6pm tomorrow night."

"So we are staying in Colombia overnight?" I frown. He nods and winks, unleashing his cheeky, boyish grin.

Huh? Is he telling me this so that they can hear or is he telling me this because he wants me to know?

I just want to get out of here with my diamonds. The sweat

runs down between my breasts. "It's so fucking hot," I whisper in annoyance. "I can't handle this shit."

He raises his eyebrow sexily. "Who are you kidding? You invented hot."

I smirk and drop my head as my heart flutters in my chest.

Stop it. Stop being so damn likeable, asshole.

Our turn finally comes, and Stace takes the reins and hands over both of our passports. "How many ships have you done in the last few days?" he asks as a distraction.

The two men reply with something. I don't know what they are saying because all I can hear is my thieving heart trying to escape from my chest. The guy looks at our two passports and smiles and hands them back before waving us through the turnstile.

Oh my God.

I'm through.

I bite my bottom lip to stop myself from breaking into a broad smile.

Stace ushers me into a waiting cab and then surprisingly climbs in behind me. Huh?

The driver turns. "Where to?"

"Bogota," Stace replies. "Bog Hotel."

My eyes widen. "Bog Hotel?" I ask. "Are you joking?"

He smiles with a shake of his head. "It's nice. Trust me."

I nod and think for a minute. "Are we dropping you somewhere first?"

"No, of course not." He subtly points to the driver with his chin.

I glance up at the driver as his eyes flick up to us in the rear view mirror.

Shit. I turn and look out the window in annoyance. You

can't even trust a fucking cab driver. The trip is long, over an hour, but I don't mind. I'm hanging out the window like a dog, lapping up the scenery. The place is colourful and alive... so different to anywhere I have ever been before.

With every mile farther away from the ship we get, I feel a little more of my positive self return.

I'm doing this.

I'm really doing this. I have a fake passport, the means to have a lot of money and possibility to go anywhere I want in the world unencumbered.

I have never felt so free and I am finding it hard to wipe the stupid grin from my face. As if reading my mind, Stace is looking over at me smiling, too.

Can he feel how happy I am?

Finally, after what seems like forever, we arrive and the cab comes to a halt. I peer out of the car as my bravery instantly dissipates. Stace jumps out and pays the driver, but I remain seated where I am as I try to calm my nerves. It looks okay, not at all what I imagined. I glance around at the street. It's busy and narrow with trees lining the pavement. The doormen all look respectable and this seems pretty swanky. I kind of thought I would be getting dumped off in a ghetto somewhere. My car door opens suddenly. It startles me and I jump. Stace frowns down at me in the car. "Out you get."

I nod a little too quickly.

"You okay?" he asks.

I fake a smile. "Of course, why wouldn't I be?" I jump out of the car.

I am okay when I have to pretend to be brave. I've been doing it all my life. Acting brave is my safe place.

When I act brave. I feel brave.

We walk into the lobby and Stace approaches the desk. "We have a booking in the name of Williams," he says to the sexy blonde receptionist.

The receptionist's eyes drop to his arms and then down his muscular body. Her eyes linger a little too long on him for my liking and I glare at her. I'm still here you know? How rude? I mean, yes, sure he's hot, but he's also my fucking pretend boyfriend.

Eyes off, slut.

"Yes, Sir." She smiles sexily as her eyes hold his. He smirks back knowing exactly what she is thinking.

Good grief. If this is how things work in Colombia, I may have to cut a bitch.

My eyes flicker between the two of them in annoyance.

Have they forgotten I am fucking here?

"When you are finished ogling my husband, I would like to go to our room, please," I snap, unable to help myself.

"Of course, Mrs. Williams," she mutters in a fluster and drops her attention to the computer and types furiously.

Ugh, why did I just say that? I feel my underarms heat with embarrassment. I peer up at Stace and he is smiling down at me like a Cheshire cat.

"Don't," I mouth with a dirty look. I snap my eyes away, angry that I just showed him my jealous streak.

Just leave me here and go. I really, really need you to go.

She puts the two plastic cards into an envelope and hands it over to him. "The booking is for fourteen nights and I have you in the Luxury suite as requested on the top floor."

"Thank you," he replies as he takes the cards from her.

Huh, fourteen nights? I frown as I follow him into the elevator and the door closes behind us.

"You booked me for fourteen nights?" I ask.

"Yes," he replies as he watches the dial above the door go up the floors.

"Why?"

"So you have somewhere safe until you get yourself sorted. This may come as a surprise to you, but I am not exactly thrilled about leaving you here alone."

"Oh." I smile gratefully. "Thank you."

We stay silent as the doors open and I follow him down the corridor to the room. He opens it and I stand still. Wow. It's glitzy... like, super glitzy.

A beautiful, cream upholstered king bed with a studded Head board and a huge leather caramel lounge. Sheer curtains line a back wall that is alight with natural light. Behind the bed is a coffee-coloured glass wall, and I peer around to see a huge free-standing bathtub and marble bathroom.

I laugh out loud.

He smiles a proud of himself smile. "Is it okay?"

"Okay?" If I could hug him, I would. "It's the nicest room I have ever seen."

He walks over to the window and pulls the sheer curtain back to look down at the road, as if thinking. "I will take you shopping and then I will head straight back to the ship," he replies as he keeps his eyes firmly on the street below.

My good mood instantly falls. "Oh, okay." Yes, he's right, he needs to go. Of course he does. "What do we need to go shopping for?"

"Clothes. You don't own a thing."

I shrug. "Ah, that's okay. I'm not really a things person."

He turns and looks at me in surprise. "You don't like things?"

I shake my head.

"All women like things."

"I'm not all women. I have done without things for most of my life and I know for certain that things don't make me happy."

His eyes hold mine for an extended time before he finally answers. "We will get you what you need."

"I don't have any money."

"We will open you a bank account while we are here." He fumbles around in his bag and pulls out a wad of cash and passes it over to me. "Here is five thousand to deposit."

I frown as I stare down at the thick bundle of money in my hand. "You're giving me money?"

"Of course I am. How are you going to live if you don't have money?"

I stare down at the cash in my hand, overwhelmed at his kindness.

"I-I will pay you back," I stammer.

"Not necessary. I earn a lot."

Regret swirls in my stomach. I have stolen his diamonds and here he is being nice and giving me his hard earned cash. Well, not technically his diamonds, but the same thing I suppose. He is the boss of the ship and they are under his watch. What if he gets into trouble because of me?

What if they kill him?

Oh no, my mind starts to race. What if they do kill him? What if they torture him to death and think that he was in on this with me? No, they wouldn't. He would blame Stucco, that's what I would do. Someone was already stealing from the ship. The key went missing remember.

Fuck.

Should I fess up?

No. Don't be stupid.

The air in the room changes and I feel panicky and sick.

I look over at his broad back as he stares down at the street lost in his own world. What is he thinking about?

Is he onto me?

I don't want him to take me shopping now. I want to get as far away from him as possible. I feel guilty. I know he is feeling somewhat guilty for letting them take me, throwing money at me and all. What if he knows I took it and he is setting a trap to see if I will really go through with it?

Oh, I hate this. I am not cut out to be a fucking criminal.

My thoughts are broken by his deep, husky voice. "Come on then." He moves to the door and ushers me out.

Moments later, we are walking through the reception area and he picks up my hand and takes it in his. My heart flutters.

We haven't been intimate since he told me he was bored in the cabin and was going to Chelsea, and he hasn't tried to touch me at all. Not that I have wanted him to. He is probably lucky he hasn't, to be honest, because I may have cut off his hand.

Part of me—the insecure part—wonders if he turned off me when he heard about my fucked up family, of me being broke and hiding all of my life. Of my own flesh and blood murdering the mother of his child in front of that child. I know I shouldn't feel embarrassed and it's not my fault, but I feel as though, in the eyes of others, it taints me.

It takes away my shine and tarnishes my innocence.

I mean, how would my future boyfriend introduce me to his parents or to his friends?

He couldn't. He could never truthfully tell them my story because it will never be accepted. Nobody would want their son to marry someone like me with the emotional baggage I have. I can only bring danger to their lives and pain. I'm good at bringing that and that's why Mom kept us at a distance from normal people.

My children will never have freedom as long as I live in the United States with my father alive. He will always find me.

It is with the last thought strong in my mind that I pick up.

I need to do this.

I do deserve a new start where nobody owes me anything.

I look him straight in the eye. "Lets go shopping."

This is fucking drug money and I'm entitled to it as much as any of those bastards.

We walk hand in hand down the street and I have a huge smile across my face. We have opened a bank account, which was surprisingly easy. Stace has gone crazy and we are loaded with shopping bags. He has bought me nightgowns and swimmers, makeup and hairbrushes, underwear, dresses, a hat, and three pairs of shoes. I tried to pay with the money he gave me but he wouldn't have it. Funny thing is, the things he has picked for me are not my style at all, but because he has liked them on me, I have wanted them. As if somehow his opinion is the only one that matters. I am a new person now. I can be anyone I want to be.

He stops in front of a designer boutique. "Let's go in here." I look at the expensive furnishings. "It looks too expensive.

I don't need fancy clothes."

"What if you have a date? You will need something nice to wear."

I smile up at him in wonder. "A date with who?"

He shrugs and smiles sexily down at me. "Some lucky bastard."

My heart swells. I follow him into the store and we start to look through the hanging dresses.

"How long since you have been on a date?" I ask as he slowly flicks through the dresses on the rack.

He narrows his eyes as he thinks. "I don't know. A long time. I would have still been in the Marines. Maybe five or six years."

My mouth drops open. "You were a Marine?"

He looks down at me and smiles sexily. "Yes. I was a Marine."

I put my hands on my hips and stare in wonder up at him. "What?" He smirks.

"That's just so..." I shake my head as I try to articulate my words. "Frigging hot."

His face falls. "And being a criminal on a shipping container isn't hot to you?"

"Well." Oh crap, that came out wrong. "I just meant..."

He cuts me off. "I know what you meant." He keeps looking through the dresses.

He moves to the other rack along the window and concentrates on his task. I, however, have a million questions and follow him around like the annoying person I am.

"What did you do in the Marines?"

"I was a nautical engineer and a chopper pilot."

I get a vision of him in his grey uniform flying a helicopter, and a thrill of excitement runs through my deviant bloodstream. He would have been a fucking hot chopper pilot.

"A pilot," I gasp.

"Of choppers." He frowns.

"Choppers, planes, same thing."

"No, not really. Different aircraft." He smirks over at me and I beam a broad smile back at him.

He continues to flick through the rack, distracted at his task at hand as he pulls out a little black dress. "I like this one."

I take it from him without even looking at it. I am too busy with my Top Gun fantasy.

"How long were you in the Marines?" I ask.

"Six years."

I bite my bottom lip as I think. He hands me another two dresses.

"Why did you leave?"

"I missed home."

I frown. "But you are not home now, anyway."

He raises his eyebrows at me and my ten thousand questions.

Damn it, this is the most interesting story I have heard, and just when he is about to leave, he tells me about it. I want to hear it all.

"Do they know this on the boat?"

"Ship," he corrects.

"Ah, yes, ship." I roll my eyes.

"No. Why would I tell them anything personal about me? They are not my friends."

I smile as a warm, fuzzy feeling runs through me. "Am I your friend?"

He smiles and puts his arm around my shoulder. "I would like to think so." He pulls me toward him and gently kisses my temple. What a sweet gesture. He instantly goes back to looking at his dresses and I stand and watch him with my mind going crazy.

I don't want him to go.

I want him to stay with me and be my friend. My gorgeous, beautiful, fuckable friend.

He is the first person who I could tell about my past and now he is telling me his.

We buy two of the dresses and a pair of heels before we head back to the hotel. Silence has fallen between us as we walk hand in hand, and I wish I could act happy and joyful, but the fact is I really don't want to say goodbye to him.

This is it. I will never see him again. We get to the room and I open the door. We walk in and throw all of the bags on the floor. I'm not sure what to say, so I start with the lame stuff. "Would you like a cup of tea?"

He smiles, knowing my tactic. "No, I've got to get going."

I nod. I knew he was going to say that.

He walks over to the desk and takes the pen and paper and scribbles down a number and hands it to me. "This is my mother's phone number. If you need to contact me." He hesitates. "Call her. I check in with her every few weeks."

I nod and take the paper from him and fold it in half.

He watches me intently. "You going to be alright?"

I nod as my eyes stay fixed firmly on the floor. I'm not good at goodbyes. I've said goodbye to everyone I cared for at one stage or another.

He puts his fingers underneath my chin, brings my eyes up to meet his, and we stare at each other for a moment. It's like he feels the same... but then he doesn't say anything.

"You should go," I whisper.

He nods.

"Thank you for everything." I smile. I can feel the tears welling and I just need him to go before he sees them. I am suddenly scared to start a new life on my own.

Stop it.

He holds me in a tight embrace and I feel his large, warm arms around me one last time. We cling to each other for an extended time, and without another word he turns and walks out of the door.

It clicks softly as it closes behind him.

I blow out a large breath as the tears slowly well in my eyes. I head over to the window so I can watch him walk away one last time. I stare down at the street below at all the people merrily going by with their lives.

I feel a sense of closure... of who I used to be.

I feel a beginning of who I want to be and I smile.

No remorse, no regrets, just a sense of gratitude that I met him for even a little while.

He gave me freedom.

I see him exit the front doors. I put my hands on the glass and lean into the window to watch him. He heads over to the cab rank and talks to the driver, and then gets into the backseat. In slow motion, the cab pulls out and drives away.

He gave me my freedom.

Three hours and a good cry later, I am lying in a semi-conscious state in the deep, hot bath.

It's okay to cry sometimes, Mom used to say. It purges the bad to make way for the good. I think I was crying for the loss of my life rather than the loss of Stace.

Although that feels pretty shitty, too. He would be back on his boat now. Ship, I correct myself with a smile. My diamonds are all packed safely away and I have an appointment tomorrow with a master jeweler to sell one of them. I have to sell them one by one to not raise suspicion. I've also made an appointment to get a safety deposit box. I can't keep the remaining diamonds here. I need to have them somewhere secure.

I smile in my heated, relaxed state. Everything is going to plan and how it should be... finally.

Once I get the diamonds all sold off and money into an offshore account, I'm off to Europe to start my new life.

Far, far away from my father, where he will never find me again.

I climb out of the bath and put on my robe and wrap a towel around my head. I pick up the room service menu and scroll through. I glance outside as the sun is beginning to set. I really should go out tonight to celebrate my new life, but I honestly can't be bothered. I will stay in and then tomorrow make the effort to spend the day sightseeing.

Knock, knock, knock.

Shit, who's that?

My heart rate picks up and I sneak over and peer through the peephole.

It's Stace. What?

I open the door in a rush. "Hello." He smiles nervously. I frown at his demeanour.

"I hope you don't mind me asking." He seems so nervous that it brings a broad smile to my face. "I saw you downstairs having dinner with your parents."

My heart freefalls from my chest. He remembered.

"I spoke to your father."

I smile.

"The doctor."

I put my hand over my mouth in shock. He remembered everything.

"It took a lot of convincing, but he said you could go on a date with me tonight."

I stare at him through blurry eyes. He swallows nervously.

"What's your name?" I whisper.

"Stace." He smiles softly. "What's your name?" he asks.

"Roshina."

A frown crosses his face at my real name.

"What do you do, Stace?" I ask.

"I'm a Marine."

A broad smile crosses my face.

"What do you do?" he asks.

"I'm an intensive care nurse."

He holds his hand out and we shake hands as the electricity jolts through me from his touch.

"Can I pick you up at seven?" he asks hopefully.

I nod as my eyes hold his. He has no idea how much it means to me that he remembered what I told him.

"You're playing along with my lifeline?" I whisper.

His eyes hold mine. "Maybe it's my lifeline, too."

12

Roshelle

I STARE at him as a clusterfuck of emotions whirl around me like a tornado.

"Asking my dad if you can take me on a date is your life-line?" I whisper.

"Taking you on a normal date is," he answers as his eyes search mine. He's genuinely nervous. Maybe he thinks I'm going to say no.

"Seven sounds wonderful."

He smiles. "I'm staying downstairs on the next level."

I smile. He even booked a room for himself.

He stands awkwardly in front of me. "I will..." He pauses as if not knowing what to say next. "I will see you at seven then?"

I nod through my smirk. He turns and walks up the hall and I watch him. The elevator doors open and he disappears, looking very pleased with himself.

Holy shit!

I jump up and down on the spot. He asked me on a date, he asked me on a date. I run into my room and punch the air. Oh my God, what am I going to wear?

I have to look good. Irresistibly good.

I open the closet and find the two date dresses that we bought today. Damn it... I wasn't even paying attention to them when we bought them, I was too distracted by my Top Gun fantasies. I pull out the one that was his favorite—a flowing, backless, ice-pink number. It has shoestring straps and a cowl neckline that dips low into the back. I can't wear a bra with it.

If I'd have known I was actually going to get this date I would have paid more attention to his choices and maybe picked something better. I slip it on and look at myself in the mirror. I turn to check out my behind. Butterflies flutter in my stomach and I smile broadly. I pick up the phone and ring reception.

"Hello, reception," they answer.

"Yes, hello." I smile. "It's Mrs. Williams from 1204."

"Hello, how can we help you?"

"Is your general store still open?" I ask.

"Yes, Ma'am."

"Would I be able to get a razor and a hairdryer brought up to my room, please?"

"Of course."

I glance down at my toes. "Oh, and... and some nail polish," I stammer. I don't think I have painted my nails since prom.

"Of course, Mrs. Williams. Which color?"

I shrug. "A natural pink, or a color not too bright if you have it. Just something pretty and feminine."

"Okay, we can do that."

I smile broadly. "Can I also have a toasted sandwich?" I am starving already and I don't want to look like a pig on my date.

I fumble around with the menu. "Um." I scan the choices. "A club sandwich, if that's okay?"

"Yes, no problem. That will be about ten minutes."

"Thank you." I hang up, and with a twirl of happiness I flop onto the bed.

———

I stand in the mirror and look at my reflection. He was right, this pretty pink dress is amazing, although something that I would have never picked for myself. It's feminine and yet sexy. I have nude, strappy stilettos on and I'm pimped to the nines. My long, dark hair is straightened and I have smoky eye makeup with pink glossy lips. My fingers and toenails are manicured and painted.

I look good, I know I look good... but then that could just be because I looked like total shit for the last two weeks. Who could tell?

The only thing missing is perfume, but Stace picked my deodorant so I guess that will have to do. I sniff my underarms and shrug. Smells okay, I suppose. He seemed to like it.

I stare at my reflection.

This is it. Unlike any date I have ever been on before, there are no preconceived ideas. I know for certain that I will never see him again after tonight. Butterflies rise in my stomach. Maybe that's why it feels so important.

This is all we have.

This night is all we will ever have. I want to make it good for him.

I close my eyes as reality sets in.

I desperately want my memory of him to be happy and

good, because that's what I feel he could have been if he hadn't got...

I cut myself off. Stop it, you idiot.

He is a criminal and you have one night. Stop thinking, stop fucking feeling, and look at it for what it really is.

My thoughts are interrupted by his knock on the door. I put my hand on my stomach to calm my nerves and take one last look in the mirror.

Go time.

I open the door and there he stands, six foot four in a navy dinner suit and dress shoes. His sandy curls are styled, and he is clean-shaven. My eyebrows rise by themselves as I inhale his heavenly scent.

He wore a suit. Oh my God, he wore a suit.

He must have gone out and bought it after we organized our date. The night is perfect already.

"Hello." He smirks.

I smile broadly. "Hello." The electricity zaps between us.

His eyes drop down my body. "You look beautiful," he whispers.

My poor heart won't be able to bear much of this, and unable to speak, I smile goofily. He makes me giddy.

"Are you ready to go?" he asks.

I smile and grab my bag and he leads me out into the corridor.

The restaurant is dark and moody with candlelit tables. We are seated in the alfresco area in the courtyard that sits between two tall buildings. Fairy lights are hanging diagonally above us from building to building creating a romantic canopy. Large plants in pots are surrounding the border. We held hands as we walked all the way here, deep in discussion about our surroundings. It seems Stace is quite the Google traveler and could tell me all about the scenery and buildings as we passed them. Salsa music is piping throughout the space and the crowd are all late twenties and above. Loud, relaxed chatter echoes all around.

"Thank you." I smile to the waiter as he fills my glass with champagne. He then fills Stace's.

I hold my glass up. "A toast."

He brings his glass up to meet mine.

"To new beginnings."

He smiles. "To new beginnings," he repeats We both take a sip.

"So what do you think of Bogota?" he asks.

"It's gorgeous." I can't hide my surprise. "I'm not sure what I expected, but it wasn't this."

"I thought this would be better for you than in Colombia itself. It seemed safer and easier for you to get your bearings."

I smile softly as I imagine him Googling places to drop me off. "My safety isn't your concern, but thank you." I sip my champagne. "This is so good." I hold my glass up to him.

"Hmm, yes it is," he replies as he eyes the bubbling liquid in his glass.

"So you bought a suit for me?" I smirk. He smiles bashfully. "I did."

Our eyes are locked on each other. "It looks really good," I whisper.

"I had to try and match my beautiful date. I had an advantage. I already knew what she was wearing."

His beautiful date. Oh, my.

"Well, you haven't had a date in six years." I smirk cheekily.

He laughs. "You caught that, did you?"

I smile. "Yes, I caught that." I take a sip. "Why haven't you taken a woman on a date for six years?"

He shrugs and rearranges his napkin on his lap. "I don't know. Things haven't gone as planned, I suppose." "What were the plans?"

He licks the champagne from his bottom lip and I feel my insides clench. "I just..." He hesitates as he thinks. "I just always imagined I would meet the right person and everything else would fall into place."

"The right person?" I ask.

He nods.

"You say the word person as if you didn't mind if it were a male or female?"

"Would it bother you if it didn't matter to me?" he replies. I shrug. "Not really."

He smiles sexily as his eyes drop to my lips. "I like women, if that was the hidden question. But, you already know that."

"And you haven't met her? Your person."

His eyes hold mine and he shrugs. "I had a serious girlfriend in college and then when I went into the marines it got too hard to be faithful. I was young, dumb, and full of come on different continents of the world, away from her. The stopovers became..." He pauses as he thinks of the wording. "Complicated."

"You broke her heart?"

He nods once and I can see the remorse in his eyes.

"You haven't been in a relationship since?"

"No."

The waiter walks over with a huge entrée platter of grilled seafood and Stace quickly reshuffles the table so it can fit.

"Oh, wow." I smile.

"Thank you." He nods as the waiter leaves.

"And you? You have had five boyfriends?" he asks.

My mouth drops open and I slap his hand on the table.

"What? How do you know that?" I pick up the huge spoon and start to dish out my prawns. "Oh, this looks so good."

He laughs. "Yes, the ship food leaves a lot to be desired, and I told you I checked you out."

"Dick Tracey, now?" I smirk as I hand the platter to him.

His face falls serious. "Are you going to contact your boyfriend?"

I screw up my face. "Hell, no. He's a twat."

"Did you love him?"

I drop my head and he picks up my hand over the table. I shrug sadly. "I kind of thought I did."

"Just thought?" he repeats.

"He was my first serious boyfriend."

"The others?"

"They were nothing really. Just kid stuff."

He waits for my answer.

"We had fun, but it wasn't until I met..." I stop myself.

Fuck. I load my mouth full of food to shut myself up.

"Until you met who?"

I shake my head and drink my champagne and then refill my glass. Oh God, stop talking you big mouthed jabber jaws.

"Until you met who?" His eyes tell me that he already knows what I was going to say.

I frown. How do I put this? "Let's just say that you have taught me that there is more to a relationship than someone making you feel safe."

He frowns as he takes his first mouthful of seafood. "Is that what he did? Made you feel safe."

I nod.

"Is that what you need from a man?"

I shake my head. "No..." My voice trails off.

"What have I taught you?"

I laugh. "Why are you so serious? Can we change the subject, please?"

He shakes his head, picks up my hand, and cups it around his face. "Tell me. Please."

I get goosebumps seeing my hand cup his beautiful face. "You taught me what it was like to be unable to..." I frown as I swallow the lump in my throat.

"To what?" He rolls my hand over and kisses the inside of my wrist, his tongue gently caressing my skin.

If I was a cat I would be purring. "To defy all logic. To want someone so bad that you don't care about the consequences," I whisper.

Our eyes lock and the look he gives me feels like it could get me pregnant. I'm not even joking. Get here, straddle me, and ride my fucking cock are its precise words.

Well, that's what it says to me anyway.

As if reading my mind, he rolls his lips to hide his smile. "I think I know how that feels," he mutters under his breath.

I drain my glass in one gulp. Stop drinking, fool.

"How did you...?" I hesitate. "How did you go from a marine to working on that ship?" I ask.

He blows out a deep breath as if knowing this question was coming. "I took a two-year gap from the Navy and was looking to pick up some casual work."

I frown. "So, you just thought oh fuck it, I will go and work on a drug ship."

He looks at me deadpan.

I bite my bottom lip to stop my champagne guzzling mouth up.

You really need to stop talking now, stupid.

"I was offered a job to fly a Japanese businessman on and off his ship on his private chopper. The pay was good and it was casual. Just the type of thing I was looking for. I didn't want to be locked into a position because I was eventually going back to the Navy, and I could live in my home town while I did it."

I sip my champagne as I listen. "Where is home to you?" I ask.

"New York."

I smile. New York... who knew? I clink my glass with his to celebrate my new found information.

He smirks and sips his drink.

"What then?"

He shrugs. "I did that for about twelve months and it was the perfect job. I worked three days a week with no hassles."

I frown, feeling like this story isn't adding up.

"I got to know the guy I was working for and he seemed alright. Anyway, one day I was waiting at the helipad for him to arrive in his limo and I was approached by another man. His private pilot had recently become ill and he needed someone he could trust to take him to his ship urgently."

I sit back in my seat, disturbed.

"He offered me fifty thousand dollars." I frown.

"F-for one trip?" I stammer.

He nods.

"So you did it."

He nods. "I was getting three grand a trip from the other guy."

My heart sinks.

He shakes his head in disgust in himself. "I knew for him to offer me that kind of money he had to be into some pretty heavy stuff." He pauses.

"But you did it anyway."

He nods. "I was saving for a house and that would be the final deposit that I needed."

I smile in surprise. "You own a house?"

"Yes."

"Where?"

"Manhattan."

I clink our glasses together again in celebration. "Well done." I smirk. "How amazing. Go you."

He smiles proudly.

"Anyway," I say as I continue eating.

"Anyway." He pauses. "On the way to the ship, we got to talking and he asked me what I did and I told him I was a marine engineer. He seemed like an okay guy."

I sit still, unsure if I want to hear the rest of it. It's like I am hearing the story of his life unravelling.

"I took him to his ship the next day and I sat in the chopper for two hours while he did whatever he did and then I flew him home. He paid me fifty grand cash."

I frown.

He shakes his head. "I was gone from home for a total of six hours and I made fifty thousand dollars."

"God," I whisper.

"Anyway, I did the job and that was that. No strings, no questions asked, and I went back to working with the other guy and bought my house."

I smile. "What an achievement."

He smiles sadly into his glass and I know there is more of the story to come.

"Three months later he called me again."

A lead ball starts to bounce in my stomach.

"I was living in my house, but it was shitty and needed renovation, and I was scratching for money."

"So you did another job?" I ask.

He nods. "It started with one and then a week later another

and another. It was never actually discussed how long I would work for him. He just gave me the cash and I didn't ask questions."

I watch him as he sips his drink.

"You knew he was bad, didn't you?"

He shrugs. "I knew he had to be involved in some serious shit by the money he threw around and the guards he had."

I feel sick.

"Usually I would just sit in the chopper and wait for him, but one day when we were on the ship, some shit went down and one of the crew got killed. His guard that flew in the chopper with us shot this guy dead, right in front of us."

I frown, this is the guy Angela was telling me about.

He rubs his forehead as he remembers it. "I didn't know what to do." He hesitates. "I had knowingly taken them there. I had to fly them back to the mainland and then I realized that I was on his payroll. My bank accounts showed huge cash injections for over eight months. If they went down, so did I. Basically, if I didn't fly them home and shut my mouth, I was either in jail or a dead man walking."

"So, in effect, you were already one of them."

He drops his head in shame.

I grab his hand over the table. "Why don't you just leave? Make a new start." I smile. "You could do it. I know you could."

He fakes a smile. "You don't just leave."

I frown.

"The only way out is death. I've seen man after man get killed."

My blood runs cold. "What do you mean?"

"They pay you so much that you get used to a certain lifestyle and you can have holidays and time off when ever you want." He sips his drink. "It's a perfect job on paper."

"But you can't leave?" I murmur.

He shakes his head. "They always find you."

I put my head into my hands on the table. "God, Stace, bloody hell. What a mess."

He smiles. "I'm no angel. I got what I deserved. I knew they were no good, and yet I was seduced by the forbidden fruit."

His phone dances across the table. He frowns and turns it over, the word Mom lighting up the screen. He turns it back over and ignores it.

"Answer it." I push it over to him.

"It's okay. I will call her back tomorrow."

"I insist, answer it now." I pick the phone up and pass it to him.

He answers. "Hey, Mom." His face breaks into a breathtaking smile. I feel myself flutter a little and my face mirrors his.

"Are you okay?" he asks, his voice is gentle and caring.

"I'm so glad to hear your voice," she replies. I can hear her through the speaker across the table. "Me, too, Mom." He smiles.

"Where are you?"

"I'm in Bogota. Colombia."

"Oh my God, Stace, are you safe? Are you with your friends from the ship?"

He smiles broadly and his eyes flicker to me. "Actually, Mom, I'm on a date."

"A date?" she shrieks and he holds the phone out from his ear.

I giggle into my champagne glass. "Who is she?" She laughs in excitement.

"Just this really cool chick I met."

I hold my glass up to him in a cheers symbol, he grabs his glass and clinks it with mine as he throws me a sexy wink.

"What's she like, Stace?"

His eyes hold mine. "The most beautiful woman in the world."

My stomach does a somersault and I try to wipe the goofy grin from my face.

"Oh, let me speak to her," his mom pleads.

He laughs out loud and I know it's because we are drinking this champagne like water. "No way, you will scare her off." He laughs.

"Oh, Stace."

I hold my hand out for the phone and he shakes his head.

"No," he mouths.

I open and close my hand out for the phone. He laughs and shakes his head again.

I stand and walk around to his side of the table and snatch the phone from him.

"Hello." I smile nervously as I fall back into my seat.

"Hello, dear. You are out with my Stace?" Her voice is warm and loving. Oh, she sounds so nice.

"Yes." I smile. "I'm a lucky girl."

This time it's him who smiles goofily.

"Is he okay? I worry about him so much."

I fake a smile as my heart drops. She has good reason to worry. He has gotten himself in the shit up to his eyeballs.

"He is wonderful." I smile. He picks up my hand and kisses the back of it.

Oh God, he is just so...

"Please look out for him, dear."

Stace rolls his eyes and holds his hand out for the phone.

I smile at his embarrassment. "I will."

"Promise me."

I laugh as he tries to snatch the phone back.

"I promise to look out for him." I laugh. "He's snatching the phone back from me. Nice meeting you." I laugh.

"Goodbye, dear. Hopefully you will come meet me in person one day."

He takes the phone back from me and winds up the conversation, but my mind is still on the meet her in person one day parting. What I wouldn't give to meet her in person one day.

Reality—the bitch—comes back with a thud. Stop it, it's just one night. He hangs up the phone and I fake a smile.

He shakes his head as if embarrassed. "Sorry, my mom is..." He hesitates.

"Lovely?" I smile.

He rolls his eyes. "She is always worrying since Justin." He cuts himself off as his face falls.

"Since Justin what?"

"Died."

"Who is Justin?"

"My brother."

"He died?"

He nods solemnly as he picks up his drink. "Six months ago."

I grab his hand over the table. "Oh, Stace, I'm so sorry. What happened?"

"He was a year older than me." He smiles sadly as he remembers. "A cop."

I frown as I listen. "He was always the good kid, did his chores first, looked out for me and Mom." He sips his drink as he thinks, sadness falling over him. "My dad died in a car accident when we were six and seven, so Justin took on the man of the house role."

"Did he have a family?" I ask.

He smiles and his face lights up. "Yes, Cindy his wife and Sebastian his son."

I sit still as I watch him struggle through this conversation. You can learn so much about a person by the way they grieve. A piece of the puzzle clicks into place. The family in the photo were his brother and his family.

"We were always best friends."

I smile and I can tell the affection he had for his beloved brother.

"Man, we got into some trouble as kids. We rode around on our bikes looking for mischief." He smiles sadly. "I was the only one who ended up finding it and yet it was he who was taken."

I frown. "You say that like you feel guilty that he died and you didn't?"

He nods. "I do."

We sit for a moment in silence. "How did he die?"

"He got caught in a case at work and wouldn't let it go."

I frown.

"I told him." He shakes his head. "I told him time and time again to let it go, but he wouldn't."

His eyes cloud over as he remembers his brother's death. "He thought he could bring them down and went to a warehouse alone in the middle of the night to talk to an informant."

I sit still as I imagine the scenario, alone at a cold warehouse in the middle of the night. How terrifying.

"It was a trap. They tied him up and tortured him. Electrocuted him to death."

My hands fly over my mouth in shock.

His eyes are cold, distant, and he stares into space. I know he is imagining his beloved brother dying alone and in pain.

"Stace," I whisper. "I am so sorry."

"We all have our baggage, Rosh." He sighs sadly as he picks

up my hand and re-cups his face with it. I don't know if my hand on his face is a comfort to him, but it's definitely a comfort to me. I dust my thumb back and forth over his bottom lip. Our eyes hold each other's and I feel so stupidly close to this man, it's crazy.

He shakes his head as if trying to remove the dark thoughts from his mind and raises his glass again. "Another toast."

I smile broadly and raise my glass to meet his. "To new beginnings." Our glasses clink and he widens his eyes. "And non-depressing dates."

I laugh out loud and repeat his words. "To new beginnings and non-depressing dates."

Stace

We are seated at a bar in a cocktail lounge. It's late, around 2am. We have had way too much to drink, but I don't want to go home. Because then I have to let her go and knowing that I can't even do what I want when we do get home only adds to the torture. Her lifeline was a dream of a respectable date, and damn it, I am going to give it to her if it's the last thing I do.

I get to kiss her goodnight. Once.

Only once.

We have talked and laughed with ease and I am surprised at just how much we have in common.

She may just be the coolest chick I have ever met.

A song comes on and I hold my hand out for her. "Would you like to dance?"

She smiles sexily. "You said you don't dance?"

"I don't dance on drug ships."

"Only on dates?" she whispers in surprise.

I throw her a wink. "Only on special dates."

We make our way to the dance floor and the song changes to some weird song I haven't heard before.

Play that song
The one that makes me go all night long
The one that makes me think of you
That's all you gotta do.

We sway to the music and she smiles up at me. "Look at you, dancing all date-like."

I shake my head with a grin and twirl her away from me violently and she laughs out loud.

"Stop talking, you're distracting my moves," I reply as I twirl her again.

We come close again and she looks lovingly up at me.

"What is this weird, hippy song?" I ask.

"I don't know, but it's my new favorite." She smiles innocently.

I stare down at her and so many emotions run through me, but the overwhelming one is regret.

Regret for what I did to her. Regret for how we met.

Regret that this feeling she gives me can't go on forever.

She starts to sing up at me and I know it's the champagne singing, but it just may be the most perfect thing I have ever heard.

If only.

Cut it out. I have to get out of this sappy mood. This isn't me.

This isn't who I am. I don't do sappy.

I twirl her violently again and she laughs out loud.

I will remember this, dancing to this hippy song with this beautiful girl, her laughter ringing loud around me.

The way she looks up at me, the way she feels in my arms. With one last twirl the song ends and the dance floor empties.

She walks over to the DJ.

"Excuse me, what is the name of that song, please?" She asks.

"Play That Song, by Train," The DJ replies.

"Thank you," she replies. "Can you put that in your phone for me so I don't forget?" she asks me.

I smirk as I type the name into my notes. "You like that song?"

I ask.

"My favorite." She smiles.

We walk into the foyer of the hotel and into the elevator. Just walk her to the door and kiss her goodnight.

That's it.

Nothing else.

Just a kiss. One kiss.

She has dreamed of a perfect date for all of her life, and damn it, I am going to give it to her if it's the last thing I do... and it might just be the last thing I do. I could die tomorrow because my balls are already hurting from what they know they are missing out on.

We hold hands and I stare at the floor, focused on the task at hand.

One kiss. Just one kiss.

I can do this. Of course I can do this.

"Oh, look, there's a pool," she whispers excitedly. "Can we go see it?"

"Ah." I hesitate. Oh, that's not a good idea. More alone

time. "Sure," my mouth replies before consulting my brain or my dick.... the control centre of this male body.

She pushes the button before waiting for my reply and soon the elevator doors are opening. The pool area is on the roof and the lights from the surrounding buildings glow in the distance. The area is darkened with spotlights in the water.

"Oh, isn't it perfect," she cries.

She is tottery on her feet and I smile at her inebriation. "It is."

She wraps her arms around my neck. "Let's dance again."

I wrap my arms around her and hold her close. "We don't have any music," I whisper.

She stares up at me and starts to sing the words to that song we danced to.

"Play that song, the one that makes me go too long."

We start to sway and I laugh because she doesn't know the words and her voice is so off key.

"The one that makes me think of you."

I swallow the lump in my throat. This is too much.

"That all you gotta do."

She giggles into the silence. "You know all dates are going to be woeful after this one," she murmurs as her eyes search mine.

"They better be," I whisper.

"This is the part where you kiss me."

13

Stace

I STARE DOWN at her and if I didn't know better I would swear I am 13 again and this is my first kiss. "You want me to kiss you?"

I ask.

She smiles lovingly and nods.

I bend and softly take her lips in mine. Her eyes close and her lips are soft and open, just like I imagine she is under her dress.

Cut it out!

My cock thumps in appreciation at the last thought, but it's my tongue that brings me back to reality. We kiss again and again, and with my eyes fused shut, I have no idea how to control myself.

Cut it out. No!

My arms crush her and I bring her to me, and she melts

into my arms, her hands going to the back of my head as she groans softly.

Don't groan or it's all over.

Her tongue gently dances with mine and I move closer and closer.

How much can a man fucking take?

"Oh God," she murmurs into my lips.

Fuck!

The kiss deepens, and this time, unable to help myself, I grab her behind and grind her body against mine so she can feel how hard I am for her. She needs to know.

"Stace," she whimpers. "You feel so good." Her lips drop to my neck and I close my eyes as my knees nearly buckle from beneath me.

Fucking hell, I feel arousal start to pump hard through my bloodstream.

Stop, stop, stop. Stace, stop!

She looks up at me with those perfect innocent eyes and she smiles softly. "Thank you," she whispers.

I softly brush her hair back from her forehead as I look down at her. "For what?" I ask.

"For showing me what it was like." My eyes hold hers. "Now I know how it feels."

My heart drops and her lips connect with mine one last time, her tongue rims my lips and then dives deeper. She's right, this night is perfect. This kiss is better than perfect.

I need to give her...

I stop myself.

Her lifeline... I need to be a man and give her the lifeline fantasy she deserves. This isn't about my fantasy and I have no right to want her as much I do.

I pull back from her in a rush as we both pant, trying to catch our breath.

Her face falls. "What's wrong?"

My chest rises and falls as I try to control my erratic heartbeat and I shake my head.

"I should walk you back to your room, Rosh," I pant.

"Why?" Her eyes darken and she moves closer and gently untucks my shirt from my pants. My breath hitches.

"Because." I tip my head back and look to the sky for divine guidance. I can't think when she is pulling on my shirt like that.

She runs her hand over my chest.

"Because this is a nice date. A well behaved date." I murmur, distracted.

She undoes my top button on my shirt. "Is that so?" she breathes into my ear so close I can feel her hot breath dust my skin. Goosebumps scatter.

I nod, unable to make my mouth say the words.

"Is that because I'm a nice girl?" she whispers.

I nod again.

"And you're a nice guy?"

I shrug. "That's the illusion we are trying to achieve here."

She laughs out loud and I frown.

"You honestly think we are nice? I think the opposite." She pauses and I frown. What's she talking about? "You see, I think we are a little bit different, you and I." Her sexy eyes hold mine and I know I am close to my breaking point.

"How so?"

"We both think that we want good."

I watch her with hungry eyes.

"But the reality is, we both crave bad," she whispers.

I stand still and a frown crosses my brow.

"I think, in each other, we see a little bit of bad," she whispers sexily. "That little bit of fucked up we both desire."

I smirk.

"And it's the crazy in you that I crave." She grabs the hem of her dress and pulls it over her head to reveal her bare breasts and a white, lace G-string.

Her perfect, toned body is plump for picking, so close I can almost taste it.

Game over.

"Fuck, yeah," I whisper as I start unbuttoning my shirt.

She slides her panties down her legs and steps out of them seductively.

"I'm going for a swim. Well behaved, boring boys aren't allowed in the pool."

I smirk as I rip my shirt over my shoulders and throw it onto the ground. I jump on one foot as I take off one shoe, and then the other, tearing my pants down.

She wants a bad boy? She's going to fucking get it.

She laughs and dives into the pool and I dive in after her. I pin her aggressively up against the wall and kiss her violently.

Her legs wrap around my waist. My hands are on her behind and I rub her up and down over my hard cock. God, she's so fucking hot and tight.

The heat she is omitting is burning me alive.

"Give it to me," she pleads. "Give me the crazy I need."

I put my hands over the back of her shoulders for leverage and drive home in one hard pump. Her head falls back and she cries out in both pleasure and pain.

"Ahh," She whimpers.

I grab a handful of her hair and drag her head back so that her eyes meet mine. With one hand on her shoulder slamming her down onto my cock and a handful of her hair in the other, I'm going out of my brain.

So good.

So fucking good.

I grab her legs and bring them over my shoulders and hold her in a vice-like grip.

Tearing her up and down as she groans in pleasure, I watch her eyes close as she deals with the pleasure.

This is when she is at her best, when she is helpless. Owned.

Owned by me.

When I have her in a grip and I can fuck her as hard as I want.

And fuck... do I want it hard.

With her back against the tiled pool wall and her two legs over my shoulders I have complete control, and I drive home hard with piston pace.

I feel her insides quiver and I know she's close. I go harder, deeper, and she throws her head back and screams out loud as she comes in a rush, which sets me off, my cry matching hers.

I keep lifting her to empty myself completely. I don't want it to end. I want more. So much more.

Our violent kiss turns gentle and loving and she cups my face in her two hands. Our cheeks rest against one another and she smiles softly against my face.

We both pant as we try to catch our breath and she giggles into my shoulder and waves up at the wall.

I frown. "What are you doing?"

She laughs out loud. "Wave to the camera."

"Huh?" I frown and turn to see a security camera attached to the wall. "Oh my fucking God," I stammer. I point to her with an over exaggerated arm. "It was all her doing. I was trying to be good," I mouth to the camera.

"Was not." She laughs as she splashes me, and my mouth drops open. "He was making me do it," she calls loudly. "It was all him."

"That's it, you're going to get it." I take off after her through the pool to the sounds of her laughter. I grab her and dunk her hard and she laughs out loud as she chokes.

It's been a good night.

In fact, the best.

Roshelle

I rub my forehead back and forth over the hard yet soft surface, my pillow of Stace's warm chest. His arms are wrapped around me, and his lips rest at my temple, his chest rising and falling as he sleeps deeply.

This is Heaven.

I wince with my eyes still closed. My body is sore. Sorer than sore. In fact, I would go so far as to say it is painful. My head is hurting from the champagne, my feet ache from those stupid high shoes, and then my girl parts... well, they are just shredded to oblivion.

I smile. God, what a night. Stace and I were like animals with each other, and knowing that we had no future only added fuel to the out of control flames.

We couldn't get enough of each other. We went from violent fucking against the wall then to love making in bed, back to fucking in the shower, and then to gentle tender love making again and again until, in total exhaustion, we fell asleep in each others arms as the sun was coming up.

I still haven't had enough. Could I ever get enough of this man? I doubt it, to be honest. This is what it feels like.

I need to go to the bathroom, but I know once I step foot outside of this bed that that will be it.

Our time will be over. Dread fills my every cell.

He rustles around and I feel him smile above me before he tenderly kisses my forehead. "Morning, babe," he whispers sleepily.

I smile softly. "Morning." I kiss his chest.

He moves and groans. "I'm fucked." His voice is scratchy from our copious amounts of alcohol last night.

"Um, I think it's me who is fucked," I mutter dryly.

I feel him smile broadly as he kisses my head again.

We lie still for a moment as reality starts to sink in, knowing he has to get up and leave.

We both know he does, but that doesn't make it any easier.

His lips drop to my neck and he kisses me as his hand finds his favorite spot between my legs. "I need you one last time, Rosh," he whispers as he runs his jaw whiskers back and forth gently along my skin.

I nod, unable to speak because the lump in my throat has blocked out all sense. "I know," is all I can eventually muster.

He slides his finger in and hisses in approval. "Oh, baby, you feel too good. How am I going to live without this?" he whispers.

I close my eyes to block him out. I don't want his last memory of me to be crying like a baby.

"Open for me."

I drop my legs back to the mattress and he rises above me, onto his elbow. His fingers slowly pump in and out of my body as he watches me intently.

"You are just so...." His voice trails off.

We kiss and it's nothing like the kisses of last night. It's a goodbye kiss and it breaks my fucking heart.

He rises above me and slowly slides his length back and forth between my lips. "Are you going to remember me?" he asks in a whisper.

Through glassy eyes, I nod.

Horror crosses his face as he sees my emotions boiling over.

"Baby, don't," he whispers.

I grab his behind and pull him down so he penetrates me hard, and we both gasp.

He's so big, so hard, and so fucking perfect. He stays still to let me get used to his size.

If only he could stay still to let me get used to his love.

And, to the sound of my heart silently breaking, we make tender and beautiful love.

I'm ruined.

Utterly fucking ruined.

And it's all Stace's fault.

I am in the bathroom pretending to go to the toilet and he is packed, ready to go. I just need a minute to pull myself together.

We have had breakfast and laughed some more, although it has been strained because we both know what's coming.

What's worse is that I know he feels it, too. I'm not imagining it.

It's here and it's palpable. It feels real.

But I'm not being the needy chick that he left in Bogota. I'm going to rock this goodbye if it's the last thing I do. I stare at my reflection in the mirror.

"You can do this," I whisper to myself.

I close my eyes and inhale deeply. Ten minutes. Just be strong for ten minutes.

I blow out the breath and head back into the room. His suit is in its bag on the bed.

"All ready?" I smile.

He nods and gives me a lopsided smile. "I don't know if I want you to stay here alone. Can you not go back to the US?"

I shake my head. "No, I've chosen my path."

His eyes hold mine. "And it's alone?" he questions.

I nod once. "Very alone."

As if feeling dejected by my answer, he picks up his suit and slings it over his shoulder and we walk over to the door before he continues out into the hallway.

We gently kiss and both of our faces screw up in pain.

He pulls back and his eyes search mine. "What if you're my person?" he whispers.

My eyes tear up because I know for certain that he is mine.

"I'm not," I whisper.

We stare at each other as mixed emotions swirl around us.

"I'm a girl you kidnapped." I hesitate. "I'm a girl who deserves more from her person."

He drops his head in shame and regret fills me that I said that... but it had to be said.

It is what it is.

He smiles sadly. "Goodbye."

"Goodbye." I smile through my tears. He silently leaves.

As if on autopilot, I walk over to the window and place my hands on the glass and wait for him to appear down on the street below.

He appears from the building and tears roll down my face as he gets into a cab and without hesitation, leaves my life.

That hurt.

What a crazy day. What a crazy, crazy day.

This morning after he left, I took the smallest of the yellow diamonds to three different jewellers and paid for valuation slips. It cost me five hundred dollars, but the valuations came in at over a million, so it was worth it. I then had to catch a cab an hour away to see a guy. I don't know who he was, but apparently he is the only person who deals with these sorts of things. That's code for he's a shonky criminal.

After bartering with him for over an hour, we agreed on a cash price of two hundred and fifty thousand dollars. I got ripped off, but I need some money to get me through until I find a real buyer.

It gives me hope for what is to come, though. The other diamonds are nearly twice the size of that one. So my quarter of a million is now in my bank account and the other diamonds are in the safety deposit box.

Not a bad day's work for a nice girl like me.

My mind goes to Stace. Beautiful Stace. He will be on his ship by now, and I get a vision of him in his work uniform that makes me smile.

I am in a cab on my way back to the hotel. I'm tired from my all night carnal activities, but know I won't be able to sleep when I get back there.

The diamonds are weighing heavily on my conscience.

What if he gets the blame?

He won't, don't worry, I keep telling myself.

I go over the night before I got off the boat. It was all such a blur. I thought he went to Chelsea and I fought with him. Then he had me checked out and I told him about my past. I didn't even know I was getting off the boat until an hour before I actually did, and then he was in the room all morning.

A sickening thought comes to me.

I didn't hide the guns that I had hidden under the bed.

I should have thrown them overboard. In annoyance, I glance out the window of the car.

Oh my God.

They are going to know that I was in the shipping containers. They are going to know I have the diamonds.

You fucking idiot!

I close my eyes as my blood starts to pump heavily through my bloodstream.

Fuck!

For the rest of the cab ride, I feel sick. Sick with worry over my stupid oversight.

Stace will blame Stucco, I know he will. I hope he kills him when they fight.

Hang on a minute...

Horror dawns.

I didn't tell Stace that Stucco is planning on killing him. I forgot all about hearing that conversation outside the container. Things were so hectic and then the fight and then...

My hands go to my hair in a panic. They were going to call for a maintenance call in the middle of the night.

I get a vision of Stace walking the ship in the dead of night alone.

And those fuckers...

Oh my God. I put my head into my hands. What do I do?

Nothing. You've got away with it. Don't do anything stupid.

This is drug money, fucking take it. I feel sick. They will kill him.

They will kill him and throw him overboard and then blame him for the diamonds.

He will get the blame for something he never did I push my thumbs into my eyes as I think.

No, no no, this can't be happening. Stop thinking about it. Get on a plane and go to Europe now. The diamonds are there for twenty-four months if I want. For half an hour, I sit in the back of the cab with my mind in overdrive until finally the driver turns to me over the seat, breaking my thoughts. "We are here, Miss."

I glance in at the hotel and after a moment I make the stupidest decision I know I have ever made.

"Can you wait here for a minute, please, while I run in and get my things? I need another ride."

"Where you want to go to, Miss?"

I glance at the clock on his dashboard. I don't even know if I have time to make it, but damn it I have to try or I will never forgive myself.

"The shipping dock."

———

I lie on the bed in silence. It's 8pm and Stace hasn't come back from his day's work. I made the ship and boarded, unnoticed.

We have been sailing for two hours and I have been in the cabin waiting for him to come home.

Part of me knows that I didn't want him to know I was on board until it was too late because I'm scared he wouldn't want me here.

Part of me knows I will die a little if he doesn't.

I'm not here for him, anyway. I'm here as a humanitarian, I remind myself. I may be messed up, but I can't live my life with his murder on my conscience. What kind of a human being would I be if I knowingly let him die? It should be no big deal that I'm here, anyway. It's only two weeks until we get to Puerto Rico and then I will have time to dispose of the guns and warn Stace about the planned attack.

It was a smart decision to come back. I'm just covering my tracks, that's all.

I'm pacing. It's 10pm and Stace hasn't come back to the room.

What if he didn't even get on the boat... ship, or whatever the fuck it is.

What if he went back for me and I put myself on here? My hands run through my hair in a panic.

Oh God, what the hell have I done?

For over an hour I pace back and forth with my heart beating hard.

He's not on the ship.

I know he's not on the ship. He would have come back to change for dinner for sure.

I start to feel sick about my decision. Nobody knows I am on here and he couldn't find me in Bogota even if he was trying. If they know I am on here alone, it's going to be open slaughter. But then... maybe not now that they know me. I know Angela and her boys would protect me.

Calm down, calm down. I walk into the bathroom and stare at the girl staring back at me. "What the hell have you fucking done?" I ask my reflection. "I don't know," I answer. "You idiot," I mouth.

More importantly, what am I going to do now?

The key sounds in the door and I put my hands over my heart in relief.

He's here. Thank God, he's here.

I hear the keys put down on the drawers and I step into the room, his back is to me.

"Hello."

He turns and his face drops. "Rosh?"

I smile hopefully. "It seems I missed the nautical life."

His face falls. "What the fuck are you doing here?" He snarls.

"What?" I whisper, shocked by his venom.

"You can't be on here! I docked the boat to get you to safety and you fucking came back?" He's angry, furious, in fact.

"I missed you, too," I whisper through my hurt.

He shakes his head. "This ship is about to become a fucking nightmare and I can't protect you. I got you off this boat for that reason." He growls.

"I came to protect you," I whisper.

"What?" he screams. "I don't need fucking protecting."

"Y-yes, you do," I stammer, trying to calm him down. "I forgot to tell you that I overheard Stucco planning with someone else to murder you."

"What?" His face screws up as if not believing my story.

"It was the night that you went to Chelsea and I was so upset."

"I didn't go to fucking Chelsea," he snaps. "Stop going on about Chelsea. You are pissing me off with it."

"They are going to call a maintenance call in the middle of the night and push you overboard."

He frowns.

"And I remembered that I didn't tell you and I was freaking out." I pick up his hand and hold it in mine. "I had to warn you and coming back onto the ship was my only choice. I didn't have your number to call," I whisper.

"I don't need your protection. I can handle myself." He sighs and I can see a glimmer of forgiveness.

"I know you can." I pause and try to sweeten the deal. "I wanted an excuse to see you." My eyes search his.

He stares at me as the last words I said roll around in his brain.

"You wanted an excuse to see me?" He narrows his eyes. "I thought I was just the guy who kidnapped you?"

I smile softly as I gently cup his face in my hand. "Maybe not. Maybe you're more."

He moves close and I know I may be forgiven. "How much more?" he whispers against my lips.

I smile up at him. "Stop asking stupid questions and thank me."

He roughly grabs my behind and kisses me, and I laugh into his lips.

"Stop doing stupid things." He growls.

"I can't, it comes naturally," I reply.

He throws me onto the bed and I bounce with a laugh.

"So, you are here by choice now?" he asks darkly as he slowly undoes his belt from his pants.

Desire runs through my blood and I nod. "Aha."

"Here for me." He pauses and raises his brow. "By choice?"

"Yes," I breathe as I watch his pants slowly slide down his legs.

"So, I can legally do whatever I want to do to you now." He purrs sexily.

Shivers run down my spine. "Yes," I whisper in anticipation. "What do you want?"

His dark eyes hold mine. "Fucking everything."

The pager wakes us from our sleep. I glance at the clock to see it's 4am in the morning. Stace rolls over and looks at the clock. I know he's thinking the same thing as me.

He gets up and reads the message on his pager.

I sit up. "What does it say?"

He doesn't answer and goes to the bathroom, flicking the light on. "What does it say?" I call after him.

"There is a problem in the engine room," he replies dryly.

Oh no, I jump out of bed. "It's a trap. This is it. I'm telling you, it's a trap. This... this is what I heard them talking about," I stammer.

"It could also be a problem in the engine room," he replies.

"Don't go. You can't go."

He zips up his pants and pulls his shirt around his shoulders. "I can handle myself."

"I'm coming with you," I snap as I try to find some clothes.

"You are not fucking coming with me. What are you going to do?"

I put my hands on my naked hips in an outrage. "I can fight, you know."

He smirks and kisses me quickly on the lips. "I can fight better. Go to bed. I will be home soon." And with that he leaves the room.

Oh no. Oh no, no, no. I grab some clothes from the drawer and pull them on, and then I get down on the floor and slide my rifle out and attach the silencer.

I click it up to ready the ammunition.

I warned that fucker not to mess with him.

I open the cabin door and peer out into the darkened hallway.

Game on.

14

Roshelle

I CREEP up the hall in the darkness until I get to the staircase, then look back down from where I came from, relieved there's still nobody around. I glance at the staircase going up, and although it feels like the safer option, I know that side of the ship is the enemy at the moment. If you go overboard, you're toast. The thought of the cold, hard maintenance level is freaking me out, but I head down anyway with my gun gripped tightly in my hand. I tiptoe down the stairs that are lit only by the exit sign. The sound of the engine is loud and obnoxious. My heart is beating so fast and I have no idea what I am going to be faced with when I get to the bottom. Fuck's sake, why did I let him come back here to this hell ship?

I arrive on the bottom step and slowly peer around the corner to see there's nobody around. The engine is loud and whirring. With my gun in my hand, I walk farther into the room.

What if he is already dead?

No, the call was only moments ago.

I hear someone coming down the stairs from where I just came from and I duck into a darkened hallway.

Shit. Who is that?

I stand flattened against the wall as I listen, and then I see Stucco walk past. Shit, it is really true.

This is it.

My heart begins to hammer and I see him stuff something in his back pocket.

Was that a knife? I frown. It wasn't big enough to be a gun. I peer around the darkened corner and he calls out, "Mac, you here?"

I listen and I know that Stace is down here doing the exact same thing as me. Flattened against a wall somewhere listening to the fucker. I wonder how fast his heart is beating?

"Mac!" He calls again.

"What's the problem?" Stace eventually replies as he appears around the back corner.

"The gasket in the rotator is gone." Stace's knowing eyes hold his.

The tension between them is thick.

"No, they aren't. That's a blatant lie," Stace replies calmly.

"But..."

"There are no buts. I just fucking checked them." He sneers.

Stucco stares him down.

"A little birdie told me you plan on knocking me off?" Stace smiles sarcastically. "Good luck. I'm waiting pretty boy."

"Fuck you," Stucco hisses.

"I'm sick and tired of your fucking shit. You got something to say or do." He pushes Stucco in the chest as a silent dare. "Do it now."

Oh shit.

Stucco runs at him and Stace punches him hard in the face, but Stucco comes back and connects a hit to his jaw and Stace staggers back.

Oh no. What do I do? I grip the gun. What the hell do I do?

Stace runs at him and tackles him to the floor and then he is on him and they struggle for a while rolling around. Over and over they roll and Stace gets the upper hand and smashes him hard in the face repeatedly.

I step back to my hiding place around the corner. Holy fucking shit.

"What are you doing?" Mac screams in his face. I call him Mac because that's who he is at the moment. There isn't a trace of my beautiful Stace here.

He slams his head on the concrete. "What do you fucking want?" he screams again.

Stucco struggles and tries to punch up at him, but he doesn't stand a chance against Mac's strength.

As if losing control, he slams him continually until Stucco is out cold.

I stay hidden, disturbed by what I have just witnessed, and yet sickly proud.

He was right. He didn't need me at all.

I watch as Stace rolls him over and checks his pocket and pulls out a syringe filled with something. He eyes it suspiciously.

I hear someone coming down the steps. Oh no. I flatten up against the wall in the darkness.

"What's going on?" I hear a male voice ask. I peer around the corner to see one of Stace's colleagues from the control tower.

"This fuckwit just jumped me and I found this on him." Stace holds the syringe up and the guy takes it from him.

Oh no, don't trust him. Don't trust him. Don't give him the syringe.

"Fucking idiot." He sighs. "We will put him in the lockup and deal with him tomorrow," he replies dryly.

They grab an arm each and pick him up and half carry and half drag him up the stairs, no doubt to the lock up in the control tower.

I lean back against the wall and let out a deep breath. That was close.

———

An hour later I lie in the darkened room and I wonder who I am sleeping with.

He was cold and calculating tonight. No remorse, no empathy.

No fear.

He smashed Stucco's head on the floor until he was unconscious, I know how Stace's story started out, but how does it end?

My mother told me that my father started out with petty crimes, and look what a monster he turned into. Is this how she felt about him when they first met? Did she know he was into some bad shit, but didn't care anyway? Was she blinded by the percentage that was good and thought that he was going to leave this life behind? But then, what was Stace supposed to do? It was attack or get attacked and even I was prepared to shoot Stucco dead.

Maybe it's me.

Maybe I am the one who is fucked up.

I don't even know anymore.

My thoughts are interrupted by him coming back to the cabin. He walks into the bathroom and gets into the shower, not saying anything. Does he honestly think I'm asleep?

Ten minutes later he gets into bed beside me.

"What happened?" I ask.

"Nothing," he replies quietly.

I frown into the darkness. "Was Stucco there?"

"Nope."

Why is he lying?

We stay silent as my mind begins to spin.

"Are you okay?" I ask.

He rolls over and takes me in his arms. "I am now that I am next to you." He kisses my shoulder gently.

A lie and a truth in the same sentence. My pleasure and my pain.

———

"Remember that time in Mexico when the border control had to be bribed?" one man says and the table all laugh out loud.

We are at dinner and the men are all swapping Vikinos stories. He arrives tomorrow and the ship has been in overdrive to prepare. Apparently this is the first time he has been on the ship in over eight months and he is flying in for the day to check out operations. From what I can tell, Stace is the only one who knows him personally. The other men just don't know how personally.

I have questions myself.

When he said he went on to work for him, was that as one of his hit men or have I just watched too many movies?

The way he lied to me about fighting Stucco the other night

has only planted the seed of doubt in my mind. Was he telling me the truth about his past or what he wishes were the truth? Has he really been innocently blindsided into this life, or is he a lifelong criminal, as I first thought?

I don't know what's going on with him this week, but he is getting more and more agitated at Vikinos's impending arrival. He must have told me a thousand times that I am not allowed out of the cabin while Vikinos is on the ship. He even sat me down this afternoon and told me that if he leaves the ship suddenly, I am to stay with Angela and the boys until we get to dock and they will keep me safe.

Is he thinking he is going to leave with Vikinos?

I'm confused, but I'm not bothering asking questions because they will be met with lies. It was only a white lie, I keep telling myself, and he was probably trying to stop me from worrying about him.

But a white lie is a black lie to me. They all hurt the same.

I am brought back to the moment with the conversation going on around me.

"Oh, and he hates cops," one guy chips in.

"Yeah," someone else says. "Remember that warehouse he had?"

"The Pig Fryer, they call it," says another.

The men all erupt into laughter and Stace drops his head and clenches his jaw in anger.

I frown as I watch him. He is visibly rattled by this conversation.

Why?

"Why do they call it The Pig Fryer?" I ask. I want to know why it is affecting him so much.

"He ties up cops and tortures them to death. Electrocutes the fuckers. Cooks the fucking pork."

The men all burst out laughing and Stace drinks his beer and stares at the floor with a murderous look on his face.

The floor sways beneath me as I join all the puzzle pieces together.

Oh my God.

Stace's brother. Vikinos killed Stace's brother.

He is here for revenge.

My eyes search his, and he knows that I know. He looks away angrily.

I stand. "I'm tired. I'm going to get going. See you all." I glance at Stace. "You coming?"

He nods and without a word follows me. We walk to the room in silence and he opens the door. We walk in and he slowly closes the door behind us.

"You're here for revenge?"

He nods once.

"You're going to try and kill him?" I whisper angrily.

"Yes."

I shake my head. "Stace, no. He will kill you. He has guards."

"I don't care."

"What?" I shriek. "What do you mean you don't care?"

"I don't care if I die. That's why I got you off the ship. I don't want you here to see this."

My face falls. "Stace, no."

He stands solemnly, as if resigned to his fate. "I have waited on this fucking ship for six months to get my chance and I'm taking it. I can't get him on the mainland but here..." his voice trails off.

I shake my head nervously. "Let's just go. We can start somewhere new." I grab his two arms as I try to talk sense into him. "We can run away and..." I fake a smile and pause as I try to sweeten the deal. "And your mom can come with us."

"No," he says flatly. "He died because of me, my brother died while trying to get me off this ship. He stupidly thought he could bring him down. But I know the only way he can be brought down is by his death. I've made my decision. He's going to pay. An eye for an eye."

My eyes tear up. "What about me?" I whisper.

His eyes hold mine and he brings up his hand and gently cups my face. "I'm grateful that I met my person before I die," he whispers.

My tears break the dam and roll down my face. "Stace, no." I shake my head. "Please, for me... don't do this."

He wraps me in an embrace.

"Don't make me lose you, too," I sob into his shoulder.

He holds me for an extended time and eventually he replies, "Baby, I'm not yours to keep. He owns me. I have nothing to lose."

———

I sit in the dawn light alone at the desk in the cabin. Stace started work at 5am this morning in preparation for Vikinos' arrival at 10am.

I'm soul searching, praying to my mother to save him. He has forbidden me to leave the cabin today and has already brought me back enough food for a week.

As if I can eat any of it. I feel sick.

I can't imagine what is has been like for him, to live on this boat knowing its owner murdered his brother when he was trying to save him.

The guilt he must feel.

———

He takes the knife and slices her neck and she lets out a garbled wail.

My eyes widen in horror. "No," I cry. "Stop it, stop it. Let her go!" I scream as the tears run down my face. I slam my head from side to side frantically as I try to break free from the ropes that tie me to the chair. The chair rocks as I try desperately to escape.

"You, animal. Let her go!" I scream. I shake my head harder. "No, no, no, no, Mom. Mom, look at me. Look at me," I cry. "Mom, hang on. Just hang on."

Her stare becomes vacant and I screw up my face in pain. The room starts to spin as my eyes drop to the sea of her blood that runs down her body and onto the floor.

"Mom. Mom!" I cry. "Let her fucking go!" I scream. "Kill me. Kill me," I cry. "No, you can't do this! Please, don't do this," I sob.

"This is what happens when you disobey me, my Roshina."

His deep voice growls.

She shudders as she tries to say something.

"I love you, Mom," I cry.

A trace of a smile crosses her face and then her head drops as the last of her life drips out.

I turn to the Devil. My father. "I hate you. I fucking hate you. I will kill you!" I scream as I go ballistic and try to break free from the chair.

His hard hand hits me across the face.

I lick my bottom lip like I can still taste the blood from his hits. My eyes fill with tears at the horrific memory, and six years later, I can still feel my beautiful mother's life drain from her body.

I know what Stace feels. Better than anyone, I understand.

I stare at the wall for hours until eventually I know what I have to do.

I need to do this for him today. I need to kill Vikinos.

The sun dances on the water, and the reflection from the metal railing is off putting. I stand up against the wall on the far end of the walkway.

The women are hidden, the men are all at their stations, and Stace and another two men are on the deck flagging in the chopper.

I can hear it hovering above the ship and I close my eyes as I prepare for what I am about to do.

All hell is about to break loose.

I slowly close my eyes, and when I reopen them, I am at my mother's murder.

Kill or be killed.

The chopper slowly comes in, and as soon as they pass where they can see me, I walk forward and lean my rifle on the handrail to look through the glass eyepiece.

I rearrange my finger on the trigger and I wait. I have gone over every possible scenario in my head a million times, and I honestly believe this is the only way I stand a chance to catch them unaware. If I wait, I risk Stace trying to take him out first and then it may be too late. This is the only way I can guarantee Stace's safety.

Ten years of practice in a shooting range and it all comes down to this.

If I miss, I'm dead.

If I hit, I'm also dead.

But Stace will be alive, and he will know that I love him. My eyes cloud over and I shake my head to remove the fog. Focus.

I stare through the lens and I count three men in the chopper. The pilot, a guard and then him.

I take aim and watch as the pilot goes through the shut down technique.

"Just get out of the chopper," I whisper.

I tighten my grip on the trigger as my heart hammers heavily in my chest.

"Kill or be killed," I breathe.

Stace approaches the chopper and then opens the door and I narrow my eyes as I steel myself.

Holy... fucking shit.

The guard gets out and shakes Stace's hand, and I follow his head with the gun. I go back to the chopper and follow the next head. Wearing a dark, clearly expensive suit, he slowly gets out and shakes Stace's hand.

I narrow my eyes. "Just a little to the left," I whisper as my hand shakes nervously. He moves over a little. "That's it." He moves to the left and I take aim and pull the trigger. I miss and confusion sets in. The men all start to run.

Fuck.

I take aim again and with my heartbeat furiously pumping, I pull the trigger, and this time, the man in the suit falls to the deck.

I take aim at the guard and shoot him in the thigh. He also crumples in a heap.

I did it.

With adrenaline pumping hard, I sprint down the metal stairs.

The alarms start to sound and I know everyone is watching. With my gun in my hands I run across the deck toward them.

Stace looks up at me in horror.

"Rosh!" he screams. "No!"

The pilot grabs a handgun and I lift my rifle and shoot him in the leg.

"Get in the chopper!" I scream.

"What?" Stace yells.

"Get in the fucking chopper!" I scream over the sirens.

"What the fuck are you doing?" he yells.

"Saving your life." I point to the chopper with my gun. "Get in."

I look down and frown. What the hell? I kick over the man in the suit so I can see his face and I step back as horror dawns.

Oh my God!

Oh my fucking God!

With renewed panic, I point the gun at Stace. "Don't make me fucking kill you, too, asshole. Get in!"

"No!" He screams. "What the fuck are you doing?"

The sirens are screaming over us and I know I have minutes before backup is here.

I shoot the ground only inches from Stace's feet. "I swear to God, get the fuck in."

He shakes his head and climbs into the chopper and I climb in after him.

"Take us up."

He frowns. "What?" he screams.

"Fucking go. We are about one minute away from being killed."

He scratches his head in a panic and starts the chopper, and I slam the door behind me. We shakily lift off just as two of the crew appear on the deck with guns.

We lift higher and higher and higher, and I hear bullets zoom past us.

He takes off and we fly into the clear air and I put my head in my hands and screw up my face in panic.

"What the fuck are you doing?" he screams over the engine.

I pant. "I'm saving your life, asshole." I run my hands through my hair. "You are most welcome, by the way."

He shakes his head and drags his hand down his face.

"That wasn't Vikinos you killed," he screams.

"I know!" I yell back in frustration. Oh my God, how could I be so stupid?

He frowns as his eyes flick over to me. "How do you know that? Who are you?"

I look him square in the eye.

"My name is Roshina Vikinos. I'm his daughter."

15

Stace

MY EYES WIDEN before they flicker to her, and then back to the sky, then back to her, and then back to the sky, again and again.

"You are fucking who?" I scream over the engine.

"You heard me," she yells.

I shake my head in disbelief. "His... his... his daughter?" I stammer. "You are Vikinos' daughter?"

She nods.

"I don't believe it," I cry as we fly higher and higher.

"Y-you think I can?" she stammers.

Realisation sets in and I put my head into my hands. The chopper dips a little.

"Stace?" she yells.

I grab the control lever and lift the chopper back up.

My eyes flick over to her angrily. "So you set us up. This whole thing was a set up to get to him."

"What?" she yells. "You took me, you idiot! How could I have set this up?"

"You really expect me to believe that this is a coincidence." I shake my head. "I'm not that stupid." I sneer.

"Apparently, you are," she fires back.

I glare at her, and then we both turn to stare at the sky in front of us. The engine is loud and drowns out all other noise.

She turns and looks over our shoulder at the disappearing ship in the distance. They would be calling for backup right now.

"What would possess you to shoot three people in front of everyone?" I fume.

She shrugs. "I thought it was him. I thought I was going to just knock him off before there could be time for it to go wrong. I'm not giving him the chance to kill you."

"It wasn't him," I snap.

"I know!" she yells in frustration. "It was my uncle."

My face falls in horror as my eyes flicker to her again. "You shot his brother?"

"Like he tortured yours. Stop acting all fucking innocent. It was kill or be killed and that guy I shot is just as evil as my father. I have no remorse. None!"

Good point.

I stay silent and turn to look over my shoulder at where we came from.

The sound of the chopper blades rings loud through the cabin. "You said you were going to kill him. You said you thought you were going to die. I couldn't let that happen!" she yells over the engine.

"At least you would have been safe!" I bark angrily.

"Who are you kidding? I will never be safe as long as he is alive."

I run my hand through my hair in frustration as my brain begins to go wild.

"What now?" she asks.

I don't answer. I just keep my eyes on the sky.

"What are we going to do, Stace?" she yells in a panic.

"Shut the fuck up and let me think!" I yell back.

I stare out at the sea below us as we fly way up high. Such a beautiful, tranquil setting and yet we are in the midst of a nightmare. I turn around and look over my shoulder again, half expecting a chopper to be chasing us. I know they don't have the resources, but my military training leaves me on stand by every time.

"Why wasn't it him? Why wasn't he on the damn chopper?"

She runs her hands through her hair in frustration.

My angry eyes flick to her. "Something you could have checked before you raised hell."

She glares at me. "You are a fucking wimp. Do you know that? Drop me off. They saw me point the gun at you. Go running back and beg for forgiveness." She shakes her head. "Blame me." She seems to come to a decision before she lets me speak. "You need to get away from me, anyway. You are in more danger with me around."

I shake my head with fury. Unfucking believable.

"I mean it," she yells, her eyes continually switching between the sky in front of us and back to me.

My face remains solemn and emotionless.

"I made a promise to your mother," she snaps.

My eyes fall her way and I screw up my face. "What?"

"I told your mom that I would look out for you."

"That was just a figure of speech," I snap. "She didn't mean for you to literally look out for me."

"Yes, she did. I know she did." She pauses for a moment. "What were you going to do? What was your brilliant plan, huh?" she yells over the loud sound of the blades above us.

I shake my head. "When I got him alone, I was going to break his neck or smother him or something less fucking dramatic than your Lethal Weapon strategy. He trusted me, and I could have killed him when I got him alone, but you have fucked up every chance of that happening, haven't you?" I tap the side of my head angrily. "So stupid."

She rolls her eyes. "Oh yes, that sounds really safe. Like his guards would have let that happen. You would already be dead if it were up to your plan."

"At least I would have targeted the right person." I sneer. She fakes a sarcastic smile.

We sit in silence for twenty minutes and I continually glance behind us at the ocean.

Nobody is following us, but I know it's a false sense of security.

The storm is brewing.

"What are we going to do?" She sighs.

I shrug and we fly for a while longer as I troll my brain for a logical plan. If I bring us down on the water, we have more chance of not being found, but then I have to get Rosh to dry land safely which would be risky. If I fly directly to the mainland we will continue on the radar of the ship. I know they can still see us now and know exactly where we are. I have to fly up the coast for at least a couple of hundred kilometres and then go inland. There is no other choice. I glance over my shoulder and finally come to a decision. I hit the satellite navigation system and wait for my coordinates. They come up and I make a turn to the right.

"We will land and hide the chopper. There is another small chopper on the ship, but there isn't another pilot on board and you took out the other one. We have about an hour, I reckon, before someone can get in the air to look for us."

She watches me intently.

"There is probably a tracking device on this one."

Her eyes widen in horror and she starts to look around frantically.

"You won't find it, but they will know where we land."

"So we land and run?" she asks.

I nod as I remain deep in thought.

"Where are we landing?"

I flick some switches and put the headphones on as we veer even farther to the right. "Colombia."

———

An hour later.

"Brace yourself," I warn her as she holds onto the straps of her seatbelt.

She closes her eyes.

"Easy... easy," I woo the chopper.

She grips the belt with white-knuckle force. We have been flying over land for a while now as I looked for somewhere safe to land.

This looks as good a place as any. It's deserted, nobody for miles, with a relatively flat paddock.

"Woo, girl," I murmur to the chopper.

The chopper hovers above the ground and I gently place

her down. Rosh drops her head into her hands in relief. "Thank God," she whispers. "How the hell do you do this for a job when it's scary as Hell?"

I reach over and undo her seatbelt before I take mine off.

We wait for the blades to stop. I open the door and then climb down to go help her out.

"Hang a second, let me grab my backpack." She bends down and grabs her backpack and handgun.

"You brought a backpack?" I frown.

"Yes." She shakes her head. "Do you think I'm stupid?" She jumps out onto the ground.

"No comment," I mutter dryly as I walk off.

She hurries to keep up with me. "I have your two passports and mine and our wallets and your phone."

I narrow my eyes at her. How does she know I have two passports? I turn and begin to run. "Keep up," I snap.

"I am," she bites back.

She's a ballsy little bitch, I will give her that. I turn and take the backpack from her and put it onto my back. "What's in here?" I ask as I flick the long grass out of my way.

"Just what I told you," she calls. "Oh, and I bought you a sweater," she adds from behind me.

I stop still and turn to her. "You brought me a sweater?" I frown.

She nods quickly. I smirk.

She smirks back. "It does seem kind of ridiculous now, come to think of it."

I burst into laughter—deep, bellyaching laughter. This fucking woman will be the death of me.

"You don't think twice about shooting your uncle who you thought was your father, but you remember to pack me a sweater."

"It could get cold," she cries out in embarrassment.

"That will do me." With a shake of my head, I turn and start to power walk. The terrain is too rough to run. We will end up breaking a leg. We walk quickly at the edge of a forest under the canopy of trees for protection from the skies above.

We have walked for over an hour and it's hot.

"I stink," she calls from behind me. "I need deodorant." She swats the bugs as she walks. "I don't suppose you have any in your pockets?"

Fuck's sake. I keep walking and ignore her. Nothing new. I've been ignoring her the whole way.

I'm so pissed off. All of my plans were ruined in three minutes of crazy.

"Do you think it's much farther?" she asks. I don't answer.

We keep walking for another half an hour. "Are you going to keep ignoring me?"

"Yes," I snap.

"Why?"

I turn and raise an eyebrow and glare at her for a moment before I return back to my power hiking. She has got to be kidding?

Another hour we walk.

"How much farther, the town looked closer than this. Are we even going the right way?" she calls.

"Stop fucking jabbering and walk faster," I yell.

We finally get to a farmhouse and I duck down low to do a risk assessment of the area. A large stone house and three cars sit idly. I wonder if anyone is home. I'm squatting down behind the building as I look around, and then, without hesitation, Rosh walks straight up to the car parked in the drive way and gets in.

I look around nervously. Shit. What is she doing now? I glare at her and shake my head angrily.

This chick has a fucking death wish... and I may be the one to kill her.

She pulls the cover off the front of the car and hotwires it. It starts on the first go.

"Get in," she mouths.

I glance around. This is just great. When they find the chopper, they are going to door knock the closest houses. She has just effectively told them where we are. With one last look around, I run to the car and get in and she speeds off just as a man and a woman come running out from the house.

I can't control my anger any longer. "What the fuck are you doing?" I scream.

"Right now?" She glances at me. "I'm stealing a car."

"Do you discuss anything before you do it or are you just in this alone?" I yell.

He eyes flash to me and she frowns. "What's that supposed to mean?" The car veers around the corner at speed and she nearly loses control. The car swerves as she straightens it back up.

"Stop the fucking car!" I yell. "Can you even drive?"

"Yes, I can drive."

"Get out! I'm driving. Stop the damn car now."

Her eyes flicker between the road and me.

"How do you know how to hot wire a car?" I yell.

"I had a boyfriend once who didn't have keys to his car, so we hot wired it to use it." She shrugs. "I never knew it would come in handy."

She pulls over and I run around to the driver side as she jumps across the seats. I take off fast.

We sit in silence as I concentrate. The roads are filled with dirt and rough terrain, hilly with lots of corners.

Her hair is flying around from the air blasting through the open windows. "Don't give me a lecture on discussing things with you. We both know you discuss nothing with me! In fact, you straight up lie."

I glare at her. I don't think I've ever been this pissed off with a woman in my life. She is absolutely fucking infuriating. "When did I lie?" I yell. "When?"

"Was Stucco there in the maintenance room?" She sneers sarcastically. "No, stucco wasn't there, nothing happened," she imitates me in a fake, deep voice.

I narrow my eyes.

"I was there, asshole. I saw you fight him."

"What were you doing there?" I yell.

"Waiting to back you up with my gun." She shakes her head angrily. "Like I was backing you up today."

"Doing something without a plan is not backing me up. It's fucking me up, Roshelle!" I yell.

"It's Roshina," she snaps.

I cannot believe it. I cannot fucking believe it.

We keep driving for a while and eventually we get to a sign. Colombia—60kms

Finally

"We will go back to Colombia, dump the car, and catch a cab to Bogota. You still have the booking for another ten days in the hotel. We can lie low there until things die down. Make a plan," I suggest.

Her face softens and she smiles her first smile of the day. I have to stop myself from reaching out and grabbing her hand. "Okay," she murmurs as her scared eyes hold mine.

There is something breathtakingly beautiful about her bravery—her unbelievably stupid kamikaze bravery. She calls to me on a level I don't understand, and even though I am beyond furious with her, my urge to protect and nurture her is at an all time high.

She was prepared to die for me today... for her cause.

She's brave enough to be dangerous and yet vulnerable enough to die.

My worst nightmare.

It's the last thought that I can't stand and I know I need to get her safely out of the country as a priority.

Vikinos is not getting her. He's not laying a damn finger on her. The damage he has already done to her is immeasurable. If I am honest with myself, I know why she shoots first and asks questions later. She has been pushed past the point of return and she doesn't care what happens to her anymore. The need for revenge has consumed her just as much as it has consumed me. What are the chances that we both have the same target? Two people who randomly meet and have a connection, both with a thirst for the same man's blood.

I'm not sure what to do with all of this. It's information overload. I need to get my head around the fact that she is his daughter. The thought of him killing her scares me more than anything else.

This is not good.

A complication I don't need.

As planned, we dump the car in a deserted street and grab a cab to Bogota. Two very silent hours later we arrive at the hotel.

Roshelle

We walk through the reception of the hotel and I drop my head. I wanted to come back here with Stace one day, but not under these circumstances. As if he can read my fragile mind, he grabs my hand reassuringly. We walk into the elevator and he wraps me in his arms and pulls me to him. I put my head against his chest and close my eyes.

I'm home.

I don't care what I did today, he is here with me. He is alive.

The rest is just semantics.

We get up to the room and we walk limply. Without a word, he walks into the bathroom and turns on the shower and I make my way over to the window and pull the sheer curtains back and stare down below.

I have a heavy feeling hanging over me, like I'm carrying the weight of the world on my shoulders. Beyond exhausted, I feel like I could sleep for a week.

We are living on borrowed time.

He comes behind me and wraps his arms around me. "You okay?" he asks. This is the first time he has touched me at all since this morning. I didn't realize how much his touch means to me.

"I don't know," I murmur as I stare out over the city. "Who have I turned into, Stace?" I whisper.

He kisses the side of my face as his eyes join mine to look way below, and after a moment he replies, "Someone I care for."

I turn to him and the lump in my throat becomes really big. My eyes fill with tears at the warmth of his touch and the softness of his words. "I didn't mean to shoot the wrong person today," I whisper as my eyes search his for forgiveness.

He kisses me gently. "I know, babe."

I shake my head as the tears break the dam. "I can't let you die at his hands." I shake my head nervously. "I can't lose you, too."

"Shh," he whispers as he pushes the hair back from my face. "Let's get in the shower."

He leads me to the bathroom and slowly undresses both of us before we get under the cool water. He holds me in his arms with my head on his chest as the tears roll down my face.

He knows.

He knows this is the beginning of the end.

———

I wake in the semi-lit room, knowing it's early evening. After our hour-long shower today, we laid down and I must have fallen asleep. The adrenaline has hit me like a truck. Stace is lying on his side facing me, his hand on my naked hip.

"Hey." I smile bashfully. Why does he always watch me sleep?

He leans forward and gently kisses my lips. "Hey." He kisses me again. "You were zapped."

I smile softly and bring my hand up to his face. "Did you sleep?"

He shakes his head. "No."

I watch him, knowing he has something on his mind.

"What is it?" I ask.

He narrows his eyes as if trying to put the words together in his mind, and after a moment he replies. "I have to go back."

I frown. "What?"

"I will never get the chance to kill him if I don't go back now."

Fear instantly fills me and I sit up violently. "We will never have a chance to be happy if you do."

"Listen. Calm down. You stay here."

I shake my head. "No."

"You stay here where it's safe and I go back and pretend that you kidnapped me. He has no reason to doubt me. I can still do it. I know I can."

"He's not going to buy it. You have been sleeping with his estranged daughter. You will be killed straight away."

"Maybe not."

I stand in an outrage. "Can you hear yourself? Maybe he won't kill you? Why would you take the fucking chance?" I cry.

"Because I need to kill him for my brother. For your mother." He shakes his head as he tries to articulate his wording. "So I can fucking live with myself."

My eyes tear up as empathy fills me. "Stace, no." I step toward him and kiss him gently and he snakes his hands around my naked body. "Stay here and fight for us. I need you to fight for us," I whisper against his lips.

His hand goes to the back of my head and he kisses me deeply. It's one of those goodbye kisses that I have come to hate so much.

"I have to do this," he murmurs into my mouth.

"Why?" I scream as I pull out of his arms with renewed vigour. "So you can have the last word?"

"I'm not spending my life hiding from him."

"Then we fight," I yell. "One day he will come for me and when he does we will be ready. Don't go into the dragon's lair looking for death. It's not needed, Stace. I only did that this morning to get you away from him. You are a danger to yourself."

He shakes his head. "You stay here so I know you are safe."

"No."

He glares at me. "Yes."

"I'm going to Europe and I'm going to forget all about my father." I hesitate and shake my head as my eyes tear up. "I'm starting again and I'm going to forget ever meeting you."

His eyes hold mine.

"I want a man to fall in love with me, one who wants to be in a happy family and isn't hell bent on revenge for evils he can't change."

"I need to do this."

"You can't bring Justin back, Stace!" I yell through tears.

His eyes lose focus and drop to the floor.

"You can't bring him back and he wouldn't want you to do this. He would want you to move on," I whisper through the lump in my throat. "Start again."

He stays silent as he processes my words and eventually, after a long pause, he replies, "I can't."

I turn my back to him and fold my arms.

He puts his shoes on. "Stay here."

I don't answer him.

Moments later, I hear the door click closed and I turn.

He's gone.

———

It's 2am and I'm numb.

Stace is gone. He's already dead. I'm grieving now.

I'm lying propped up in my bed with my Scotch and Coke in his honor, watching bad television.

We were so good together.

I'm furious with him, furious for him taking me, furious with his seduction, furious for letting myself fall for it.

All of it.

He had to go back.

What a crock of shit. If he cared for me, he wouldn't have left.

He would have stayed and fought because the fight will come to me. It always does.

I lie back and stare at the ceiling as the sound of silent regret hangs around me.

Jiggle, jiggle.

What's that? I look to the door and see the handle move. Someone's trying to get in.

I stand and walk over to the door and watch the handle jiggle again in the darkness.

Someone is trying to get in.

16

Roshelle

I STAND BACK, wondering what I should do. What am I going to do?

Shit. I race over, pick up the gun, and shuffle behind the door. The lock clicks as if a key has been used, and then a figure comes into view. I frown as I try to focus.

I know that silhouette.

"Stace?"

"Hey." He sighs.

"What the fuck are you doing? You scared me half to death," I whisper angrily.

He turns to me in the semi-lit room, takes the gun from my hands and lays it on the desk.

I watch him for a moment as he stares at me, despite the darkness.

"I don't know how to do it," he murmurs.

"Do what?"

He hesitates. "Walk away from you."

I smile softly. "I hope you never learn," I whisper.

Then he is on me, his large lips over mine, his hands roaming up and down my naked body.

"Did you miss me?" he whispers.

"No." I smile against his lips. "I decapitated your voodoo doll."

"Smart ass," he breathes against my lips with a smile. He picks me up and throws me onto the bed. I bounce as a thrill of excitement runs through me. He's in that mood—the crazy, fuck-all-night mood he gets in.

"Where have you been?" I ask.

He rips his shirt over his shoulders. "In the bar trying to make myself leave."

I smile and bite my bottom lip as I watch his pants slide down his legs. He's semi-hard and my eyes linger on his groin.

Oh, he's just so...

He walks around to the side of the bed as he watches me from above. "Legs open," he snaps.

I lie on my back and spread my legs, and he smiles darkly as his eyes linger on my sex.

"There she is," he whispers in wonder. He spreads me wide with his fingers so he can see everything, and I close my eyes. No matter how often he looks at me like this, it always seems too intimate, too close for what we are supposed to be.

He bends and licks my flesh and I see his cock harden instantly. His eyes meet mine as he bites my clitoris, forcing me to nearly jump from the bed.

Oh dear God, he's good at this.

"You taste so fucking good," he whispers before his lips lower down to suck me. His eyes close in pleasure and my knees start to lift off the bed by themselves. Oh God. My body starts to quiver and he grabs my thighs in both hands, pushing them back to the mattress.

"Open." He growls. "I want it all. Give it to me."

He bites me again and my back arches off the bed. He starts to really eat me—face whiskers, pleasure and pain—and all I can do is hold on to the back of his head and whimper. He takes his fingers and slides three in. I flinch.

"Ouch, take it easy," I whisper.

"No," he answers as he starts to really give it to me hard.

His fingers pump in and out and the bed starts to hit the wall with force.

Holy... fucking fuck. My insides start to liquefy.

He watches me as he gently kisses my inner thigh, but his fingers continue to rip aggressively into my sex. The sound of my wet body sings loudly through the air.

In, out, round and round, and I'm going out of my head in pleasure.

He licks me again and I start to quiver when he pulls all fingers out immediately.

"Roll over. I want you on your knees," he commands.

I frown. "Huh?" What for?

I shuffle over and he pulls my knees farther apart.

"Lean down onto your elbows."

I drop to my elbows and he kisses each of my ass cheeks tenderly as his hand gently trails up and cups my breasts.

"So fucking beautiful," he whispers, almost to himself. He runs his whiskers softly back and forth over my behind.

My eyes close.

Jeez, I would never let anyone do something like this to me before. What has he turned me into?

A crazy sex maniac, that's what.

He gently pulls my cheeks apart and then I feel his hot tongue burn my behind.

Oh...

I close my eyes tight as my mouth hangs open. This is not my style, but holy hell if it isn't the hottest thing I have ever experienced.

For fifteen minutes his tongue laps at me, coaxes me, and tempts me to do things I've never even contemplated before. I feel myself lifting towards his face for a deeper connection.

I can hardly breathe; I'm so turned on.

He pulls back and I feel him lube my behind with saliva. I breathe out to try and calm myself.

Shit. Oh my God. Oh my God. Is this happening?

He disappears for a second and I hear the telling tear of a condom packet being ripped open. He arranges himself at my opening.

"You're not going to ask for permission?" I ask, joking, but half serious.

He slowly sinks two fingers into my sex. "You belong to me now. I don't have to ask before I take what's mine." He pushes forward and drives me hard into the mattress.

"Ahh." Oh fuck, that hurts. Holy... shit... ahhh!

"Relax." He growls. His fingers start to slowly pump my sex and my mouth drops open with a deep arousal. Oh God, this is a new sensation. I've never done this before.

I pant to try and deal with his claiming.

"Let me fuck you the way I want to fuck you."

He slowly slides out and drives back home in one deep pump. We both groan.

Oh dear God. This is Bad Boy Heaven in all its glory.

He slides in and out, again and again.

After a few uncomfortable minutes, my body finally loosens and the sensation turns to enjoyment. As if sensing the exact moment I begin to enjoy it, he smacks my behind. "That's it, baby, ride me home."

He lifts my hips and starts to take what he wants, deep hard pumps with his fingers just at the right tempo into my sex.

I have never felt something so naughty, so forbidden, and so fucking good in all of my life.

He pinches my clit between his fingers and I nearly go through the roof.

"Oh, yeah," he purrs in a deep guttural growl. "You feel so fucking good. This ass. This beautiful fucking ass."

Our bodies slap together and I'm close... Oh God. This orgasm is going to be so strong, it's going to hurt.

He slaps me hard on the behind again and it's the smart of the slap and the depth of his cock that sends me spiralling over the edge. I fall forward as my body convulses, and I scream out face down into my pillow.

He picks up the pace and pumps me hard and fast and my legs turn to jelly.

I can't... I can't take any more.

Hard and deep. Hard and deep... so hard and deep.

He grabs my hipbones and slams brutally to stay buried deep inside. I feel the deep jerk of his cock. "Oh... Rosh," he calls.

He slowly slides in and then back out, and I stay still with my face buried deep into the pillow.

Holy fucking shit. What was that?

He eventually pulls me back and sits me up on his lap and kisses me over my shoulder. His kiss is tender and caring.

I fall back on his chest with my head on his shoulder as I look up at the ceiling, panting, breathless, and completely overwhelmed. My heart is beating so fast. He is still deep inside me and his lips are worshipping every inch of my face.

His words come back to me about me being his.

"When did I become yours?" I whisper into the darkness.

He kisses me gently over my shoulder, his lips tenderly claiming mine. This is the most intimate sex I have ever had. I feel so... cherished.

Sexual perfection.

He slides out and lays me down on my back, rips his condom off, and crawls over me again. My legs wrap around his waist and my arms around his broad shoulders. His hair falls messily over his forehead as he looks down at me. "When you came back for me on the ship," he murmurs.

I smile and he kisses me softly.

"When did you become mine?" I whisper up at him.

He kisses me again, his tongue slowly moving against mine. The feeling behind it nearly brings me to tears. "When I couldn't leave you tonight."

Our eyes are locked and, unable to help myself, I say the words I know I shouldn't.

"You know I'm in love with you, right?" I whisper.

He smiles sexily. "I kind of hoped you were." His lips take mine as he slides his slick body back into my sex.

I smile into his lips. This guy is going to be the death of me.

"Legs up, baby." He growls. "I need to fuck my girl."

"Didn't you just do that?" I pant.

"I'm just warming up."

There are three cardinal rules that any self-respecting woman should adhere to if she is going to acquire any hand in her relationship—and by hand, I mean upper.

Rule number one: never let him fuck you up the ass without asking.

Rule number two: never say the words I love you first while still drunk on an orgasm high.

Rule number three: never sit on the edge of the bathtub and watch him shower with love heart-shaped eyes.

It's just plain embarrassing because, right now, at this minute, I am the world's biggest One Direction fan and Harry fucking Styles is in my shower.

He knows it, too. His eyes occasionally flicker up to meet mine as he rubs the soap all over his muscular physique.

"Get in with me." He smirks.

"No, I'm happy watching the show." I smile.

His huge, tanned body fills the shower, and his dark, trimmed pubic hair is the focal point of the masterpiece. He is manicured all over and everything is where it should be.

Muscles, dick, hair, tatts... those naughty but nice dimples.

I'm totally screwed.

Stace Williams is a piece of art. He's valuable and adored by any woman who is lucky enough to ever experience the pleasure he bestows upon them.

I feel grateful that I have had the opportunity to meet him, to touch him, to have had him touch me, and I wonder if we hadn't been locked in a room together if we would ever have had our connection. Would he have even looked my way? I wonder what kind of women he normally pursues out in the real world.

Bringing me back to the present, he tries to sweeten the deal by giving himself a few long strokes with his soapy hand. My mind goes back to the first night we had sex and the masturbation show he gave me. I've never seen anything like it before. It's an all time top memory in the bank. One I will revisit again and again.

"We need to get out of here," he replies casually as he soaps up his chest.

"Hmm." I'm preoccupied as my eyes follow his hand.

"We can't go to any airports because they will be looking for us there. We are safe in Bogota for the time being, but we can't stay here for long." He thinks for a moment as he washes himself. "The problem is I don't have any money in my real name bank accounts, but if I access my Mac accounts, they will know where we are."

I nod. "Hmm."

"Where do you want to go?" he asks.

I shrug. "Wherever." My eyes drop to the large muscle between his legs. God, he's hung, even when soft.

"Will you concentrate?" He interrupts my thoughts.

"Oh, huh?" My guilty eyes flicker back up to his face. "I am concentrating."

His eyes darken. "Yes, I know what you were concentrating on."

I smile because there is no denying it. How am I supposed to carry on as normal when I have a bonafide god in my shower?

I'm in awe of his sexual prowess because, well...he's, just damn ridiculous.

"We will move on today," he continues.

"Yes, you are probably right. I need to stop by and pick something up first."

"From where?"

"A safety deposit box."

He frowns. "What do you have in a deposit box?"

"Umm" I hesitate. This is going to go either of two ways. He's going to lose his shit... Or... I don't know. I'm thinking he's going to lose it.

I stand and pace for a moment. "Well, you know when I was on the boat?"

"Ship," he corrects.

I roll my eyes. "Yes, whatever." I pause again.

"Yes?" he snaps.

"I didn't know I was actually going to like you."

He looks at me deadpan and stops washing himself.

I fake a smile. "You see."

"You were sleeping with me," he replies flatly.

"Yes, but you had kidnapped me and I was going to come here all by myself, remember?" His emotionless face tells me nothing. "Which... I-I would have hated, by the way." I stammer. "Coming here alone, it's much better with you."

He rolls his eyes at my bad cover up. "Go on."

"I broke into a container and stole the diamonds," I blurt out in a rush.

A frown crosses his face.

I screw up my face as I wait for the eruption.

He stares at me blankly as he processes what I have just said and then his mouth nearly drops open.

Oh shit, here it comes. I run out into the room from the bathroom and he chases me, wet and nude.

"You... you stole the fucking diamonds?" he stammers.

I nod quickly. "You're wetting the carpet, you know," I murmur as I point to the floor as a distraction.

He puts his hands on his naked hips. "You are telling me that you stole millions of dollars worth of diamonds and got off the ship straight-faced, and now they are in a safety deposit box." He points to the floor. "Here? In Bogota?"

"Uh-huh," I whisper.

A trace of a smirk crosses his face and he shakes his head. "Just when I think you can't possibly shock me any more than you already have." A smirk crosses my face, matching his. "Then you go and get all sexier and even more shocking on me." He rushes to me and I squeal in laughter. He throws me over his shoulder and slaps my behind hard.

"Put me down," I yell. "Put me down."

He turns the shower to freezing cold and I kick to try and get away.

"You..." He slides me down his thick body. "Have been a very bad girl and you need to be punished."

The water is freezing and I laugh out loud as he pins me up against the wall with his body.

"Who's going to punish me?" I breathe as I smile up at him.

"I am."

———

"Can I have the bacon and eggs, please?" I ask the waitress.

"I will have the same thanks," Stace adds.

"Oh, and two coffees, please." I smile.

"Is that all?" she asks as she scribbles on her notepad.

"Yes, thanks."

We are sitting in a café having breakfast. I had to come out alone this morning and buy Stace new clothes. His high visibility work wear was like a beacon and not something one would wear if trying to blend in. I got us both a few outfits and toiletries. I also picked up a wig for me, and a pair of sunglasses for both of us.

I'm wearing a little pink dress with spaghetti straps that hangs just above my knees while the blonde wig sits below my shoulders. I have a pink cap on. I kind of look like a Spice Girl, to be honest. Stace is harder to disguise. How do you hide a giant made of pure, hard-ass muscle? His tattoos are easily distinguishable so I have him wearing a long-sleeved, cotton, white shirt, and a cap to cover his hair.

He picks up my sunglasses from the table and puts them on then looks around. "These are better than mine," he mutters.

I frown, pick up his glasses, and put them on. "Why? What's wrong with these?" Oh, everything does seem a little blue. I glance around at our surroundings. Mine are better than his, he's right.

"I just like these better," he tells me.

I hold my hand out to him. "Don't, you are going to stretch them."

He looks over the top of the glasses at me. "The only thing I'm going to stretch are your orifices."

I smirk and stare at him as my brain misfires. Does he have any idea how hot he is with this sexual innuendo he just casually throws into our conversation? Stretching my orifices. How does he even think of this shit? But he is onto something... I have been stretched to the hilt, and then some. I turn to see the waitress standing next to our table with the coffees. She doesn't know where to look, and it's obvious she heard what he just said.

I laugh and my eyes flicker to Stace who has dropped his head in embarrassment.

"I'm sorry, please excuse my friend. He's an idiot." I fake a smile.

Her eyes widen and with shaky hands she places the coffees down on the table then scurries out to the kitchen, no doubt to tell her work friends about the hot, dirty talker at table nine.

"I'm an idiot?" he asks with an arched brow.

"If the shoe fits." I turn the page of the newspaper in front of me, embarrassed that he makes me swoon like a teenager on heat, and that he bloody well knows it.

"Oh, it fits," he replies darkly. I lift my eyes to meet his.

"The shoe fit perfectly." He pauses for effect. "Like a glove." He widens his eyes.

I smirk. "Perverted," I mouth as I turn back to my paper and pick up my coffee.

"Just how you like it."

I smirk as my eyes rise to meet his. He's on to something there. I do like it... Very much.

"I need a computer," he tells me, changing the subject. "I need to do some research."

"Maybe we should just buy one?"

He nods. "Yes, good thinking. That can be our next stop and then we hire a car and go to the deposit box."

I hold my coffee up and he clinks his with mine.

"We make a good team, you and me." I smile.

He smiles into his coffee cup as his eyes drop to my lips, and I feel my insides clench. "In more ways than one."

Two hours later and we are at the rental car company. Stace is sitting on a row of seats at the back of the office while he connects the Wi-Fi on our new laptop. I'm standing next to him as I wait to be called to the desk. His left hand runs up and down my leg as he sits deep in concentration while he boots up our Internet. His hand slides up my leg, and then back down, back up and under my dress and back down again. I have my arms folded as I stand and wait my turn.

"What kind of car should I get?" I ask.

"Something inconspicuous."

"Where are we dropping it off?"

"I don't know yet. Maybe Chile."

I look around nervously. "When will you know?"

"When I get this fucking Internet working and find out where we have to go to sell the..." He widens his eyes.

"Oh, right," I whisper. Of course.

His hand slides up my leg again as I watch him over his shoulder and I glance over to see a middle aged woman sitting in the row of seats watching us. What's she looking at?

His hand slides up my leg again and I drop my head to hide my smirk.

Oh... that.

Look at me. I've gotten so used to his hands on me all the time that I don't even notice he does it anymore. What must we look like? Me in a short, slutty dress with a blonde wig, and him being his edible self, running his hands up and down my leg in public while he concentrates.

"Rebecca Williams," the girl at the desk calls out. I walk over to where she is sitting.

"Yes, I would like to rent a car, please." I slide over my passport.

"Drivers license."

I slide Stace's international license over the counter and her eyes lift to find him in the room. She goes back to her computer and types for a moment. "What kind of car would you like?"

"Um." I glance at Stace. "I need something with really, really dark, tinted windows." I pause for a moment. "Like black windows. Oh and air conditioning."

She raises her brow. "Sneaking around are we?"

My eyes widen and I glance back at Stace. Oh shit, what can I say? "Yes, on my husband... with my lover." I tilt my chin towards Stace and her eyes rise to him again. He sits with his legs spread and his muscles on show, the epitome of an alpha. She smirks and widens her eyes. "Boy, I don't blame you," she whispers.

I smile. "I know," I whisper back.

She types into her computer. "Have fun while you can, I say."

"I am." I smirk. If only she knew how much.

She reads her computer screen. "Okay, so we have a SUV, a sedan..."

"Hmm." I pause for a moment. "Anything else?"

She hits a few more buttons and raises her eyebrows. "We have a black Ferrari."

I smirk. "A Ferrari?"

She looks up at me and raises her eyebrow. "If you're going down, you probably should do it in style, right?"

I bite my bottom lip to hide my stupid smile and she smiles back. We are thinking exactly the same thing. "Exactly," I whisper as I glance back at Stace. "How much is that for two weeks?"

She widens her eyes and she types into her computer and waits for the reply. "Twenty thousand dollars."

I think for a moment. If I'm going down I should do it in style. This is crazy, but fucking hell, so is my life.

"I'll take it."

Fifteen minutes later Stace is sitting in the parking lot waiting for me to pick him up as he works on our computer, and I am out the back getting instructions from the maintenance guys for our Ferrari. I am like a little kid at Christmas and my heart is racing. After many instructions, I finally get the keys. I climb into the lowered vehicle and drive around to the front to see Stace sitting on an outdoor chair. I pull up slowly and rev the engine. When he looks up, his eyes widen.

I wind down the window. "Going my way?" I smile with an over exaggerated wink.

He stands and puts his hands on his hips and shakes his head.

I laugh because I knew that would be his reaction.

He walks around to the driver's side and bends down.

"This is the inconspicuous car you rented?" I rev the engine again. "Yep."

"You're fucking crazy. You do know that, don't you?"

I rev the engine again. "Yep."

He smirks as he looks over the car.

"If we're going down, we're going down in style." I smile cheekily.

He bends to the window. "Do I have to fucking punish you every hour?"

"Yep." I beep the horn to annoy him more. He slowly walks around the car and opens the driver's side door.

"I'm driving," he snaps as he unzips his jeans. "While you go down in style."

17

Roshelle

"I WOULD LIKE to access my safety deposit box, please?" I tell the cranky receptionist through the glass security screen. My nerves are high and I'm panicking that she is going to call the police or something. It doesn't seem real that I have gotten away with it so far.

Her beady eyes flicker up to Stace and she eyes him suspiciously.

He raises a brow in a silent dare and I subtly stand on his foot. What is the problem between these two? She seems to hate him and he apparently hates her more from the looks they're exchanging.

"Identification, please," she demands flatly.

I slide my license over the counter along with my two bank cards. She studies them for a moment. "I need to photocopy these and the one out here is broken. I will be back in a minute. I just need to go into the other office."

"Yes, of course." I smile gratefully.

She disappears out of sight.

"What's her problem?" Stace whispers.

"You are her problem. Why are you glaring at her?"

"Because she's a fucking bitch."

I roll my eyes. "Will you shut up," I whisper.

She reappears and rings a bell. A man comes out and gestures to the doorway. We follow him down a long corridor until we get to the end where it opens out to a large square room where the walls are covered in lockers. "Bottom left in the corner," he murmurs as he points us in the right direction.

"Thank you." I smile. "I would never have remembered where this was."

He nods and disappears from where he came from. I smile broadly and take my key to slowly open the safety deposit box. Stace stands behind me and puts his hand on my hips as he watches me over my shoulder. "Careful of the cameras," he whispers in my ear.

"I know," I whisper back. I open the door and see the sock encasing our treasure.

I stand back to let Stace peer in. "My sock?" He raises his eyebrow in question. "A sock is what you chose to put them in?'

"It's all I frigging had," I snap quietly. "Beggars can't be choosers." I reach in and try to untie the sock while it's still in the locker. I don't want the cameras to see what we are doing. It's dark and my arms are confined.

"How many?" I whisper.

He thinks for a minute. "The five smallest. How long did you say we can keep this here?"

"Two years."

"Do you reckon five?" he asks.

I think for a minute. "Yeah, maybe. I don't want to take them all at once in case we get caught."

"Fuck, don't say that."

I struggle to untie the sock in the darkness of the locker.

"What are you doing?" he whispers.

"Trying to untie the damn thing."

He shakes his head. "Let me bloody do it." He takes over. "I can't believe you lied to me and took these," he whispers as he concentrates on the untying sock challenge.

I screw up my face. "Oh, because you have never lied to me... Mr. Mac." I sneer sarcastically.

He rolls his eyes. "If I am Mr. Mac, then you are Mrs. Mac. In fact," he whispers. "You are the Mac Daddy of all Macs."

I smirk. He's got me there. I have told some porkies in my life.

He finally gets the sock undone and fiddles around before he takes them out of the sock and lays them out in the bottom of the locker.

"Holy fuck," he whispers in amazement.

I smile proudly. "I did good?" I know I did, but I just want to hear him say it out loud.

He kisses me quickly on the lips. "You did great, babe."

He points to the five smallest and I nod as he picks them up. I put my purse into the locker and he loads them into the change compartment.

I smile broadly and his hand drops to my hipbone before he kisses me again, his lips lingering over mine. "We should celebrate tonight."

"What do you want to do?" I smile.

He shrugs. "Find a bar where they play that hippy song you love so much."

I smile goofily at him as hope blooms in my chest. Another

date. This is the first time that I can remember being truly happy. He knows my story, my fucked up story, and yet he likes me anyway. Nobody has ever known my truth about my life on the run and the shame I feel for having such an evil, fucked up father. Stace and I laugh, we have fun, and I have never had this sense of belonging before. It seemed to happen to everyone around me, but I always thought it was out of my reach. I want to talk to him, I want to tease him, and God I want to fuck him stupid.

But mostly, I just want to call him mine.

He loads the diamonds back into the sock, reties it, and then locks the locker. We gently kiss again and walk back out to the reception hand in hand. I pause and my eyes flicker over to the cranky receptionist. "Just a sec." I drag him over to the desk. "Excuse me," I call.

She looks up as if I am annoying her. This chick is so lazy.

Do your job, stupid.

"Yes," she replies flatly.

"I would like to add my husband to the safety deposit box, please." My eyes flicker between Stace and her.

Stace frowns and he shakes his head subtly.

"Do you want him to have full access or just to be a double signatory?"

"Full access, please," I state.

She raises her eyebrows as if surprised and then she stands. "You will have to sign some release documents granting permission. I'll go and get them." She gestures to the other office and pauses for a moment. "We normally have another girl, but she is off work today. Oh, and I will need your license and identification again, please."

"Okay." I nod as I take out my purse.

"I don't need access," Stace whispers as he takes my hand.

"Yes, you do." I pause as I try to think of the right wording.

"We both know that my days are numbered."

His face falls. "They are not. Don't say that."

I reach up and cup his face. "He will get me. One day he will get me. I already know my fate. So in that instance, I want you to have the diamonds."

"I won't let that happen."

I smile as a sinking feeling of dread fills the pit of my stomach. I have tried my hardest to not let the past week worry me, but the feeling of pre-empted horror awaiting me is overwhelming. "I will be ready for him when he comes." I pause. "I'm going to give it my best shot." I shrug. "You never know. Stranger things have happened, right?"

Stace watches me as a frown crosses his face. "How long have you lived like this?"

"Like what?"

"In fear?"

I swallow the lump in my throat as I contemplate his question. "I guess that's the thing, I'm not scared anymore. The ship changed me. You changed me." I hesitate as I try to articulate my thoughts. "I just want to live my life like every day is my last because it could be." I shrug and am suddenly overcome with emotion, the tears welling in my eyes. "I don't want to be scared anymore."

Stace's eyes hold mine and he bends to gently kiss my lips.

"I got your back, babe."

I run my fingers through his stubble and smile into his warm lips. "I know you do and that's why I feel brave."

"Ahem," the woman interrupts.

We both turn back to her guiltily and she slides the papers across the counter. "Sign here." She points to a line. "And here." She points to the next page. "I need you to fill out your email details and you will need to empty the locker on the 15th of June in 2019 by 2pm."

I smile and watch on as Stace signs his documents and hands them back to her. "I will give you both a copy." She stands and leaves the room to photocopy the documents and Stace's eyes find mine.

"You remember that date in case you come back alone," I whisper.

He kisses me. "It's not happening. Nobody on Earth could tear me away from you."

———

I laugh as I spin. Stace is twirling me as we dance alone in our hotel room. It's 8 pm and we have been drinking cocktails since 2pm. After researching for most of today, we have found out that the man we need to speak to about selling our diamonds owns a bar two suburbs away. He doesn't buy them, but he knows people who know people. His bar, The Snake Pit, isn't open tonight, but he will be there tomorrow night so we have delayed our moving on plans for two days until we get to see him. I'm kind of glad to be honest. I feel safe here in our little bubble. We have decided that after we sell the diamonds we are heading to Chile and catching a private plane out of South America.

He dips me and holds me down. "How about this move?"

"You're going to drop me." I squeal as I laugh.

"That's the plan." He dips me farther. We go back farther and farther as he laughs in his cheeky boy way, and suddenly he trips and we go flying onto the floor.

We land with a thud and burst into laughter. Oh, this is so much fun. I'm spread on my back and he hovers over me holding my hands above my head. His face falls serious as he looks down at me. "You didn't tell me you loved me today," he says softly.

I smirk. What? "I didn't know I had to."

"You do."

I raise my eyebrows. "At least I said it once."

He kisses me playfully. "It's not in my vocabulary."

My mouth drops open and I laugh out loud. "You are completely shit at this."

"Am not." He ravages my neck with his mouth and I squeal in laughter.

"Stop it." I laugh as I struggle to get away from him.

"Say it," he demands.

"No." I laugh as I try to buck him off me.

"Say it."

"Take me dancing." I laugh as he bites my neck hard.

"I'm taking you to bed." He growls into my skin.

"You're taking me for granted." I squeal as I try to get him off me.

His mouth drops open and he pulls back to look at my face.

"Is that what you think?"

"Well, I do seem to spend a lot of time underneath you." I smirk.

He grabs me roughly on the behind and drags me underneath him. "I don't hear you complaining, and for the record, I'm often underneath you, too."

"I'm not complaining. I'm saying I want to go dancing on a date with my man."

He watches me for a moment and finally stands to pull me up by the hand. "Let's go then. See if we can hear that hippy song again." We've been ready for two hours, but keep getting side tracked by each other.

I glance down at him and my hot pink lipstick is all over his shirt from our drunk dancing. "You need to change your shirt."

He looks down at himself. "Yeah, okay." He unbuttons his shirt and slides it off. His sun-kissed, broad chest and chiselled abs catch my attention and I have to immediately stop to look at him. He is, without a doubt, the most perfect man I have ever seen. Unable to resist, I bend and kiss him on the ribs just under his chest. His hand instantly drops to the back of my head and I could just keep going down his body. Stop it, focus. Dinner. He's so damn kissable.

He smirks. "You want it again, nympho?" His hand holds me down and I laugh as I try to escape his claws. I stand and my eyes drop to the lipstick marks that I have left on his body. "Just marking what's mine." I smirk.

He glances in the mirror at himself and then lifts his arms and turns to look at the lip marks I have left.

He smiles sexily and throws me a wink.

"What?" I smirk.

"Let's go. I got an idea."

"You are totally fucking crazy," I whisper.

"Crazy for you." He smirks.

———

My eyes lift up to the tattoo artist as he holds the needle in his gloved hand. "So you just want the lips tattooed exactly as they are?"

Stace lies on the bed with his arm above his head. "Yes." He thinks for a moment. "And the same colour as the lipstick." He pauses for a second. "Actually, can you write the words Mrs. Mac underneath it."

My mouth drops open. "You wouldn't."

He smiles broadly. "Just watch me." He grabs my head and brings my face down to meet his. "I want to be marked as yours, too," he murmurs against my lips. Our eyes lock and something changes. I have no idea what it is, but it feels good.

I fall back into the chair, half shocked, half elated. I spend the next hour watching Stace get my lips and the words Mrs. Mac permanently inked on his side.

Game over.

My life is complete.

Stace

I wake as a wave of nausea hits me. "Shit," I whisper with my eyes still closed. I feel sick.

What a night?

I close my eyes and smile to myself. Now that was a date. Rosh and I laughed, danced, and drank cocktails for hours until we came home and had mind-blowing sex.

She's got me.

She's got me by the balls.

I've never met anyone like her, and I've never felt like this before. She's brave and beautiful, funny and sexy as fuck. I turn on my side to face her and my hand gently trails up over her naked body. My mind goes to yesterday when she told me that she lives every day as her last. It resonated with me, as if somehow I also know our time is limited. I can't stand the thought of Vikinos getting to her. Her childhood was stolen because she spent her whole life on the run. The thought of him killing me and making her watch as punishment turns me inside out.

Because that's how it will go.

They will catch us both and torture me to death in front

of her, as he did to her mother. I get a vision of my brother being electrocuted to death and my blood runs cold. I don't want her to have to go through that again... and I know I can't go through it again.

To be honest, I don't think he would kill her, but he will make her suffer as punishment for not loving him.

She has suffered enough.

Maybe he does want her dead? I can't begin to imagine how his mind works.

I need a plan. I have to kill him first, but how? I had my plan and it was on the ship until she completely ruined it. He trusted me then, but I have no way of getting to him now.

She slowly opens her eyes and smiles shyly up at me. I lean in and kiss her gently. "Good morning, my Mrs. Mac."

She smiles broadly and frowns sleepily as if remembering something. "Did you get a tattoo last night?"

"I did."

She screws up her face with her eyes still closed. "Oh God. You're batshit crazy."

"I am." I bend and take her lips in mine. "We already established this."

She smiles sleepily up at me and I feel my heart somersault.

Even her smile affects me.

"Tell me something." I pause, I'm not sure if now is the right time to bring this up. "If you dared to dream of a future, what would it be?"

She frowns. "That's a bit deep for this time of the morning, isn't it?"

"I'm just wondering." I bend and kiss her lips. "Humor me."

She rolls onto her back and thinks for a moment and I

put my open hand onto her stomach as I wait for her answer. "I suppose I would just want all the normal things any girl wants."

"Like what?"

She shrugs. "A husband who loved me, white picket fence in the country, two kids." She smiles wistfully. "A dog." Her voice trails off. "I always wanted a dog."

I watch her. "You never had a dog?"

She shakes her head softly as if ashamed. "No."

Sadness fills me. A simple thing like having a dog is her dream. We lay in silence for a moment and I stare up at the ceiling and pull her body across mine. I kiss her forehead. "Sounds nice," I murmur. "Where would this white picket fence house be?"

"I don't know, somewhere with rolling green acres," she murmurs, as if far away.

I flicker my eyes over to her. "Could we build my mom a house on our land?" I smirk.

She pulls back to look at my face and smiles broadly.

"Depends."

"On what?"

"On whether she likes dogs."

I laugh out loud and she leans up on her elbow above me. "Stop dreaming, Stace. That future isn't our reality."

My face falls. It's true it's not. "It's a nice dream, though, huh?"

I ask sadly.

She kisses my chest. "Let's just try to get through today, baby. Dreams only bring heartache."

Roshelle

It's 10pm and Stace is in the shower. We've had a wonderful day in each other's arms and have spent most of it in the rooftop pool. He went out this morning and bought us both a few new outfits and phones with prepaid data and credit. I couldn't go. I was feeling too seedy from last night's activities. Tonight we are going to try and find this guy who apparently knows where you sell things—the one who owns The Snake Pit. It sounds pretty dodgy if you ask me, but Stace assures me that it will be okay. He asked me to stay here and wait for him, but I am not letting him go alone. I would go crazy waiting here not knowing if he was safe.

I'm happy—God, I'm so happy—and I am petrified that my bubble is going to burst. I'm in my wig and my little pink dress.

I smile as I turn and look at my behind in this dress. Stace doesn't particularly like it when I have the wig and this dress on. He thinks I look like a hooker and I'm pretty sure he is quite familiar with that look. My mind flashes to Chelsea and my skin prickles with jealousy. I pick up my phone and scroll through the Internet as a smile crosses my face. I can check emails now. Who knew something so trivial could be so exciting? I log into my email account and sip my wine as they load.

"Babe, can you get me the razor from the drawer, please?" Stace calls from the bathroom.

I look around. "What drawer?" I call.

"The stuff I bought today is in the top drawer of the desk. There is a razor in there."

"Okay," I call. I grab the razor and take it into him. I am rewarded with a wet kiss from my shower god. I return to my place on the bed as I wait for the emails, and finally, I get the ping that they loaded. The heading of the first one brings a frown to my face.

From: Downtown Storage Solutions
Subject: Activity

I frown and I click on the email.

Safety Security box was accessed today at 12.32pm.

I sit up in my seat. What? I check the date. No, that's todays date. The email must have been sent yesterday after we were there? I scroll down the messages with a flutter in my chest. Don't do it... no, don't do it.

A second email.

From: Downtown Storage Solutions
Subject: Activity
Safety security box was accessed today at 11.10am.

The air leaves my lungs. That's a different email to the one that arrived this afternoon. Stace went to the safety deposit box today without me. I stand and walk to the window and look down at the street below as my heartbeat hammers in my ears.

Really?

Are you fucking kidding me?

My eyes close as the all too familiar feeling of betrayal washes through me.

He's taken the diamonds and like a fool, I led him to them.

Tears fill my eyes. I thought his feelings were real.

Oh God.

I'm just a stupid girl blinded by love.

I trusted him.

Stace

I shave, shower, wrap myself in a towel and head into the bedroom.

"Rosh?" I call out as I glance around.

Hmm, she's not here. She must have gone down to the restaurant to get some takeaway to eat. Weird, I thought we were getting something on the way out.

I take my time and dress then lie back on the bed as I wait for her to return. I glance at the clock knowing we need to get going soon. My mind runs over the conversation I am going to have tonight at The Snake Pit. I need to ask where to sell something without telling them what I have to sell. It's a fine line. I'm just going to ask where to sell jewelry. I think that that seems like the safest option. For half an hour I wait. Where the frigging hell is she? I thought she wanted to come? I could have gone and been back by now. I take out my phone and message her.

How long are you going to be?
We have to leave?

I wait for a reply, but it doesn't come. I text again.

I'm coming down.
We will eat down there?

I watch my phone as I wait for a reply. For fuck's sake. I grab my wallet and keys and head down to the elevator. My phone beeps as the door opens and I get in. It reads:

I will sort the diamonds.
Don't worry yourself.

I frown and text back.

What are you talking about?
Are you at the restaurant getting us dinner?

I wait for a reply. It doesn't come. The doors of the elevator open and I enter the foyer and glance around in search of her. What's going on? Have they got her? I start to panic. I dial her number and it rings out, no answer. I walk into the restaurant and glance around nervously, but she's not here, either.

Shit.

I half run to the reception desk. "Excuse me, did you see where my wife went?" I ask.

The girl frowns. "Carlos," she calls the doorman and he comes over from his place at the door.

"Did you see where Mr. Williams' wife went?"

He frowns as he thinks for a moment. "Yes, she caught a cab."

"Was she alone?" I frown as a million thoughts run through my mind.

"Yes, I believe so, sir."

"Do you know where she went?"

"She asked the driver to take her to The Snake Pit," the doorman replies.

My face drops. "Are you sure?" I frown.

He nods. "Yes." He hesitates for a moment. "I thought it was odd."

What is she doing now? Why does she go crazy and ruin

my plans every fucking time? I hurry out the front and jump into the backseat of the cab.

"Where to?" the driver asks.

"The Snake Pit." I glare out the window as the cab drives me through the night. I cannot believe her. I cannot fucking believe her. I shake my head in annoyance. Every time she gets a pea brain idea in her head, she runs off on a tangent and ruins everything. My mind goes to Vikinos and her damn stupid shooting spree that nearly got us killed—still could get us killed, if we are being honest. I had that all worked out. I was going to poison him quietly and nobody could have ever blamed me.

But no.

She didn't even shoot the right guy.

It infuriates me just thinking of it. What a fuck up.

And now, just when we are about to actually meet someone who could make a huge difference in the price we get, she goes and does this.

She will fuck this one up, too. I can already see it coming.

She thinks she's so gangster and can handle herself, yet when it comes down to it, she has no idea what she is playing at.

She could be up to an hour in front of me. Like a fool I waited for her to come back to the room.

I'm so fucking mad that when I do see her, she had better run. The cab finally pulls up in front and I slowly get out and look around. The club is in a slum area and looks run down. The bouncers on the door are as seedy as all hell.

I blow out a calming breath and walk in through the dark wood double doors in the dimly lit foyer. The club is large and has circular tables scattered throughout. The music is loud and sounds like Cuban style. The place is about half full. I can see through an archway leading into another room and there are pool tables with low hanging lights hanging over them. My eyes scan the room for her. Where is she?

Where the hell is she?

The whole back wall is a bar and the waitresses are scantily dressed. One attractive brunette immediately catches my eye and she smiles sexily in my direction. Back in the day, she would have been right up my alley, but that was before I met Rosh and her ten personalities. I like about four of her personalities. I'm in love with about three of them and the other three I hate with a passion.

She's doing my fucking head in.

I blow out a deep, steadying breath as I keep searching. A thick cloud of smoke hangs low in the air. Every person in this club is smoking some kind of cigar. My eyes roam from table to table, then I see her. Sitting at the back table with three men. My fury ignites. She's going to fucking get it. I storm straight over to where she is sitting with three middle aged, overweight men, and I stand at the end of the table. She looks up at me from under her hideous blonde wig. "What are you doing here?" she asks flatly.

I glare at her. "I should ask you the same thing."

She sips her drink sarcastically and it's all I can do not to rip her by the hair from the table.

She raises her eyebrow. "Meet my friends." She gestures to the three men she is sitting with. "This is Carlos, Santiago, and Mateo." They fake smiles and reach up to shake my hand.

"This is my friend." She pauses and narrows her eyes momentarily as she thinks. "Judas." A trace of a smirk crosses her face, proud of her sarcasm.

I glare at her and start to feel fury run through my bloodstream. "Birds of a feather." We glare at each other and I have no idea why she is so pissed at me, but holy fuck she's about to know how pissed I am at her.

"Won't you join us?" one of them asks.

"I'm going to the bar first." I turn and head to the bar and straight to the hot brunette.

"What will it be?" she asks sexily.

I stare at her. Yeah, she's hot. Smoking actually. I bet she is uncomplicated and normal.

Unlike somebody else I know.

I glance back over to the table and Rosh's eyes are on me like a hawk. Screw her, she can sweat for a bit. I take a seat at the bar.

The waitress leans her elbows onto the bar and bends down to talk to me. "What's your name? I haven't seen you here before?" Her accent is as hot as hell.

I stare at her and without thinking lie. "Andre."

She smiles sexily. "I'm Camilla."

I smirk and nod. "How do you do Camilla?"

She smiles broadly and picks up the cloth and starts cleaning the bar. Her breasts are near hanging out of her skimpy top and I watch them bounce as she moves her arm. "What do you want, big boy?" she asks.

My eyes hold hers and I know what I want to say—what the old me would say—and then I am reminded of the infuriating woman sitting at the table with three other men. My eyes flicker to Rosh, and as if she can read my mind, she narrows her eyes and gives me the filthiest look she can muster.

I turn back to the brunette with renewed incentive. "I will have two Tequilas, please."

"Sure." She pours my drinks and I down them straight up.

Her eyes drop to my lips as I lick them, and hell it's so fucking tempting to cleanse the Rosh from my pallet with this hot piece of ass. I blow out a breath and my eyes flicker to her again. She's laughing with the men now and I feel the hairs on my neck prickle in jealousy.

"Where are you from?" the waitress asks, interrupting my thoughts.

"All over," I reply, then I think for a moment. Maybe she will know something. "Tell me, if I had some jewellery to sell, where would I sell it?"

"What kind of jewellery?" she asks.

"I have an inheritance to sell. Gold, diamonds, a few rubies and sapphires."

Her eyes dance with delight. "An inheritance?"

I nod and I know she knows that there is no inheritance.

"Most people sell things to Big Al."

"Big Al?" I ask. "Where is he?"

"Teusaquillo."

I nod, knowing that's not far from here. "Do you have a number for him?"

She smirks as her eyes hold mine. "Don't you want my number?"

I lick my lips; it would be so easy... stop it. "Not really," I reply. "I'm here on work."

She raises her brow in disappointment.

"Can I have the number?" I ask.

"Sure," she replies, dejected. Camilla disappears into the kitchen and my eyes flicker over to Rosh.

What?

She is sitting on one of the men's laps, laughing out loud. I start to see red.

Uncontrollable fucking red.

Camilla comes back and passes me a card

BIG AL 0436990135

I fake a smile and take the card from her. "Thanks." I stuff it in my pocket. I glance back and see Rosh and the guy now has his arms around her. "I will be back," I snap, and before I can help myself, I'm marching over to the table.

"Get your fucking hands off her."

"Hey." The men all laugh. "Calm down, brother."

I reach over and grab her by the arm and drag her across the table, sending one of the drinks flying. "Get outside," I snap.

"I'm staying here," she replies.

"The hell you are." I push her in the back toward the door and she stumbles forward.

"Don't touch me," she yells.

"I will fucking touch you when I want." I push her again and she shuffles forward.

We burst through the front doors and out onto the street and stumble down the road a bit.

"What is your fucking problem?" I yell.

"You!" She screams. "You are my fucking problem!" She folds her arms in front of her. "I know you have the diamonds, asshole. You can stop lying."

18

Roshelle

MY HEART IS HAMMERING hard as we stand on the sidewalk. "I... I can't believe I trusted you." I stammer through tears.

His face screws up. "What the hell are you talking about?"

"Don't insult my intelligence!" I scream as I lose the small amount of control that I had.

"Don't flatter yourself because you don't have any."

He has got to be kidding. Who the hell does this dick think he is? "That's it, I'm done." I turn and storm up the road.

"What are you raging about?" he yells as he follows.

"Go away." I pause and look up for a moment as the skies open and huge raindrops start to fall sporadically. Oh great, it's going to pour down now. I keep power walking up the road.

The downpour comes loud and heavy and we start to run to find cover. I cross the road to stand under an awning from a bakery, and he follows and stands next to me.

We stand in silence as we watch Mother Nature cause her havoc.

"What the hell are you angry about, Rosh?" he finally asks. My eyes fill with tears again and I drop them shamefully to look at the cement in front of me. "I know you went to the safety deposit box today."

He stays silent and the air hangs thick between us.

"Did you take them all?" I ask over the sound of the heavy rain.

After a long silence, he replies. "No."

I look up the street through blurred vision. This is it. This really is it for us. He did take them. I knew he did.

"I didn't steal from you."

My eyes meet his. "Yes, you did."

"I need you to trust me."

His silhouette is blurred. "I can't," I whisper. "Trust is earned."

"Haven't I earned it?"

"No," I reply flatly. I put my arm up and hail a passing cab and it comes to a slow halt. I bend down to the window. "Bogota, please?" I ask.

"Sure, hop in."

I climb in and he pushes in after me. I scoot over in the seat to allow him the room. I wrap my arms around me protectively and stare out the window. I just want to get away from him. I can't take this. I can't take fucking deceit anymore. His silence is stifling.

"You going to sell them? Is that it? Did you get the contact that you needed?" I glance over at him. "Maybe you are going to set up your wife and kids at home."

He sits with his hands linked on his lap and shakes his head dismissively with an eye roll. "I have a wife and kids now?"

I shrug. "Why would I believe anything that you have told me so far?" He glares at me. "Lie to me once, lie to me all the time, it's all the same. I will never believe anything that comes out of your lying mouth now."

He doesn't fight back and the car trip is made in silence. Part of me wants him to deny it, to fight for us, to tell me it's not true, to beg me for forgiveness, but then... I need the truth.

The painful truth.

At least I have that little bit of money in my account. I start to go over my options on getting out of here. The cab comes to a slow halt before he pays the driver and we climb out.

He glares at me, still furious, and it's like he is waiting for me to say something.

"Come and get your things and get out." I sneer.

"So, that's it?" he asks.

I feel the tears behind my eyes and I nod. "That's it," I whisper, barely able to push out the words.

He shakes his head, and with renewed anger, opens his wallet and frantically flicks through it. He takes out a business card and tosses it at me. It hits me in the face and falls to the floor.

"When you pick it up, flush it down the toilet." He growls. "I'm done with living my day as if it's my last."

He storms off. I stand and watch him disappear into the darkness down the busy street. I let out a deep, sad breath and my eyes fall to the card on the cement and I bend and pick it up.

Downtown City Jewellers
Engagement Ring Specialist

What? I frown. "What does this have to do with...?"

I close my eyes. Oh God. He took one diamond. Just one.

"Stace," I yell as I look up. I take off in the direction he walked in. I look around frantically through the busy street. I can't see him.

"Stace," I call through the people. "Stace!"

What have I done? I run to the end of the street as I frantically search for him. I look back to where I came from. I can't believe I just...

With my heartbeat hammering fast, my face screws up in tears. Oh no, what I have I done?

"Stace," I cry. I take out my phone and ring him, but it rings out, so I text him.

Talk to me
What's going on?

I call him again and no answer, damn it. Why do I always fuck things up? I bounce my legs up and down as I cry. I text again.

Stace, I'm sorry
I don't know how to trust people.
Please talk to me.

No answer.

For an hour I walk the streets in tears as I look for him, knowing I have no one to blame but myself.

I try to call him again and this time his phone is switched off.

I really did it this time. I pushed away the first guy who was actually worth keeping.

I sit on a seat in the busy street for half an hour as I try to figure out what to do. Finally, with a heavy heart, I head back to our room. I only hope that when he calms down he will come home, although the sinking feeling in my stomach is telling me he has gone for good.

Sometimes, when I close my eyes, I see the haunted look on my mother's face as she bled out.

Sometimes, when it's really still, I hear her cry.

I feel like tonight she's crying in Heaven for the mess I have made of my life.

Mess is an understatement. This is a total disaster.

I have a heavy, sad feeling on my shoulders. It's guilt and regret all rolled into one.

I retrace the last month of my life. The memory of my ex-boyfriend and best friend kissing in the nightclub makes my eyes tear up as the betrayal iron brands me once more. The murder I witnessed and how they consequently took me. Stace... I smile when I think of my beautiful Stace. He protected me from his crew when I was at my most vulnerable. Then the nightmare when I stupidly thought I could take out Vikinos. It all seemed so clear at the time, like nothing could go wrong, but it did.

I shot the wrong man. I thought I could get revenge for Mom's death but... I don't know how I...

I screw up my face as the pain becomes too real to cope with.

I try my hardest to be brave, but I just never seem to get it right. I clutch the white card tight in my hand as I sit on the floor near the window in the dark, desperately hoping my love returns to me. I read the card for the millionth time.

Downtown City Jewellers
Engagement Ring Specialist

I smile as I get a vision of him on bended knee, proposing. What a fairy tale it would be. How badly I wish that dream had come true.

It wasn't our reality and I knew that all along. Maybe I don't deserve happiness.

People with families like mine don't get happy endings.

I stare out at the city below. Where are you now, Stace?

I watch the people bustle along on the street below. This place never seems to go to sleep. It's after 1am.

Where is he?

I frown as my eyes fix on two men on the street. They aren't acting like everyone else. They keep stopping, looking at the people around them. I sit closer to the window and really concentrate

Is that...?

I sit back. Stop it, you're imagining things now. My eyes stay glued to the two men and as they come under a street light, my worst nightmare becomes my reality.

It's Stucco and one of the men from the ship.

I scurry back from the window as my heart begins to hammer. They found us. Oh my God.

I go back and stand behind the curtain and watch them. They seem to be looking around and talking and then pointing and discussing something. They obviously don't know which hotel we are staying at, and in slow motion, I watch them turn the corner and walk towards town... where Stace is.

Oh no.

I run to my phone and dial his number frantically. Pick up. Pick up. Please pick up.

No answer. Shit.

I throw the phone onto the bed in frustration and it bounces onto the floor.

What do I do? I begin to pace back and forth. It's only a matter of time until they find us. Stace will be sitting in a bar somewhere and they will find him. He will be unprepared and have no defense.

Fuck. Why didn't I just ask him if he took the diamonds? "Why do I have to be such a fucking idiot?" I cry out loud.

For twenty minutes I pace as I try to figure out what to do. I need to find him. I have no choice but to find him. I run to the wardrobe and put on my wig, a dress, and some fake glasses. I grab my phone, our passports, and find the gun and put it all in my handbag. I walk out of our room and into the elevator. I push the button with my heart hammering hard in my chest. I scroll through my phone to try and find a map satellite. I have no idea where I am going. I look through the apps and I find one.

Find My Phone

Huh? What's this? Stace must have put it on my phone unless it came with it. I click through and it seems to be some kind of tracking device. Hang on, I wonder if he put it on his phone, too? I quickly type in Stace's number and watch the screen. Low and behold, like magic, a little red dot lights up the screen.

Yes!

He's not far away, just four blocks from here. The doors of the elevator open and I bounce out with renewed optimism.

I know where he is.

The street is busy and bustling and I make my way out, knowing the little red dot is here somewhere, I just have to find it. I think it's just up here on the right. I keep my head down and walk as fast as I can, aware that at any moment I may be spotted.

The red dot seems to be underneath me, and I frown as I do a full circle on the spot.

Where the hell is he? I walk into the bar on the left hand side of the street and search with no success. I stare at the phone and frown. It says he is literally above me. I look around, and over by the wall I find a staircase and tentatively walk up. I smile broadly when I get to the top.

A bar. I walk through and the first person I see is Stace, sitting alone at a bench seat at the back with a beer as his companion.

I approach the table. "Mind if I join you?" I ask.

His eyes rise up to meet mine and he shrugs without answering.

I slide in next to him. "They've found us."

He frowns as his eyes flicker to me. "How do you know?"

"I saw Stucco and one of the others in the street below our hotel looking for us."

He exhales deeply and sips his beer.

I wait for him to say something but he doesn't. "I think we should go," I whisper.

"I'm not going anywhere with you," he replies flatly.

My heart drops. "Stace," I whisper as I put my hand on his thigh.

He flicks it off. "Don't touch me. I'm so fucking angry with you, I can't see straight."

"I know. I'm angry with myself."

We stay silent for a while and he orders another drink.

"We really should go," I whisper. "We don't have time to be sitting in bars."

He shakes his head. "Right now I got bigger problems than fucking Stucco." He growls.

A smirk crosses my face. "Me?"

"Yes, you," he snaps.

"I should have asked you if you took them."

"You should have."

"I just..." I pause as I try to articulate my thoughts. "I'm not very good at trusting people."

"You said you loved me."

"I do," I whisper.

"That's not love, Rosh." He pauses. "Not the kind I give, anyway."

"I don't have your love yet, Stace, we both know that."

His eyes meet mine. "It would be much easier to walk away from you if you didn't."

He's going.

My eyes tear up. "Please don't walk away from me." The lump in my throat gets really big and I find it hard to speak. "I'm much better when I'm with you. I can try harder."

"I just don't need this," he whispers.

I sit with resignation, understanding exactly where he is coming from, and after a long pause of silence I speak quietly. "When we get out of here, you can go." The tears burst from my eyes and I wipe them away shamefully. "You are better off without me."

He continues drinking his beer, void of emotion.

"But at this moment we need to go," I whisper. "Stace, they are going to find us. We are in danger. You can leave me later."

He downs the rest of his beer.

"I have our passports and the gun in my bag," I whisper.

"Give me the gun."

I pass it to him under the table.

"You walk in front of me. We are more noticeable if we are together." He thinks for a moment and hands me back the gun. "You keep it."

I frown.

"I can handle myself without a gun," he explains. I nod and put it back into my bag.

"Just remember that we are on land now. If you shoot someone, you are going to jail." He widens his eyes. "So don't shoot anyone."

"Okay," I murmur, distracted as I stand. "So straight back to the hotel?" I ask.

"Yes, and then we will go."

I nod. "Please be careful." I look up into his eyes and I just have to say it. "I love you," I whisper as I grab his hand.

He squeezes my hand in his as his eyes search mine. "Then start acting like it."

I smile softly, and in that split second, I know it's going to be okay between us. Relief mixed with adrenaline starts to pump through my bloodstream. We need to get out of here. Damn this drama. Why can't we just be in our love bubble somewhere on a secluded luxury island? I stand and make my way out onto the street. I drop my head, and without looking up, I walk fast. I continue without hesitation until I get to the hotel where I turn and wait in the shadows of the trees next to the entrance door.

For fifteen minutes, I wait.

Where is he? I glance at the time on my phone. He has been way too long. Something is wrong.

Shit.

What do I do? Do I wait here? He gave me the gun for protection, but who's protecting him? I slide my hand into my bag to check that it is still there and I feel the cold, hard metal. I blow out a grateful breath. I bite my thumbnail as I stare out into the darkness.

It must be after 2am.

Where are you? Come on, come on.

He's not coming. I walk to the edge of the curb and stare down in the direction I came from. I can't see anything odd going on.

Fucking hell. I have to go back to see where he is. I glance back up at our hotel room window. Did he go in another door and I didn't see him?

There is no other door, stupid. Shit.

I walk back down the hill toward town, careful to keep in the darkened shadows, and I'm positive this isn't bloody safe. Forget about Stucco. Who knows who else is here? I become super sensitive to all the sounds around me. I hear a can kick across the ground in the distance and I turn suddenly. My footsteps are magnified from the earlier downpour as I try and listen for unfamiliar sounds. I hear a woman scream in the distance and I stop still as I battle the fear in my throat. I turn and look back up at the hotel, and then back in the direction I am going. I slide my hand into the bag and grip the gun. My heart is trying to escape from my chest.

If you shoot anyone, you are going to jail. Stace's words from earlier echo in my mind. I don't want to go through all this shit to end up in a Colombian prison for life.

Don't shoot anybody. Just don't shoot anybody, I remind myself.

Where the frigging hell are you? I get to the row of shops and start to look around frantically. The street is still so busy. Why are there so many damn people around? Actually, that's a good thing. I can't imagine how frightening this would be if the town were deserted. A police car drives slowly past and I feel like jumping out in front of them and asking for their help, but I know they can't help us. Nobody on Earth can help us. I walk past an alley between two restaurants and I peer up into the shadows. I frown and stop on the spot.

Three men are up the other end in the darkness, and one of them is Stace.

Fuck.

I immediately slink up against the wall in the shadows near the opening and listen. I strain my ears as hard as I can, but I can't hear what they are saying. I need to get closer... but what if he gets out of it and then I am here and ruin the whole thing? But, what if they kill him?

That's it. I'm getting closer. I slowly tiptoe towards them in the darkness, until finally I can hear what they are saying.

"I'm giving you one last chance. Where the fuck is she?" Stucco growls. Oh God.

"I told you, I don't fucking know. She took me hostage to get off the ship. I haven't seen her since we landed."

"Bullshit. That's an outright lie."

"Go to fucking hell. I don't know where she is."

"Get him," Stucco says to the other man.

The other man grabs Stace and a scuffle breaks out.

"Get your hands off me," Stace snaps.

A punch is thrown and I screw up my face as I slowly get the gun out.

"Vikinos wanted you alive, but I don't care for that. You are better off dead." Stucco growls.

"Fuck you," Stace yells as he connects a hard hit to Stucco's jaw. He staggers back and then regains composure and runs at Stace and they fall to the ground.

I grip the gun with white-knuckle force.

The other man starts to kick Stace on the ground as he fights with Stucco, and I step forward. Don't shoot anyone. I step back into the shadows.

Stace jumps up and does some kind of round kick and

connects with the man's jaw and he instantly drops to the ground, out cold.

Good one.

Then he turns on Stucco and goes ballistic. The sound of the hits are so brutal, I have to shut my eyes. Stace gets him on the ground and hits him and Stucco pulls out a gun.

Oh no. I step forward and point the gun at the two of them.

"Don't move," I yell.

Stucco looks up and the momentary distraction allows Stace the crucial break he needs. He hits him hard and fast four times in succession and he slams his head on the concrete. Stucco falls back dazed and incoherent. He doesn't move again. I walk over to Stace who has blood running down from his eyebrow.

"Are you okay?" I whisper.

He looks down the alley and nods as he wipes the blood from his lip. Stucco's phone rings and we look at each other. Panting, Stace bends and retrieves it from Stuccos pocket, he answers it, but doesn't say anything.

The voice on the other end is loud and clear. "Where are you, we're coming through town now."

Stace hits the end button and looks at me. "Run."

19

Roshelle

"WHAT?" I whisper.

"Run." He growls as he grabs my hand. We turn and run as fast as we can to the end of the alley and then stop still in the shadows as we peer around the corner and onto the street.

A cab is slowly coming down the road. "I'm going to try and get it." I glance at Stace and the blood running down his face. "Clean yourself up or he won't let you in."

"Yeah, okay," he murmurs as he takes his t-shirt off and begins to wipe the blood from his face. I run out onto the road and put my hands up in front of the cab. "Stop, please stop," I mouth in desperation.

The driver slows and I open the back door and jump in, I gesture a come here signal to Stace and he runs from the shadows and jumps in the back of the cab.

The cab driver frowns and turns to eye us suspiciously. "Is everything alright?" he asks.

"Yes, bar fight," Stace replies quickly. "Can you take us to the Marriot hotel please?"

He nods cynically and turns and pulls out into the traffic.

I frown. "The Marriot?" I mouth.

Stace shakes his head subtly and grabs my hand in his, the warmth of it instantly calming me. He then lies down and puts his head on my lap and I know it's so nobody can see he is in the cab. "Come down here and cuddle me," he says out loud.

He wants me out of sight, too. I lie down across his back and we stay silent for the rest of the trip until it comes to a halt. He pays the driver and we sheepishly get out of the cab. He grabs my hand and we walk across the road in the opposite direction and along the backstreets until another cab goes by and we flag it down. "Now we can go back to the hotel," he says softly as it comes to a halt. We climb into the backseat.

"The Bog Hotel, please."

"Yes," the driver responds, uninterested.

We drive a little way and Stace interrupts my thoughts.

"Can you let us out at the side street?"

"In this street here?" The driver gestures.

"Yes, please," Stace replies. The cab slows and we climb out again.

"What are we doing?" I whisper.

"We will go in through the parking lot. I don't want anyone seeing me like this."

I turn to look at him and he's right, his face is a mess. "Shit, are you okay?" I frown.

"Yeah, that fucker laying the boot in didn't help."

I run my hands through my hair as my apprehension rises.

"Oh God, Stace. What are we going to do?"

"Let's just get to the room safely."

"What if they know we're staying here?" I whisper as we walk down the ramp to the underground parking lot.

Stace slides his key into the scanner and the security doors slowly rise.

"Then we're fucked."

I shake my head as my nerves start to really thump. We walk through the darkened parking lot as we both scan our surroundings. This could be the perfect place to murder us. "This doesn't feel safe," I whisper.

"It's not."

I screw up my face. "Can't you lie and pretend we are safe?"

He shakes his head and keeps walking. "No." We get into the elevator and push the button for our floor. "Give me the gun."

"Why?" I fumble through my bag. "What do you think is going to happen?" My eyes widen. "Do you think they are going to be up here?"

Oh God, shit just keeps getting worse and worse.

He shrugs as he pulls the gun open to check the ammunition, and then he turns to me. His eyes scan my face and he smirks.

"What?" I ask.

He grabs my hair and straightens it. "Your hair is on crooked."

I instantly grab the wig and straighten it up. "That's the least of my fucking problems," I whisper.

The elevator comes to a halt and Stace tucks the gun in the back of his jeans and we slowly exit into the hall. Looking both ways down the long and scary corridor, we walk quietly to our room, and when we get to our door Stace puts his finger up to his lip to order my silence. He then points to the other side of the hallway. "Wait over there," he mouths.

Oh God, he thinks they are in the room. I take my place over at the far wall and he swipes the key card and opens the door. He peers in as I hold my breath. The room is dark and silent.

Are they in there?

He waits for a moment and then he disappears into the darkness.

"Please don't be in there, please don't be in there," I whisper again and again.

He turns on the light and then checks the room and comes back to the door. "The coast is clear."

I let out a deep breath and walk into the room before he closes the door behind me. We stand still for a moment looking at each other as we process what just happened.

"We are going to have to stay here for the night." He sighs. "Try and get some sleep."

"Are we safe?"

He shrugs. "Safer than we are out there."

It's at this time I get a good look at his face and I think that guy has kicked his cheekbone in. One half of his face is swollen. "Stace." I frown as I put my hand up to his face. "Your cheekbone is broken."

"It's fine." He winces as I touch it.

"We need some ice," I murmur. I think for a moment and then pick up the phone and call reception.

"Hello, room service," the bored operator answers.

I fake a calm voice. "Can I please get a bottle of champagne and a bucket of ice brought up to our room, please?" I glance at the clock. It's 3am. God, what must they think?

"Yes, of course."

"Thank you."

I walk Stace into the bathroom and sit him on the side of the bath and he winces. A deep cut is above his right eye and is still trickling blood, but it's his left cheekbone that I am worried about. I wet a cloth and start to clean him up and he sits and watches me.

"You okay?" I ask as I wipe his forehead and push his hair back to look at him. "You're very quiet. Are you really hurt?"

He nods and rolls his lips as if he wants to say something but is holding it in.

"What?" I ask. "What is it?"

He shrugs. "I just wonder why you are so worried about a little blood when you are the only one…" He stops himself midsentence.

"The only one that what?"

"Nothing." He grabs the cloth from me and stands and walks back out into the room.

I follow him. "Say it. Just say it." I hold my arms open. "I want you to tell me what you were going to say."

He turns angrily. "You are the only person who hurt me today." My heart skips a beat. He shakes his head. "And it fucking pisses me off that you have the ability to do that."

I don't know what to say.

"Stace," I whisper softly. "I am sorry for not asking you if you took them, but what was I supposed to think?"

"That I wouldn't steal from you," he barks angrily. "Why do you tell me you love me when you obviously think so little of my character?"

"I do love you," I murmur.

"Well, you know what I don't love?" he sneers angrily.

My heart drops. "Me?" I whisper.

"Being made to feel like a piece of shit."

"I never said that," I fire back.

"Yes, you did."

"When?"

"When you put me in the same category as your ex-boyfriends and your father."

My eyes tear up, because he's right on target. That's exactly what I did today. "I'm sorry," I whisper.

A knock bangs at the door. "Room service," The waiter calls. I look through the peephole and see him standing with our champagne and ice. Stace walks back into the bathroom frustrated that we have been interrupted, I blow out a deep sigh as I open the door. "Thank you," I murmur as I take the tray from him and lock the two deadlocks as he leaves.

I wrap a handful of ice in my t-shirt and walk back into the bathroom where I find Stace now in the shower, his back to me as he soaps his body up. I take off my clothes and get into the shower and hold him from behind. I wrap my arms around his large body and squeeze him tight. I press my face on his back and the water that runs down the drain is a shade of pink, tinged with blood. We stay silent for a long time, both lost in our own thoughts.

"I'm not an easy person to be with, Stace," I murmur.

He stays silent.

A large lump forms in my throat. "I understand if you don't want to fight for us. I'm damaged goods. I couldn't be with me."

He turns to face me. "Don't say that," he whispers.

"It's true." I shrug sadly. "I have more baggage than a 747."

He pushes the hair back from my forehead and then, with his finger under my chin, lifts my face to meet his. "You're my damaged goods."

My eyes tear up at the words I so desperately needed to hear and he kisses me softly. "I have fallen in love with you, Rosh," he whispers against my lips.

"You have?" I whisper in hope.

He kisses me again. "It's annoying really." I smirk.

"Annoying?"

"Well, right now my face is a mess and I should be making an escape plan, but the only thing that is on my mind is being inside my girl." He grabs my behind and drags me across his hard body.

I smile, wrap my arms around his neck, and I kiss him.

Oh, I love this man. He knows me. He knows how fucked up I am and he is willing to try. Our kiss deepens and he really starts to grind me against the tiles.

"I'm sorry for today. I was so hurt, I couldn't see straight," I murmur.

He lifts me and wraps my legs around his waist and holds me up against the tiles. I can feel his tip at my opening.

"I'm not going to hurt you." He growls.

He brings my body hard down onto his and I groan as I struggle to accept his size.

We stay silent, our eyes locked on each other, and he slowly lifts me and then brings me back down hard so that he hits the end of me. "Trust me and let me love you. Let me protect you," he whispers.

I nod, unable to speak as his body takes full possession of mine.

"Because I fucking love you and I need you to survive this." Our kiss turns frantic and I can't see straight. He raises his arms to the tiles above my head and really starts to slam into me. The burn is so intense, I can feel every vein of his thick shaft. Every ripple of his muscle deep inside of me makes me crave more. I can't get enough. I will never get enough of the way he makes me feel, of the way he touches me. He stops suddenly and cups my face with his hand. The water runs down our faces and I feel like I can't breathe. Our eyes are locked on each other and with the way he is looking at me, it feels like anything is possible. His hand on my face is gentle, his eyes are filled with love, and yet my sex is throbbing from the beating it is taking.

This is love... Stace style.

———

"So, you know the plan?" Stace asks me for the tenth time as he sits on the end of the bed watching me.

"Yes," I reply as I stuff my shoes into the overnight bag.

"Tell me what it is."

"I already told you."

"Tell me again."

I roll my eyes in frustration. "I walk into the bank, withdraw all of our money, and then I get into the waiting cab."

He nods. "Then what?"

"Then I catch the cab here and walk through reception as a decoy and get into the lift, but instead of coming up to the room, I go straight to the basement and get in the car with you and we leave."

"But I am following you to the bank in case anything happens."

"Nothing is going to happen. They were searching for us all night. They won't be up at the crack of dawn stalking banks."

"They might be."

"Will you please say the glass is half full for once instead of being so damn negative?"

"I'm realistic, not negative."

I roll my eyes as I continue packing. "Whatever," I mumble under my breath. Honestly, there is no use even arguing with him when he's like this. We have decided that if we want to really disappear, we need to fly to Vegas where Stace has another fake passport contact. Unfortunately, we need money to do this, and if we don't withdraw all the money now they will easily be able to trace where we go. The guy who made my last passport has obviously ratted us out. It's no coincidence that they found us. They have traced my bank card usage by matching it with my fake name.

"Are you sure that they don't know who you really are?" I ask.

"Positive. I have a house and everything set up in Mac's identity. They think that's me and my house and have no idea who I really am."

I shrug. "If you say so."

"What's that supposed to mean?"

"It means my father is an intelligent man. An evil, intelligent man and if he smells a rat he will find out your real identity as easy as pie."

"He won't."

I zip up my bag and Stace rings reception. "Hello, can you please tally up the bill and let me know the amount, please?" He waits for a moment. "Yes, of course." He waits again and then scribbles down an amount onto the notepad next to the phone. "Thank you. My wife will be down shortly to settle the bill. We are checking out this morning." He listens to the receptionist. "Yes, we have had a very pleasant stay." He smiles. "We'll be back."

I watch him and feel myself swoon. My wife. How I wish that were true. He hangs up and sits down on the bed. I sit on his lap and kiss him gently. "How's the face feeling?" I ask.

"Tight." He screws his face up and I touch his eyebrow gently. It's a dark shade of purple and his face is still swollen, the harsh bruising appearing. I can see a distinct shoe mark on his cheek.

"Tell me something," I say.

He kisses me, distracted by me being on his lap.

"Do you think my ring would be ready to pickup today?" I ask hopefully.

"No, not for another four days."

My heart drops. "Do you think we can—?"

"No, Rosh." He cuts me off. "We can't wait for it. We don't have time."

My face falls. "Oh." I sigh sadly.

"I will get you another one."

"When?"

He smirks. "When I can."

"When do you think that will be?"

"I don't know."

Hmm, I don't like that answer at all. I stay silent, still hoping to get my way.

He lifts me off his lap. "You ready to do this?"

I nod. "As ready as I'll ever be."

He picks up my wig and puts it on my head. He then passes me the fake glasses and I slide them on. "I hate this fucking wig," he mutters to himself as he adjusts it on my head.

"I thought fake blondes were your type." I smile sweetly as I remind him of Chelsea.

"Not ones with horse hair," he replies, distracted as he combs his fingers through it.

"Although horse heads are okay?" I tease.

A trace of a smirk crosses his face. "Do you need to be punished today?"

I smile broadly. "Probably."

———

The cab pulls to a halt. "So you will wait here?" I ask the driver.

"Yes."

I point to the road underneath us to make sure he understands me through the language barrier.

"Wait here?" I ask again.

He nods an over exaggerated nod. "Yes."

"Right here?"

He rolls his eyes in frustration. "Yes, miss, I wait here."

I nod quickly, embarrassed at my pushiness. "Okay, I will only be five minutes."

"Yes."

I glance left and then right. The coast seems clear. The black Ferrari is parked up the street across the other side of the road and I know my love is watching over me. Somehow, I feel even closer to him today. It's as if our huge fight last night has only brought us closer to one another. I blow out a steadying breath. Let's do this shit and get it over with. I slowly get out of the cab and walk into the bank. I take out my identification and slide it over the counter and the bank teller smiles warmly.

"Hello," she greets as she types my information into the computer.

"I would like to make a withdrawal, please?" I ask.

"Sure. How much would you like?"

I roll my lips. "Two hundred and twenty-seven thousand, please?"

She frowns. "Cash?"

I nod.

"Umm." She scratches her forehead. "Did you ring ahead and tell us you would be withdrawing this amount of money today?"

Panic starts to set in. I don't have time for this. "No, I shouldn't have to. It's my money. I would like it now, please," I demand nervously. Shit, why didn't I think of that?

She frowns. "I will have to see my manager."

I nod as my heart starts to beat hard. I turn and look out the window as she disappears.

Fuck.

I glance up and down the street nervously. I can't see anyone suspicious. She reappears. "That will be about fifteen minutes. Please take a seat in one of the offices." She smiles and gestures to an office to the left.

Shit.

I fake a smile and walk into the office. At least I am out of sight in here. I take out my phone and text Stace.

It's going to take about fifteen minutes

A text bounces back.

What the fuck?
We don't have time for this.

I roll my eyes and text back.

Feel free to come and rob the bank.
Because that will be so much quicker.

I turn and peer out the glass panel in the door to see if I can see anyone lurking around. I wonder where Stucco is this morning. My nerves rise to another level.

A text bounces back.

Don't tempt me!

I sit and bounce my foot up and down impatiently. Come on, come on. My phone beeps a text.

We got company

My eyes widen.

Who?

A text bounces back.

They are walking up the street, two men.
I recognize one of them from Vikinos' team.
Stay where you are.

I put my head into my hands. Oh no. This is a disaster. I text back.

What if the cab leaves?

A text bounces back.

Then we are screwed.
Tell them to hurry the fuck up!

I peer around the door jamb like a mouse and smile sweetly at the bank teller. "Excuse me, I have a plane to catch and I am in a really big hurry. How much longer will it be?"

"Of course, my apologies. Another teller is just cross checking it now. You are so lucky that we just had a delivery of cash this morning or we wouldn't have had that amount here for withdrawal."

Oh hell, that would have been a disaster. "Okay." I gesture back to the office. "I will just wait in here."

She fakes a smile.

I sit back down and text Stace.

I watch my phone as I wait for him to answer. I wait and wait.

What's he doing? Why is he not answering if he's sitting in a damn car? My mind goes to last night and how they broke his cheekbone. Cowardly bastards. Who kicks a man in the face at full force when he is fighting another man and has his hands full? I text again.

What's going on?
Answer me!

No reply. Oh God, this is fucking stressful. I start to perspire. I put my face into my hands. What if they have him? The windows are so black that you can't see inside the car... unless, they know what car we have hired. It is a possibility, a strong possibility. Shit.

The bank teller comes into the office with a large box and starts to unload the money onto the table and her assistant follows her with a note counting machine. They start to count the money out in front of me. I sit still pretending to watch, but my mind is far from money.

Where is he?

Why isn't he answering? I dial his number and it rings a few times.

"Hi," he answers, and my heart flips.

I fake a smile. "Why aren't you answering your phone, sweetie?" I act nice in front of the bank tellers when all I really want to do is scream at him for worrying me sick.

"Sorry, I took a call."

"Ha, what a time to take a call." I pretend to laugh.

"It was my mother," he snaps. "She was getting worried and I thought I may not be able to talk to her again for a while."

My heart drops. "Oh, fair point." I stand and walk away from the table. "What are we up to?" I speak in code.

"All good, the cab is still there. Walk out and get straight into it. Continue with the plan."

"Okay?" I ask hopefully.

"It's still okay, see you soon."

"Bye," I whisper through my dread.

I sit for another five minutes as they count the last of the cash and I load it into my small overnight bag. "Thank you." I smile as I sling the bag over my shoulder.

I push through the double glass doors and put my head down and go straight to the cab. "Hello, thank you for waiting. Back to the hotel, please."

"You took a long time. I nearly leave."

"I know, I'm so sorry. I will pay you extra." I glance through the back window and down the street in front of me. I can't see anyone suspicious. The cab pulls out into the traffic as my phone beeps another text.

> **They have seen you.**
> **Keep your head down and stick to the plan.**

I drop my head as fear starts to make me nauseous. Holy fuck.

I see the Ferrari pull out into the traffic and turn back towards the hotel. The cab comes to a stop at the hotel, and with shaky hands, I pay the driver and get out. I walk straight to the lift and push the button as planned.

The lift doesn't come. Why is it taking so long?

Hurry, please hurry. I watch the numbers above the doors and they are going so slow. I push the buttons again and glance outside to see a car pull up out on the street and two men get out. I push the up button on the lift and run into the fire stairs. I take two steps down at a time, nearly frantic. The bag of money is heavy and swinging around and hitting me as I run. I burst through the door at the bottom and see the black Ferrari sitting over by the lift where he is expecting me to come from. I run through the parked cars and open the door and dive into the seat.

"Go," I yell.

Stace revs the engine and we fly through the parking lot.

"Come on, faster," I yell. "We need to get out of here now."

20

Roshelle

WE FLY through the underground parking lot and up towards the exit ramp. Stace slides the parking ticket into the machine and the roller door slowly creeps up.

"Get down," he says as his eyes flick over to me.

I nod nervously and bend down over my knees as he drives the car out slowly. "This car was probably a good idea after all."

He turns out of the driveway and onto the street as I watch him from my crumpled hunched position. "They aren't expecting us to have money. They won't be looking for this kind of car," he replies as he drives down the street.

"Can you see anyone?" I whisper.

His eyes flicker up to the rear view mirror. "No." He pauses. "They are still inside the hotel."

"Do you think they know that we have the diamonds?" I ask.

"I doubt it," he replies as he reaches over and pulls the wig from my head and throws it onto the floor. "The ship is still at sea. Nobody would even know they are gone yet."

We drive for a while longer in silence and his eyes continuously flash to the mirrors to check if anyone is following us.

"See anything?" I ask again.

"No, it's okay." He reaches over and rubs my back and I blow out a breath and shake my head.

"I-I didn't think the bank was going to give me the money," I stammer.

"What happened?" he asks.

"They were just taking so long and I was freaking out. I thought they had called someone to let them know I was there."

"But you got it?"

"Yep, it's in the bag."

He smiles sexily. "Good girl."

"Stace." My eyes search his from my hunched down position. "What are we doing? What are we going to do?"

He blows out a deep breath and pauses as if thinking. "At this stage, trying to not be found is the main priority. We're not safe until we have new passports and can go in between countries without being detected."

"Can we go to Sweden? They won't find us in Sweden." I have always had it in my head that I will be safe in Sweden. I don't know why but I just do.

He smiles sadly as he takes my hand in his. "We will go somewhere. It's going to be okay, Rosh. I got you."

I nod and bring his hand to my face and kiss the back of it.

"Thank you," I whisper.

"For what?"

"For helping me."

His eyes meet mine and for a split second his mask slips and I see fear. My face falls, and as if knowing what he has just revealed, he lifts them and concentrates back on the road and to the rear view mirrors.

He thinks they are going to get us.

We drive for fifteen minutes out of the city in silence until finally he speaks. "You can sit up now. Nobody is following us." I unfold my body from its hunched position.

I stare out the window as my mind goes to my mother and the horror she went through. I can't stand the thought of him having the same fate. I won't allow it.

"Stace?" I hesitate as I try to get my wording right. "If they do catch up with us..."

"Yes."

"I want you to run. Don't try and save me because you will die. Look what they did to you the other night? I need to know that you won't try and be Captain America."

His eyes stay fixed on the road. "I won't let anything happen to you, Rosh," he murmurs.

"Yes, but..."

"Stop it!" he yells, cutting me off. "I'm here till the fucking end. Get that shit out of your head right now. I'm not leaving."

"I don't want anything to hurt you."

His eyes snap to me angrily. "It's a little too late for that. Do you think it wouldn't fucking hurt me if they got you? I'm saving you for me as well as you!"

A lump forms in my throat. I just want this to be over with.

I don't know how much more I can take of this running. All of my adult life I have been on the run. Now I'm scared and I'm so damn drained. I don't know what to say. I have no words. No words that will undo the last week. I had it, I had escaped with a fake passport and then I went and ruined it when I went on that damn shooting spree. But then Stace would probably be dead now if I hadn't.

I did the right thing. I just wish I killed the right man.

I blow out a deep breath as my eyes wander back out the window. If I'd killed the right man our troubles would be over.

———

I feel the soft touch of his hand swipe the hair back from my face. "We're here, babe."

I struggle to open my eyes and readjust myself in the uncomfortable car seat. "This car is shit." I scowl.

He smiles sexily. "It's pretty good to drive." He revs the engine as he throws me a sexy wink to show me just how much he loves it.

"What time is it?" I yawn.

"About 8pm."

"Are we stopping here for the night?" I ask. "Yes, we will find somewhere to stay."

I smile and lean over and kiss the side of his face. "Thanks for letting me sleep," I whisper into his strong face.

He turns and kisses me gently on the lips. "I have an ulterior motive. I need you to stay awake tonight."

"Why is that?" I ask.

"Because I need to relax."

"And?"

"And I need you to suck my dick." He kisses my fingertips. "Among other things."

I smirk. "I'm your relaxant, your all night sucker?"

His dark eyes hold mine and he nods.

"That could be arranged I suppose." I hesitate. "What's in it for me?"

He grabs my hand and places it over his crotch and I feel

the hard steel beneath it. I feel my insides start to pulse. He's as horny as hell. Fuck, I love this man.

"What have you been thinking about while I have been sleeping?" I smirk.

"You." His eyes flicker over to me. "You on me. Me on you." I smile broadly. He knows exactly what I need when I need it.

We pull into a swanky looking hotel and the luggage men all swoon at the car. I smile as I watch their reaction. It's so much fun having money. The bellboy opens the car door and Stace climbs out.

"Do you have any rooms for tonight?" he asks.

"Yes, sir."

He leans back into the car. "This will do. Out you get."

I nod as he opens the trunk, retrieves our bags, and I climb out. "Do you have any money in your wallet?" I ask.

"Yes, I think so." He quickly opens his wallet and checks. "All good."

He passes the keys to the bellboy and the young man's eyes widen in excitement. It's not every day you get to park a Ferrari.

"Be careful with it," Stace tells him.

"Yes, of course, sir."

We walk through the lobby and up to reception where the three girls behind all take a double take at my beautiful companion. Wearing tight black jeans and a white t-shirt that hugs every muscle, he is looking mighty fine, even if he does have a banged up face. "I would like a room tonight, please," he tells them.

The beautiful brunette smiles nervously and begins to type.

"Yes, of course, sir." Her eyes linger on his face.

"He's a boxer." I interrupt. "His face is bruised from fighting."

"Oh." Her eyes flicker to me and she seems embarrassed

that she forgot that I was here. Stupid bitch. What is it with slutty reception chicks?

"What kind of room would you like?" she asks. "We have an executive suite, a terrace room, a master suite, or a penthouse."

"The penthouse, please," he replies without thinking. He looks at me and I smile. What an amazing life this would be? Being married to him, crazy rich without a care. We could travel the world. There isn't a thing we couldn't do. For a moment, I let myself imagine what it would be like and I smile stupidly.

It takes about fifteen minutes to check in and head up to find room 2102.

He swipes the key into the reader and the double doors open. We are hit in the face with exuberant luxury. There's a large lounge room with a mini grand piano and three luxurious leather lounges. Another sitting room branches off to the right, it has two large, wingback chairs and ottomans. The back wall of the sitting room is lined with bookcases that are filled with beautiful books. The bedroom is to the left and a huge king-sized bed sits in the centre. The whole back wall of the bedroom is glass that overlooks the gorgeous city where the lights twinkle down below. A marble bathroom and walk in wardrobe veer off to the left. "Wow," I murmur as I walk in slowly. "This is..." My voice trails off. I don't even have words for this.

Stace takes me in his arms. "Only the best for my wife." He kisses me, his lips are strong and soft, and tonight I can feel the want in them as they linger over mine. He stares down at me and he pushes the hair back from my face. "You okay?" he asks softly as his eyes search mine.

I nod with a fake smile and pull out of his arms. Don't ask me that because in all honesty, I just don't know. "Yes," I lie.

"You haven't eaten much today."

I blow out a breath as I throw my bag up onto the bed to get some fresh clothes out. "Not really that hungry," I murmur.

"Let's go out for dinner."

I frown as I look over at him "Is it safe?"

He shrugs. "Who cares?" He grabs both my hands in his. "We are living each day like it's our last, remember?"

I really needed to hear that. "You always know just what to say."

His eyes hold mine as he tucks a piece of hair behind my ear. "I love you."

My stomach drops, realizing that's the first time he has ever just said it openly and honestly, without thought. "You do?"

He takes me in his arms and kisses my forehead. "Why do you sound surprised?"

"I'm not…" I pause. "I just…" I stop myself.

"You just what?" He frowns.

I stare at a painting on the wall over his shoulder so I don't have to look him in the eye. I have been thinking about this all day. He is safer without me. "I just don't know if I'm good for you. Maybe we should separate."

"Look at me."

I keep staring at the painting as I try my hardest to show no emotion.

"Fucking look at me."

I drag my eyes to his.

"I want to live in the moment. Right now."

"Was the engagement ring…?" My voice trails off because I'm not sure if I want to know the answer.

He cuts me off. "I got an engagement ring because I wanted to live in the moment."

"But would you have bought it for me if we were under normal circumstances?" I ask.

"If I felt this way about you in normal circumstances, yes."

"Stace," I whisper.

"If I planned out my perfect life tonight, you would be in it. I know this seems fast, but we have been together and alone every day for a month. I feel like I have known you for forever. I've never..." His voice trails off.

I smile softly, that's how I feel. "Is this real between us?" I shake my head and step back from him. "How can we fall in love under these circumstances?"

"I don't know."

"So you are having trouble believing this as well?" I ask.

He nods subtly. "I am."

My eyes search his. "I don't know how to let myself believe it."

I see the moment a thought crosses his mind. "Are you doubting your feelings? Is this what this is about?"

I stare at him as a clusterfuck of emotions swirl through my brain. I should end this. I should make him leave me so I know he is safe.

"No," I reply on autopilot.

"No, you don't believe this or no you don't doubt your feelings?" He steps back from me to distance himself.

"Stace..." I hesitate as I try to get my words together. "I love you, you make me feel like I never have before, but I worry." I touch his eyebrow and he flinches. "Look what they did to you to try and get to me."

"I'm fine."

"This time. You're fine, this time."

He wraps his arm around me and holds me tight. "I'm fine as long as I am with you." He gently kisses my forehead.

I feel the ice start to melt from around my heart.

"You know what I want to do?" He smiles into my forehead.

"What?"

"I want to take my girlfriend on a date."

"Girlfriend?" I smile.

He nods as he widens his eyes. "Sounds weird, doesn't it?"

I shrug. "I could get used to it I suppose."

He puts his finger under my chin bringing my face to meet his. "Stop over thinking. Let's just get through each day and get our new passports, then disappear and start again."

He kisses me softly, and then again harder. His lips part and he slides his tongue slowly into my mouth. His hand cups the back of my head as he holds me the way that he wants me. "Put your date dress on and blow my mind like you did on our first date."

I smile. "I blew your mind?"

"Like an atom bomb. I went crazy back on the ship knowing that I wouldn't see you again. That was the first time..." He stops himself.

"The first time what?" I ask.

"That was the first time that I knew we were more," he whispers against my lips.

I smile as his lips take mine. "Then I knew before you," I whisper.

"I know." He kisses me again. "I'm slow at these things." Our kiss turns deeper and I begin to feel the heat between my legs. "When did you know?"

"When you remembered my lifeline. Actually, it was earlier than that." I correct myself. "It was when I got hurt that you slept with Chelsea."

"I didn't sleep with Chelsea. I haven't touched another woman since I met you."

My eyes search his.

"Maybe I knew the night I met you," he whispers. "I believe we were meant to meet."

I smile. "If it's okay with you, I'm going to stick with the first date where you asked my father if you could take me on a date as our meeting story."

He grabs my behind and drags me over his hard cock. "You're going to leave out the kidnapping bit when we tell the kids?" His lips drop to my neck and he nips me with his teeth.

I laugh out loud. "You want kids?"

"Yes, I want fucking kids." He picks me up and throws me onto the bed and I bounce with a laugh. He crawls up over me and rests on his elbow as he looks down at me. We fall serious suddenly.

"What kind of father will you be?" I ask.

"The kind that protects their mother." He bends and kisses me tenderly as his hand slides up my leg, underneath my dress, and finds that spot between my legs. He circles and then slides beneath my panties and slips his two index fingers into my sex.

"Oh, God," I whisper as my legs part without permission.

His fingers slowly pump in and out, and I clench to give him a taste of what's to come.

He inhales sharply. "I can make you happy," he whispers as his eyes hold mine. He picks up the pace and the sound of my arousal hangs in the air. "I can make your children happy." He lifts my top leg over his body to spread me more.

My eyes tear up. I have never heard anything so beautiful in my life.

This is all I want. All I will ever want. "Promise me we can make this work, Stace," I whisper as I put my hand onto his forearm and feel it flex as he pumps me with it. He stretches me as he adds another finger and we both groan in pleasure. "I don't care about money. I just want to be with you. I just want a future with you." He picks up the pace and his hand becomes almost violent as the bed starts to hit the wall.

"You have it." We kiss again and I think it is the most heart felt kiss he has ever gifted me with. "I've never felt this close to anyone," he murmurs.

"I'm so in love with you," I whisper as my body quivers on the edge of orgasm.

Suddenly desperate, he stands and rips his shirt over his shoulders and slides his jeans down his legs. I am blessed with the sight of his large cock hanging heavily between his legs. Pre-ejaculate drips from the head, and I can see the veins that run down its thick length. He pumps it three times to give himself some kind of release. I reach up and brush my fingers over my lips that are branded to his side. I'm still in awe that he did that.

His beautiful, brown eyes hold mine as he crawls over my body and nudges my opening with his cock. He keeps me waiting as he slides it back and forth through my wet sex. We both smile in pleasure and I know it is taking all of his resistance not to slide straight in.

He leans back onto his knees and spreads my legs. His eyes drop down over my sex and then back up to my eyes as he thinks.

"What?" I smile softly.

He lies over me and kisses me softly. "Marry me."

Our eyes lock as he slowly slides in. My body struggles to take his size and he levers himself from side to side to loosen me up. "Oh... God," I whisper.

"He's not going to help you take this cock, baby." He groans through his pleasure.

I laugh against his lips as he slams me and tears through my flesh. He pulls out and slides back into me, forcing me to cry out. He pumps me again and it knocks the wind from my lungs.

Oh, my man's in the mood to fuck hard. He grabs my legs and holds them up over his shoulders, and then with straightened arms, puts his hands above my shoulders to give himself leverage.

In. Out. Slam, and oh so fucking good. His eyes hold mine and it's almost too much. This intensity is nearly too much to cope with.

The bed is hitting the wall hard as he really lets me have it.

"You feel so good. Fuck me. Fuck me hard." He growls as the perspiration sheens his skin.

I clench as hard as I can, his eyes close, and he groans deeply.

He leans down to kiss me and we are like animals with each other. Both taking what our own body needs from the other. I hold him tight to me, and in all honesty, the world could end right now and I wouldn't care.

"Come," he demands as he pumps.

"More," I cry. "I want fucking more of you."

He picks up the pace and I scream out as I am hit like a truck with an orgasm, but before I have time to react, he pulls out and shoots semen across my stomach. His head tips back to the ceiling and his mouth hangs slack as he empties his body onto mine.

We both scramble for air and then he sits up onto his knees between my open legs and slides his three fingers back into my sex. He slowly strokes me as his other hand rubs his semen over my stomach and breasts. It feels so intimate having his fingers back inside me so quickly and his semen all over my skin.

His eyes hold mine and I know I am going to get him again. I'm going to get him again. I'm going to get him forever. "Kiss me," I whisper.

"Marry me," he replies as his fingers slide in and out.

"Why?" I whisper.

"Because I need this every day. Because you are the only person I want to do this with." He frowns as if thinking of something else. "You make me want to be better and I need you."

He brings his fingers up and sucks them and I feel my arousal start to pump heavily. I'm swollen and wet, and hell, I want him again.

"Answer me." He growls as he crawls over me.

"Yes," I whisper as I curl my arms around his broad back. "Yes, I will marry you."

He kisses me tenderly and with the feel of his smile against my lips, I am lost.

Stace

I hear the shower turn on and then wait for Rosh to get under the water. I shuffle through my bag for the crumpled piece of paper. After finally locating it, I dial the number I have scribbled down.

Ring, ring.

"Hello," Chris answers.

"Hey, it's me."

"Hi. I've been thinking. What do you need this for?"

"Long story." I sigh.

"I got time."

"I don't. Have you got it or not?"

"Stace, what the fuck have you got yourself into?" He sighs.

I blow out a deep breath. "I just need someone reliable who can get the job done."

"This guy is FBI."

"Does he miss?"

"Never. He is only one of four who does jobs on the side."

I think for a moment. "How trustworthy is he?"

"He works for Uncle Sam. He's the best of the best."

"So, how do I do this?" I ask.

"You call this number and they put it into the system anonymously and then they all bid for the job."

"Okay." I roll my lips as I walk to the window and pull the curtain back to peer out into the darkness. My mind is racing, but I have been thinking about this all day. I know it's the only way.

"Are you going to do it?" he asks.

"I have no choice."

"Are you sure?"

"Positive."

"You could spend your life in jail."

"It will be worth it."

"Okay, man, it's your funeral. Call me when you can."

"Thank you. Goodbye."

I hang up and dial the number as my heart hammers in my chest.

"Hello," the male voice answers.

"I would like to post a job, please."

"Yes. How much are you paying?"

I pause as I try to reign in my nerves. "Thirty million dollars."

Silence falls over the line. "Who is it?" he finally asks, knowing it's someone big.

"I want two snipers and they will receive fifteen million each, twenty-four hours after his confirmed death."

"Who is it?" he asks again.

"Mario Vikinos."

21

Stace

ROSHELLE SITS with her hands linked under her chin. Her big, brown eyes look across the table at me lovingly and I feel my chest constrict. She is, without a doubt, the most beautiful woman

I have ever known. Every day I fall deeper under her spell.

I smirk to myself, wondering how the hell I got so lucky to cross her path.

"What?" She smiles.

I shake my head. "Nothing."

"Why are you looking at me like that?"

"Like what?"

She shrugs as she picks up her wine and sips it as she thinks of a fitting answer.

"Like I want to eat you?" I ask with a raised brow.

A broad smile crosses her face. She slips her shoe off and

lifts her foot so that it sits on my crotch. I reach down and tenderly place my hand over it.

"Do you?" She wiggles her toes and I squeeze her foot in my hand.

"That's a given. You are my staple diet these days."

She giggles into her wine glass. I pick up my beer and sip it. We are in the restaurant of the hotel and it's about 10pm.

"This is a beautiful hotel, isn't it?" she asks.

"Yes," I murmur as I look around at our surroundings. "Stace."

My eyes flicker back to her.

"Let's do this. Let's get away with it." She widens her eyes hopefully. "We could be so happy together if we can just get out of this mess."

I smile and pick up her hand across the table.

"That's the plan." I open my mouth to tell her that I have ordered the hit, but I quickly close it. I don't want to give her false hope when I'm really not sure if it's going to happen. She doesn't need a false sense of security. I know she won't care about the money I've offered if he's dead, but we will cross that bridge when we get to it... and I sincerely hope we do.

"I was thinking that maybe we should try to get a flight to Vegas from here tomorrow," I add.

She frowns into her wine glass. "I thought you said we were going to Chile to fly out?"

I nod as I sip my beer. "It's a long way from here and it means a lot more time on the road and out in the open."

She bites her thumbnail as she thinks. "You think it's more dangerous to stay here?" I nod.

"Can we charter a plane from here?" she asks.

"I did some research tonight while you were in the shower, and

I think it will be easier to be picked up if we do that."

She frowns. "So you think we just catch a commercial flight?"

"I think so."

"But won't they be able to find us?"

I shrug. "We will buy the tickets in the airport at the last minute with cash. The international passport website is a lot harder to hack and it may give us some time. I'm assuming, up until this point, they were tracking our credit card."

"But what if they do track us and are waiting at the other end?"

My eyes hold hers. "It's a possibility."

She rubs her forehead with both hands as she thinks. "Stace, I don't like this."

I grab her hand over the table. "I know, baby, but it's going to be harder for them to take you from an international airport than it is from a deserted country road in South America."

Her eyes rise to meet mine.

"I feel like I need to get you back on American soil."

"Why?" she whispers.

"I just do. We have no contacts over here and the police don't know your circumstances. Hell, the police are probably on his payroll. I don't know the dynamics of this country and it makes me fucking nervous."

She closes her eyes as she grapples with the concept.

"Do you get where I am coming from?" I ask.

"I suppose." She sighs as she looks off into the distance.

"Hey." I squeeze her hand. "Look at me." She drags her

eyes to meet mine. "It will be okay. We will get the passports and disappear."

"Promise?"

I hold my glass up and clink it with hers. "On my life."

The sound of Rosh's breathing is comforting. She's fast asleep on my chest and tucked safely under my arm. Every night, around this time, is when the dark thoughts creep in. I start to worry, just after she has drifted off to sleep before me. I rub my cheek back and forth over the top of her head as I think. She nestles closer and kisses my chest in her sleep.

I've never had this before. I've never felt so contented, so connected to one person. My mind goes back to Mandy, my childhood sweetheart, and a heavy sense of regret fills me.

I haven't let myself think of her much over the years. I guess I've always been too disappointed in myself to let my mind go there. I loved her. I loved her so much, and yet on trips away I would sleep with other woman at different ports around the world.

Why?

I think back and I can remember how aroused I was all the time and how badly I needed the touch of a woman when I was away... any woman. Why didn't I just break up with her? I think on it for a moment. It was because when I went home she was the only woman I wanted in my bed. She was the only one I wanted to talk to. It went on like that for a while. I would go away for six weeks and be home for six weeks. In the end it was the guilt I felt when I looked in her eyes that brought me undone. I wonder if I hadn't finally 'fessed up, would we have married? Would I have gotten over the young and stupid stage, or was there something lacking in our relationship that made me do it?

She would have done anything for me, and I for her. Except the obvious: Loyalty.

I couldn't do that.

She moved on quickly and was dating within a year, hooking up with a nice stable guy. She married him and they have two small children now.

I don't think I ever recovered.

I've never let myself get close to anyone since. I never want to cause anyone that hurt again. My mind goes to the moment I told her I had slept with someone else and the haunted look on her face. She didn't believe me at first, and then her heart broke as she wept on the bed as I sat helplessly at her feet.

I will never forget it as long as I live.

I get a lump in my throat still, seven years later. Along with my brother's death, it is the most painful memory I have, and I caused it for both of us. I gently kiss Rosh's forehead as she throws her top leg over mine. And now I have this woman. I'm head over heels in love with her, and yet we only met because I kidnapped her.

What kind of man have I turned into? My brother would be so ashamed.

I lie for half an hour in the dark staring at the ceiling as I go over and over all the mistakes I have made. My lips rest on her forehead.

For some reason I need to physically touch her or I can't relax. Why do I feel so different about Rosh? Why is this love incomparable to anything I have felt before? I feel like an out of control schoolboy who would die on the sword for his all consuming first love.

The thought of being with someone else turns my stomach.

She's strong, crazy, unpredictable, and yet vulnerable like a child. I feel like, with her, I need to be the adult in the relationship. The urge to protect her is almost primal and I've never experienced anything like it before. Sexually, she blows my mind. Mentally, she constantly challenges me, and yet I know that she would leave me in a heartbeat if she thought it was for the best.

Her strength scares the hell out of me, partly because I know I can't control it. The first woman I can't control and she's learned how to detach herself if she needs to. What if she walks away from me to save my life?

Or worse.

What if she dies?

I couldn't bear it. I can't bear the thought of living without her.

I squeeze her that little bit tighter in my arms and I know it's going to be another long night in the dark alone. I'm certain that if nobody accepts the job to kill Vikinos, it will be one of our last together.

They are closing in.

We are running out of time.

Roshelle

Stace sits at the other end of the row of seats opposite me. My eyes meet his and he snaps them away. I am wearing jeans with a large black hoodie, and a red wig that is plaited down my back with a baseball cap shielding my face—another disguise. We are at the airport and, true to Stace form, he is being super careful and won't even let us look at each other. He's edgy. We had to leave the guns. This is the first time since it all happened that we have been completely unprotected, but we have no choice if we want to board an airplane. He is on his phone and I know he is searching to see if there are still flights available on the next plane to Vegas. The plane starts boarding in an hour. We only have half an hour to get on if we are going to make it. What is he waiting for?

I text him.

You need to get the tickets or
they are going to close the flight.

He reads it and then runs his hand through his hair in frustration and texts back.

Five more minutes.

For God's sake. I text back.

Stop procrastinating and just fucking do it!

His eyes flicker up and he raises a sarcastic brow. I smirk and drop my head. He doesn't like me telling him what to do, but that's too bad. He needs to get us on this flight. He waits for a few minutes and then stands and goes to the counter with our two passports. I go and stand behind him in the line as if I don't know him.

"Two tickets to Vegas, please." He shuffles around in his bag and gets out our two identifications. "Seated separately, please."

The stewardess frowns as she types in her computer. This could be a disaster. If we can't get on the plane, then we have alerted them to where we are for nothing.

I hold my breath as we wait for her answer.

"The next flight is boarding in forty minutes, but you have missed the luggage."

"We only have carry on."

She glances to the two small bags we have with us. "Oh, okay. I can get you on that one then, if you want."

"Yes, please."

Relieved, I glance around at our surroundings. Life on the run isn't as fun as you would imagine. I feel fifty.

He gets the ticket and leaves mine on the counter to collect, then he goes to walk in the doors and I walk up to the counter as a decoy. "Excuse me?" I ask the stewardess as I slide my ticket off the counter. "Do you mind me asking where you got that watch from?" I ask.

"Oh, it's nice isn't it?" She smiles.

I glance over at Stace as he disappears into the early check in lounge.

"Harrods in London," she replies.

"Great, thank you," I call as I take off after my love. That was so rude, but I don't really want to know where she got her crappy watch. I walk through the check in gates and hold my breath as I walk through the scanners. Our five diamonds are scattered around the bottom of my bag with a handful of beads as if they are junk jewellery and the plan is, if I get picked up, to say that they were in a costume jewellery necklace I had bought. They wave me through and I see a trace of a smile cross Stace's face as he slowly waits for them to check his bag in front of me. Happy with the result, he turns and walks in, and I follow and sit down two seats down from him. I take out my phone and text him.

Can we sit together now?

He texts back.

You know we can't.

I blow out a frustrated breath and he looks over at me before he texts again.

You can sit on me when we get home.

I frown as I read his text and reply.

Where is home?

A text bounces back.

Wherever you are, is my home

I smile, and for some stupid reason I tear up. I reply.

I love you.

I watch him smile as he reads it and texts back.

I love you more xx

I tuck my phone into my backpack and clasp my hands in my lap and smile to myself. Not long now. We are nearly there.

"Cabin crew, prepare for landing," the captain's voice echoes through the cabin. The flight has been long and uneventful. I am looking forward to getting Stace alone. It seems ridiculous that I could miss him after not being able to sit with him on the flight. I turn in my seat to look back at him. He is seated four rows behind me with three guys. They seem to be getting along famously and I have sporadically heard them laugh as they talk. Better than my damn trip. I'm sitting next to an old lady who had five strong drinks and then went to sleep and snored the whole damn way. It annoys me that I depend on him so much. For a month now, it has just been him and me.We haven't had anyone with us, no family network. I think that's why it feels so intense. Our life together isn't reality... although it is for me, I've always been kind of alone. I just hope that when we get out of this mess we work out, I can't see how it won't. We are crazy about each other. I wait for the lights to go on and I immediately take my phone off airplane mode. I text.

Nice flight?

A text bounces back.

Yes, you?

I smile.

Dull.

The plane slowly travels down the runway to our destination and with it my nerves begin to rise, they could be here waiting for us in the airport. A text comes through.

You know the plan?

I text back.

Yes.

I love you X

A text immediately pings.

Tell me the plan.

Fuck's sake.

The plan is I'm going to kill you
if you don't stop making me repeat the plans

A ping sounds as the woman next to me struggles around in the overhead.

Don't make me come up there. Tell me what the fucking plan is!

I blow out a breath and shake my head. This man is infuriating, I'm not a child and I'm bloody nervous, too.

I walk out and go straight into the
ladies restroom and wait for your okay.

"Do you want me to get your bag?" The lady asks me.
"No, I got it, thanks." Why is everyone treating me like a damn baby?

Good girl.
Wait for my instruction. xx

The plane comes to a slow halt and I shuffle through the line to exit the plane. Funnily enough, the walk up the makeshift corridor into the airport is the longest walk I think I have ever done. My mind is racing. What if they're out there waiting? What if they just shoot me on sight in front of everyone? No, that won't happen. What if the police are here and arrest Stace? Does anyone even know we are here? I could be worrying for nothing. I try to calm myself down knowing this is not helping me act casual. Don't be stupid, they won't shoot us, of course they won't. Stace said I'm safe in the airport. Hell, maybe I should just live here forever? My stomach is churning, I'm starving and tired, and I don't bloody need this shit. We just have to get through customs now and hopefully everything will be fine. Stace has the money strapped around his body and if he does happen to get searched we are totally screwed. It was the only way to get it into the country, and seeing I am carrying millions of dollars in stolen diamonds in my handbag, it was unfortunately left up to him. Thank God sniffer dogs don't pick up cash. Our eyes meet as we wait in line to get through customs and he looks away. He's nervous.

I'm nervous.

He's in the line in front of me and I stand and flick through my phone as if I haven't a care in the world. Oh, how I wish that was true.

Stace gets his passport stamped and then goes through the walk through scanner machine. I stuff my hands in my pockets to hide how much they are shaking.

Please wave him through. Please, please, please.

The guard calls him over to the side and my heart starts to hammer.

Shit.

Stace stands with his arms lifted as they run the scanner up and down his body, and then he turns and they go down the back of him. He must be so nervous because I am nearly beside myself here. A little girl in the line in front of us suddenly projectile vomits and chaos erupts. The guard looks over and with a roll of his eyes, he waves Stace through the gates. The next man is ushered through quickly as the staff scramble to get a mop and bucket, and then it is my turn.

The woman ushers me over and I walk through the scanner unnoticed. In a fleeting moment, I glance up to see Stace picking up his bag. His eyes meet mine before he looks away. Right, I need to get to the bathroom and quick.

I walk to the bathroom as I see Stace drop into a seat at the back of the lounge area. He is going to sit and check that nobody is here to find us, and from that position, he will be able to see everything around us once the crowd dies down. I walk into the bathroom stall and drop the lid, nearly falling onto it with relief. I'm sweating profusely. This is no good for my heart. I send him a text.

Are you okay?

An answer bounces back.

Yeah, babe, you?

I puff air into my cheeks as I type.

Can you see anyone?

He answers.

The coast seems clear.
Wait for a ten minutes and then walk straight out and get into a cab
to the Venetian.
I will be right behind you in another cab.

I smile because maybe we can get away unnoticed. I text back.

If something happens... Don't come after me

I take out my hairbrush and re-comb this stupid, itchy wig as my heart bangs heavily in my chest. God, I hate this shit. He answers.

I will see you at the hotel in the foyer.
We can have a hot bath and
order room service tonight.

I smile broadly. He always knows exactly what to say. I reply.

Bring it on. xoxoxo

"It's just up here." Stace smiles proudly.

———

After a good night's sleep in the beautiful Venetian hotel in Vegas, we are on our way to the passport guy in a car we have hired. Things seem to be going to plan and last night was uneventful. We checked into a room and had a big deep bath together and got that beautiful room service dinner he promised me. For a short time, we were in Heaven. Hopefully, this time tomorrow we will be on our way out of here. I don't know if Stace slept all night. It seemed that every time I woke up, and that was a lot, he was awake, staring at the ceiling deep in thought.

We pull into a printing shop parking lot. "What are you doing?" I ask.

"This is it."

I frown. "This is a printing shop."

"Oh, because being a fake passport dealer is such a reputable business."

"R-right," I stammer. "I suppose so."

I follow him in through the front doors and the receptionist smiles. "I'm here to see Vernon," Stace announces.

"He's in the back office."

Stace nods and grabs my hand as we walk through a dingy hallway until we get to a closed door.

"This is sketchy," I whisper.

"You think," he whispers back as he knocks three times.

"Come in," the voice calls.

Stace opens the door and we are greeted by the sight of a huge, overweight man sitting behind a large, black desk. His hair is long and in a ponytail, and he has a whole biker gone wrong vibe going on.

He sits back and shakes his head as he smiles smugly. "Well, well, well... if it isn't the dead man walking? I was wondering when you would show up."

Stace glares at him. "I need two passports."

"Not a chance in Hell, man."

Stace glares at him.

"Vikinos himself came to visit me and said if I made you and her..." His eyes flick to me. "A passport, I'm dead, too."

"Nobody will know." Stace growls.

"I need to be alive for my kids," he fires back. "Death isn't on my to do list this week."

"When was he here?"

"A couple of days ago. He has a lot of men with him."

Stace glares at him as he processes his words.

My eyes flicker nervously between the two men. Please let this work out.

Stace leans over him on the desk. "Maybe you didn't understand me."

Vernon's eyes narrow.

"I said... I want two fucking passports and you are going to make them for me. Now!" Stace sneers.

"The answer is no." His eyes hold Stace's for an extended time, and eventually he fakes a smile. "I estimate you have about six hours to live."

Stace dives over the desk and grabs Vernon around the throat. "Make the fucking passports or I will kill you myself."

My eyes widen in horror. God, he's losing his shit.

Vernon chokes and coughs. "Let me go. Let me go," he cries.

Stace holds him, one hand around the throat and squeezes.

"I want the fucking passports."

"I can't." He coughs.

Stace bangs his head down on the desk. "Don't make me fucking kill you." He growls.

My hands fly to my head in a panic. This is getting out of control.

22

Roshelle

"THERE....THERE... IS SOMEONE ELSE," he stammers through his fear.

"Where?" Stace replies.

"He calls himself Wesley Snipes."

I roll my eyes. "Now I have heard it all," I mutter under my breath.

Stace slams his head again into the table. "Where?"

"You'll find him in the high rollers room at the casino. You can't miss him. He has bright red hair and dresses like Usher."

"Do you think this is a joke?" I snap. "I'm not risking my life by going to the high rollers room in the casino and looking for Wesley Snipes dressed as Usher. Let's go," I order nervously as I watch Stace hold this guy in a death grip. He's going to kill him if I don't get him out of here. "Stace! Let's go," I urge again. We have got enough shit to deal with already without him going nuclear on me.

"How long does he take?" Stace snaps.

"Same day."

Stace thinks for a moment as he holds him in his grip.

"If I could help you, you know I would," Vernon adds. "You have already put me in shit just for being here. I'm supposed to ring him the moment you arrive."

"Give us twenty-four hours before you do." Stace growls.

"Or I will be back to finish you off."

Vernon nods once.

We turn and Stace grabs my hand. We walk as fast as we can up the corridor, through the office, and out into the sunlight of the parking lot. We both look around nervously as Stace unlocks the car and we dive in. He starts the car with a roar and throws his phone at me. "Google gun shops."

With my heart hammering, I quickly Google Gun shops in Vegas. I wait for the page to load. "There's one called A-ammo," I stammer.

"Where is it? Hit maps," he instructs me.

I hit maps and wait for the little red dot to load. "It's just up here," I cry excitedly. I turn and look behind us. Are we being followed? "Second on the left, after this street."

Stace races toward the shop, and with a couple of turns and with renewed purpose, he parks the car in the street.

"You stay here."

I look around nervously. The street seems industrial and deserted. I can't see a soul. "I'm not staying out here on my own. I'm a sitting duck."

He watches me for a moment and then his eyes flicker around. "Okay, come on, let's go."

We get out of the car and casually walk into the shop and straight up to the counter.

ı "I would like to look at your hand guns, please," he asks the man behind the counter.

He nods emotionless and retrieves a gun from the glass cabinet and hands it to Stace. He pulls it back and inspects it, and then hands it to me. I look at it and turn it over.

I nod. "Feels good."

"We will take two with ammunition."

The guy nods and still while showing no emotion retrieves two boxed up guns. "That will be $389.00, thanks."

Stace hands him the cash, and before I know it we are on our way.

The drive back to the Venetian is made in complete silence.

We're both lost in our own thoughts, our own dread of what's to come. I hold the loaded gun in my hand on my lap in case the unimaginable happens. Funny how the unimaginable has turned into the most probable.

They will come for us eventually, and with no passport, I have no idea how we are going to get out of this.

"What are we going to do?" I eventually ask. Stace keeps driving and doesn't answer. "Did you hear me?" I repeat.

"Yeah, I heard you." He thinks for a moment. "We can't go anywhere undetected without passports. We need to be able to get around between countries or we can't sell the diamonds."

"I don't care about the money." I frown.

"I know, neither do I, but it will make it a lot easier to disappear forever."

I turn back and stare out the front windscreen. "We shouldn't even need to be thinking of this, Stace." My eyes fill with tears. "We are good people. Why have we had to deal with such shit in our lives?"

He grabs my hand and brings it up to his lips. "Shh, it's okay. It's going to be alright."

"H-how?" I stammer. "How is it going to be alright?" The tears are now running down my face. "You heard Vernon. He is threatening peoples lives if they help us. How the hell are we going to get out of here? We can't catch planes. We have millions of dollars in diamonds in another country that we can't get to." I shake my head in disbelief at the situation we are in.

"We will run out of money sooner or later. What then?" I ask. "What the hell are we going to do?" I cry.

He thinks for a moment with my hand still in his. "We have two choices."

I watch him as he drives. "Which are?" I ask.

"We stay and try to get passports to disappear forever." His eyes flick to me. "Or we run."

I stare out the car front window as raindrops start to fall.

"If we run." I pause at just how final this feels. "We will always be running."

"Yes," he answers honestly. "That's why we stay and sort this once and for all. I'm not spending our lives on the run. Fuck that."

Nerves flutter around in my stomach at how angry he is. What's he going to do if the next guy won't give us passports?

We drive for ten minutes in silence.

His eyes glance between the road and me. "Prepare yourself. This could get ugly."

His eyes meet mine and I know he is trying to give me an option to run.

"Stace, I want a life with you. A normal fucking life, not hiding and running, and being unable to hold a job or have children out of fear."

His eyes watch me as he processes my words.

"We find fucking Wesley Snipes and we get the damn passports and get your mom and we get the hell out of America."

He nods as he grips the steering wheel, his eyes staying on the road. "I've done something."

What's he talking about now? "Like what?" I frown.

"I don't know if it will happen and I didn't tell you because I didn't want to get your hopes up."

"But?" I snap.

"I ordered a hit on Vikinos."

My mouth drops open and I screw up my face. "How?"

"My friend works for the United States Government. I offered thirty million, fifteen million each to two snipers, if they could kill him."

I watch him with my face filled with horror. What?

"They get at least half of the diamond money if they kill him," he adds.

I swallow the lump in my throat. "I don't care about the money," I whisper.

"I know you don't, and that's why I did it."

I put my head into my hands as the rain starts to really come down. "Do you think they are going to pull it off?" I ask hopefully.

"Nobody had accepted the job last time I checked."

"Fuck," I whisper.

He shrugs. "By the time someone accepts it, it may be too late."

I close my eyes and my mother's death runs rampant through my mind. "Stace, promise me if they catch up with us that you won't try and be the hero. I need you to run and not look back. It's me that they want."

"And you are a part of me. You're the part I can't live without."

Tears fill my eyes and he kisses my hand again. "We will go

back to the hotel and tonight we hit the high rollers room and get those passports."

I nod as the rain comes down around us, bringing with it a sense of doom.

The end is coming and I know that soon, I will either kill my father... or I'll be killed.

Either is a nightmare. God, help me.

Stace lifts his chin triumphantly as we travel in the elevator up to the high roller room in the casino. We are both dressed to the nines and I have my boobs out to sweeten the deal. The stupid blonde wig is back on. I may as well look the part, I suppose. This is the one place it does suit the surroundings.

"You look beautiful." Stace smiles as he leans in and kisses me gently on the lips.

I smile stupidly up at him as an idea comes to mind. "If we get passports tonight." I kiss him again. "Can we get married tonight by Elvis in the chapel?" I widen my eyes in excitement.

He frowns down at me and wraps his arms around my waist. "You want to marry me in an Elvis chapel in Vegas?"

I shrug. "Well." I laugh, it does sound ridiculous when he says it out loud. "Yes, kind of." I kiss him again. "We haven't done anything traditional so far. It seems like a shame to start now?"

His hands drop to my behind and he squeezes me hard.

"No."

I frown. "No?"

"No. I am not getting married in a seedy Vegas chapel by fucking Elvis."

My shoulders slump in disappointment.

"We will get married in a traditional wedding. Somewhere that is..." He pauses as he thinks of the appropriate wording.

"Nice. I hate fucking Vegas and you deserve better than a shotgun wedding."

I smile softly.

He kisses me and as the heat from his lips permeates through my body, I feel myself hover above the floor.

I deserve better. He's right, I do. I forget that myself sometimes. I'm so in love with this man.

I love the way he makes me feel and I'm totally addicted to the buzz I get from his touch. Our relationship is unconventional, but somehow this is the most normal I have ever felt in my life. It's weird how it's turned out, but for as long as I can remember, all I wanted was a normal, happy life with my soul mate, and it turns out that I just needed unconventional and to be kidnapped to find him. Who knew it was this simple?

The elevator doors open, and we are greeted by a security guard as he steps in our path, effectively blocking our way.

"Minimum ten thousand dollar bets on this floor," he announces coldly.

"Yes, of course." Stace smiles casually as if it's lunch money. Shit, ten thousand dollars. That's exuberant. I better get this right or we could drop fifty grand in five minutes. I will be doing the gambling tonight while Stace tries to find Wesley Snipes. I still can't believe this guy actually calls himself that. It's kind of ridiculous, if you ask me.

I glance around at the glamorous people buried deep in their own world, hardly looking up from the tables. This is hardcore. I've never seen anything like it, from their clothes, to their shoes, to the young gorgeous women with old sleazy men. Everyone smells of money and security guards line the wall. Waiters are walking around with trays of food and drinks. It all seems to be on the house up here. This is like another world.

Stace smiles and takes my hand and we casually stroll

around and look at all of the tables. There is Poker, Roulette, various card dealers at tables playing a wide assortment of games. The air is thick with smoke and clearly the universal occupational health and safety guidelines don't apply to high rollers. Large lounges sat in pairs line the perimeter, and the whole back wall is a giant fish tank complete with huge sharks and tropical fish. It's like a James Bond movie. I smirk to myself. Wow, isn't this something? People are laying chips everywhere like candy—chips that are at least ten thousand dollars each. The room has an entitled feel to it. Everyone in here clearly thinks they are a somebody.

Maybe they are?

Stace walks over to the cashier booth "I would like fifty thousand dollars worth of chips, please."

She smiles and slides five chips across the table.

I look at the five puny chips on the table. Is that it? Holy shit, that is it. Fifty thousand dollars in five freaking chips. You have got to be kidding me? Stace smiles and takes his five chips and passes them to me. "Where do you want to play, darling?" he asks.

I look at him blankly. I have never even been to the casino before, why on Earth is he trusting me to do the gambling?

"Umm." I look around at all of the tables as I try to locate something that I have at least seen before. Shit, how do I act like this is normal for us? Cards with important looking men playing, what looks like, a large hopscotch kind of thing, and people are throwing dice and seeing what they land on. Over in the far corner is a roulette table. Ah, I know this game, sort of. I have seen it in movies.

"Roulette?" I smile sweetly.

He takes my hand and leads me over to the Roulette table. A beautiful, older brunette woman is playing, and she is accompanied by a much younger looking, handsome man. He is sitting on the stool next to her and has his hand on her leg. They are both dressed to the nines and she is laughing out loud with the table cheering her on.

Sugar momma.

We stand for a moment and watch. "Thirty-two," she asserts and claps her hands together in excitement as it spins. The ball goes around and around, and I hold my breath as we wait for it to land. The ball bounces a few times and then finally lands on number eleven. The table all laugh and sigh and she snaps her fingers in disappointment. "Again." She smiles to the dealer.

My eyes drop to the pile of betting chips in front of her and I count. Twenty. Holy shit. She is betting with two hundred thousand dollars.

What is wrong with these people?

I am brought back to the present as Stace squeezes my hand, and I drop my head and smile bashfully. I wonder what my facial expression just revealed to everyone surrounding us. This is so far from the life I had, some days I couldn't even afford credit on my phone and would have to wait until payday to top it up. She goes again and Stace puts two chips on the table amongst the others. Oh crap, now I have to do it. Stace wraps his arm around me and smiles as he kisses my temple from behind. He knows damn well that I'm disgusted at this money wastage.

Stace points over to the corner with his chin and pretends to kiss my ear.

"There he is," he whispers.

I glance over to the lounges in the corner and see a man who is sitting with a woman. I try to hide my smile, but I can't. He is just as I imagined. Red hair and geeky, but dressed in cool rap clothes that don't suit him at all.

"Back in a sec," Stace whispers in my ear with a kiss to my cheek.

I nod, distracted by sugar momma and her boy scout who just had a huge tongue kiss in front of everyone when she won.

Ew, God, some people are such show ponies.

I watch Stace approach the man across the club. He shakes his hand and they begin talking. My concentration goes back to the table and I watch as sugar momma loses a cool fifty grand. Another man seems to be cleaning up, though.

A waiter approaches and she smiles as she takes the champagne from his tray. "I'm out." She smiles in her toffee accent.

The dealer nods to me.

Huh, me? Oh crap. "Okay." I smile as I pretend to know what the hell I'm doing. Umm. I nervously look around at the numbers. What the heck number should I pick? "Umm."

The table all wait for my answer. Oh shit.

"Ten, please," I announce.

My heart starts to race and I watch the wheel spin around and around until, unbelievably, it lands on ten.

"You win." The dealer smiles.

Really?

I jump up and down in excitement and clap my hands like a child. "Again." I laugh. I put my chip on number eight.

The dealers have to do a shift change, and as we wait, Stace comes up and wraps his arm around me as I sit on the stool. "Hope you have your vows written?" he whispers in my ear.

My eyes flicker up to him over my shoulder.

He smiles sexily. "Let's find that chapel, Mrs. Mac. I don't think I want to wait for another day." My eyes search his and he grins and shrugs.

"Won't hurt to have two weddings, I suppose."

"Oh my God." My anxious eyes flicker back to the dealer as

a stupid smile covers my face. Hurry up woman! Is he serious? She spins the wheel, but my mind is far from stupid Roulette. It goes around and around for forever as we wait and then bounces onto twenty.

"I'm sorry." The dealer smiles. "Again?" she asks the table.

"No, thanks," I reply. I couldn't care less about this stupid game.

I'm getting married. Tonight!

Stace takes me by the hand and we walk straight out of the high rollers room without looking back. "What happened?" I whisper.

"We have to be at his office first thing in the morning. He can have them done by 2pm. He was actually a decent guy."

My eyes widen as we get into the elevator. "Oh my God, that's fantastic," I whisper excitedly.

He kisses me and his lips hover over mine. "This time tomorrow night, we'll be on our way out of here."

I smile against his lips, knowing things are going to work out.

"Are you sure you want to get married now?" I ask as he wraps his large arms around me.

"Uh-huh." He smiles as my hand wraps around his shoulders.

"Why tonight?" I ask. "What's different?"

"Because who knows what tomorrow holds," he whispers.

"Live in the moment, remember? Sometimes I forget to."

He smiles down on me and, at this moment, I know he wants this as much as I do. "We have to go back and get our passports from the room. We need three pieces of identification."

"Okay." The elevator enters onto the main floor and we walk through the area and then catch another elevator up to our room. Stace has my pinned to the wall with his pelvis and my arms held over my head.

"Stop it." I giggle. "I don't want you to have a raging hard on in my wedding photos."

"Why not? It's a promise of what's to come." He smirks.

We walk down the corridor and see a commotion way up ahead in the hallway with a few men coming in and out of a room. Stace's face drops.

"What?" I frown.

"That's our room."

"Huh?"

I glance up and see the door just open, and one of Stace's shoes holding the door open.

"Who is in our room?" I whisper.

A man appears in a dark suit distracted as he talks to another man and they stop in the doorway for a moment to discuss something. They seem to be talking to someone else in the room.

Oh my God, they've found us.

Stace turns us and we start to speed walk down the corridor in the opposite direction.

"Hey, you!" a man calls. "Stop right there!"

23

Roshelle

"DON'T RUN, KEEP WALKING," Stace replies calmly. "Just keep walking."

My heart is hammering in my chest as we quickly walk down the corridor.

"Don't look back." He growls.

Thankfully, the corridor turns a corner, and for a moment we are shielded. I'm not sure if they are coming after us, but damn, we are doing a bloody good job of acting like we don't have a care in the world. We start to run.

We pass by a cleaning cart parked in the hallway. The maid is in the adjacent room with the door propped open and a lanyard with a card key is hanging from the top of her tea and coffee tray. Stace casually picks it off and we continue up the corridor a bit and he swipes the key and the door unlocks. We scramble inside and he closes the door quietly. He immediately looks through the security peephole.

"Fuck, that was close?" he whispers.

I stand still for a moment, in shock. "Stace. They... they are in our room and they have our things," I stammer. I put my hands on top of my head as I try to grasp the situation.

He continues to look through the hole. "It's definitely them," he whispers and he moves back from the hole to let me see. I stand on my tiptoes and peer through the small glass hole and see the three men walking down the hall looking for us.

"It's one of the men from Bogota that was outside the bank," Stace whispers.

"Shit." I look around the room and, thankfully, it doesn't appear to have anyone staying here. The room smells of cleaning fluid and has obviously just been turned over by the maids.

"What are we going to do?" I whisper. "All of our money, our clothes." My eyes widen. "Our fucking passports are in that room."

"Where are the diamonds?" he asks.

"I unscrewed the light fitting in the room and hid them in there. Nobody should find them."

"We get new passports tomorrow and you still have our chips, right?"

"Yes." I scramble through my bag and retrieve the chips and hold them up to him.

I start to pace as Stace continues to stare through the peep-hole. My heart is hammering. "What if someone checks into the room?"

"Then we're fucked," he snaps.

"Holy shit." I drop my head into my hands. "How did they find us?"

"Vernon."

I shake my head. "Fucking Vernon." I continue pacing with

my fingers on my temples. "I fucking hate that guy. I knew I hated that guy."

For the next hour, Stace watches through the peephole as the men walk up and down the corridor looking for us.

I'm nearly in a fetal position on the bed.

"They're not leaving, in fact, more and more are arriving. They are all waiting in and around the room for us to return."

A heavy sense of dread hangs over me. Like mice, we are trapped. "Stace, what are we going to do?" I whisper in despair.

His eyes hold mine for a moment and I know he feels as desperate as I do. "Just turn the television on and try to rest for a bit while I think of something." He walks over and brushes my hair back from my face. "Just try and rest, baby." He gently kisses my lips. "It will be okay. Try not to worry."

With a deep exhale, I go to the mini bar and take out a can of Coke and a chocolate bar. I need to try and fill my stomach. I feel sick I'm so hungry. This is supposed to be my wedding night, but no... my prick of a father had to ruin that, too. I lie back on the bed and try to calm myself down as I flick through the channels. Suddenly, a face I know all too well comes across the screen with the headline.

Breaking News

My mouth drops open. Oh my God. "Stace," I whisper with wide unbelieving eyes. "You might want to come and watch this, honey."

He turns from his pacing and walks into the bedroom, his face falls as I turn up the television.

Breaking news in the
Roshelle Myers kidnapping case.

Key suspect Joel McIntyre has been sighted in security footage from Las Vegas airport on Tuesday night where he landed on a plane from Colombia. He was travelling with a female passenger who is believed to be Roshelle Myers. She may have been under the influence of drugs and grave concerns are held for her safety.

Joel, who goes under the alias Mac, kidnapped Roshelle at gun point in the middle of the night 31 days ago from a nightclub parking lot. The ground search for her body has been extensive.

It is believed he is on the Las Vegas strip and police are combing the area. If seen, do not approach the suspect. He is armed and extremely dangerous. Please call 911 immediately for police assistance if sighted.

The newsflash ends but we both still staring at the screen, bewildered by what we have just watched. My mouth hangs open and my eyes flicker to him. His face is solemn with no expression.

I shake my head. "Stace," I whisper. "How did they know about the kidnapping?" I shake my head. "They've been looking for me this whole time?"

He storms past me into the bathroom and shuts the door behind him and I put my head into my hands.

This is a nightmare that just keeps on giving out nightmares.

———

It's 3am, and Stace and I lay facing each other on the bed. We can both sense the end is near. The corridor outside the room is buzzing with Vikinos's men, there is no air-conditioning vent large enough for us to get out of. There is no exit from this Hell.

The men are guarding the lift doors, probably on every level as they wait for us to arrive back to the room. If we do get out, we have no money and we can't even cash our chips in because the police are probably combing the casino floor. They would have watched the CCTV footage by now. They know we have chips that need to be cashed.

Stace brings his hand up, cups my face, and kisses me tenderly. My eyes fill with tears. "I'm sorry," I whisper. "I'm sorry you got caught up in this."

He holds me close to his chest. "I was already in it. It's me who's sorry. I shouldn't have brought you back here."

"Some wedding night, hey?" I smile sadly.

His face falls and I know what he's thinking.

I shake my head. "Don't think that."

"Shh." He tries to calm me.

"We will get married," I whisper. "Promise me, we will get married."

"Rosh." He pauses and the emotion in his eyes breaks my heart.

"No," I whisper.

"I need to hand you into the police, babe."

The tears break the dam and run down my face toward the pillow. "No."

"You will be safe with them."

"And you will be dead. If you go to prison, you will be killed immediately. We both know how many men are on his payroll."

"I can't protect you," he whispers.

"And who will protect you?" I cry. "I will not leave you out here where they will kill you."

"But you will be safe. That's all I care about."

I put my head into his chest as the lump blocks my throat. "There's another way, Stace. We just have to think of it. Stop thinking like this." I kiss him softly through my tears and he holds me tight.

———

"Rosh." He shakes me awake. I squint as I try to focus, and I glance at the clock. It's 5am. "The coast is clear. I'm going to go and see what's going on."

I sit up. "No. What?" I try to make my brain wake up.

"I will be back soon."

I frown. "Where are you going?"

"I just want to go and see where the fire stair exits are so we can get out of here. I will be back, but you need to stay here."

I grab his arm. "No." I shake my head frantically. "I'm not staying here without you."

He grabs my face in his two hands. "Listen to me. Let me go and see if I can find an exit. We are more of a target together." He kisses me as he holds my face in his two hands. "I love you."

I watch him through tear filled eyes. "I love you, too," I whisper.

"If I don't come back, stay in the room and call the police."

I screw up my face in tears. "No, Stace, don't go." I try to grab hold of his arm to make him stay where he is safe, but with one last long look he disappears from my sight. I hear the latch on the door quietly click shut.

He's gone.

Stace

I glance down the hallway toward our original room. Silence. The men are still down there. I just went and checked as Rosh slept. More men are waiting at the elevators and the

bottom of the fire stair exit. Only one door opens on a fire door exit. The ground floor, and they know that... everybody knows that. I'm under no illusion that the ground floor won't be crawling. There is no getting out of here undetected.

After thinking on this all night, I know more than ever I need to ensure her safety.

That's all I care about now.

Unfortunately, there is only one way to do that. I creep along the hallway until I get to the fire stairs, and I know if I go in I will probably never see my Rosh again. They will put her back into witness protection, and if I am able to fight my way out of this mess with Vikinos's men, I will be a wanted man from the police. I won't be able to find her. My chest constricts at the thought of never holding her in my arms, of never touching her again. His men will be waiting for me at the bottom of the stairs.

But she will be safe.

I slowly open the door and walk in and shut it behind me. It clicks with a cold heartbreaking click.

I retrieve my phone from my pocket and dial 911. "Police, Fire, or Ambulance," the receptionist answers.

"Police."

"Putting you through."

"Hello, Police," the policeman on the other end answers.

I frown and pinch the bridge of my nose. We were getting married tonight. Emotion overcomes me and my throat constricts. I take a deep breath and force the words from my mouth on autopilot. "This is Joel McIntyre. I kidnapped Roshelle Myers from Carpenter parking lot at gunpoint and held her captive for thirty-one days. She is in room 3590 of the Venetian in Las Vegas."

"Are you armed?" the policeman asks.

"No, I'm no longer with her."

"Is she alive?"

"Barely. She needs medical attention. You should hurry." I hang up and shakily sit down on the steps underneath me as I am overcome with emotion.

Thanks, babe.

That was the best month of my life.

Roshelle

I lie in the silent darkness and stare at the ceiling. My mind is ticking and I have sick feeling in my gut. Stace has gone looking for an exit, but something else is bothering me.

His mother.

She hasn't called and yet his face has been plastered all over every news station.

Why hasn't she called?

Stop thinking the worst, I chastise myself. I close my eyes as I try to block out the vision of my own beloved mother dying.

Stop it, just stop thinking about it.

I get out of bed, make myself cup of tea, and walk over to the window to peer through the crack in the curtain. The sun is rising. A new day. A new opportunity.

How did my life come to this?

What did I ever do in my last life that was so bad that it warranted this kind of torture?

Stace. My beautiful Stace. My face screws up in pain as I walk to the door and look through the peephole. Do they have him now?

Please, no. Please, God, protect him. Please, please, please. I begin to pace back and forth in the fading darkness.

Why hasn't she called?

For ten minutes, I pace, so filled with fear for my love that I can hardly stand up.

Crippled at the thought of what they might do if they catch him.

It's me they want.

Stace, where are you?

I begin to go over the times when Stace's mom has called. She calls him every few days. If he was on national television as a wanted man, she would call him. I know she would.

But then... I frown. I don't even know what's going on anymore. Am I imagining this? Maybe it just seems magnified because I am here in the middle of it, and what if she just hasn't seen the damn news?

I pick up my phone and scroll to my contacts. I have two. Stace and his mom. I narrow my eyes as I stare at the phone and I click on her number, it rings.

Ring, ring.

Ring, ring.

It picks up and I stay silent.

Nobody answers, but I know someone is there listening. Fuck.

I frown as I listen.

Why isn't she saying hello?

I close my eyes as I think. What if this is a trap?

What if they are going to trace my phone? What the fuck have I done?

I instantly hang up. I stand up and throw my hands around in the air in a panic. Oh my God, oh my God. I have fifteen minutes before they can trace where I am. What am I going to do?

My phone beeps a text on the side table, and goosebumps scatter all over my body. I watch it for a few moments in the dark silence with one hand over my mouth. Slowly, I pick it up to see that a video has been sent as a text. I click it open and the blood drains from my face.

A middle aged woman is tied to a chair in a darkened factory. She is black and blue.

Stace's mom.

Oh dear God. Tears fill my eyes. They have her. They're going to kill her.

I'm jolted back to life to the sound of my father's strong voice through the video.

"Roshina. Hand yourself over or she will have the same fate as your mother. You have ten minutes."

The screen goes black.

My heart starts to thump at my loss of power. Déjà vu.

How does he do this? How does he manipulate me and gain control over every damn circumstance? I taste the hot, salty tears as they run down my face. This isn't an idle threat. I know he will kill her without a second thought. I walk into the bathroom and stare at my reflection in the mirror where a scared child stares back at me—the same scared child who lost her mother at his evil hands. I can't. I won't let that happen. Stace has already lost his father and brother. I can't let him lose her, too.

His whole family will be gone, just like mine.

The loneliness... Oh, I can't even think of it. It hurts my heart to remember my mom and the way she died.

For a moment, I sit on the edge of the bathtub, knowing that somehow, all along I knew this was coming. I begin to mentally prepare myself for what's to come. All those days at the shooting range, all those early morning kickboxing classes, the weekly grief counselling and anger management. It starts a fire in my stomach.

I've had it.

He's got it coming to him... and I'm going to give it.

How fucking dare he try to ruin my life, yet again? Fury starts to pump through my bloodstream. I go to the bathroom, straighten myself up, and without a thought, I head out the door and into the corridor. I turn and walk down to our old room where I can hear the numerous men's voices on the other side.

Knock, knock, knock.

A tall man in a suit answers and a trace of a smile covers his face, as if he was expecting me.

I glare at him, the hatred for my father so thick in my blood that it clogs my arteries. "My name is Roshina Vikinos." The men all glance at each other. "Take me to my father."

I sit in the car with a man on either side of me and another two in the front. I'm not tied or bound. He knows he has me, I have no choice but to be here and I have no choice but to kill or be killed. I won't let her die at his hands like my own beautiful mother did, and I'm sure as shit not letting my Stace come to try and get her out of this.

He would be dead on sight.

I have more of a chance than he does.

We drive for over an hour. It's early morning and I watch as the people in cars around us all head off to their day at work like everything is normal. It is for them. I wonder what normal feels like? My whole world is collapsing again. It's like I'm watching it play out in a movie... all my worst fears brought to life.

Armageddon.

The farther we drive from my love, the more I feel the sanity leave my body.

I've never felt so fucking crazy.

At least his men are with me and Stace is free to try and escape.

Run, baby.

I close my eyes. Even though I have distanced them away from Stace, I know the police will be chasing him down. He has no money. What's he going to do?

Where will he sleep tonight?

"I need to go to the bathroom."

"No," the driver snaps.

"Where the hell am I going to go?"

"We are nearly there." He growls.

"I'm going to piss in your car, asshole."

"Do it and see what happens to you."

The man next to me smirks and I elbow him hard in the stomach. He doubles over and the man on the other side of me bursts out laughing.

"Shut up or you're next," I snap.

They are all so happy with themselves. They came up with the goods. Makes me sick. Their pay increase for bringing me in will be substantial.

Fucking assholes.

My anger simmers beneath the surface and I clench my fists in front of me. If I'm going to go down, I'm going down fighting. He has no idea what I am capable of, and in all honesty, neither do I.

I am his daughter.

We drive into an industrial estate with huge factories on large lots of land, and I study the surroundings carefully, still hopeful that I can fight my way out of this mess. Stace's mom is a whole other problem. I have to get them to let her go first and then I can fight. If she is there with me, I have no chance of escaping. How do you run and hide with an elderly lady who is injured?

I hope she's okay.

The car turns into a long driveway and we travel off the main road and across open land through a windy dirt road for a few kilometres. How the hell am I going to get out of here?

There is nowhere to hide, acres for as far as I see. I feel my apprehension rise. We come to a slow halt in front of a huge, old warehouse, and are greeted by three men holding semi-automatic guns, guarding the door and waiting out the front for our arrival.

I feel the adrenaline start to pump through me and I close my eyes in dread.

The men get out of the car, but I stay seated. I don't want to get out.

"Get out." The man I elbowed growls.

"Go to fucking hell."

He reaches in the car and grabs me by the hair and I kick him hard in the face, but his grip is too strong. After a few moments of struggling, the other men help to hold me down and he drags me out. The pain in my head shoots through me and as I stand he hits me in the face and I stagger back.

"Don't fucking hit me again." He growls.

I look him square in the eye and fake a smile. "You pathetic piece of shit. He will kill you next, you're just a number."

He pushes me in the back toward the door and I stumble forward. I really wish I had something more appropriate on. I'm in a black, skimpy, tight dress and my tits are half hanging out. Two of the men grab my arms and drag me through the door and suddenly fear takes over and I fight to break free.

"Let me go," I yell.

I get my arm loose and I punch one of the men in the face and we begin to violently struggle. The other man hits me again, and I turn and kick him as hard as I can in the groin. He doubles over and falls to the ground. The other two men grab me and, as hard as I try, I can't seem to break loose. They push me farther into the room and that's when I see her.

Oh dear God.

Tied to a chair with her hands behind her back, her eyes so swollen from being beaten that they are closed, she looks near death.

"What have you animals done to her?" I scream.

I run to her. "Annette. Annette are you okay?" I cry.

Her head is slouched and she is semi-conscious. She lifts her head slightly. "Stace," she whimpers.

I bend and kiss her face so that they can't hear me. "Stace is safe," I whisper. "I'm here now, I'm going to help you." I put my hand tenderly on her head. "I'm here to help you."

I turn as if possessed by the devil. "Let her go!" I scream.

The gutless men all stand still as they watch me.

"Untie her now!" I scream. "It's me that he wants. Tell him I'm here."

The men all continue to stand still.

"Tell him!" I scream.

My father steps out from the shadows and my heart drops as the air leaves my lungs.

The little girl in me is terrified.

His eyes hold mine, and he steps toward me, wearing an expensive dark suit he is the epitome of evil. "Hello, Roshina," he replies flatly, his voice is calm and collected.

I don't answer as the fearful tears fill my eyes. There's no air in here. I feel like I can't breathe. "I hate you. I hate you."

He smiles as he stares at me and after a long pause he replies, "You are as charming as ever."

I stare at him through bleary tear filled eyes. How could I possibly be half of this man?

"Where is he?" he asks calmly.

My blood runs cold. "He's dead," I murmur.

He smiles. "No, but he will be very soon."

His words knock me. "What do you want?" I whisper.

"Something only you can give me."

I stare at him.

He puts his hands behind his back and links his hands together and begins to pace. "I'm dying, Roshina."

I frown.

"I have brain cancer."

I step back and his man grabs my arm and I yank it from his grip. "Don't fucking touch me." I growl.

"Good. I'm glad you're dying. It will be a blessing to the world," I snap as I lift my chin in defiance.

He tips his head back and laughs out loud. "I do love your drive."

I glare at him. "Just die already."

"There is something I want from you before I do, and then you can die right along side of me."

My eyes hold his.

"You will marry the man that I have picked to take over my empire."

Fear pumps through my body and I begin to hear my heartbeat in my ears. "No, I won't," I snap.

He smiles darkly. "Yes. Yes, you will."

I shake my head. "You are fucking crazy. Why would you possibly want me to marry your understudy? What could you possibly gain from such an arrangement?"

"A bloodline heir. I want your son."

24

Roshelle

I SMILE FROM SHOCK, I think. That is the craziest, fucked up thing I have ever heard.

A frown crosses his face and I see a trace of a weakness.

"You think this is funny?"

I laugh a deep belly aching laugh. "Your stupidity insults my intelligence."

He watches me intently and he lifts his chin in defiance.

"You didn't think to check with me on that arrangement?" I smile.

He glares at me. 'I don't need to check anything. You will do as I say and you brought this on yourself when you killed my brother."

"I will do nothing of the fucking sort!" I yell. "Who the fuck do you think you are?" He narrows his eyes. "Now untie her and let her go, or I am going to kill you."

A broad smile crosses his face and he raises his eyebrows.

"You?" He smiles, his eyes flicker around to his gophers and he points. "She's hilarious." He laughs and his monkeys all start laughing, too. "Is that a threat Roshina?"

I step forward and spit in his face. "That's a promise."

He slaps me hard across the face and I smile darkly. "How does it feel to have your own flesh and blood hate you with everything that she has?"

His face drops as he wipes the saliva from his cheek with his forearm. That disgusting act felt better than it should.

"Mom left you." I lean forward and raise my eyebrow as I whisper. "Do you want to know why?"

His eyes flicker to the men around us and I know I have hit a nerve.

"Let her go." I gesture to Stace's mom.

His eyes flash to her tied to the chair.

"Let her go and we can go to your house to discuss this grandchild."

"I'm not stupid."

I smile. "Neither am I."

"Where is Mac?" He growls.

"Let her go. It's me you want. You have me." I hold my hands up. "You let her go or you can shoot me dead as I fight." He glares at me. "I can't procreate when I'm dead." I pause and smile sweetly. "Can I, Daddy?"

His eyes narrow in fury and I know that my sarcasm is getting to him. I've got him. He needs me alive.

I walk over to Stace's mom and I begin to untie her hands from behind her back.

"Stop right there," he yells.

"Nope." I keep going.

"This is your final warning."

"And I'm warning you. You want me to stop, get one of your monkeys to kill me."

I struggle with the knots and finally I wriggle her free before I help her stand.

The roof cracks and I look up into the darkness overhead at the big timber beams. The men's eyes rise to the ceiling and two walk around as they hold their guns in the air.

Somebody is on the roof. Stace?

I force my eyes down. Distract him.

Two of the guards step forward and grab her by the arms.

I turn to look at him. "What's it going to be?" I sneer. "Me or her?" He glares at me. "You let her go, I do what you want," I reply.

He hesitates and lifts his chin in thought.

"Your plan worked, you got me here. Now she's not needed anymore. If you keep her or hurt her, I will fight till my death." I shrug. "I'm happy to die today and then where will you get your heir?"

"No, dear," she whispers. I grab her hand and squeeze it.

I walk her toward the door and the guards step forward and he puts his hand up in a stop signal. "You can have your way this time, Roshina," he says calmly. "As a show of my good faith." The men stop on the spot where they are and I usher her over to the door.

"Go, run. Hide in the grass."

She shakes her head in fear. "Come with me," she whispers.

"Run, hide," I whisper again so only she can hear. I open the door and push her out before she can argue and close it behind her before he changes his mind.

I turn and face my father. "Now, let's get down to business."

Stace

I sink to the floor and sit on the step for a moment as I let my actions sink in. I've done it.

That's it.

I close my eyes in regret. Deep down I always knew we couldn't be long term. I always had that annoying little voice in the back of my psyche letting me know how it would go. How could I possibly have ever imagined a future with her when we met through the kidnapping?

She was right all along. She did deserve more from her person. I get a vision of her laughing out loud underneath me and I feel a sharp, swift kick to my stomach.

Knowing what I am missing out on is going to make it so much harder to go on.

Damn Vikinos for treating her the way he has. How in hell could he treat his own daughter like that? A daughter as special as she is. My blood starts to simmer, and with renewed fury I stand and turn the handle to get back out onto the floor.

Locked. Fuck it.

I stare at it for a moment, knowing I have to go to the bottom to get out. My adrenaline starts to pump. I am going to have one of two welcoming parties.

The police or Vikinos' men.

I want the men. I want my revenge and I'm going to fucking get it.

I'm furious. I glance at the time on my phone. The police should be here within fifteen minutes to pick Rosh up, hopefully sooner, and then I can start my attack.

With Rosh safe and out of harm's way, I can go back to the original plan. I start to jog down the steps. We are on the tenth floor, so it is a fair way down. Two flights down I hear a noise in the level underneath me and I stop on the step. I peer over the handrail as I try to see what's coming up the stairs.

Bang, bang. Clatter.

I frown. What is that? I lean over the rail again and see a maintenance man cleaning the rail and I pick up the pace. I jog down and come face to face with him.

"Oh, hello." I smile casually. "I came into the stairs by mistake and now all the doors are locked."

"It's the fire stairs, the doors don't open until you get to the bottom floor," he replies with a shake of his head.

"Damn, I didn't realize." I look around as I wait for him to offer to open the door. "So you have to walk all the way down the bottom floor every time, do you?" I ask.

"No, I got a key."

"Great." I fake a smile.

He keeps cleaning. Am I going to have to jump this dude to get the bloody key or what? "Do you mind opening the door so I don't have to walk all the way to the ground?" I ask.

"I'm not supposed to. It's against policy."

My eyes hold his as I sum him up.

He shrugs. "Why not?" He shuffles over and opens the door for me.

"Thank you." I smile as I walk calmly into the hallway. I wait for ten minutes and then head straight toward the lifts. I watch the dial above the doors and as it opens I step out into the corridor. I look left and then right. I walk down the hallway toward our original room and I hesitate and swipe the card key across the lock. I brace myself.

I open the door and glance around. Nobody is here. Huh?

I walk through the room and they have been here, but it looks like they have just left.

Why have they left?

My eyes search the room as I try to work out where they have gone. Are they coming back?

I go to the wardrobe and open the safe combination and my gun is still in there.

What are the chances?

I take it out and walk to the window and glance around the room again. Then I see it.

The blonde wig, it's on the chair.

Rosh was here. They have her.

I kick the wall as hard as I can. "Fuck!" I yell. I run my hands through my hair in frustration. Why did I leave her alone?

My phone rings and I look at the screen. Chris. I close my eyes as I think and then I answer.

"Hey."

"Oh my fucking God. Where are you? Have you seen the fucking television?"

I pause for a moment. "Yeah, I saw it."

"Do you have her?"

I nod. "Yes."

"Fuck me!" he screams. "Hand yourself in. What the fuck is going on?"

I rub my hand through my hair. "It's not how it looks. I kidnapped her to save her life and now Vikinos is after her."

"W-what?" he stammers.

"Chris, listen to me. I need you to do something."

He stays silent.

"The hit I ordered. It's on Vikinos."

"The drug lord, Vikinos?"

I nod. "That's him, he's her father."

"What the fuck, Stace? Stop it. Stop acting fucking crazy and hand yourself in. This girl is fucking trouble, she's going to get you fucking killed."

"Chris, listen to me. If something happens to me, you need to look after her."

"What? No. I want you safe. Hand yourself in."

"I'm in love with her."

"Stace. You've lost it."

"If the hit comes through and I am not here, tell the agency that their payment is the diamonds that are hidden in the light fitting in room 3590 at the Venetian," I reply.

"Diamonds. What fucking diamonds?" he yells. "I can't fucking believe this. You have stolen fucking diamonds from Vikinos. Jesus Christ, Stace!"

"They are worth more that the thirty million I offered."

"I'm not doing it," he snaps.

"I love you, man." I sigh sadly.

"Stace, stop. Listen to me, hand yourself in. We can get you off. I need you to hand yourself in. Don't do anything fucking stupid."

"Goodbye, Chris." I hang up before he can say another word and put my phone on silent. It rings immediately again.

I close my eyes as I try to pull myself together. Damn it. I leave the room and run down the hall and jump in the elevator. I take it to the underground parking lot and calm myself as we get to the bottom. I can't bring attention to myself.

Where were the fucking cops? They were supposed to have her, the stupid fucks. I am so fucking angry right now.

The doors open and I walk casually out into the parking lot and make a beeline for the back row of cars. I take out my gun and smash the window of a sedan and climb in. I pull the cover off the front dash and hotwire the car. I check the gas, nearly a full tank. That's going to have to do. I reverse out and then floor it through the parking lot and drive straight through the gate that is down. The car smashes through out into the early morning and I floor it up the highway.

I take out my phone and put on the Find My Phone app and I hold my breath as I wait.

Finally, the little red light flashes. Got you, baby.

Hold on.

Roshelle

Relief hits me. I did it. I got her out of here. I turn to face my father; my murdering, cold-blooded father.

"What do you want?" I ask.

"I want you to marry Antonio."

My eyes hold his. I need to distract him long enough for her to run. "Why?" I ask.

He starts to pace again as he puts his hand behind his back.

"I told you, I'm dying."

Can't come soon enough.

My eyes turn to the men around me. Six in total. Four I was in the car with, and then the two guards with guns. His bodyguards.

I start to slowly look around for the exits. "Why do you need me?" I ask.

"I want to hand what I have worked so hard for down to my blood son."

"He doesn't want your filthy money."

His dark eyes hold mine, and he steps forward toward me. The fear rises in my throat. No matter how much training I have done, nothing can cure the fear I have of this monster.

"Your son will take over the family business."

"I don't have a son."

"Yet." He smiles darkly. "But you will."

I shake my head. "I would rather die than hand a child to you."

He smiles. "And you will as soon as I get my child."

Fear starts to close my throat. "You're pathetic, can you hear yourself? Can you hear how fucked up you are?" I shake my head. "I don't know an Antonio and I'm as sure as shit not going to marry one," I snap.

"Antonio," he calls.

A man steps out from the shadows and I step back. Tall dark and European, his black eyes scan me up and down.

"Meet your new wife, my son." My father smiles.

He smiles darkly and walks up to me. I feel his breath on my face. He smells like cigars and whiskey. "Very nice." His eyes drop to my breasts as if I'm his next piece of meat, and he picks up my hand. "It's nice to meet you, Roshina."

I frown as the air leaves my lungs.

He bends and kisses the back of my hand and I'm no longer able to hold it as I slap his face hard. The sound echoes through the space and his head turns with the sting of the slap.

He steps forward and puts his hand around my neck in a chokehold. "You will learn your place," he whispers as his hand squeezes hard.

"The hell I will," I whisper back.

I snap his hand away and turn to my father. "You are insane. You have killed so many innocent people. You killed your own wife!" I scream. I shake my head as tears threaten to fall. "What kind of fucking animal are you?" I whisper.

My father lifts his head. "One that gets his own way."

I turn back to Antonio. He's huge. He doesn't need a gun

and I know he must be pure evil to hold such esteem in my father's eyes.

"Here is how it's going to go." Antonio smiles. "We have a minister that is going to marry us today."

I frown.

"And I will be taking my marital rights immediately." He smiles as he licks his bottom lip. "Repeatedly." His eyes meet my father's and they exchange some kind of sick smile of acknowledgement.

I shake my head quickly. "No. I won't."

He grabs my face and squeezes it hard. "Oh yes...you will." He smiles. "And you will enjoy it." He leans forward and licks my face. "I will make sure of it," he whispers as he nips my cheek hard between his teeth

My heartbeat starts to sound in my ears. I've got to get out of here.

I push him away from me. "Go to Hell." I turn to the men guarding the door. "Is this the kind of men you want to work for?" I scream.

The men stay silent, I need one of them to cross sides to try and help me.

"A man that arranges the rape of his own daughter?" I cry.

The man closest to the door drops his head slightly, and I know he is my target.

The roof creaks again and our eyes all fly up above. Who is up there?

"Put her in the car," Antonio demands.

Two of the men step forward and I back away from them. One comes forward and I punch him as hard as I can in the face. He falls back. I turn and round kick the other man, and he staggers back allowing me to try and grab the gun.

"We have your boyfriend," my father announces. I stop dead in my tracks.

Dear, God, no.

"No, you don't. He has been arrested. That's a blatant lie."

I lie.

Distracted, they grab me and push me into a sitting position on a chair.

My father smiles. "You are a terrible liar, but we already know that, don't we, Roshina? Tie her." he demands.

I struggle and fight as the three men hold me down and tie me to a chair.

"He's with Stucco right now." My father smiles.

I shake my head as the perspiration runs down my forehead. "You are so fucking stupid."

"Quiet!" he yells.

"Do you know you've got a traitor in the camp?" I ask.

The two men glare at me.

"I caught Stucco stealing your diamonds. Did you know he helps himself to your cargo?"

For a moment my father's mask slips and he frowns. "That's not true."

I smile broadly. "Oh, but it is. They planned to kill Mac and blame it on him."

"Liar." He sneers.

"I heard it with my own ears. How else would I know that diamonds are on the ship?"

Antonio and my father's eyes meet.

"I heard them talking. The plan was to take the diamonds and kill Mac before you arrived."

"Nonsense." He yells.

"You heard about the syringe he got caught with, didn't you?"

Antonio and my father's eyes meet and I know that they had.

"Think about it. What possible benefit could they have had at that time to kill Mac if it wasn't to frame him for a crime they were about to commit?"

My father thinks for a moment.

"I heard him talking to another man," I continue.

"Who?" Antonio growls.

"I don't know. I couldn't see him but there were two men talking on the deck one night when they didn't know I was there. It was about the diamonds they were going to steal in some container or statues or something. I-I don't even know if it's real," I stammer.

Antonio looks out into the darkness of the factory and I can see his evil mind ticking.

They know I'm telling the truth... in a roundabout way.

"That's why I went crazy on the day you were supposed to arrive. I knew that they were going to blame him for their crime." I shake my head as I try to talk my way out of this. "I knew he had literally hours to live."

"He still does." My father sneers.

"He didn't do anything wrong. If anything, you owe him. He saved me from your animals. He's going to jail for a very long time. Leave him out of this," I plead.

Antonio glares into space. "Bring Stucco to me." He growls.

"He's minutes away," one of the other men replies. "He just texted through."

Antonio and my father's eyes meet again. I fiddle with the rope tying my hands behind my back as I try to subtly break free.

"Walk the perimeter." Antonio growls. Two men immediately walk outside to check our surroundings. He dials a number on his cell phone and he waits for an answer.

"Hello."

He listens for a moment.

"Check the container." He growls, then he listens for a moment and his eyes flash to my father. "We have a thief in our camp."

He listens again.

"Call me back immediately." He hangs up.

Think.

I hear a car pull up on the gravel outside and I close my eyes. Fuck, here we go.

I hear the two men talking and the door opens and Stucco walks in smiling.

Antonio takes a gun and aims it straight at his head. Stuccos face falls and he holds his hands up in the air. "Do you have something to tell us?" Antonio growls.

"W-what's going on?" Stucco stammers frightfully.

It's really hard not to smirk as I watch these fuckers all turn on each other.

Antonio's phone rings and he answers immediately. Stucco stands still with his hands in the air.

Antonio listens and his eyes flicker with fury before he hangs up. He drops his gun and shoots Stucco straight in the leg.

The gun shot rings loudly and he falls to the ground, screaming out in pain.

"Where are the fucking diamonds?" Antonio growls.

"Ahhh," he cries as he writhes around in pain. "What are you talking about?"

"Do not lie to me!" My father yells. He walks over and kicks Stucco hard in the stomach.

I scrunch my eyes shut. Oh no, I don't want to see this. "Who is working with you?" he yells.

"I don't know what you are talking about?" he screams. He kicks him again and I drop my head as tears fill my eyes.

This is brutal.

I hear a bang outside and a commotion, and then a gunshot rings out.

What?

Someone is here. Someone is outside.

Antonio lifts his gun and points his finger in the air and rotates it. The three remaining men all lift their guns and disappear out the front door.

Oh no. Oh no. Who is that?

Stucco writhes in pain as he bleeds profusely, and I drop my head once more so I don't have to see the suffering.

I can't deal with this.

I hear a bang and then a crunch and I hear another man cry out.

Oh fuck, what's going on out there?

Antonio lifts his chin to the last remaining two guards and they walk over to the window to try and see what is going on. After a moment they walk to the other end of the factory and disappear out another entrance.

I stop breathing.

I sit tied to a chair, alone in a room with two of the most evil men on the planet. Is that my Stace out there fighting? He needs my help? I begin to frantically try to untie the rope. I have to get out of here. I need to help him.

I hear another gunshot and my father disappears into the darkness of the factory.

Tears of fear run down my face.

The door bangs open and Stace comes into view covered in

blood. Oh my God, he's taken out the four men outside with his bare hands.

He holds his gun up at Antonio. "Untie her." He growls.

Antonio smiles darkly. "Not a chance." He raises his gun and points it at Stace. I rock my chair back and forward. I need to distract him. The chair falls and in that split second Stace runs at Antonio and tackles him to the ground. They go flying onto the hard concrete with a thud. He hits him hard three times and smashes the gun from his hands. Antonio rolls on top and hits Stace and blood spatters up everywhere. The sounds of the hits are so brutal.

Stace gets the upper hand again and rolls on top as he smashes his head on the concrete and my father walks out of the shadows with his gun drawn on Stace.

No... dear, God, no.

"No!" I yell.

He turns and shoots me in the upper thigh and I scream out in pain.

The fighting immediately stops and Antonio is only semi-conscious as he lies on his back.

I scream in pain. Oh God, I'm going to die.

Stace stands covered in blood and holds his hands in the air in surrender.

"No," I yell. "Run, Stace!" I scream as the burn of the bullet burns my skin and I see the large sea of deep, dark red blood puddle around me on the floor.

He has a deep gash on his cheekbone and his nose is obviously broken, the blood trickling down his face.

"Don't kill her," he whispers.

"Why not?'

"Kill me instead."

Vikinos holds the gun at Stace. "On your knees."

"Stace, no," I cry.

Not again. No, not again.

Stace drops to his knees.

"Hands behind your head."

Stace slowly brings his hands up to behind his head.

"I love you, Rosh," he whispers almost to himself.

My father walks around behind him and places the gun to the back of his head.

"Stop it!" I scream. "No, please," I beg.

Two gunshots ring out.

"No!" I cry.

But it is my father that drops to the ground.

A bullet hole right through his forehead and another through his chest.

My eyes fly up to the ceiling above to see two men in black with sniper rifles hidden in the beams.

My face screws up in tears of relief and I drop my head and weep. Stace falls back to the ground from his knees.

He is covered in blood and exhausted.

A siren rings out from outside, and suddenly, after a commotion, ten policemen come storming through the doors in full swat gear.

They run to me. "Roshelle." The policeman unties me. "Are you okay?" He lifts his face to meet mine.

"What happened?"

"A man came in and shot him," I whisper.

"What man?" the policeman asks.

"He left in a car," I whisper as my eyes find Stace. The hit men came through.

I need to cover for them because they just saved our lives.

25

Roshelle

I INHALE DEEPLY as I try to get comfortable. I'm half asleep, groggy, and incoherent.

"Shelly," a familiar voice whispers.

I frown in the semi-lit room. Who is that?

"Shelly," the voice whispers again. "Come back to me."

I frown as I drag my eyes open and the pain in my leg throbs. It's semi-dark, dusk, maybe. I glance around at my surroundings. I'm in a hospital room.

What? Where am I?

"Shelly. Oh my God. I thought I was going to lose you," he whispers as he drops his head to rest on the bed.

I frown. What the hell? "Where?" I stop myself.

Todd takes my hand in his. "You're safe now."

I shake my head as confusion sets in. Stace. Where is Stace? My thoughts are interrupted by a nurse as she walks into the room.

"Oh, she's awake." She smiles, she walks over and takes my blood pressure and vitals.

"Do you know where you are?" she asks.

I look around the room in despair. "Hospital?" I whisper.

She smiles broadly and Todd picks my hand back up in his. I cough. My throat is so dry. The nurse passes me a glass of water and I sip it slowly.

"What happened?" I whisper. Todd brushes the hair back from my forehead and I swat his hand away. "Don't," I whisper, annoyed.

"You have been through a horrifying ordeal," Todd replies softly. "You are home now."

My eyes hold his, and although I'm still foggy, I know I didn't imagine him and Melissa at that nightclub. "Home?" I ask.

"Yes, I'm here, and I'm not leaving your side. I've been frantic." I frown. "I thought I had lost you forever." He smiles softly.

My eyes flicker to the nurse in confusion and she smiles. "I will go and get the doctor." She leaves the room.

"I know about your father." Todd pauses. "I know about everything." I stay silent as the tears fill my eyes. "Why didn't you tell me?" he asks.

I stare straight ahead, unable to make myself look at him.

"I could have helped you deal with this. I could have protected you."

"What happened?" I whisper. What does he know? "I don't remember much."

"You were kidnapped by your father's men." I frown. "He tried to kill you again, but thankfully he was shot dead."

I swallow the lump in my throat as I see him lying on the cold, hard factory floor. The pain pumps hard in my leg. "My leg?" I whisper.

"You were shot."

I frown and my eyes meet his for the first time.

He wipes the hair back from my forehead. "I'm so sorry, Shelly. We will get through this. I love you, we will get through this."

"Melissa?" I ask.

He shakes his head angrily. "It was a mistake, a one-night, terrible mistake. We haven't seen each other since. She has moved out of the apartment. I have been frantic and going out of my mind searching for you."

I turn my eyes straight ahead again and stare into space.

The doctor comes through the door. "Well, hello." He smiles broadly. "You are looking much better."

He picks up my chart and checks my vitals that the nurse has just taken. "From one to ten, what is your pain level?"

"Ten." I wince as I try to move.

"I will give you some stronger pain medication." He turns to the nurse. "Can you give her some morphine, please?" He turns back to me and smiles. "We operated, and thankfully the bullet has made no permanent damage. You will be up and about in no time."

My eyes hold his. "Do you know where the man who saved me is?" I whisper.

The doctor's eyes flicker to Todd.

"He didn't save you Shelly. He was the man who kidnapped you," Todd replies. "You're confused, angel." He bends and kisses my forehead.

I frown. "No."

The doctor takes my hand in his. "You have been to Hell and back over last month. I don't want you to think about it now. I need you to concentrate on getting stronger, getting well."

"Where is he?" I whisper. "I need to see him—"

"Shelly, listen to me," Todd interrupts as he brings my face to meet his. "You are traumatized. I'm here. I'm going to get you through this."

My eyes fill with tears. I feel weak. I'm confused. "Where is my love?" I whisper.

"I'm here, angel," Todd replies. "I'm right here." He picks up my hand and kisses the back of it.

The nurse injects me, and as the tears roll down my face, I somehow drift into sleep.

I wake in the early hours of the morning. My room is darkened and the hospital is silent. I buzz for the nurse and stay staring at the ceiling for a while until a new nurse comes in. She's young, younger than me.

She smiles sweetly. "Hello. You buzzed."

"I feel like I need to go to the restroom," I whisper.

She checks my catheter. "I will just empty your bag." She fusses about and empties my bag and then tops up my meds.

"You are a nurse?" she asks.

I smile softly and nod. "Yes."

She stands at the side of my bed in the darkness and picks up my hand in hers. My strength breaks down and my eyes fill with tears.

"Do you want me to sit with you for a while?" she whispers in the darkness.

I nod, unable to speak.

She pulls up a chair and sits with my hand in hers. The tears start to run down my face.

She doesn't speak and neither do I, but having her here with me is enough.

———

I am woken up by Todd. "Good morning, Shelly." He smiles broadly.

"Hi."

"You look better today. How are you feeling?"

"Fine."

I stare at him for a moment. I have to know. "What happened to the man?"

He frowns. "That animal has been charged with your kidnapping and rape. He has been deported to Colombia for trial."

My face falls.

"I hope they give him the death sentence."

"He didn't rape me."

"Yes, yes, he did. His semen was found in a rape kit test carried out on you. DNA testing has come through."

"It was consensual," I snap.

His face falls. "You don't know what you are saying, angel."

"Yes, I do."

"No, you don't. You have been kidnapped and beaten into submission by that freak."

"His name is Stace," I snap. "Don't speak about him like that."

His eyes meet mine.

"I'm in love with him," I whisper.

He screws up his face. "You're not in love with him. He has brainwashed you. You are traumatized."

"I'm not in love with you."

"Yes, you are," he commands. "You have been through a lot."

"I've seen what it's like," I whisper. Todd buzzes for the nurse.

"I don't need a nurse," I snap. "I need to know what happened to Stace. Tell me what happened to him!"

The nurse walks in. "Can you give her something please to calm her down. She's delusional."

I frown. "No, I'm not. Get out!"

"I won't be going anywhere." He puts his hands on his hips in an outrage. "She is obviously having some kind of mental episode."

"Where is he?" I yell. "Take me to him."

The nurse buzzes for back up.

"I wasn't raped. He would never do that!" I snap. "You need to tell the police. Get them. Get the police for me now," I whisper.

———

"And then what happened?" The officer's eyes glance up from his notepad.

"I snuck onto the boat," I continue. I have to get him out of this. He is rotting in a prison somewhere for something he hasn't done.

"We know that's not true, Shelly."

I cut him off. "My name is Roshina."

The officer's eyes meet and then the other one interjects. "We have been over this a million times over the last week. We have video footage of you being taken against your will and put into the trunk of a car."

"I wasn't raped."

"You have been brainwashed. It's not unusual for victims to become attached to their attacker," the officer soothes.

"I'm not... I'm not fucking brainwashed," I stammer in frustration. "Listen to what I am saying. He didn't touch me. He took me to save me from the other men. He helped me escape. I want him set free."

The officer's eyes hold mine.

"He isn't even in the country anymore."

"Where is he?"

"He has been extradited to the Colombian authorities and charged with your kidnapping and drug offenses."

"It was on American soil. Why has he been extradited? I don't understand why nobody is listening to me."

"That is not your concern," Todd snaps from the doorway.

I glare at him. For a week now he has been pretending we are something that we're not and that I'm simply going crazy. What he doesn't know is that day-by-day I am getting stronger, and as my strength builds, so does my hatred for him.

I haven't forgotten what you did, asshole.

"We understand you are getting released next week," the policeman replies.

I nod. "Yes."

"You can't be released out on your own. Where are you going to stay while you recover?"

"In my apartment."

"You can't. As the doctors and psychologists have told you numerous times, you are not well enough to look after yourself just yet. The doctors have instructed us that you are not of sane mind to be left alone and you are physically incapable of caring for yourself." The policeman frowns. "Perhaps you should take the rehabilitation center option."

"I'm going home and I know my options. You can't keep me against my will."

"I will be with her," Todd replies.

"No, you won't."

"I'm looking after you whether you like it not."

I roll my eyes. Fuck's sake, why won't anyone listen to me? The policeman blows out a frustrated breath and shakes his head. He takes out his wallet and hands me a business card. "If you need me, just call." I take the card and stare at it. My thoughts go back to the engagement ring specialist card that

Stace had.

I was so happy then.

"The case has been closed from our end. I will not be in touch with you again unless you contact me."

I nod as I stare at the card.

"Todd." The policeman turns to him. "If you need our assistance, here is our card." He hands him another card. "Here is the mental health crisis centre line, in case you need it."

Todd nods as he takes the two cards. "I think I'm going to."

This is bullshit. "I'm not a child. I'm not unstable," I snap.

Todd's eyes flicker to me. "Thank you, officers. I have it handled from here."

The officers leave and Todd falls into the seat along side of me.

"Todd..." I pause. "We have to talk."

His eyes hold mine. I know I can't tell him the truth because they will put me into a mental institution.

"I don't love you anymore."

"Yes, you do. We can get through this."

I shake my head and smile softly as my eyes fill with tears.

"I've been through enough."

"I know, and that's why you need me."

"I need to be alone. For the first time in my whole life, I want to be alone."

His eyes hold mine.

"I'm sorry about Melissa, I'm so, so sorry. I love you. Please let's work through this."

I shake my head and take his hand as empathy fills me. "I don't think I ever loved you, Todd." He frowns.

"I am incapable of loving you."

He stares at me as he thinks.

"I want you to walk out that door."

He looks to the door.

"And I don't want you to come back."

"I don't want you to deal with this alone."

"I have been alone my whole life."

"Shelly," he whispers sadly. "I fucked up, but I can fix it."

"It's broken for good, Todd," I whisper. "We can't be fixed."

———

A knock bangs at the door. "Hello, Shelly. My name is Erica and I am a psychologist. We had an appointment booked for this morning."

Grateful for the interruption, I smile. "Yes, of course. Come in, please."

I've been in rehab for two weeks. It's been six weeks since I was shot. I finally got the message through to Todd and he stopped coming to see me, although he still rings me every morning and night. The psychologist has diagnosed me with Stockholm syndrome, and so, for now, I am just playing along and agreeing with them.

Six long weeks since I lost the other half of me.

Does he think about me all the time, like I do him? Sometimes I wake up and I feel like I won't be able to survive another hour without him.

Are they right? Am I crazy?

It doesn't really matter anymore, I suppose, and I just need to concentrate on my health for the time being. One of the nurses from work is flying in to pick me up today and then fly back home with me. I'm assuming it's my closest friend Moira, I think my boss would have sent her. I'm excited to be seeing familiar faces. It's been a lonely six weeks and I've had no contact with anyone at all.

I sit on my bed as the nurse goes through the last of my medication and discharge notes with me.

"And this one here is the one that helps you to sleep." She scribbles onto the box, sleeping.

I nod. "Okay."

"But remember, you can't drive when you are taking these."

"Okay." I smile. "Thank you. You have been wonderful." I smile.

"You going to be okay?" she asks.

I shrug. "Yeah, I'm tough."

"No shit." She smirks and leaves me to it. I walk over to the window and stare out over the city.

I don't like Vegas. I don't think I will ever come back here.

"Hello, love," a familiar voice rings through the room. I turn. Annette, Stace's Mom.

Tears fill my eyes.

"Are you ready to go home?" she asks softly.

"What?" I whisper.

"I've come to get my daughter-in-law and take her home."

I frown, confused.

"You can stay with me for a little while and I will take care of you. You can then move into Stace's house in Manhattan"

I stand still.

"Where is he?" I whisper.

"He's in prison in Colombia."

My face screws up in pain. "Is he okay?" I whisper.

"He will be better when he knows you are being looked after."

I smile through my tears. "Does he know you're here?" I ask hopefully.

She wraps her arms around me. "He sent me to come for you." She kisses my face. She holds me in an embrace, and for some stupid reason, the skies open up and I cry stupid howling-to-the-moon tears.

"Come on." She eventually smiles. "Let's go home."

———

I bounce down the street in Bogota in the ice-pink dress I had made. It's a mirror image of the one Stace bought me for our first date. I wonder if he will remember. It has been two long years, but today he finally got out of prison. He was originally sentenced to five years, but we got it reduced to two on appeal. That was the best we could do with the cash that we had.

He wouldn't let me pick him up this morning. He said he has a surprise for me.

I moved to Colombia as soon as I was well enough. I needed to be closer to him. I live in a beautiful house in the hills and life has been good.

I needed this time alone, to find myself. To find out who I am supposed to be when I am not living in fear. I've finally forgiven myself for my mother's death.

It wasn't my fault. I know that now.

I've visited Stace in prison three times a week, every week. It was the maximum amount of visits he could have. The time has only brought us closer.

We are so in love.

He didn't have the privilege of conjugal visits. The prison he was in was too overcrowded and didn't have the facilities.

Every time I said goodbye and put my hand on the glass,

and he did the same, we both died a little without each other's touch.

Not even a kiss.

He's done it, though. The conditions were atrocious and yet every time I visited, he was more concerned about me and how I was doing. At first, I was petrified that Vikinos would have men in the prison. But, thankfully, that hasn't seemed to be a problem at all. It would have been a different story had he been put into an American one.

I'm not only in love with him.

I like him.

He's a good man. My hardened criminal is a good man.

I'm buzzing, buzzing with excitement. Buzzing with anxiety.

What if things have changed between us, and the chemistry has gone?

It hasn't. I know it hasn't, but hell, two years is a long time to have a best friend and not be able to touch him.

I turn the corner onto the safety deposit box street. We arranged to meet here and get our diamonds out together. I didn't want to come back here without him. These are his diamonds, too. I keep walking and I catch sight of him. He looks up, our eyes meet, and in that moment my heart completely stops.

He's waiting out the front on the steps and he has a golden little puppy on a leash.

An over the top smile breaks free on my face, and I walk faster. I skip and then I start to run. He laughs and walks toward me, and I jump into his arms where he spins me around. Our lips connect and I laugh through my tears.

We kiss as his hands wrap tightly around me. Oh God, he feels so good.

We kiss again and again and I feel my arm being tugged by the little, sandy friend.

I bend and pat him on the head. "Hello." I smile through tears. "What's your name?"

The little Labrador pulls back on his lead to try and escape this new form of torture. He does this pathetic little woof and I laugh out loud.

"You got me a puppy?"

Stace nods as he drags me to my feet, his hand holding my jaw the way he wants me and his tongue caressing my lips.

Oh God, I've missed this.

"We need to go home," he whispers.

"Diamonds." I smile as I wrap my arms around his broad muscular shoulders. He's much bigger than he was before.

He walks me backwards until I am up against the wall, his hands on my face, his hard length up against my stomach. "I couldn't care less about the diamonds," he breathes into my mouth. "It's you that I want."

His mouth drops to my neck and I close my eyes in pleasure as his whiskers dust my skin. We kiss again and he's right, we really do need to get home. I could come on the spot.

"Diamonds and home," I breathe.

He bends and picks up our new family member and we walk into the office and up to reception.

"We are here to empty our deposit box," he says. He hands over his identification and I watch him. He's different. Harder, yet softer, if that makes sense. His body has changed from all of his weight sessions and now, when I look at him, I only see the Stace that I am in love with. The beautiful man who saved me, both physically and mentally. My attention goes to the little puppy as he grabs his lead in his mouth and pulls backwards as hard as he can. I smile as we play tug of war with his lead and he lets out a squeaky little bark again.

I have a puppy.

We follow the guard down to our locker and Stace hands me the key. I open the box and his lips drop to the back of my neck as his hands skim up and down my body.

"I've missed you," he whispers.

Goosebumps scatter up my arms. I turn and kiss him over my shoulder.

I love this man. I love the meaning and the sense of belonging he has brought to my life.

He kisses me again and I turn in his arms, and we forget where we are once more.

The lead gets pulled from Stace's hand and our little friend runs around our feet. He fake growls and barks in his squeaky little voice.

"Just get them and we can go." He smiles as he bends to pick him up again. Our puppy fights and wrestles, clearly he thinks this is playtime.

I open the locker and see the tied sock sitting inside. I smile broadly and Stace shakes his head in amazement.

We got away with it.

When I first got to Bogota, Stace didn't want me to come here alone in case it put me in danger. I had enough money and, after thinking on it for a while, decided to wait for him. We will face the challenges together as they come up.

We walk out of the building and flag a cab.

"Hello." I smile as we climb in. I slide over to give my two companions room. "Can you take us to the lower mountains, please?" I ask.

He nods and turns as he pulls out into the traffic.

Staces hand goes straight to my thigh and he slowly slides it under my skirt. His lips drop to my neck, his fingers subtly slide up and up and then slowly circle over my sex.

"I need you," he whispers in my ear. "I can't wait until we get home."

My eyes close as my arousal hits new levels. How could I have thought that the chemistry might be gone between us?

It's explosive.

"How do you feel?" he whispers. "Show me how you feel." He lifts my leg and hooks it over his so I am effectively half sitting on his lap.

Oh shit. I hold my breath as his fingers slip underneath the side of my panties. He slides the back of his fingers through my wet flesh. He hisses in approval into my ear and readjusts himself as he opens my legs further.

Fucking hell. We are in a damn cab.

"Open," he whispers.

I can hardly keep my eyes open, I'm so aroused. "Stace," I breathe onto his open lips. "Just wait."

"I can't."

He pushes forward and slides a finger into me and we both nearly convulse. Two years is a long time to go without each other's touch.

His breath quivers as he slowly slides his finger out and then back in. His open lips are on the side of my neck. My eyes stay firmly fixed on the rear view mirror. Thankfully the driver hasn't looked our way at all. He has headphones in.

"You're so wet," he whispers in my ear.

I nod, unable to speak as his magical fingers slide in slowly again.

"You need to be fucked, baby." His breath brushes my ear and goosebumps scatter everywhere, whether it's from the words or the sensations, I can't be sure.

I shudder, no shit. An orgasm is dangerously close and I feel him smile underneath me.

"I'm going to blow so hard," he whispers. He pushes three fingers into me and I lose control and lie back across him.

I need him to fuck me. I need him to fuck me now. A rush of arousal floods me and he hisses in appreciation.

His thick fingers slide in and then slowly out again.

"Here we are," the driver says flatly.

Oh shit. I jump off Stace's lap and shake my head. What the bloody hell are we doing? I widen my eyes at Stace and he smirks as he puts his three fingers in his mouth and sucks them. I freeze as I watch him and my insides begin to liquefy.

This man is so fucking hot, he fries my brain.

As if reading my mind, Stace smiles sexily and takes my purse to pay the driver. I don't have one coherent thought in my head right now. He drags our puppy and me from the cab and it drives off. He looks up at the house in front of us. It's a two-story terrace kind of house, white with blue doors and trim. The windows have the same blue shutters around them. The ivy is overgrown and all over the wall, and we have a fountain is in the front garden

"This is it." I smile nervously.

He smiles as his eyes roam over the house. "Looks nice."

I shrug, smile, and struggle to pull our little friend on his leash. "He hates this leash."

Stace follows me as he continues to stare at our surroundings.

What must it be like to be locked away for two years? I can't imagine what is going through his head right now.

I open the blue, arch-shaped door and we walk inside. The flooring is tiled in all different shades of green in big diamond shapes, and the walls are a warm terracotta colour. It is the epitome of South America and exactly why I wanted this house when I first looked at it.

It's warm, earthy, and inviting.

"This is the lounge room." I gesture to the lounge room and we walk through the hallway. "This is the kitchen."

He looks around the timber kitchen and smiles. "Where is the laundry?" he asks.

"Oh, through here." I walk through the hallway and show him the laundry and he looks around. His dark eyes come back to my face.

"Where is our bedroom?"

Nerves flutter through me. It's been a long time. "Upstairs," I whisper.

He takes me by my hand, leads me back to the staircase, and we continue upstairs.

"Last door on the right," I murmur.

He puts the puppy down and walks me up the hall to our bedroom. His eyes scan the space.

There's a large bed with white linen and timber furnishings. It's simple.

I stand nervously and he turns to face me. "It's nice." His lips meet mine and he kisses me softly.

I smile. I can't believe he is actually here with me... in our home. I've waited so long for him to come home.

"I have something for you." He wrestles around in his pocket and pulls out something wrapped in tissue paper.

I frown as he unwraps it and then he drops to his knee and holds up a ring.

I stare at him, overwhelmed with emotion.

"Marry me."

I'm speechless. I have no words.

"I want you to marry me."

"I know." I smile as I bend and kiss him. "I want you to marry me back," I whisper through my tears, onto his lips.

"Is that a yes?"

I nod. "That's a hell fucking yeah." I laugh. He stands and lifts me, and then throws me onto the bed. I bounce hard.

He stands, and as his dark eyes hold mine, he takes his shirt off and then slowly slides his jeans down.

My breath catches. He was muscular before, but now... there are no words to describe his physique. Tall and broad with a chiselled, cut stomach, and a distinct V of muscles that go down to his groin.

I've never seen anything more beautiful.

His huge cock hangs heavily between his legs and my sex clenches in appreciation.

Good God. Bad Boy Heaven in all its glory... and he loves me.

He sits me up, takes my dress over my head, and then lies me back and slides my panties down my legs.

I can hardly breathe as I lie naked before him. His eyes roam all over my flesh as if memorising every inch of my skin.

"Open your legs," he whispers.

I open my legs slightly and he pushes them back to the mattress and stares at me for a moment as I see a myriad of emotions cross his face.

"What's wrong?" I whisper.

"Nothing."

I frown.

"You don't know how long I have thought of this moment."

"What have you thought about?" I ask as I bring my hand up to cup his face.

"To have you wearing my ring. To have you naked in my bed. To have you love me."

"And I do," I whisper. "I love you so much."

He kisses me softly and crawls over me, sliding home in one deep thrust. We both groan out in pleasure.

He pulls out slowly and slides in deep again, and as he lifts his body up onto his straightened arms, he smiles broadly. "Honey, I'm home."

I laugh out loud as he slams into me again. Fairy tales do come true.

Super heroes are real.

EPILOGUE
FIVE YEARS LATER.

Roshelle

"AH BABY, CAREFUL." I run to the bottom of the stairs as the little diaper behind tries to climb up. I pick her up and put her onto my hip.

Molly is two, cheeky as hell, and into everything... just like her dad. She squeals in delight and tries to wriggle free.

We live in Oyster Bay Cove on Long Island now, in a large, beautiful, two-storey house. We have a swimming pool and a double lot of land, and thanks to our diamond heist, we want for nothing. After toying with the idea of living overseas, we decided against it. We have exotic holidays a couple of times a year, but that's about as far as it goes. When it really comes down to it, what makes us the happiest is family. Stace wanted to be here for Sebastian, his nephew.

He figured the best gift he could give Justin, his brother, was to bring up Sebastian as his own.

And that's just what he's doing.

We have bought Annette, his mother, a house in the same estate, and also one for his sister-in-law Cindy, Sebastian's mother. We are all very close. They have become the family I didn't have. They looked after me so well in those first few months when I came to live with them while Stace was in prison. I will be forever grateful that they adopted me the way that they did when they didn't even know me. Cindy has recently remarried and is pregnant with their first little one. Her new husband Andrew is nice. I know it kills Stace to see his brother's love move on, but he wants her happy, like we all do. Seb, as we call him, is eleven now and lives with us half the time just as he would if he was Stace's son. He is at an age where he wants to be around Stace, and when Cindy started dating Andrew we had him more often to give them time alone. Seb has insisted it stays that way and his mom is only around the corner if he needs her.

Stace is at every ball game, training session, every school function, every birthday party. They fish, they fix things, they camp, and Stace loves Seb with everything that he has. They have a beautiful relationship and Seb really does see him as his father.

I smile down at the little blonde haired girl staring up at me. Cheekiness personified.

This one has her dad wrapped around her finger. I hear the electronic gates open and I know the boys are home. I glance out the kitchen window to see Stace's big, black pick-up roll into the driveway. I bought him that black Ferrari that he loved so much. Funnily enough, he hardly ever drives it. It's a trophy car and a waste of money, if I'm totally honest. Stace has started a development company. If he had his time again, he would have gone back into The Marines, but now that he has a crim-

Play Along

inal record, that wasn't an option. He's doing well and has four men working for him. Sometimes he flies a helicopter for fun on the weekend if he has the time.

Like a whirlwind, they come through the kitchen back door. Seb is bouncing his basketball and Stace is carrying groceries in bags that they have just bought.

"Dada!" Molly screams in excitement and he laughs and scoops her up and spins her around in excitement.

The ball bounces continually and I shake my head. What is it about ball bouncing that drives me so mad? "Stop bouncing that ball, please, Seb," I call.

"Yeah, okay," he replies from the lounge room as he turns on the television.

Stace puts Molly down and she runs off to play with Seb, and Stace wraps me in his arms.

"How is my beautiful wife today?" His hand gently rubs over my heavily pregnant stomach.

I smile up at him as I kiss him softly. We got married in Bogota the day after he got out of prison. We couldn't wait any longer.

I look at him deadpan. "Huge."

"Hugely hot."

"You know it." I smirk against his lips as he kisses me softly. I have five weeks to go until this little one comes.

"What have you got for me tonight?" he whispers as his hand cups my behind and his lips drop to my neck.

"I thought maybe we could do a little role play." I smile.

"Oh yeah, I like the sound of that." He breathes and I feel him harden up against my hip.

"To stay alive you have to play along and pretend you're pregnant," I whisper into his ear as I nip it with my teeth.

His eyes meet mine and he smirks.

"And we can strap a ten-pound bag of potatoes to your stomach and see how sexy you feel."

He pushes me backward until I am up against the wall. His arms surround me, effectively trapping me in, and his erection digs into my hip.

"You've never been sexier," he whispers onto my lips as his tongue slowly ploughs though my mouth. "I've never wanted you more than I do now."

My breath catches. "You have a pregnant woman fetish?"

He smiles darkly as he pumps me with his hips. "Maybe I do."

"Sick," I mouth. "You better get your kids to bed early then." I smirk.

"Why is that?" He smiles against my lips as his hand explores under my skirt.

"Because I want to have pregnant sex with my husband."

His fingers slip underneath my panties and I pull back and shake my head. "Kids in bath," I mouth.

He rolls his eyes and steps back. "Bath time, guys," he calls.

"I'm super tired and I want an early night."

He grabs my behind and drags me across his large cock. "You have an hour and a half, Mrs. Mac, before you are going to be fucked. Hard." His eyes drop to my lips and he grabs himself through his jeans to release a bit of tension.

I smile and slide my hand down his jeans and cup him in my hand. "Two children, dinner, and bed first," I remind him.

He tips his head back to the ceiling in frustration. "Bath time. Now," he snaps as he disappears up the stairs.

I hear the shower and bath turn on and I smile as I continue to finish dinner.

This is life.

This is love.
Stace style.

The End.

Read on for an excerpt of The Italian.

THE ITALIAN EXCERPT
AVAILABLE NOW

Olivia

I stare up at the sign above the door, and I smile.

When in Rome

That's me, in Rome, loving myself sick.

The weather is warm, the scenery is breathtaking, and Rome is everything I dreamt it would be.

I'm in week two of a five-week Italian vacation. I've been to Venice and I've been to Tuscany. I may also be in the middle of a small midlife crisis, but whatever. It's forced me out of my comfort zone and into this Heaven, so I'll take it.

I push open the dark, heavy, timber door, and I walk into the bar and restaurant. It's dusk outside, and the restaurant is large with a huge back garden area. Fairy lights are lighting up the space, and it has a party feel to it with jovial laughter echoing loudly around me. A three-piece band are playing at the front, and the place is a hive of activity. One man is singing, while two others play guitar. I can't understand what they're saying but I don't need to. It sounds so good—*so Italian.*

I take a seat at a table for two outside in the courtyard.

"Buona sera." The waiter grins as he approaches.

I smile nervously. "Do you speak English?"

"Ah, yes, Madame. How can I help you?"

I quickly peruse the menu. "May I have a Prosecco, please?"

"Ottimo." He nods and takes off in the direction of the bar, leaving me to look around in wonder at the gorgeous surroundings.

Everything is exaggerated in Italy. The hand gestures, the laughing, the story telling.

The beauty of the language. I could sit and listen to people speak Italian all day, and I have done so for fourteen days straight now.

It's been the best trip. I thought I would have been nervous traveling on my own, but I've found an inner bravery I didn't know I had. I've eaten out every night by myself, and I haven't once felt self-conscious or unsafe. The people are all so lovely and friendly that I feel totally at home.

I glance around the crowded bar and see people drinking, laughing, and having the time of their lives. I find myself smiling as I watch them talk with their friends.

The waiter comes back with an entire bottle of Prosecco, and my face falls. Oh jeez,

I meant a glass, not the whole damn bottle. I'm going to have to pace myself.

I watch on as he pours me a glass. "Grazie." I smile.

He nods as he gestures to the food menu. "I back soon, okay?"

"Yes, okay." I open my menu and look down at the choices as he runs off to tend to other customers.

Everything is written in Italian. Some choices I can make out, and others I have no idea about. I look at the people at the tables around me to see what they are eating.

There's pizza, pasta, something in a hot pot. Everything does look delicious, though. I look up to the bar and stare straight into the eyes of a man. I didn't notice him before. He's standing with a group of men. He's huge, towering above the others around him. His black hair has a little length to it, with a curl, and his eyes are dark. Those eyes are unmistakably locked on me, and he doesn't look away. Instead, he dips his head and gives me a slow, sexy smile.

My stomach flips—his gaze is intense... hungry.

Is he doing that to me, or is his girlfriend behind me?

I sip my drink and casually look at the surrounding tables. I drag my eyes back to my menu and scan back through the choices. He has me flustered from just one look. From my peripheral vision, I feel him still watching me, and I glance back over.

Our eyes meet and he smiles again, prompting me to give him a reaction. I have no idea if he's smiling at me or not, but I decide to play along with the fantasy that is him.

I give a weak smile, and then in slow motion his lips curl into the sexiest damn smile I've ever seen. How can a smile be so fucking sexy?

He's absolutely drop dead gorgeous—tall, dark, exotic. He's everything I'm not.

I look back down at my menu.

Focus fool.

Abbacchio alla Cacciatora

Abbacchio Brodettato
Bistecca Fiorentina
Braciole
Braciolone
Bresaola
Brodo
Cacciatore

I frown as I look down at the choices, and I turn the page. A million delicious things on the menu, and I'm about to no doubt order something crap that I'll hate.

I glance back up to the Italian Stallion and he's gone. My heart drops.

"Looking for me?" I hear a deep voice say from behind me.

I jump and turn and see him standing behind me. "W-what?" I stammer as I stare up at the god.

His eyes hold mine. "I asked if you were looking for me."

I stare at him, electricity zaps through the air between us. I'm unable to think because of his close proximity. He's even more delicious up close, if that's even possible.

"Ahh." I pick up my drink and take a big gulp. "No, actually."

He chuckles, the sound deep and raspy. It does things to my insides.

He holds out his hand for me to take. "My name is Enrico Ferrara."

I place my hand into his. Its big, warm, and holy hell, is this happening?

Enrico sounds *so exotic.*

"I've been watching you from the bar," he says with a heavy accent.

"You have?"

"Do you need some help?"

Help with what? Kissing? Undressing? Unzipping your trousers?

Stop it.

He smirks to himself as if knowing exactly what I was thinking. "Help with the menu." He gestures to the menu in my hand. "I saw you frowning while reading it."

"Oh, of course." I giggle nervously and drain my glass. *Idiot.* "Yes, that would be great, thank you."

He sits down opposite me and steeples his hands under his chin. His eyes are assessing me. "Come ti chiami?"

I don't know what he just said, but fuck, it sounded good. "I don't speak Italian, I'm sorry."

"What is your name?" he repeats in English.

"Oh." I shake my head, flustered. Honestly, this guy needs to go away, I'm embarrassing myself here. "Olivia Reynolds."

He picks up my hand across the table and slowly kisses the backs of my fingers, leaving me to watch on. "Olivia," he purrs. "What a beautiful name."

Oh jeez. "Thank you."

We stare at each other, and my heart is beating hard in my chest from the feeling of his lips. A trace of a smile crosses his mouth, and he's clearly amused by my physical reaction to him.

Annoyed with myself, I snatch my hand away and open my menu. Unexpectedly, he does the same.

"What would you like to eat, bella?"

You. I would like to eat you. "What would you suggest?" I ask casually as I pretend to read through the choices. I can't see a thing. I have double vision from the smell of his aftershave. Why does he smell so good?

He raises his brow at me. "You like meat?"

I swallow the lump in my throat. "Yes."

His eyes drop to my lips, and I feel my insides clench.

Okay...what the actual hell is going on here? This guy is insanely sexual.

"When was your last meal?"

I look up into his stare...what are we talking about here? Food? Sex? It's been twelve hours since food and twelve months since sex.

I'm basically fucking starving in all areas. "Too long."

Arousal flares in his eyes, and I know in that very second that we *are* talking about sex.

He sits back and steeples his hands under his chin again. "You're beautiful. Where are you from?"

"Australia."

"Where is your man?"

I frown. "I haven't met him yet."

Our eyes lock as tension bounces between us. I've never encountered a sexual attraction to someone like this before. You read about it, but it's never actually happened to me.

I break the silence. "Where is your... other half?"

"I don't have one."

"Oh." I pretend to read the menu once more.

"What are you doing in Rome?" he asks.

"I'm on vacation."

"Alone?"

"No. My girlfriends are back at the hotel," I lie. Rule 101: never tell anyone you are travelling alone. See, Mom, I do remember some rules.

"Why are you here alone... in this bar?"

"You're very nosey." He frowns as if not understanding the term. "Inquisitive," I add.

"I don't understand."

"You want to know everything."

He breaks out into a broad beautiful smile. "I do." He reaches over and picks up a piece of my shoulder length, honey-blonde hair. "So fair," he says. "Is your hair fair like this everywhere?"

I swallow the lump in my throat as my heart has an epileptic fit.

He smiles as if fascinated and takes my face in his hands. "Blue eyes."

"The opposite to you," I breathe.

"Opposites attract." His eyes drop to my lips again.

Okay, what the actual fuck is going on here?

I pull out of his grip and open the menu in a fluster. "The food," I remind him.

He sits back, clearly annoyed that I pulled away from him. "I already know what you are eating tonight."

"You do?"

His eyes hold mine. "And so do you."

I begin to hear my heartbeat pounding in my ears. Is he thinking what I'm thinking? "What's that?"

"Pasta."

"Pasta?" I frown.

"Yes, of course. What did you think I meant?"

I giggle and refill my glass.

"What were you thinking, Olivia?"

"I don't know. You have me all flustered."

He frowns. "Flustered?" I can see him trying to translate the word. "Like a chicken? You mean plucked?"

I laugh. "Yes, plucked like a chicken."

He smiles and holds his glass up to clink it with mine. "I hope to pluck you many more times tonight, Olivia."

The word play between P and F has never been so high. I smile goofily as we stare at each other, electricity buzzes between us, our glasses touch.

I need to change the subject. "What do you do for work, Enrico?"

"Poliziotto."

"Huh?"

"Policeman?"

"Ah." I smile. "Law enforcer."

"Yes."

I feel myself relax a little. If he's a policeman, I'm safe.

A man approaches the table and says something in Italian. Enrico answers him, and then turns to me.

"Olivia, meet my brother Andrea."

"Hello." I smile as we shake hands.

"Hello, nice to meet you." He smiles. He's slightly younger than Enrico, but with the same gorgeous bloodline: dark hair, olive skin, and big brown eyes. He, too, is deliciously handsome, though in a completely different way to his brother. He seems softer but the family resemblance is strong.

"Andrea is a doctor here in Rome," Enrico says proudly.

"Oh, wow, that's amazing." I begin to feel at ease. He's a cop and his brother is a doctor. Maybe Enrico isn't a serial killer after all.

"Thank you. Are you English?" Andrea asks.

"Australian."

"Ah, I see." He smiles and turns to his brother. "Are you coming with me, Rico, or are you staying? I have to go now. I have work in the morning."

Rico. They call him Rico. *I like that.*

Enrico's eyes come back to me. "No, I'm going to eat pasta

with Olivia, and then show her why I'm the best dancer in all of Italy."

Andrea rolls his eyes, and I smile into my drink.

Sounds so fun.

"All right then, good luck, Miss Olivia." Andrea bends to kiss my cheeks. "You will need it. It was nice to meet you."

"Goodbye, Andrea."

He disappears, and Enrico turns back to me with a satisfied smile. "What am I feeding you, bella? You need energy for dancing."

I giggle and open my menu, this is the best night of my life. "Pasta," I remind him.

"Ah, yes." His eyes dance with delight. "That's right. Pasta it is."

———

"So, tell me about yourself." He drops his chin onto his hand as his elbow rests on the table. "What is the Olivia Reynolds story?"

We've eaten, drank two bottles of wine, and now we're sitting in the darkened courtyard, fairy lights are lighting up the space and the music now soft and romantic. I'm feeling very tipsy indeed.

"Well." I sip my wine. "I'm here on a holiday... I guess to try and find myself."

"Are you lost?"

"Perhaps." I smile bashfully across the table at him.

"Why?"

"I don't know." I contemplate his question. "I feel like I'm searching for something, but I don't know what it is yet. I'm here to try and figure that out."

He gives me a slow sexy smile. "Maybe it's me. Maybe you're looking for an Enrico Ferrara?"

"Oh yes, that's the logical answer, how many of you are there?" I giggle.

"Just one." He smiles. "One is enough."

"How long have you lived in Rome?"

"About ten years. I moved here when I joined the police force. Where do you live in Australia?"

"Sydney. Have you ever been?"

"No, it's on my list, though. I don't travel far."

"Really, why not? I love to travel."

"I prefer Italy. I travel around Europe regularly, but Australia is a long way from here. How long does it take to travel there by plane?"

"Twenty-one hours."

"Twenty-one hours," he scoffs. "On a plane? You must be crazy, woman."

I giggle at his horror. "We're used to it. Australia is on the opposite side of the world from everywhere. If we want to travel, it's a twenty-four-hour plane trip to most places. That, combined with the terrible jetlag from time zones, it turns a lot of people off."

He frowns and sips his drink. "Do you work at home?"

"Yes, I'm a fashion designer."

He smiles, as if surprised. "Really?"

"Uh-huh."

"What do you design?"

I shrug, embarrassed. "Well, I'm designing pyjamas at the moment for Kmart."

"Kmart?" He frowns.

"It's a department store."

"What pyjamas would you put me in?" he asks. I watch his tongue dart out as he sips his drink, and my sex clenches in appreciation.

"I don't think pyjamas would do you justice. I imagine your birthday suit is enough."

His eyes have a tender glow to them as he watches me, and my heart constricts in my chest. He really is a beautiful man.

Embarrassed by my forwardness, I change the subject. "But it's only temporary. I would love to work in fashion one day. That's the ultimate dream."

"Who's your favorite designer?"

"Umm, let's see." I narrow my eyes. "Valentino or Dolce and Gabbana."

"And you've applied to both of those houses?"

"Yes. Nothing back from them yet, though."

"One day," he replies.

I smile. "One day."

"Finish your drink, bella. I'm taking you dancing."

"Bella?" I frown. God, he doesn't even remember my name.

He takes my hand over the table and lifts it to his mouth. "Bella means beautiful."

He kisses my fingertips. "And you really are very beautiful, Olivia. I can't take my eyes off of you."

Oh, I like him.

"To be honest, I'm having a hard time staying on my side of the table. I want us to dance so I can have you in my arms," he says softly.

Nerves dance in my stomach. "Then take me dancing, Mr. Ferrara," I whisper.

He smiles darkly, tips his head back, and he drains his glass. "Let's go."

———

Three hours later and the room is spinning to the sound of my laughter. Enrico and I are dancing and he's throwing me around like a rag doll. He is holding me by the hand and is spinning me around and around.

We've drunk way too much, and now it's late—3:00 a.m., to be precise—and we've come to our third bar of the night. I don't remember the last time I laughed so much. He's funny, smart, and seriously gorgeous. He's also making me feel like the most beautiful woman in the world.

I couldn't tell you if anyone else is here, because all I can see is him.

He's the epitome of tall, dark, and handsome, with his square jaw, dark, wavy hair, and the biggest brown eyes I have ever seen. His lips are pouty and a beautiful shade of red. He has this joyfulness that seeps out of him, as if he doesn't have a care in the world. His laugh is loud, echoing, and his voice has a deep huskiness that speaks to something deep inside of me.

A slow song comes on. Enrico pulls me close and wraps his arms around me. "Finally," he whispers as he kisses my temple.

"Finally?" I smile, liking the way his lips feel on me.

"Finally, a slow song that allows me to hold you close."

He towers above me. He's so tall that I only come up to his shoulder. One of my hands is in his, while he holds me by the waist with his other. The air between us is electric. My heart is pumping hard and fast.

What would it be like to have sex with a virile, intense man like this?

Imagine fucking him.

A deep ache begins to grow inside of me. I can feel myself

getting wet as my need for his body grows. Enrico slowly dips his head, and his lips softly dust mine, his tongue gently asking for permission to enter my mouth. I grant him access. His kiss is slow and erotic, and it does things to me as I get a visual of him on top of me. Naked. Fucking me hard—so hard. Our bodies wet with perspiration. I'm aching for him to touch me.

His hand tightens around my waist, pulling me closer as we kiss. I lose control and my hands go to his hair, bringing him closer to me.

For fifteen minutes, we stand on the dancefloor, kissing like we are the only people in the room. I can feel his hard cock up against my stomach. His eyes have darkened to nearly black, and I can feel the want in his vice-like grip.

He's different to any man I've ever met. It could be the whole Italian thing, of course, but I feel like it's more than that. There's more to him than meets the eye. Perhaps that's just my inexperience with gorgeous men speaking. Maybe all players make women feel like this. Maybe it's a spell that only a few men know how to cast.

A special kind of black magic.

Suddenly, achingly aware that I'm dripping wet and acting like a horny ho, I whisper, "I should get going."

His eyes hold mine, and some kind of silent acknowledgement runs between us. He bends and kisses me softly, a promise of more.

After a beat, he replies, "I'll walk you home."

———

Half an hour later, we arrive at my hotel, hand in hand. "This is me," I say nervously.

He turns toward me, takes my face in his hands, and he kisses me again, waiting for an invitation to come in. Our lips dance as my mind runs at a million miles a minute. Visions of us naked together play like a perfect porno in my mind.

But... I can't. I can't do it. As much as I want to, I can't sleep with a stranger. It's not who I am.

Damn you, conscience.

"It was nice meeting you," I say.

His face falls as he stares at me, his chest rising and falling as he battles his arousal.

"I'm sorry," I whisper. "I..." I hesitate, because damn, saying it out loud seems so lame. "I'm not the type of girl who sleeps around."

Tenderness crosses his face but he remains silent.

"You make me wish I was." I smile bashfully.

We kiss, and then he holds our foreheads together as we both try to come down from our high.

"Can I see you tomorrow?" he asks. "I have the weekend off. I can take you sightseeing."

"Really?"

He takes a step back from me, creating distance, and I know he's trying to calm his throbbing body down.

"Okay." I smile.

"I'll pick you up at ten?"

I look at my watch. "That's only six hours away."

His eyes dance with mischief. "I know. It seems stupid to go all the way home. I can just stay here until then."

I giggle. "Nice try. Go home, Ricki."

He chuckles, and with one last lingering kiss, he opens the front door of my hotel. I walk in, trying to act cool and hide the over the top smile on my face.

I turn back to him through the glass. He has his hands

tucked in his pockets as he watches me. I give him a wave, and he blows me a kiss. I get into the elevator with my heart jumping all over the place. I smile broadly at my reflection in the elevator mirrored wall.

Holy shit.... what the hell just happened?

To continue reading this story it is available now on Amazon.

Thank you so much for reading and
for your ongoing support
I have the most beautiful readers in the whole world!

Keep up to date with all the latest news
and online discussions by joining the Swan Squad VIP
Facebook group and discuss your favourite
books with other readers.
@tlswanauthor

Visit my website for updates and new release information.
www.tlswanauthor.com

ABOUT THE AUTHOR

T L Swan is a Wall Street Journal and #1 Amazon Best Selling author. With millions of books sold, her titles are currently translated in twenty languages and have hit #1 on Amazon in the USA, UK, Canada, Australia and Germany. Tee resides on the South Coast of NSW, Australia with her husband and their three children where she is living her own happy ever after with her first true love.

Made in United States
Orlando, FL
12 March 2025